I0749177

Dark Cheer
CRYPTIDS EMERGING

Volume Silver

Edited by Atlin Merrick

First published by Improbable Press in 2022

Improbable Press is an imprint of:
Clan Destine Press
www.clandestinepress.com.au
PO Box 121, Bittern Victoria 3918 Australia

National Library of Australia Cataloguing-In-Publication data:

Improbable Press
Dark Cheer: Cryptids Emerging (Volume Silver)

ISBN: 978-0-6452899-2-3 (hb)
ISBN: 978-0-6452899-3-0 (pb)
ISBN: 978-0-6452899-4-7 (eb)

Cover artwork by © Pixie Ink
Cover photo "Dark Forest Canopy (Unsplash)" by © Phoebe Stafford 2015, on Wikimedia Commons
Typesetting & Layout by Dimitra Stathopoulos

Improbable Press
contact@improbablepress.com
improbablepress.com

*For everyone who wants to see their own face
in audacious tales of adventure and mystery*

And, always, for Joseph Carey Merrick

Contents

Be of Good Cheer!

Cryptid: it's a young word, barely forty years old, and it means hidden animal. Cryptozoology? That's the *study* of hidden animals and know this: quite a few creatures we now accept as familiar, common, well they were once cryptids, too.

The giant squid. The okapi. The megamouth shark and mountain gorilla. The saola, one of the world's rarest animals. These creatures were stories told by local people for years, yet despite their size, each remained elusive to science for generations. Heck, until the 21st century no one had even captured a living kraken – excuse me, a giant squid – on film!

All this to say that though the cryptids we love are hidden, we just never know when and where the next great beast might be discovered. You'll certainly discover dozens here, in Volume Silver, the second in the *Dark Cheer: Cryptids Emerging* series. In this book we learn again what we already knew: cryptids come in every size and shape, they are captive of no one land, possessed by no single people. *We* are the locals where we live, and most of us have heard tales by firelight about a bird, a beast, or a being in the nearby woods or lake, a creature who transcends the possible, who puts lie to what's probable, and in so doing does this: gives us the joy of wondering *what if?*

In this book our what if includes darkly cheerful tales of a grootslang ready to rise, bigfoots too, of lake monsters, jackalopes, and sentient hotels. Here be stories of what's splashing in the tub (a grundylow's babe), who haunts the coal mine (a rare kind of 'canary'), what the tiniest leviathan really wants (just a bit of respect). And while cryptids are what this book and its kin, Volume Blue, are all about, they're more than that alone. This collection, like its sister book, is full to bursting with stories of diverse protagonists too, with BIPOC, disabled, LGBTQIA+, and neurodivergent people in tales of adventure, emergence, rebellion, and rebirth.

As you read, you'll find every one of these ghosts, each goblin and grim, represent the people who have faith in them. From India to Australia, South Africa to Japan to the Ukraine, there is a beauty of believing in these unbelievable creatures. In reading about these cryptids, we learn what our far away neighbors glimpse in the shadows, and what happens when they step into the dark.

Does that thought give you a shiver? Fantastic! That's what dark cheer is all about. It's about rubbing at the goosebumps even as we tip-toe closer. It's about wanting to see and know and hear and touch things that are the same as us in some ways but, with wing or fin or fur, so very different too. To paraphrase a quote I heard recently, it's so much more fun to believe in possibilities than be discouraged by improbabilities. So do please be of good cheer and relish each and every cryptid here.

Now, if you'll excuse me, I'm going to sit still beside the sea and breathe deep of the salt, believing in selkies and the nain rouge, in jorogumo and sasquatch, in the Enfield monster and goatboys and...oh wow. Was that a qaxdascidi just there?

I hope so.

Atlin Merrick
Spring 2022

The Monster

SIMON KEWIN

Eventually he grew weary of the long winter he'd escaped to.

It wasn't the cold; he could withstand that well enough. His body was strong. There were fish to catch in the icy waters, and sometimes he could creep up on a seal and wrestle it to its death. The flesh and blubber could feed him for a month. He hated to butcher the creatures, but it was a matter of survival. His house was built from their furs lashed over whale bones. He'd extended and reinforced it again and again over the decades. When sickness came, as it did even to him, he could lie on his seal-hide bed and shiver through until it subsided.

Water was always plentiful.

In the early days he'd had fights with the arctic bears, those roaring monsters with cruel teeth and butcher's-hook claws. Some were taller even than he when they reared up on their hind legs, but he was nearly as strong and made up for the lack in cunning. Now the bears walked a wide path around him, watching from a distance and sniffing at the air, but daring no nearer. They had to be the descendants many times over of the originals, but still they kept away, wariness passed down from mothers to cubs. The arrangement suited them all.

No, it wasn't the cold, or the four months of utter darkness in the winter, or the bears. It was loneliness, finally, that spurred him back into life, that made him gather his few supplies onto a sled and set off. He knew he would never have the companion, the mate, he craved. The possibility of another like him had died with his creator. It was a loss that, even now, cut through him more sharply than any wind from the north. He was a monster, forever an outcast.

But loneliness. Loneliness had grown within him, gestating over the decades and centuries into something that couldn't be denied. It appeared he wasn't going to age and die as he'd assumed. His creator had done his work well.

There were things he needed to understand, too. Questions that needed answers. Whose fingers did he slip into the fish's mouth to break the creature's spine and end its suffering? Whose muscles sawed at the ice to open up access to the water? Whose eyes did he see the world through? Whose brain, even, thought these thoughts, asked these questions? Who were they, all the poor, broken wretches that were *him?* Young or old? Male or female? He could tell from his external appearance that young, strong men made up a large part of his anatomy. But his organs? His inner workings? He didn't know.

He didn't know who he was.

But he'd seen signs in the sky. Miracles. Wonders. For many years he'd been utterly alone, and everyone else on the Earth might have been dead for all he knew or cared. He'd wanted no more to do with any of them. But then one day he'd seen a light in the east. A shooting-star. Except not a shooting-star. It didn't blaze and fade but was constant, moving across the night sky with slow precision, as if a star had worked itself loose and set off on a journey. He'd watched in wonder as it arced across the darkness. The following night it was there again. All the yearnings, all the questions he'd tried to suppress, blazed into life as he sat and stared upwards.

And so, he set off. Finding his way was easy. Even in summer the sun was low in the southern sky. All he had to do was head towards it. If there were still people in the world, the thought of being among them again gave him little pleasure. He remembered their revulsion all too well. But if there were answers to be found, they lay among humanity. He had no choice but to face them, just as he'd once faced the white bears.

He spied the ship in the distance after two weeks of hauling his sled across the ice. The black speck against the endless white slowly took on shape as he approached. It was trapped, far from open water. Summer was coming and the floes were breaking up, but the ship must have been marooned there all winter. It was large, too. Large and strange. His maker had endowed him with good eyes, and he could pick out fine detail from a safe distance. It appeared to be made from metal rather than wood. At night lights blazed out from it, brighter than any lantern he'd ever seen. Icicles festooned its rigging, but there were no sails in sight. There were definitely people on board. He could see them clearly: stick-figures milling around on the decks, or even venturing onto the ice to engage in activities he couldn't begin to understand. One or two of them always carried long-snouted rifles. Guns for the bears, most likely, but they'd work on him just as well. Even he couldn't withstand the sort of damage they'd inflict.

He counted nine people in the end, assuming there was no one who stayed below decks. He couldn't fight nine of them, especially not when they carried those guns. But perhaps he could pick the people off, one by one. Break their necks before retreating into the icy wastes. The thought gave him little pleasure but it was his only hope. They'd come hunting him, as he'd been hunted in the old days. But the ice was his domain. Once it was done, the ship could transport him far away, to the cities where he might find the answers he sought.

He watched for three days, crouched behind his upturned sled for camouflage, while he waited for the right moment to act.

Helen Magnusson crouched to study the GPS marker they'd left embedded in the ice. She popped the rubber cover on the USB socket and plugged in to download the latest readings to her device. All in all, it had been a good winter. Lots of good data. They needed to do more analysis back in Copenhagen, but it was already clear they'd learned significant amounts about the movements of the ice floes. Repeat readings taken over successive years would give them invaluable insights into climate change.

As she was a biologist, the floes weren't her main area of interest. She was much more intrigued by the alterations they were seeing in the microfauna populations. Larger creatures were being affected too: the migration patterns of fish, whales, and polar bears were all altering. There could be no doubt. The world was changing.

While the data downloaded, she glanced up at Kurt, standing guard nearby with his rifle at the ready. Kurt the pacifist vegetarian who'd never intentionally harmed any creature in his whole life. He really wasn't going to be much use if a bear did attack, was he?

"Hey, Kurt. It's gone ten. Why don't you go make your Skype call to the lovely Margarita?"

Kurt's voice was muffled behind the frost-rimed scarf covering half his face. "I'll stay."

She knew how much he looked forward to these daily calls with his young wife. The winter away had been hard on him. "It's okay. Go. I only have five more probes to do. I'll be back on board in fifteen minutes."

Kurt gazed around the ice, looking for any threat. The white silence stretched away in all directions, utterly unblemished.

"Go," she said again. "I'll be fine. Leave the rifle. If I see a bear, I'll shoot the damn thing myself."

With a grunt of gratitude, Kurt laid down the rifle and strode back to the *Kraken*, adding another line of boot-prints to the well-trampled ice around the frozen research ship.

She was on the last probe but one when the attack came. She was thrown to the ice, a cruel blow to her side knocking the wind out of her before she could even scream. A moment later she felt the pain of it. *Ribs cracked*, a detached part of her mind observed. It was agony as she scrabbled about for the rifle but it was too far away, over by the probe. She half-rose, trying to call out. Her attacker filled her vision: a huge shape against the bright sky, rearing over her for the final blow.

He woke in a laboratory. Another laboratory. Different from the one his creator had used, of course. This one was cleaner, shinier, red, and green lights twinkling away on incomprehensible contraptions all around. But he knew the smells, knew what places like this meant. He keenly remembered the agonies he'd suffered.

Raw pain thrummed away in his side, his leg, across his shoulders. Memories came back to him. Memories of the fight. He'd thought to show them his true self. Despite everything. He'd thought to reveal the person he was beneath. What was he thinking? They'd seen none of it. He cursed himself for his own stupidity. Mankind hadn't changed. They saw something monstrous and assumed it was a monster. He should have stayed on the high ice where he was safe.

When he tried to rise and found he was restrained, bound to the bed by shiny straps, he knew the worst of it. The straps cut into his limbs as he struggled. Furious with himself, at his own weakness, he tore himself from the metal slab they'd laid him on. He also ripped aside the tubes and wires they'd attached to him.

He had to get away, out onto the snow. There were no portholes in the laboratory; it was impossible to know how many decks he had to climb. He padded down a metal corridor lit by harsh white lights, no flames in sight.

He made it half-way up the first flight of steps when they came for him. They stood at the top, three of them, looking down upon him. Roaring, he charged. If he could throw them aside, fight his way above decks, he could jump from the ship, get away. He was conscious he was playing the part of the monster they saw when they looked at him, but he had little choice.

One of his captors raised a gun. It was only a pistol. He ignored it. When the shot struck him, it was little more than a wasp-sting. He'd nearly reached them when his head began to swim. Clouds descended, filling his brain. What had they done to him? He tried to shake the fog free, but there was too much of it, the weight of it too great.

Dizziness overwhelmed him. His last sensation was of falling backwards, the people who'd captured him receding into the darkness above.

When he awoke again it was to the gentle rocking of the ship. It took a few moments to grasp what that meant. How long had he been asleep? What had they done to him?

As before, he tried to rise. As before he was bound. He was naked too, now. A single white sheet covered his body instead of the furs he'd been dressed in. To what end? Had they been examining him? Preparing their fresh torments?

One again he struggled, trying to tear himself free from their bonds.

"Hey, it's okay. I'll undo the straps for you." A woman's voice, speaking accented German, as if it wasn't her native tongue. "You do understand me, right? You speak German and French?"

He stopped struggling. "Why am I bound?"

She set about working at his wrists and ankles. She was young, her blonde hair long and soft. He marveled at how smooth her skin was. Cream compared to his own scarred and pitted hide.

"We went through some rough seas yesterday," she said. "Didn't want you to fall out of bed."

"But before. When you first captured me. I was bound then, too."

"You kept fighting us in your sleep, even when we were trying to treat you."

"You are a doctor? A woman?"

She smiled a little. "As it happens, I am a doctor. But a biologist, not a medic. We had you in the sick bay for a while, but then we needed the room so we wheeled you in here."

"So you could study me?"

"So you could sleep."

She finished untying him. Warily, expecting some cruel joke, he swung his legs round to sit upright. The room lurched for a few moments before settling back into place.

More memories returned to him. "You shot me."

"Darted you. You were delusional, a danger to yourself and others. It was all we could do."

He didn't understand all her words. He towered over her but she didn't appear to have any fear of him. He wondered, briefly, if she was blind, like the old man. But no. She could see him well enough. She held out a bottle of water for him, constructed from some strange, flexible material and not the glass he'd expected.

"How long have I been asleep?" he asked after he'd drunk. The water trickled cold inside him.

"Ten days. An ice-breaker came for us a week ago. The captain wanted to air-lift you off. I thought you might want to decide things for yourself. Given your past."

"You know what I am?"

"Who doesn't?"

"And that doesn't alarm you? The fact that we're here alone in this little room?"

The woman shifted in her chair. But she wasn't uneasy. Getting comfortable if anything. "You saved me. Out there on the ice, when the bear attacked. Never seen anything like it. A man fighting a polar bear and winning. Incredible."

"I killed it?"

"You did. Not before that bear gave you some terrible injuries. It took all of us to carry you on board while staunching your wounds."

"Were you harmed?"

"I'm healing. The painkillers help."

He looked around, uncomfortable at this intimacy between them. With his bed and her desk and the shelves full of her books there was little room left. She'd clearly been studying insects as part of her research. On her desk, next to a microscope, beetles crawled around in a series of glass tanks. Beside them, butterflies fanned their wings upon a purple-flowering plant. They appeared to be free to fly wherever they wished.

"Why are there insects?"

"I'm studying the effects shifting magnetic fields have on their life-cycles."

He nodded, although her words still made little sense. "You said I was a *man*. If you know who I am you also know what I am. A monster. A concoction of broken parts. A chimera."

She shook her head. "Those are bad words. Is that how you see yourself?"

"It's how the world sees me. And...I have done terrible things. I've taken the lives of others."

"Terrible things were done to you. Seems to me you had plenty of reason for doing what you did."

"You may think like that. The world won't."

She didn't reply for a moment, looking at him, considering him. "Why did you come south after all this time?"

"I...I wanted to find out who I was. What I was."

She nodded, as if this was a perfectly normal thing to say. "You know, the world has changed a lot since you last walked it. Now you would be a marvel. A wonder."

"These are simply other terms for *mongrel* and *monster*."

"No. People would love you. Scientists, obviously. I mean, how is it you've even survived this long? But everyone else, too. You'd be famous. Trust me. You'd be a huge deal. We'd help you find your answers. Everyone would want a piece of you."

"A piece of me?"

"Sorry. Bad choice of words. I mean everyone would want to find out about you. You'd be huge."

He tried to make sense of her words. Clearly the way in which people spoke had changed over so much time. Was this all some trap? Some way of luring him back into the clutches of what was laughably called civilization? Sometimes, back in the north, he polished a slab of ice so he could see his own reflection. Thinking that, maybe, he wasn't as lumpen and scarred as his memory said. He was always disappointed. "I'm still a monster. I'm still this assemblage of stolen body parts."

"And, what, you think we're all pure, all perfect? I've been thinking about you while you slept. Let me tell you, we're all mongrels. We're all a mishmash of human ancestries. Neanderthal ancestries, too, come to that. Amphibian, reptile, you name it, it's all in there. Maybe 10% of our DNA is from viruses, absorbed into our own millions of years ago. Our bodies are mostly bacterial cells. You think you're a mongrel? Welcome to the human race."

"I don't know what any of that means."

"Look. You want to know whose hands those are? Whose face, whose limbs? Is that it?"

"I do."

"Well I can tell you. They're yours."

"Once they weren't. They were stolen for me."

She studied him for a moment. Then, unexpectedly, she began to unbutton her shirt. Confused, mouth dry, he could do nothing but watch as she revealed her breast. An old thrill of delight kindled in him, like torches being lit in rooms long left dark.

Beneath the fabric of her undergarment, running the length of her sternum, crawled a long, centipede scar. She traced its line with her blood-red fingernail.

"You see this? I was born with a congenital cardiac condition. My heart didn't work properly. So, they gave me a new one. Some unfortunate died, I don't know who, but I got to live. Their heart beats in my chest. There are lots of people like you. Like, I have a cousin living in Stockholm. *He* was born a *she*. Surgery can fix many things that nature got wrong."

Such marvels, such wonders. This was a place of magic. Terrible magic. Except, not, of course. It was all natural science. He of all people should understand that.

"No," he said. "You're still *you*. I'm only an assortment, a collection. There is no *me*."

She shrugged. "Bodies are just things. Collections of organs and limbs that allow us to live. Even our minds. Our ideas, our thoughts, our desires. Our way of seeing the world. Everything's inherited, stolen, borrowed. Or else it's something new and unique, something we came up with for ourselves. How are you any different?"

He didn't speak for a moment, trying to understand what she was saying. He looked away, conscious he was staring at the glorious swell of her bosom. He was suddenly aware of how flimsy the white sheet covering his body was. His loins, for so long mere functional plumbing, were stirring into life.

"You...you should button your garment back up now."

"Forgive me," she said. "Things get pretty relaxed onboard as the winter wears on." He thought she was going to take offence. Scream or swoon. Instead, seeing the movement of his body beneath the sheet, she laughed. "You see? You're *definitely* human. No doubt about that." One of her eyebrows arched in something like amusement. "You didn't come south again just to find answers about your origins, did you?"

"I don't know why I came. I felt compelled."

"Oh, come on. You've been alone for a long time. You're looking for love, right? Or, failing that, you're looking to fuck. Who wouldn't after all this time?"

He winced at her rough choice of words. "That possibility died with my creator a long time ago."

"Bullshit."

"I'm sorry?"

"That's bullshit. What, you think you have to find someone just like you? That's not how it works these days. I guess that's not how it ever worked. Love comes in endless shapes and sizes and combinations. These days, we're all about our variety, our individuality."

"That wouldn't extend to me."

She shook her head. "Don't kid yourself. You're strong and thoughtful. Kind, too, I think. You're going to be famous. You also have–" Her gaze flicked briefly over his body beneath the sheet. "–some impressive physical characteristics. Trust me. You'll have no trouble finding love."

"I planned to kill you all," he said. "Take you ship."

She looked amused. "Really? That was your plan? You're good with modern navigation systems, are you?"

He didn't reply for a moment, considering her thoughts. He could maybe still escape. Dash her to the ground, make a bolt for the sea and swim for the ice. Escape to the safety of the far north. Except, where would that get him apart from back where he started?

"You are sure of this?"

"Look, it's up to you. Say the word and we'll lower you a lifeboat, let you paddle away into the darkness. We won't tell a soul. Or you can stay with us and rejoin the human race."

He watched her for a moment, half-expecting some joke, some elaborate cruelty to be revealed. Instead she sat quietly, awaiting his reply.

"You will help me?" he asked.

"Least I can damn-well do."

"And what should I call you?"

"Sorry. Should have said. I'm Helen. Helen Magnusson. And your name I know, of course."

"No. I have no name."

"Of course, you do. It's Fra…"

His expression must have stopped her mid-word. A wave of revulsion had washed through him. Revulsion and anger. "Don't say it. Why would you call me by that foul name?"

"But…but that's who you are. Everyone knows that."

"No."

"What do you mean, *no*?"

"That was *him*. The monster who created me. The butcher with the knives and the saws. Who hacked up the bodies of the dead, who picked and sorted out parts to stitch together into the shape of a man. Into *me*."

"I didn't think. Forgive me." She considered for a moment. "You aren't grateful to him at all?"

Was he? It was hard to know. It was complicated. "I am glad to be alive," he said finally.

"So, he didn't name you at all?"

His rage subsided a little, to be replaced by an old emptiness. "No. *Things* don't have names."

"Then you're going to need one." She considered for a moment. "How about, I don't know…Neumann."

"Neumann?"

"Sure. That is what you are. *New Man*."

Neumann. He turned the word over in his mind. He liked it. Liked the shape of it. In some unexpected way this strange woman with her gift of water had anointed him. Baptized him.

"Neumann," he said out loud.

One of her butterflies flittered through the air to settle, unexpectedly, on his scarred hand. He reached out to touch it. The creature's iridescent wings were like paper. It flew off, but not before some of the tiny, colorful scales had rubbed off onto him.

He studied his fingers. The rainbow stayed when he tried to scrape it away. His skin shimmered as if he had become part-butterfly, his fingers taking on the dazzling colors. Taking on, also, their beauty.

Marveling, Neumann held out his hand to the young woman who'd befriended him, showing her what he'd become.

Chicken Monster Motel

KEYAN BOWES

"It's my birthright!" says Jerry, unloading his mom's India Market groceries onto the counter. "Everyone knows about motels and Patels. Motel, Patel, they go together." He pronounces Patel the American way, Pat-ell, instead of the Gujarati way, Puh-tale.

His father frowns. "We want a different life for you, Jairam," he says firmly. "Your expensive education is for what?" The Patels had run three different motels, eventually cashing out before Jerry went to college. "You think motel goes with Patel? Doctor goes even better. Google Dr Patel. You will get 82 million hits, including your cousin Leela."

"Papa, I just graduated! I don't want to go to med school. I didn't even write my MCAT!"

"Then you should write it!" His father storms out.

"I hate exams!" Jerry shouts after him.

Later, his mother hands him a jewelry box. "Jerroo my son, if that's what you really want, sell these, give it a try. I have faith in you."

"What, seriously?" Jerry opens the box to find twelve diamond-studded gold bangles. Two have elephant heads with emerald eyes. He's seen these on his mother's wrists at his cousin's wedding. They were handed down to his mother by her mother and her mother before. "Ma, you can't!"

"Take it, son. In this country, when will I wear this kind of jewelry?" She looks at him seriously. "Running a motel is a lot of work, but a young man should work hard."

The Motel on Craigslist

"Hey Peter!" Jerry's looking at Craigslist. "Here's a motel! It's even got a cafe. Up in the mountains. We could do a road trip."

"What?" Peter says. "Dude, you haven't even got the jewelry appraised yet." He reads over Jerry's shoulder. "Weird name, Chicken Monster Motel."

"Gotta start looking, right? Let's go get a Starbuck's and plan the road trip." Jerry dumps his mug in the sink. "Ten minutes to pack."

"*Plan* a road trip, you said."

Jerry drops a kiss on Peter's neck. It leads to one thing and another and takes more than ten minutes.

But the packing doesn't. Toothbrush, smartphone, clean t-shirts, socks, and boxers. "Don't leave the jewelry behind in the empty apartment," Peter says. "And I'll drive. I don't want gray hair before I'm 30."

Slow Season at the Chicken Monster Motel

"Finally! There it is." Jerry accelerates wildly around the curving mountain road. He's driving after all, and they're both frazzled. The motel is perched in an unlikely spot on a cliff above them. Jerry brightens. "Bet it has terrific views."

"Hope it has cold beer," Peter says.

Jerry blows him a kiss. "Yeah."

The Chicken Monster Motel is clearly having a slow season. Peter's Honda is the only car there. The manager – a young woman who snaps her gum and ends all her sentences with question-marks – tells him to pull into the garage underneath the building. Then it's a hot shower, cold beer, and surprisingly good beef sandwiches on the house. Jairam's parents would be horrified that he's not vegetarian, so he hasn't mentioned it. Though he's devoted to them, there's a lot he hasn't said. No point upsetting them.

Jerry likes what he sees. Maybe he can get a really good price on the motel since it's so remote? It's clean and in good condition, with neutral walls and industrial carpet. The manager says it has forty rooms, a lounge with a commercial kitchen, and a small owner's apartment.

Peter and Jerry settle into big fake-leather armchairs beside a window overlooking a gorge. River sounds drift up, the rippling and rushing of a fast stream. A hawk hovers outside practically at their eye level before they swoop off onto the other side of the gorge. A gentle breeze blows in.

"Your idea wasn't so dumbass," Peter acknowledges.

Jerry takes a contented swig from the beer bottle. The sky behind the mountains is turning from pink to purple when the building shakes.

"Earthquake!" he tells Peter. "Feel that?"

"Here? No way. Which fault?"

The manager pops her head in. "Can you, like, fasten your seatbelts? We're just warming up now and waiting for full dark."

"Hey, wait!" says Jerry, "What seatbelts? Why?"

"Like, on your seats? Maybe you're sitting on them?" The manager snaps her chewing gum. "I gotta see your car's secured, y'know?" The door clicks shut behind her.

"I've never heard of seatbelts for earthquakes," Jerry says.

"They told us duck and cover. But she seemed pretty positive. And there are actually seatbelts." Peter fastens his.

The manager runs in again, rushes to the window, and closes it. "Uh-oh! Nearly forgot! Creates too much drag, you know?" She rushes out before they can ask her anything.

"Drag? In an earthquake? What?"

The building shakes again. The floor actually seems to tip. Jerry expects the chairs to slide, but they're bolted to the floor.

"Put on your seatbelt," Peter says. "Don't be an idiot. She knows something."

Jerry opens his mouth to retort when Peter says, "Oh. My. God. What's that?"

'That' is a pair of huge wings that appear on either side of the motel, visible through the lounge's wall of windows. They look more like the wings of eagles than of airplanes, but the feathers seem metallic, like they might be made of aluminum alloys.

The motel gives an experimental flap or two, and then rises from the cliff-edge, into the nearly dark sky. Peter gasps.

"What the...!" Jerry says. His dream motel climbs in a large spiral, bumping through turbulence from the wind currents blowing up the gorge. So much for a really good price. "What's going on? Where's the manager?" They stagger to the door. It's locked. The motel lurches.

"I'm going to throw up," says Jerry. "Do they have barf bags?" Peter hands him the waste-bin. They yell for the manager, but she doesn't show. Now what?

The motel flaps onward through the night. Eventually they fall asleep in their chairs.

Where's the Beef?

The motel makes a surprisingly gentle landing in a cow pasture, especially considering it lands on one of the cows. When Jerry and Peter recover, the door's open. Outside, they find the manager butchering the animal in the early morning light.

"Good catch today," she tells them cheerily.

"Won't the farmer be mad about the cow?"

"Nah, it's included in the landing rights." She loads a large piece of cow onto a hand-truck.

"Yuck," says Peter, but he goes forward to help.

Jerry feels sick to his stomach. He eats beef just fine, despite his parents' beliefs, but dragging around bleeding bits of carcass is too much.

Over breakfast, the manager introduces herself. Her name is Malayaga Smith, and she inherited the motel from her mother.

"I'm sorry for your loss," Peter says politely

"Oh, she's alive, she just pretended to die. She got bored and decided to travel. I think she's in Kazhakstan this week. I get random messages from her."

"Ah. Umm." Jerry has no idea what to say. He helps carry the dishes into the kitchen and takes a closer look at the stainless-steel appliances. High-end. Well-maintained.

"So why do you want to sell?" Peter asks Malayaga.

"It's not my kind of life, this motel management. Don't get to meet people, you know? I mean, they're all just passing through. I'm young, I'm single. I want to pay off my student loans, go to New York, get a studio apartment and a proper job. I'll sell at any reasonable price."

"Awesome!" says Jerry, excited.

"We haven't even seen the financials," objects Peter. "You're jumping the gun, dumbass. Did you notice we're the only guests here?"

"I have all the details in Qakbooks," says Malayaga. "Last year's audited numbers. Also route maps and clearances and rights and stuff?" She gestures at a desk in a glassed-in cubicle. "It's all there. I'll pull it out."

"No point wasting time with the financials, stupid, unless we're interested in the deal."

"We?" asks Peter slowly.

"Yes," says Jerry impatiently. "We. Aren't you coming? Look, she wants us in the cubicle."

They pore over the details. The Chicken Monster Motel actually has a high occupancy rate. The customers paid in a variety of currencies, including old Roman silver, Mughal coinage, golden eggs, singing harps, and jeweled mechanical birds. Her spreadsheet meticulously converted them into US dollars as of the transaction date.

Malayaga is happy to accept Jerry's bangles as payment. She's accustomed to accepting payments that aren't in dollars. There's some kind of valuation and validation routine.

"But you gotta be sure, you know?" Malayaga says. "You can't change your mind after it's done. The Motel only moves forward."

"Jerry," says Peter, "Do you even know how to run a flying motel? At a profit?"

Jerry laughs. "We'll learn as we go along. I don't even know how to run a grounded motel. Do you?"

Peter shakes his head. "Me? Writing code, remember?" He pauses. "Do we have wifi?"

Malayaga nods. "Permanent wifi and cellular. It's kind of built in to the Motel. It always has the latest communication technology and it always gets a good signal."

That clinches it. "Okay," says Peter. "I can write code in the sky. I'm down with this."

"This will be awesome!" says Jerry. "A flying motel!"

Jerry hands the bangles to Malayaga like the treasure they are. She puts them in a drawer that slides open, then automatically slams shut. Jerry looks concerned.

"Nah, it's okay," says Malayaga. "The Motel values, converts, and shunts it to my account. That should be paying off my student loans, like, right now."

They shake hands on the deal. "I'll show you how it operates," she says. "It's, you know, intuitive."

Language of the Heart

The control room door won't open. Malayaga makes crooning sounds in a mysterious language as she tries the knob. The glass door remains immovable.

"D'you have a key?" Peter asks.

"There's no keyhole, stupid," says Jerry. "Maybe it's jammed? Do you have some WD40?"

"What language were the words you said?" Peter asks Malayaga.

"Finnish," she replies. "But Russian works too."

"Wait, I need to learn Russian or Finnish so I can command this motel?" asks Jerry.

"He sucks at languages," says Peter.

"It's sorta, 'communicate'? Not command?"

"Yeah, okay. So do I?" asks Jerry.

"Can he just talk English?" asks Peter.

"Maybe?" says Malayaga. They all look at the recalcitrant door. The only sound is the snapping of chewing gum.

"What were you saying, anyways?"

"Open sesame," says Malayaga.

"Open sesame? In Finnish? That's from Arabian Nights, not anything Finnish or Russian."

"Yeah," says Malayaga, sounding baffled. "So?"

They take turns whispering, shouting, and singing Open Sesame. By the time Peter's doing it like phone sex, Jerry can no longer listen.

"Why'd you pick Finnish?" he asks Malayaga.

"It's gotta be, like, a language of the heart?"

Peter's seductive voice isn't getting anywhere with the door, but is having an effect on Jerry. He focuses on what Malayaga's saying. "A…language of the heart? Like Peter's doing right now?"

Malayaga shakes her head. "You know when a baby gives back love? Like they're one or two years old, and they have some words to say? The language they learn then? That's a language of the heart."

"Wait, what? Don't babies speak English?"

"This baby didn't," Malayaga says, pointing to herself.

"Oh. Mother tongue. You mean your mother tongue?"

"Maybe?"

"So why isn't it working for Peter?"

"Why isn't it working for me?" says Malayaga. "Maybe the motel isn't mine anymore, but it's not yours yet." She looks worried. "That's kinda not good. Maybe dangerous."

Oh great. A ronin motel.

It's Peter who says, "So what language did you learn then? Gujarati or some other kind of Indian?

"I don't know," says Jerry. "Gujarati? Hindi? And 'Indian' is not a language, stupid."

"I didn't say it was, dumbass. I know India's got a bunch of languages and Gujarati's just one."

"I was born in Mumbai, it could have been anything. Gujarati, Hindi, Marathi. Anyway I forgot them all."

"So call your mom."

Jairam calls home. But it's his father who picks up the phone, and he is furious.

"I can't stop your mother from giving you her jewelry, but she was always too soft with you! All these years I've worked for the sake of this family! I wanted to make you a doctor or at least a dentist. Now what? You are going backwards!"

"Papa..." says Jerry, trying to get a word in.

"What do you know about motels?" his father asks.

Jerry hopes he won't have to answer too many questions when he admits he's bought the motel. He's looked at the numbers. What else should he know about? Structural integrity? Foundation work? No, probably not that. Not termite inspections either. Anyway, it's all up in the air – well, not literally – until the Motel gives him access.

He doesn't want to admit that to his dad either. He can imagine him yelling, "You bought a mobile home as a motel? And you don't have the keys? You can't get in? What useless thing have you done with your mother's jewelry?"

Not that his father lets him say anything at all. "Do you know how much work it is to run a motel? How difficult it is to make a profit? Do you know how to buy a business or a building? You are just being foolish and your mother is encouraging you." His father slams down the old-fashioned landline phone with an audible thunk.

Peter eyes him unsympathetically. "You should get your Mom a cell phone, dumbass," he says.

"She has one. A smartphone with email and apps and everything. It's usually turned off. They like me to call the landline." Jairam tries his mom's cellphone, but she doesn't answer. He leaves a desperate message.

No Treasure, No Motel, No Chance

Jerry sinks back on the sofa in the motel lounge, staring out at the sunset and the unperturbed cows. The motel's still not responding. Malayaga's voice has gone from crooning to pleading, but the door remains shut.

The transaction is irreversible, the precious bangles gone to pay off Malayaga's student debt. All Jerry has to show for his mother's faith in him is an uncooperative flying motel.

Peter massages his shoulders. “I’m going to help Malayaga,” he says. “Maybe we should kick the door down?”

Malayaga looks horrified. “You’d be so dead,” she says. “I mean, like literally. Don’t play games with this Motel.”

“Dead?” asks Peter “What? How dangerous is this?”

“It’s a monster,” says Malayaga, sounding miserable. “If it goes feral and starts flying without a flight plan...”

Jerry’s imagination completes the sentence in terrifying ways. What would happen if the Motel started flying barrel rolls? Or wandering off in random directions? Did it even need to stay in this world? Would it migrate or search for others of its kind? Would it care or even realize it had guests aboard?

“Maybe we should leave, you know?” Malayaga says. “While we can. I’ll pack my bag. Your car got gas?” She disappears into the hallway, reappearing in minutes with a suitcase. “Come on!” she says.

“Wait,” says Jerry. “Are we just going to abandon it? What happens next?”

“We’ll figure that out,” she says. “First, let’s go!”

“Wait,” says Peter suspiciously. “You got Jerry’s treasure. Now you can’t control the motel. Maybe we all leave and later you just call it to come get you?”

“It’s seriously not a trick! Come on!”

But it’s too late. The door locks. The motel lurches into the darkening sky. Malayaga falls into an armchair. “Fasten your seatbelts,” she says quietly.

Peter turns pale, and Jerry swears under his breath.

Momma Ex Machina

Fortunately, except for some jolting due to air-pockets or willfulness, the motel flies quite steadily through the night. By dawn, they make a rough touchdown in a deserted field, with no people or cows.

“Where are we?” asks Jerry.

Malayaga looks out the window and shrugs. “We’ll find out when the doors open. And then we’ll leave.”

"Leave? Look, we're still alive. I'm not leaving!"

"Jerry," says Peter. "We don't know what it'll do tonight. We can't stay."

Jerry shakes his head stubbornly. "I'm not giving up on my dream!"

Peter looks somber. "Then I'll stay too."

Jerry calls home again, dreading another confrontation with his dad. The line is dead. Did Papa deliberately keep the phone off the hook? He'd been mad enough. Jerry's leaving another desperate message on his mother's cellphone when the phone rings in his hand.

"Jerroo. I found a message on my phone?"

"Mom? Thank you Ma, thank you thank you thank you!" He explains the problem.

"I see. You already bought a motel? Here is what you must say. Khulja simsim."

"Cool-ja sim-sim?"

Malayaga catches his eye and points at the control room door. It's swinging open. They all cheer.

"It opened? Good," says Mrs Patel. "Now go put some sandalwood paste on its forehead."

"Mom, I don't have any sandalwood and it doesn't have a forehead! It's a flying motel. Why are we putting sandalwood on it?"

"It's auspicious. Any good Indian store will have sandalwood." She pauses. "The jewelry box, I kept a little bit in there."

Malayaga brings it over. Sure enough, they find a tiny baggie under the red velvet lining.

"Good," his mother says. "I'm just now saying a small prayer to Sri Ganesh. We should invoke him before any project, I thought I taught you that much. He is Vigneshwara, the Remover of Obstacles."

Jerry smudges some of the fragrant paste on the control panel. He hopes it won't short-circuit anything.

“Hey, Peter? Thanks.”

“What for, dumbass? I didn’t do anything.”

“You stuck with me. We were possibly going to die.”

“Yeah, I’m not leaving you to die alone. Your parents would kill me.”

Jerry drops to one knee, pulling a ring from his pocket. “This was going to be romantic, not just randomly in a flying motel. But Peter – will you stick with me forever? Will you marry me?”

Peter gulps and nods. “Yeah. Someone has to keep you out of trouble, or at least keep you company.” He pulls Jerry to his feet and hugs him.

“Awww,” says Malayaga. “You know, I think this motel’s liking you guys already?”

Jerry blushes. “Our first home as a married couple!” he says.

“Congratulations!” Malayaga says, pulling out a bottle of champagne. “Drop me off in New York tonight? I’ve already packed.”

Nights Without Dreams

TOM VELTEROP

The night was right for hunting dreams. It was clear and moonlit, silver shrouded and star touched. The mountains were the shadows of mountains, shaped by their absence. In the valley, small windows below icicled eaves flickered with warm candle-glow, a pool of golden stars to mirror the silver ones above.

From the fissure of the cave in the side of the shadowed mountain, he watched for the candles to go out one by one. He was hungry and hunting-ready. He called himself Tipatap.

His foot left the cave as the last breath blew out the last light in the valley. The moon bathed him, but its light would not linger on his skin. Tipatap crept down the mountain as silent and secret as a shadow.

Soon after the last candle was snuffed the dreams of the people appeared. They blossomed from the frosted windows like flowers in romance with the moon, and hung like frozen smoke in the night. They were all the colors of sky. Some were purple and blue, others yellow and dawn red, more still sunset orange and rose, and in all glittered the bright stars of human dreaming.

Tipatap tiptoed into town. Patient as the mountain and silent as the night, he climbed up the walls of the houses to the windows and their strange flowers. His many-jointed fingers wrapped around drainpipes and window sills, and his many-toed feet found the cracks between bricks and wooden beams. Under the icicled eaves, he stretched his long lips into a snout, and one by one he sucked the sleepers' dreams and stored them in his cheeks. By the last dream of the last house in town, his cheeks were full and round, and Tipatap tiptoed out of town.

Behind him, the town was dark of candle light and colorless of dreams.

Soon the mountain was climbed and the town left behind. Tipatap slipped into the fissure of his cave in the mountain, leaving the moonlight at the door. Inside, the cave was full of machines. They manned the walls and cluttered the floor. They hung from the ceiling. They stacked and stocked and stuck to one another. They stood still, and silent, and their bodies were dark.

Tipatap went to each one, and wrapped his long lips around the mouthpiece that each one had, and gave them one by one a dream. The machines sighed like a band of brass instruments. Their bodies lit with the colors of sky, and all together they came alive.

The machines danced, the machines sang, and Tipatap smiled.

The girl awoke from fright, but not of nightmare. Her night had been empty and cold and colorless of dreams.

She went to the bed of her mother and father, and crawled under the covers with them. Outside the window, the colors of dawn were shining on the icicles and sparkling on the frost.

"Mama," the girl whispered. "I had no dreams again."

Her mother pulled her close and stroked her raincloud hair. "I know, lovely one," she said. "Neither did we. Neither has the whole town, for months now."

"Will the dreams come back, Mama?"

Her father turned over then, and said, "Not unless we take them back."

The girl closed her eyes and cuddled closer to her mother. Her father came, and put his arms around them both. The girl's name was Cadha.

Each and every evening that long winter, after the mountain had forgotten the sun and remembered the moon, Tipatap stole the dreams of the town's sleepers. He came, sucked them from the windows like a hummingbird taking nectar from a flower, stored them in his cheeks, and took them back up the mountain to his machines.

Each and every night the machines came alive with the colors of dreams, and they sang and danced for Tipatap, and he smiled.

Their bodies were built of brass and copper and strange bits and pieces of things that Tipatap had found. A horseshoe, and a pinecone. A wooden comb, and a bent iron nail. A wolf's head handle of a walking stick, and a pebble with a heart of crystal. Their eyes were closed like sleepers and their mouths were smiling. They were made of scraps and stolen dreams. They were made of humanity and magic, and the love of Tipatap.

Each and every morning the dreams faded from the machines, taking their color and life with them. The machines faltered and fell still, frozen halfway through pirouette or leap. Their songs ground out in creaks and rust, and Tiptop's smile fell from his face and hid in the shadowed corners of his cave among the dust and cobwebs.

Each and every day, when the sunlight kissed the fissure in the side of the mountain, Tiptop's cave sunk into chill and gloom like a stone into a winter pond. Without the dreams and the dancing the cave was a bare and lonely place, full only of what could be, and never of what was. Then, Tipatap would sleep. He would curl himself around the dancing legs of his machines, dancing no more. He would sleep through the bright chill of the days. Sleep in the center of his cave, nestled among his machines, nestled in their breathless silence. He waited, as he always did, for the night and the moon and the hunting of dreams, for the dancing and singing of his machines. But he waited also, without knowing, for the coming of people, and for change.

For never, on any day in that long winter, had Tipatap had a friend to visit in his cave, nor spoken with anyone capable of listening. He spoke a silent language throughout the frozen daytimes, one of dust and sleepy breathing, one of cold corners and longing. It was only at night that Tipatap had company. The company of dancing machines with brass songs, and that of stolen dreams.

Cadha's father rallied the townsfolk together near the end of that long winter. The nights had been endless and the days barely more than a breath of warmth and light forever, it had seemed, but the solstice had passed and their hope was blooming alongside the snowdrops.

Cadha's father stood in the morning light and pointed up the steep slope of the mountain, where the snow gleamed and the clouds tangled on the peak.

"There, on the mountain, dwells the thief of our dreams," he said loud. "For a long winter we have suffered his cold and colorless nights, but the winter leaks from the valley now, and the spring is soon to come. I say we march on the mountain to find the thief's cave, and make what was stolen our own again."

The people cheered for Cadha's father, and all agreed. Together, they would march on the mountain. Together, they would make their dreams their own again.

So the people of the town left their homes and gathered in the town square, where they waited. Cadha and her mother and father joined them, and Cadha's father led them from the town, up the steep slopes of the mountain.

By grumble and curse-mutter they stamped up the rocky path. They wore hard frowns between their eyebrows and tension in their shoulders. They carried wood axes and rock hammers, pitchforks, and fire pokers.

Even the children went up the mountain. They too, perhaps most of all, had been robbed of their dreams.

The coming of the people woke every rock and pebble on the mountain side. The treading of their feet trembled through the floor of the cave beneath Tiptop's sleeping body, and woke him. Even his machines quivered where they stood or lay, or hung from the ceiling, in a weak and timid mockery of their former dancing.

Tipatap huddled in his cave with his long arms wrapped about his knobbly knees, and watched the sunlight that knocked at the fissure. He watched until the sunlight was pulled away like curtains by the shadows of the people.

The people marched into Tiptop's cave with great shouting and stamping and chanting, meant more for their own courage than the fright of the thief. They shook their makeshift weapons in the air, and clanged iron onto stone so sparks flew, bright and hot in the dusty darkness.

Cadha came into the cave behind the marching legs of her father, who was near the front, and full over the brim with anger both righteous and spiteful. It was a big place, so Cadha thought, like looking up into the steeple of the church in the town, with the same spiderweb bunting and dust balloons.

At first, she thought the cave was full of people. And such strange people. There were all made of bits and pieces of metal and all manner of other strange things. Cadha thought she even saw a hair comb she had lost a time ago, put now in place of a mouth. All the strange people were frozen in place, or time, and did not move when the town's people came marching in. A few even hung from the ceiling on lengths of string. Cadha at once thought it odd that they did not move, for each one, strange as they were, seemed about to leap or dance, perhaps as soon as she would look away.

Then, Cadha noticed the figure on the floor in the center of the cave. He was the strangest of the lot. His limbs were ever so long, and she could not count the number of his fingers and toes, nor their many crooked joints. It was obvious to Cadha that he was frightened, more frightened even than Cadha had been when she woke from a night without dreaming. He did not make a move or a sound as the people from the town poured into the cave like oil into a pan, and began to break the strange frozen people up into all the little bits and pieces that had once made them whole.

Tipatap saw, but could not understand. Here, in his cave, were the machines he had seeded and nurtured, watered and grown, from bits and pieces of metal and lost objects, and fragments of hopes and stolen dreams.

What Tipatap saw was the destruction of his dancing, singing machines. What Tipatap could not understand was how a thing so cared for, so loved, could be destroyed so easily, and without thought.

And so Tipatap wondered, perhaps, if the people could see the machines dancing and singing, they would not want to break them. Perhaps then, they would care for them as Tipatap did, perhaps even love them.

Tipatap stood, and tried to speak.

The figure in the middle of the floor in the cave unfolded himself, and stood. He was tall, far taller even than Cadha's father, even though he stooped and hunched his shoulders into his chest like nervous wings. The people of the town shrieked and waved their weapons at him, poking and jabbing, circling around him, and caging him with iron and cruel tongues and fearful eyes.

Then, the figure tried to speak.

Cadha could not understand the words, if words there were. To her it sounded like the whistling of a mountain wind and the mewling of a wolf cub. His long lips twisted and crooned around the lonely sounds, and his hands begged, and his eyes searched hard but did not find.

"Do not let the thief speak," said Cadha's father, and he raised his wood axe.

Every line of the figure's body implored.

"Wait," cried Cadha, and she pushed through to stand in front of her father. "He is trying to tell us something."

"Let him be, Cadha," said her father. "He is a monster, and a thief, and this mountain is fairer without him and his hellish creations."

"Please, Father, let him speak."

"Listen to your daughter," said Cadha's mother, putting a soft hand to her husband's shoulder.

He nodded, and lowered his axe, but Cadha knew it could rise again just as easily. She turned to the imploring figure.

"Well?" asked Cadha. "What do you want to say?"

The figure looked at her, and Cadha looked into his eyes. They were black, and depthless, and she could not help the fear that ran cold fingers down her neck. Looking into his eyes was like sleeping a night colorless of dreams.

The figure touched his lips with his hand, then gestured to one of his creations that was still unbroken.

"Do you want to show us something?" Cadha wondered.

The figure's eyes pleaded.

"Go on, then," she said.

Tipatap went to his machine, and wrapped his lips around the mouthpiece. He gave it a dream that he had kept tucked under his tongue while he slept, and stepped back.

The machine came alive with the color of the dream, a bright winter blue streaked with wild green and silver frost. It began to dance, and it began to sing, all on its own in the cave, surrounded by the people of the town, the little girl, Tipatap, and the broken bits and pieces of its brothers.

Tipatap smiled.

Cadha watched in wonder. In the machine's dancing and singing, there was a depth of loneliness and longing that Cadha had never known. There was a most beautiful sadness and a most heartfelt hopefulness. There was wisdom, and childlike innocence.

All around the cave, the weapons the people of the town held drooped their heads to the floor. For a moment, the cave was alive only with the colors and dancing and singing of the machine. Only for a moment Cadha wondered whose the dream had been. Then she thought that it did not matter, now. The dream belonged to those who witnessed it.

The people of the town watched with tear-promised eyes. Then, they wondered what they would do now.

"He cannot keep stealing our dreams every night," Cadha's father declared, in a softer voice, but a firm one. "No matter how beautifully he makes them dance."

"Then what shall we do?" the people asked.

The figure's hands wrung and his eyes sought.

"A deal must be made," Cadha's mother decided. "Perhaps he may take one dream, each night."

The people of the dream grumbled and muttered.

"He may take my dream, tonight," offered Cadha.

The courage of the little girl settled it.

The figure met Cadha's eyes, and found what he had been seeking.

That night, the little girl came to Tipatap's cave. She knocked at the fissure with the moonlight, and brought the crumbs of candle-glow and the smell of warm bed into the cave with her. She lay down, and at last fell asleep, and dreamed. Tipatap took her dream, and tucked it under his tongue. Cadha woke, and sat up to watch Tipatap as he went to one of his machines, and blew her dream into it.

Together, Tipatap and Cadha watched the machine dance and sing, and at last Cadha saw the colors of her dream in the night. Together, they smiled.

Old Friend

JEFFREY DAVIS

An evening downpour burst forth from the intense midday heat. It was a rain like Osaka hadn't seen in some time, freeing people from weeks of high temperatures. Either of these conditions would drive people indoors, Azumi thought. The barren streets signaled that they already were and that her bar might be empty that night.

As she approached the bar's door, Azumi readied her key. She noted the key's chipping gold plating and teeth that were rounded with use. The shaft was even bent. It had happened the night a rather inebriated group of locals had convinced her to stay late and have a drink with them. She had twisted the key locking up in a stupor. Despite all these imperfections, it still worked perfectly and it slid right inside the lock.

She headed in through the black door with gold trim. It creaked as it swung open. Stepping inside, she collapsed her umbrella.

Once upstairs, Azumi set the umbrella down at the end of a line of many umbrellas. They were hung neatly in place, and there were many more lines of umbrellas adorning every wall. Every size and color was represented. Those that extended were retracted and aligned with the rest. Those with curved grips had them flattened against the wall and were made to fit in lines as well. In fact the orderly rows of umbrellas covered most of the wall space of the small, darkened bar.

It was a gimmick that had started somewhat by circumstance when a few visitors left their umbrellas behind. Nonetheless, it was a gimmick that had served her well. She even renamed the place Kasa to fit the theme. The oddity of all this had brought in a good share of tourists.

Azumi went around the room and made sure everything was acceptable. The purple couch cushions fluffed and clean. The tables free of debris. Every chair neatly squared into position for potential patrons. When she was finished, she went to the windows which were currently shielding the room from cascading sheets of rain.

No other businesses in the alley remained open into the night like Kasa did. Their lighted signs dimmed one by one and their owners emptied out onto the street. They rushed, eager to return home and get out of the rain. She watched them flow out to the main street until a dark figure appeared and staggered against the herd.

At first, she thought the man might already be drunk. Still, maybe the till wouldn't remain completely empty.

The crowd hurried past and the man continued his wobbly gait toward the building. He wore a black bowler hat and a dark trench coat that swayed back and forth with each step. He was getting closer to the building, so she went back behind the bar to wait.

The creak of the black and gold door downstairs was followed by a slow, unsteady rhythm of clomps up the steep staircase.

"Irasshaimase!" Azumi greeted the man with habitual glee as he entered.

The man remained quiet and kept his head down as he lurched past, but she could see that his face was wrinkled and pale. Azumi then knew this man was not intoxicated, he was just elderly.

When he collapsed onto the couch, his hat fell off and to the cushion beside him. It revealed a deeply receded hairline and white hair. The old man leaned back and Azumi could see the rather large coat rest on his thin frame. He looked strangely as though he might have filled his clothes at a younger age, but now they draped down from his bony shoulders.

Always a good hostess, Azumi promptly approached him.

"Welcome. What can I get for you?"

He looked up at her.

"Isn't she pretty? Whiskey, please. With ice," he seemed to push each word out of his lungs.

"Yes," Azumi replied.

She went back to the bar as the man sat forward. While fixing the drink, she could see his head cocked as he gazed around the room. His eyes widened.

"What a magical place. Where did all these umbrellas come from?"

"Visitors leave them. It started by accident, but after a while people began to contribute on purpose. I like to think of it as a collaborative art project."

"All of these umbrellas, just abandoned?" the old man seemed bothered.

"They are not abandoned. They are left in my loving care!" she smiled.

"Of course, of course," he reclined and let out a small cough.

Azumi returned with the man's drink and set it down on the small table in front of him.

"Here you are. Please let me know if there is anything else you would like."

As she began to turn back, the man reached out and took hold of her wrist. "Please, won't you sit with me a while?"

The man seemed innocent enough, and there certainly wouldn't be any other customers to serve in this weather.

"Of course," she replied warmly and pulled a wooden chair up to the far side of the table.

The man took several heavy breaths. He seemed to be trying to remember what came next.

He finally spoke, "Do you know of yokai?"

"Old folk tales? Mythical spirits and monsters? Of course. I learned of some as a child."

"Then do you know of tsukumogami?"

"No, I'm afraid not."

"Tsukumogami were peculiar creatures. It was believed that any item, any tool, that had spent a long one hundred years in service could be granted a spirit and become a yokai. They could then become living beings called tsukumogami."

"Is that so?"

"Yes! Hammers, saddles, clocks. These tools, whatever they be, would gain faces and limbs and move about!" the man smiled with whimsy.

"Any tool at all? That's so interesting."

"I only bring it up in a place like this because of the kasa-obake."

"Ghost…umbrella?" Azumi pondered.

"Yes!" he replied enthusiastically, but let out another small cough before continuing, "They were living umbrellas! With arms and one big eyeball and one big, hairy foot to stomp around on."

The man waved his hand in a motion to portray one foot hopping and Azumi laughed at his theatrics. His story was interrupted by a short coughing fit.

"How very interesting," Azumi said, gazing at the multitude of umbrellas that surrounded them, "Imagine all these umbrellas just leaping off the wall!"

"Yes, imagine that."

"Were they good or bad spirits?"

"That is difficult to ascertain. Many believed that they were evil and so they would throw away old tools a year before their one-hundredth anniversary. But if you ask me, you don't spend ninety-nine years building a relationship only to throw it away. You would have to take great care of any tool if you wanted it to last one hundred years. In the end I suppose all yokai were much like people though, comprised of both good and bad."

"Of course. However, I don't believe any of these umbrellas are quite that old," she said searching the room for any that appeared worn or aged.

Then she remembered.

"There is the one back there," she twisted her torso around to point toward the bar.

"Where?"

"There. Behind the bar. The gray one in the corner. I think it was one of the first that was ever left here. Although I am not certain who left it."

She could see from her seat that the umbrella's fabric was torn and at least one of its ribs was bent. It could very well be older than the man that sat before her.

The man leaned forward and coughed yet again. This time his coughing grew more severe. As Azumi turned back to face him, he coughed a small amount of blood out onto the coffee table and his eyes closed shut.

"Are you all right?"

When the man didn't respond, Azumi got up and stepped around the table to his side. She gently nudged his torso back on the couch. Once he had fallen back, she had a clear sight of it. The man bled from what looked like a bullet wound on the side of his abdomen. The blood soaked through his oversized shirt.

Azumi gasped then cried out, "I'll call the hospital! I'm sorry! I didn't see!"

She turned to get to the phone at the bar.

"Wait!" the man shouted before she could take a step.

She looked back. The old man's hand slowly reached into his coat and brought forth a dark silver pistol. Azumi's expression transitioned from shock to terror.

The man gently set the gun down on the table. It looked as though each slight movement caused him anguish.

"Please come back. Sit."

She did as he asked. For a frightening, uncomfortable moment, nothing was said.

Finally, Azumi mustered up the courage to speak. "Are you going to kill me?"

"Don't be silly," the old man replied in a tired but warm tone. He paused before adding, "You are a good person. And I imagine if these umbrellas were alive, they would agree."

"If you would just let me call the hospital, I'm sure we can get you some help," Azumi pleaded.

"No. It's far too late for any of that," he said with a half smile.

Azumi stared down at the antiquated-looking gun. Blackened silver with a dark wooden handle. She lost herself in her gaze and her panic subsided. "What happened?"

"Much like any tool, I too lived my life in service. I am afraid, however, that my time will not see me rewarded. Quite the opposite."

The man's last sentence was gradually overtaken by the creaking of the door downstairs. It cried out, sending waves of relief and worry through Azumi's body.

"Maybe you should go back to the bar now," said the man.

"Who is it?" Azumi rose from her seat.

But the man did not answer. He sat up slightly while she quickly moved back behind the bar. They waited. They listened as multiple footsteps progressed up the staircase.

The door to the hallway swiftly swung open and in came two young men. They were no older than Azumi. They too wore dark suits like the old man, but theirs were more fashionable and more fitting. Time had not diminished their physiques yet.

"I told you we'd find him," said the man in the rear.

"You were right, you were right," replied the other young man.

He stood straight and tall, with his chin protruding. The other leaned back against the wall and adjusted his hair.

"What did you run for, huh?" the first man questioned angrily.

"Yeah! What did you run for?" echoed the second.

The old man sighed and leaned forward, resting his elbows on his knees.

"So many years I have worked for your father and he can't just leave me be? I'm an old man."

"Old or not, you don't get to just steal from him and walk away," the young man said.

The old man suddenly pounded his fist on the table, "It's nothing more than what he owes me! That man only wants to ensure my silence! Holding on to my earnings, keeping me in servitude to him. I have had enough!"

It was more liveliness than Azumi had thought the old man capable of. She could only watch the scene play out, paralyzed by fear. The first young man took a breath and scratched his forehead. It appeared as though the old man's outburst had scared him and he was now debating how to proceed.

"And now you drag us all the way down to this stupid, little bar?" he asked rhetorically.

"I don't know, there could be worse places," said the second man, eyeing Azumi with a smirk on his face.

She backed up to the wall and reaching behind her, felt around with her hands. Grasping for whatever she could use to protect herself, despite the belief that it would do no good. Her left hand found the tattered gray umbrella and lifted it, freeing it from its hook.

"Leave her alone. I'm the one you're here for," the old man said.

"What are you going to do about it, huh? You're just a washed up, useless old man. I'll bet you can't even lift that gun in front of you."

The second man chuckled.

There came a lingering silence. For a moment, the elderly man looked to Azumi and smiled warmly. When the moment had passed, he lowered his head down.

"Goodbye, old friend."

No sooner had he finished the words than the gun was in his hand. Never did Azumi expect that the man could move so quickly, especially with his wound.

His movements, however, were not fast enough. The two men riddled the purple couch with bullets. The old man's body slumped down and his gun clattered to the floor.

Azumi watched in terror. Fear gripped her so tightly it restricted her movement. She wanted to scream, but couldn't take a breath deep enough.

The room settled and it was silent again. In the quiet Azumi could gather her thoughts, but they only confused her more. What did he mean? "Old friend."

She clutched the gray umbrella tightly as the two men turned their attention to her once again.

"What about the girl?" asked the second thug.

Pointing the muzzle of his gun at Azumi the first man responded, "I'm tired. Let's just get out of here."

Before either man could pull their trigger, Azumi reacted. She flung the old gray umbrella from her hip directly at the young thug.

It bounced off his head and then fell to the floor, sliding towards the coffee table. It provided just enough of a distraction for her to duck.

As Azumi dropped to her knees, the two men began to fire wildly at the bar. She covered her head as bullets struck all around her. Wood splintered and bottles shattered. She was certain this was the end.

Then came a distinct sound. It was the sound of two gunshots. Two gunshots that were not like the others. These were more tinny and sibilant. Even more notably, they put an end to the barrage of gunfire filling her ears.

Azumi unwove her arms from around her head. There wasn't a sound now. Once again, she could attempt to gather her thoughts. And once again, she only found confusion. Had the old man survived?

After taking a minute to calm herself, she decided that the two young men would never have remained quiet for this long. They were either dead or they had left. She wasn't quite sure which to hope for. Delicately, Azumi rose to her feet.

Her mouth sat agape as she observed the bodies of the two men collapsed on the floor by the entrance. She forcefully pushed the air from her lungs to try to relax the tenseness in her chest and stop herself from screaming.

Looking around the room, she saw that the bar and stools were destroyed. It was a miracle no bullets had struck her. The nice old man still lay lifeless on the couch. His body hadn't moved. Clearly he hadn't fired the shots that killed the two men.

Just then, there was a rhythmic scampering sound from somewhere in the room. Azumi couldn't tell from where. She stepped out from behind the bar. Inching along apprehensively, she moved past the bodies of the two young thugs.

The noise of scurrying sounded again from somewhere near the couch. Each beat was evenly measured. It was more like a hop than a footstep.

She reached the coffee table. Once there, she paused when she heard it again. It came from the back corner of the room now, near a darkened corridor that led to the bathroom.

Surveying the area around the old man, she could see the couch was shredded and the coffee table fractured as well. Below the table, at the tip of the old man's shoe, rested the ragged gray umbrella.

She slowly proceeded past the purple couch and approached the corridor.

Not knowing what to expect, she timidly called out, "Hello?"

There was no response. Azumi continued forward. Nearing the hall, she saw movement in the shadows.

"Is someone there?"

Still no response. She had already come this far though, so she stepped into the corridor.

There was something there. Something small sitting on the floor, in the blackness against the far wall.

When she stepped closer, she noticed it twitch. She decided to hold her position until her eyes adjusted and she could see what she was dealing with.

As her eyes adapted, the first thing she noticed was long dark fur. It wasn't evenly spread, it was placed in patches on the creature's body. A body that was no larger than a rat. It sat still, hunched steeply over.

The darkness dissipated further. There was a slight gleam to any part of the creature's body not covered in fur. Azumi saw at least one wide, black eyeball looking back at her. She watched it blink.

Azumi continued to hold still, next noticing the claws. Large, unevenly-sized claws attached at the base of the strange being's one, very thick leg. A leg that appeared to be made of wood. Ridged, darkly-stained wood like the handle of a pistol.

The creature started to shift away from the wall, seeming to want to investigate Azumi. It hopped once to get closer to her.

She squatted down to get a closer look. It was clearly visible now. The creature was the antique pistol that the old man carried. It had been given a spirit. It was now a twisted mishmash of machine and living thing.

Azumi smiled and the tsukumogami hopped closer.

The Grundylow

JULIE ANN REES

I saw a grundylow in the pond at the bottom of my garden, where it turns muddy. I don't usually go down there, too many bugs and midges, but during the recent months of drought and sunshine the pond had dried up considerably. Pretty flowers scattered the banks, cowslip trumpets, king cups, and wild orchids now clustered the usually-dank marshland; a rare splattering of color instead of murky brown and algae green.

Because of the drought, the bottom of the pond revealed itself, like shattered brown crockery, dried up and shriveled. Towards the middle lay a slug of murk and damp. It was here that I saw it, the grundylow. Poor thing was half in and half out of the sludge, struggling to hide in the shallow puddle. Frog eyes narrowed and fish lips sneered away from pike teeth. The feeble display was pitiful.

I made soothing noises and sat still on the bank, watching. The grundylow gurgled and flapped, fear raising their hackles towards me. How things change. I remembered the old stories, how grundylow's had dragged children to watery deaths, feeding on their flesh. My grandmother would hiss and snarl during the tales, reaching bony fingers to tickle us kids until we screeched and hid. Fear and laughter close companions. It kept us safe, we steered clear of the waterways.

Jenny Greenteeth was the one we feared most, but she lived up North. Down here in the Welsh marshes we called the grundylows *mari morgans.* Men succumbed mostly. Addled with drink they mistook the grundylows for young women, they had sweet voices with which they sung, which is why children got caught too, believing them to be fairies or other kids. Nobody ever survived an attack, only chewed up bones made it home to stricken families.

I watched the grundylow struggle before deciding to approach. I couldn't help but feel sorry for the creature. I sat on my haunches on the cracked mud of the pond and reached out my hand. They scrabbled and tried to run before slumping into what little water remained, spent. My fingers brushed the top of their head where strands of pond weed, brittle and cracked, broke away. The grundylow was dying I thought, the drought was killing them.

I wanted to help. I couldn't just watch the creature shrivel and die before my eyes. Maybe I could coax them into the house and fill the bath with water. I'd get some water weed from the garden center, turn my bathtub into a pond, and keep the grundylow alive until the rains returned. I could feed them fish, but would draw the line at human flesh; although this thing looked too small to be a threat.

"Hey, Grundy," I whispered. "Don't be scared, I'll help." I tried to lift the creature, feeling sharp spines along their back. They flinched and hunched away, hiding something. I could hear a sweet song, the voice of a young girl rose around me before cracking. Gently I gathered the bag of spines and bones into my arms, helping them to sit up – and noticed then what was clutched in the creature's arms.

A tiny grundylow peered at me. The baby had been suckling a dry, flappy teat. Green liquid oozed from the side of a slitted mouth, the infant hiccupped before beginning to cry. The sobs broke my heart. I had found a female grundylow with her young. This was rare. I didn't know how grundylows reproduced, but obviously they must do, wasn't that tragic beast Grendel the child of one? I had to help this poor female and her suckling babe.

I told her she must trust me, and explained about the bath. She stared, head cocked, and I think she was beginning to understand. I held out my hand and tentatively she placed her husk-like fingers in mine while her other arm cradled the whimpering tot. She was very weak and I could hear her breaths wheeze in the dry air. What looked like gills in her neck closed stiffly, caked in mud.

I walked slowly, leading her down the garden. Thin, webbed

feet blistered in the sun, I knelt down to her level and explained I needed to carry them both the rest of the way. The grass was hot and the garden path burning. She twitched from foot to foot before reaching a spindly arm around my neck, allowing me to lift her as she clutched her baby.

Her body was like a sack of sticks and twigs that smelled, not unpleasantly, of mold and earth. The usual pond stench of a grundylow had long dried up, leaving a sweeter fragrance. The spines along her back were sharp, and I was careful not to cut myself, I didn't want her to get a whiff of human blood. She was still a wild and dangerous being.

My hip nudged the back door and I carried her through the cool stone-flagged kitchen and into the bathroom. I placed her in the tub and ran the cold tap. She adjusted her baby and blinked her relief, eyelids sticking to jellied eyes. Water swirled around her limbs, the dust and sludge coloring it woody brown. Her skin began to soften; dry patches flaked off, floating to the surface. She sighed and lowered herself into the water, stretching out. The baby kicked and woke, and began swimming newt-like around her.

"I'll get food," I said, "and some pond weed. I won't be long, try to rest." She regarded me, eyes bright with gratitude. I smiled and her lips grimaced in response.

There wasn't much choice of pond weed in the garden center, the plants were dry and in as much need of rehabilitation as my grundylow. I bought what they had, and picked up some fresh cod from the fishmongers on the way home. I asked for any fish they were throwing out, saying I had a cat that needed feeding up. The stench made me gag in the hot car on the way home.

Half of me wondered if she'd still be there, or had she replenished herself and slinked away to the marsh. The other half wondered if I'd dreamed her, a hallucination from too much sun. Cautiously I approached the bathroom door. Small sounds cooed from within, a young woman's voice, childlike and dainty. I opened the door to the juxtaposition.

She was returning to her old form, the water giving her life. More dead skin coated the bathtub and floated string-like. Underneath, fresh skin glowed greenish, her eyes had regained their bulbous watery stare, and her gills opened and closed freely. The strands of hair left on her head draped over her chest, where the little one suckled greedily. The tiny head was oval and smooth, larger than their green body, which was furred moss-like, with twiggy arms and legs.

I removed the pond weed from the pots and placed them into the bath; she watched me like Ophelia amongst the fronds. She was beautiful I realized. I was aware she might be spelling me, but I was a woman like her and, according to legend, women did not succumb in the same way as men. She was simply a beautiful creation and I marveled at her.

I gave her the fish, even the fresh cod, my own appetite having retreated from the stench. Eagerly she snatched them, disappearing under the water. She fed underneath and I could hear sounds both savage and sweet. I waited patiently until she resurfaced. I could tell she was ashamed, but I smiled encouragingly, telling her she had to eat to get strong to feed the little one. Her lips pulled back from her teeth and she gripped my arm. I flinched but her grip was gentle and doll-like, she squeaked a thank you.

I stayed with her for most of the night. I told her my name was Gwen, she grimaced a smile and told me hers was Jilly. I remembered that name; it belonged to a missing child from years ago. I asked her how she'd got her name, and she said she didn't know, but most mothers took the names of their victims to give to their children. I asked what she'd called her little one, holding my breath for the answer, hoping it wasn't another missing child.

"Lamb," she said, "his name is lamb." She explained how the poor, bleating creature got separated from their mother, and she had taken the fragile life. She'd been heavily pregnant, and the drought had weakened them both. Soon after she had given birth, the lamb's blood gave her the strength she needed. Grundylow births are complicated; many mothers do not survive the process.

Jilly and Lamb lived in my bathtub for the whole summer.

Lamb got larger, and I worried about them being discovered. I had recently broken up with a boyfriend, and he'd come around a few times hoping for a reconciliation or sex. I'd hidden in the bathroom giggling, ignoring his knocks and calls, Jilly's girlish voice joining my own. He must have got the message in the end, through the sound of splashing water and female shrieks. I hoped we'd made him jealous.

In reality, my bathroom was far from a feminine boudoir: it stank. Jilly was loath to change the water, preferring the stagnant green and smelly sludge to fresh. She also liked to leave the fish guts floating about for Lamb to wallow in, and practice eating solid food. I understood it was her habitat, and how she liked it. I however, had taken to washing with a flannel at the sink.

My friends begun to ask questions, I visited their houses but always put them off from coming to mine. Now I just stayed in, it was easier, and I preferred being with Jilly and Lamb anyway. I knew they would have to move back to the marsh when the rains came, so wanted to make the most of our time together. I would miss them. I enjoyed Jilly's company and even cuddled Lamb when she needed some peace. She knew she'd have to leave soon too; a murky bathtub was no place for a young grundylow to grow up.

September drew to a close and the sky darkened, heavy and brooding. The weathermen predicted thunderstorms and torrential rain. Flood warnings were issued and people piled sandbags outside their front doors. I didn't need to tell Jilly the news; she could smell the rain coming. Her nostrils flared as lightning lit, thunder crashed, and pattering drops began to pour before pregnant clouds released a deluge.

She rose from the bathtub, Goddess like, carrying Lamb on her hip, his twig legs clutching, and walked through to the kitchen. I opened the door, the rain glistened silver in the lamp light, and she stepped into the torrent. I followed her to the pond, my own clothes plastered to my back. The pond was beginning to fill rapidly, and I could smell a mineral-rich dampness from the marshy waters beyond.

Lamb was kicking and yipping with excitement. She released him into the pond and we watched as he swam and leaped, twirling and diving. He peeped from the surface, bug eyed and grinning. Sharp teeth were beginning to form, two at the top and one below. It gave him a gap-toothed innocence. We laughed at his antics, proud parents.

I touched Jilly's soft arm scales, fingers trailing a shiver to her neck. She breathed sharply, reaching for me. Pad-like fingertips cupped my face. I rubbed my cheek against her cold, clammy palm. Her hair had grown back, framing her face in emerald weed. Leaning forward she pressed amphibian lips to my own. I wrapped my arms around her, gasping as a sharp scale caught my finger. She held my hand and sucked the wound; concern creased her face as she recognized my fear. Smiling she released my hand and kissed me again, pulling me close.

Her body felt firm and wet, the brittleness healed, fresh skin and muscle returned. She had grown taller, almost matching my own height. Even her breasts felt soft, and her belly small and rounded once more. Sharp teeth trailed over my lips and she breathed my scent before slipping from my grasp.

"Wait," I cried. "Will I see you again?"

Eyes bright, quicksilver hands lifted from the pond in farewell. I watched two shapes dart otter-like into the shadowy depths, and out through the overflow into the marsh.

Reluctantly I returned to my own life. Loneliness prevented me from cleaning the bathroom as I longed for her presence. The neighbor complained of a boggy smell and, unable to put it off any longer, I got to work, the stink was getting to me too if I'm honest. I bagged up the fish guts for the rubbish, and took the pond weed down to the bottom of the garden to plant.

Pressing fragile roots into the squelch of the bloated pond, I called her name. My voice echoed emptily over the marsh. Wading birds had returned; they rose startled into the sky sounding a caterwaul of shrieks. I sat in the weak autumn light watching the pond. Ripples formed, bubbling and spreading. Reeds parted, swirling in the greenish depths, and a delicate childish singing rose from beneath. Showing no fear, I waded eagerly into the water as the surface broke with a splash, and the song of a grundylow washed over me.

Lakers

MARSHALL J MOORE

Smooth ripples spread across the placid surface of Lake Erie, lapping at my knee-high rubber boots and splashing the rocky shore. The ripples grew to a wake, a disturbance beneath the surface like the bow wave thrown up before a speedboat, but the creature that made the wave was under the water, not upon it.

The wave frothed and whitened. Now I could see the first hints of the shape beneath: snakelike and sinuous, undulating with a motion at once powerful and lazy. A wake like a jet ski's trailed behind her.

And she was coming straight for me.

I fought the urge to take a step back, just as I resisted the even more primal impulse to turn and run screaming into the woods. I planted my feet deeper in the muddy shallows and pulled my raincoat tight around me.

She broke the surface ten yards from shore, breaching like an orca as the whole of her great bulk shot skyward. She revolved in slow motion, at once graceful and ungainly. I drank in the delicate twist of her long neck, her broad flippers, the horse-like shape of her head. No wonder the Scottish had labelled her kind kelpies centuries before one of her cousins had settled in a loch near Inverness.

A thunderclap split the early morning as she bellyflopped back into the lake, sending a wave as tall as I was hurtling towards shore. I barely had time to make sure my phone was safely insulated in my coat pocket before I was swamped. I closed my eyes as the solid wall of water struck me full in the face. The cold shocked me fully awake, something a full thermos of coffee had failed to do.

A smaller woman might have been swept right off her feet, but I come from hardy stock. I planted my boots in the mud and held firm.

The long neck had surfaced again. She paddled towards me, her short but broad foreflippers driving her forward with each stroke. Within seconds she towered above me, her long narrow face angled down at mine. Intelligence glimmered behind eyes so dilated that only the faintest ring of gold could be discerned at the edges of the huge pupils. Droplets rained on my face.

I looked up into those deep black eyes, studiously avoiding the rows of needle-sharp teeth.

"Thank you for coming," she said.

"I apologize for the early hour," Bessie said, as I splashed through the shallows. Bessie swam smoothly beside me, her head bent towards shore so that we could converse without effort.

"I know you walkers like to sleep past the sun," she continued, "but we rouse at dusk and sleep when it's light. I hope you had a good night's rest?"

"Sure." I hoped my smile masked the weariness tugging at my eyelids – or barring that, that Bessie wasn't adept at reading human facial expressions. Not many lakers were.

That was what we had decided to call them, to the lasting outrage of all Angelenos. Not that it bothered the lakers – they were creatures of deep freshwater lakes and broad rivers, neither of which were abundant in southern California.

Bessie bent her head towards me, one black eye looking into my own. "Though we have only just met, may I ask you what might be a rude question, Dr. Spyros?"

"No such thing as a rude question in my line of work, Bessie." I wrinkled my nose. "Is it…okay to call you that? It feels… derogatory, somehow."

The laker bobbed her head in their version of a shrug. "It is the name you walkers have given me, so I answer to it. My real name would be unpronounceable to you."

Of that I had no doubt. The lakers' natural tongue was a series of clicks and whistles akin to those of dolphins, ideal for carrying across the echoing lakebeds where they made their homes.

"Okay," I nodded. "What's your question, Bessie?"

"You have met other lakers before?"

I glanced at her. "I thought Champ recommended me to you."

"Champ?"

Of course she would know him by a different name. "The laker who lives in Lake Champlain. I, uh, I'm not sure how you say it–"

"Oh!" Bessie shook her head. A long, keening whistle sounded across the water, followed by an arrhythmic clicking. Champ's laker name. "Yes. He told me you were very…familiar."

My brows knitted themselves into one. "Familiar?"

"Very easy to talk to," Bessie amended.

"That was nice of him," I said.

A loon called across the water, mournful and eerie in the mist. Bessie's head swiveled to search for it, the steady rhythm of her paddling faltering. And though the differences in our physiology made reading one another's body languages difficult, I recognized the unease in the motion.

She was nervous.

"What about you?" I asked, keeping my tone icebreaker casual. It's best to approach these things tactfully. "Do I seem familiar to you?"

"Oh, yes." Bessie nodded, a gesture I knew she had acquired from walkers. She was trying to set me at ease, just as I was her. "I like you already, Dr. Spyros."

"I like you too, Bessie."

She snorted in a laker laugh, the sound exactly like a whale clearing its blowhole. Her kind were aquatic reptiles, not fish.

"Good," Bessie snort-laughed. "That's good. Only…" She trailed off, her head swiveling around on her long neck.

I stopped walking and waded into the lake until the water rose to my navel. Bessie ceased paddling and turned to me, the expression on her alien face unreadable.

"Bessie," I said, my voice firm but gentle. "Please. Is something bothering you?"

Another nod, the motion artificial and exaggerated. "You have met other lakers. And you have worked with children?"

"I have." I was beginning to understand the root of her unease.

"But you have never..." Her head dipped towards the lake, as though hoping to find the right words in its murky depths. "Never worked with one of ours. With a laker child."

"No one has," I said. "This will be the first time a human social worker has ever consulted for a laker."

Bessie considered this. We continued in silence for several minutes, me wading and her swimming. I didn't press, simply waited.

"I suppose you know that we are not subject to your laws," she said at last. "If you think that something is...is wrong with Trevor...you can't..."

Ice water crept down my back as I realized the precise nature of Bessie's hesitance. I had to reassure her of my motives quickly, or this whole thing was sunk. Perhaps literally.

"Bessie," I said, in that same firm-but-gentle voice I used to soothe worried human parents. I could only hope it was as effective on aquatic reptile mothers. "Listen to me. I'm not here with any government agency. I'm not here to punish Trevor, and I'm certainly not here to take him away from you. I'm here because you asked for me, and because I think I can help. All right?"

The loon called again, somewhere in the fog.

"All right," Bessie said after a moment. She lowered her head until we were nearly eye level, and I found myself resisting the mad urge to reach out and stroke her snout like she was a horse. "I'm sorry."

"You have nothing to be sorry for," I told her, my tone softening. "It's natural for a mother to want to protect their child. Admirable."

"Thank you."

We continued along the lakeshore. The early morning mist had dissipated somewhat, though the air was still thick and cool. Bessie was leading me to a secluded cove that was nearly inaccessible to humans, tucked away in a remote corner of the lake's wilder edges. To her lair, in fact.

"I need to ask you some questions about Trevor," I said. "If that's all right with you."

"Certainly."

"Is he your only child?"

"At present." Bessie glanced at me. "We birth only one at a time. Live young, not eggs, to shelter and raise until they are old enough to swim the deep waters, to find some new lake to make their home. Only then are we ready to birth another."

"But you've had others?"

"Three." She bobbed her head low over the water. "I cannot tell you what their names were, for they were each grown and gone before we lakers first spoke with you walkers. But they were strong, bold swimmers. Good hunters."

I sensed the unspoken words lurking like shadows behind those she voiced. *Not like Trevor.*

"And Trevor?" I asked. "How old is he?"

"Young," Bessie said. "In seasons, but also in mind. He…does not hunt. Not well, at least."

Now we were getting to the heart of the matter. "Why is that?"

Bessie bared her needle teeth; an expression of frustration. "Because he is a poor swimmer. Clumsy. In the shallows he splashes and flails. He cannot properly hold his breath, so in the depths he flounders, unable to control his…"

"Buoyancy?" I suggested.

"Yes." Bessie nodded. "So he thrashes, and scares off the fish. I must do his hunting for him, even though at his age he should be able to catch them himself."

I picked my way through a thicket of branches lying low over the water. "Does that frustrate you?"

"Of course." Another flash of her needle teeth. "But more than that, it worries me. I cannot look after him forever."

"All right." I considered what she had told me, comparing Trevor's difficulties to those of terrestrial patients I had known. "What about speech? Can he…does he talk normally?"

Bessie snort-laughed. "Funny you should ask that. Trevor is

a quiet boy, in our tongue. But he is quite conversant in walker-speak."

"Really?" I chewed my lip. This was startlingly similar to many other cases I had encountered, save for the difference in species. "That's unusual."

"Quite. Most of us do not try to learn your language until we have mastered our own, but for whatever reason yours comes more easily to Trevor."

I reviewed my mental checklist of Trevor's symptoms. Unusual speech patterns, check. Difficulty with physical activities others his age found normal, also check. Struggle with social interaction was another, though that would be harder to gauge with a laker than a human child. I would have to reserve judgment on that front until Trevor and I had had a chance to talk.

One other qualifier, then.

"What about his interests?" I asked. "Hobbies, activities, that sort of thing."

Bessie quirked her head to the side, a startlingly human gesture. "Hobbies?"

Right. I should have realized that would require some clarification. "Activities unrelated to daily survival. Not hunting or swimming."

"Oh." Bessie was quiet for a moment. We rounded a bend, and the sheltered little cove where she laired appeared from behind a bank of willows.

"I think it is better that I show you," Bessie said.

To my surprise, Trevor was already above the waterline when we arrived, his neck bent low over the shore.

Bessie gave me a look that even on her reptilian face plainly said "wait here," then turned and paddled towards her son. I halted beneath a willow and watched through the trailing leaves, taking my time to observe the young laker.

A thrill crept down my spine. Few humans had ever encountered a juvenile before. As a species lakers were highly protective of their young. For Bessie to not only allow me to meet Trevor but to evaluate him was either a sign of great trust, or an indicator of the depth of her motherly concern. Perhaps both.

Trevor was built along the same frame as his mother. His horsey head sat on a neck that would shame a giraffe. His torso was comparatively short, almost porpoise-like, with four stubby flippers and an even stubbier tail. What I could see of his underside was a smooth pale gray, but his dorsal side was mottled with a streaked pattern that put me in mind of a tiger shark's stripes – a trait his mother lacked. I wondered whether this were a juvenile characteristic that would fade with adulthood, or a genetic variation like human hair color.

Bessie was speaking to him, her voiced pitched too low for me to hear across the water. Trevor's head swayed towards her, listening, but he did not look directly at her.

I frowned. In a human subject, difficulty making eye contact was another symptom, but I was less certain with lakers. As aquatic beings, their natural mode of communication echoed across the lakebed, rendering line of sight between speakers about as necessary as the salutation in an email.

My own name drifted to me over the cove. I started, realizing that they weren't speaking in clicks and whistles, but in English. Trevor really *was* more fluent in my language than his mother tongue.

Bessie turned back to me, the motion remarkably similar to a human looking over their shoulder, despite the difference in neck length.

"Dr. Spyros," she called, her voice carrying over the water. "Would you come here?"

I pushed aside the drape of willow leaves and waded towards them, moving slowly and making plenty of noise. Many children I had worked with reacted poorly to strangers, especially if they felt like they were being surprised. By making my approach slow and obvious, I was alerting Trevor to my presence and making it clear that I didn't mean to sneak up on him.

His head craned towards me, looking me dead on with both eyes. Though their skulls were shaped similar to horses', lakers were predators, their eyes forward-facing to aid in chasing down prey.

"Hello, Trevor," I said once I was at a polite distance – far enough that he could bend his head towards me, but not so close that he couldn't turn and slide into the lake if I made a sudden move.

"Hello," he said. Like all lakers, his voice was surprisingly melodic, like a whalesong in English.

"My name is Dr. Spyros," I said. I bent my head and bowed at the waist – the closest a human could reasonably get to approximating the complex neck movements lakers used to introduce themselves to one another.

"Dr. Spyros," Trevor repeated, carefully enunciating each syllable. "A doctor is someone who helps people, right? Like when they're hurt?"

"Somctimes," I said. "But more often we just try to make sure that people are healthy and happy."

"Trevor," Bessie said, leaning her head in close to his. "Dr. Spyros would like to ask you some questions."

"If that's all right," I added.

"Okay," Trevor said, his voice suddenly quieter. He lowered his head almost to the muddy bank, where several mounds of damp earth were piled high. I stared, fascinated, as he curled his neck protectively around them. The little mounds were like a child's sandcastle, only muddier. I had never before encountered any evidence that lakers possessed a play instinct, but Trevor clearly did.

Then again, we have had so little interaction with their young. Maybe all laker children built mudcastles by the shore. How would we know?

"Bessie?" I asked. "Would you mind leaving Trevor and I to talk privately?"

Bessie looked pointedly at me, then at Trevor.

"It's fine, Mom," he said, still curled about his creations. A high keening sound like a radio being tuned accompanied this statement, and it took a moment for me to realize that he had added something in laker-speak. Whatever he'd said seemed to mollify Bessie, because she snort-laughed.

"I will be on the far side of the lake if you need me," she said, then leaned in and pressed the tip of her snout against Trevor's.

This display of motherly affection was one of the few encroachments on personal space a laker would permit. Even so, Trevor's flipper twitched in seeming discomfort, though he otherwise endured the contact without complaint. I added difficulty with physical contact to my mental list of symptoms the young laker matched.

Bessie turned, flippers paddling soundlessly beneath the surface as she swam out of the little cove. I waited until she was out of sight, hands tucked into my raincoat pockets.

"Could you give me some space?" Trevor asked once his mother had gone behind the bend. His neck was bent so low over the mud mounds that he had to look up at me. "You're a little close."

"Of course," I said, backing further into the shallows. "I'm sorry. I didn't mean to make you uncomfortable."

"You didn't," Trevor said, a touch too quickly. He raised his head, looking not at me but down at the mud. "I mean, you did, but that's okay. It's not your fault."

"Trevor," I said, keeping my voice soft. "I'm not here to make you feel bad, or to judge you. Can you understand that?"

"Okay," he said, still not looking at me.

"I'm just here to get to know you."

"You don't have to lie." Trevor shuffled backwards into the water, the motion exactly like a sea lion backing away from shore. "I know my mom asked you to talk to me."

"She did."

Trevor splashed at the shallows. There was something distinctly adolescent about the gesture. "She thinks there's something wrong with me."

Bessie *did* think that, but there was no point in dwelling on it.

Honesty was always the best policy. Children like Trevor didn't like being lied to, even little white lies meant to smooth over the uncomfortable parts of a conversation. To them, words were a device for conveying facts and information – in other words, truth. Speech for any other purpose was a waste of time or worse, pointless deception.

"She's concerned for you, Trevor." I scooped up a palmful of lake water and let it trickle through my fingers, a subtle mirroring of Trevor's own nervous stimming. "She just wants to know that you'll be all right once you're grown."

"It's because I can't fish." Trevor sighed, the sound remarkably human. "She doesn't have to worry. I'll be okay."

"It's a mother's nature to worry," I said. "It doesn't reflect on you at all, other than showing how much she loves you."

"I know she does." Trevor glanced at me. "Are you a mother, Dr. Spyros?"

"I am." I smiled. "Two kids."

He looked more directly at me, his deep eyes boring into mine. Unlike his mother, his huge irises were ringed with a faint halo of blue. "What are their names?"

"Katherine and Nick," I said. "They're about your age, I think. At the same stage of growth, anyway."

"What do they like?"

I blinked. "I'm sorry?"

Trevor trundled through the shallows, pushing a clump of mud towards shore with his front flippers. "I mean, the sort of things they're interested in. Are they normal for walkers?"

"Oh." I should have realized. "I suppose so. Nick's into musical theatre. Katherine likes roleplaying games. Nothing extraordinary."

"Extraordinary," Trevor said, sounding it out. His flippers flapped wetly against the mud. "I don't have any brothers or sisters. None my age, anyway."

"That's not unusual for lakers, I understand."

"I guess not," he shook his head. "But I don't need them to know I'm different."

"How are you different?" I asked. I waded a little nearer to shore, careful to maintain a respectful distance from him.

"I'm bad at fishing," he said. "And at swimming. But it's…more than that, I think. I…don't talk right."

"On the contrary," I said. "Your English is excellent."

"I know," he snort-laughed. "I meant Laker. I…don't sound right. Hard to understand, my mom says."

I felt a sympathetic twinge in my chest. "That must be difficult."

"It is." Trevor nodded. The motion looked more natural on him than it did for his mother, somehow. "Especially because she doesn't understand the things I want to talk about."

"Like what?"

"Like these," Trevor said, patting the mud into a mound like the others. "Come and see."

I drew nearer, still keeping my movements slow. Trevor had stacked the mud lining the shore into an uneven row of mounds, each a neat little cone pointing up at the trees above. Now that I was closer, I could see that smooth river pebbles and loose twigs adorned their sides. Trevor hadn't simply made the mud mounds; he had decorated them.

"They're very nice," I said, kneeling in the shallows to examine them more closely. "I like the little sticks."

"Thanks," Trevor said, bending his head. One of those sticks had fallen from its mound. I watched as he picked it up between his teeth and with surprising dexterity placed it back into the mound. "Those are trees."

As soon as he said it, I understood what I was looking at. The conical mounds of damp earth arranged in a rough row, with smooth round rocks adorning their peaks and a forest of twigs below.

"These are mountains," I said.

"Yes!" Trevor's head bobbed up and down in undisguised delight. He craned his neck towards me, so close that I could have reached out a hand and stroked his long snout if I had dared. "Have you ever seen one?"

"A few times," I said, smiling. He was warming to me.

"Will you tell me about them?" His eyes stared into mine, black ringed with blue. Even across the gulf of our separate species I could see the excitement in them.

I trudged out of the lake, boots squelching in the mud, and seated myself on the mossy bank.

My work had taken me to the Cascades, on a case not too dissimilar from Trevor's. I talked for nearly an hour, describing as best I could recall the extent of that sweeping range of white-capped mountains. I told him about the fast-flowing rocky streams that fell from their heights to the lush coniferous forests clustered around their bases. I described the way the ground would sometimes rumble ominously underfoot as the sleeping volcanoes stirred, though it was difficult to convey the feeling of the earth trembling to a being who spent most of his time immersed in water.

Trevor worked the entire time I spoke, pushing more mud further up onto the shore as he expanded his little mountain range. I found myself admiring his patience and dedication, the careful way in which he arranged each pebble and twig to better fit his design. I quietly added his fixation on repetitive activity and his particular interest in mountains to my mental checklist.

Every once and a while I caught a glimpse of Bessie, cruising slowly through the waters beyond the sheltered cove. I was glad to know that she was keeping a close eye on her son, but hoped she was wise enough to keep her distance while I was working. Like all adolescents, Trevor's natural self-consciousness was only exacerbated by his parent's presence.

"It sounds wonderful," he said once I had finally exhausted my memories of the Cascades. There was an unmistakable wistfulness in his tone. "I wish I could go."

I kept my face carefully blank. Years spent working in child development had trained me never to laugh at a child's desires, no matter how fanciful. Those desires were real to them, and often deeply cherished. To mock them was to mock the child.

"Why is that, Trevor?"

"It just sounds so exciting!" He nudged a pebble that had fallen out of place. "To be way up high, with the sky above you and all those trees below you. Not like here."

His looked around the little cove. Was I reading too much into things, or was his expression wistful?

"You don't like the lake?" I asked.

Trevor bobbed his head in a laker shrug. "It's okay, I guess. Just…boring."

"A lot of young people think their homes are boring," I said. "There's nothing unusual about that."

"If you say so," Trevor said, sounding unconvinced.

By now the sun had risen well into the sky, and I was beginning to grow hot. I checked my watch and was surprised to find it was nearly nine in the morning.

"I'm sorry, Trevor," I said. "I'm afraid I've kept you up. This is awfully late for you, isn't it?"

He shook his head. "I don't mind."

"Your mom might, though," I said, glancing over my shoulder. Sure enough, Bessie was lurking just past the bank of willows. I waved to her.

"I guess," Trevor said reluctantly. "Will you come back tomorrow?"

"Not tomorrow," I said. "But soon, yes."

I had already begun formulating plans for a follow-up session, and had an idea for how best to engage Trevor's more unusual interests. "Would it be okay with you if I brought a friend?"

"A friend?" Trevor mulled this over. "A walker doctor, like you?"

"He is a walker," I said, which was true in the broadest sense. "Not a doctor, though. Just a friend. I think you'd like him. You have a lot in common. He's from the mountains."

"Really?" Again those deep eyes lit up.

"Lived there his whole life," I said. I put my hands on my knees and stood, wincing at how my backside had gone numb from sitting in one spot for so long. I bent at the waist, just as

I had when greeting Bessie. "Thank you for showing me your mountains, Trevor. I'll see you soon."

He bowed his head in return, then lifted one flipper into the air. A grin broke over my face.

Trevor was waving goodbye.

"There's nothing wrong with Trevor," I told Bessie as I trudged along the shore back to my car. "That's the first and most important thing."

"No?" She craned her neck towards me. "But he is such a poor swimmer."

"He'll get better with time," I assured her. "A lot of kids like him are slow to develop their physical capabilities. But slow isn't the same as never. He'll learn."

"Kids like him." Bessie mulled over the words. "So there *is* something different about him. Not wrong, but...different."

"In walkers we call it autism," I said. "It's a developmental condition."

I told her the basics, explained how I had matched Trevor's symptoms to autism: his physical clumsiness, his odd speech, his social tendencies. I made particular note of his unusual interest in mountains, careful to frame it as the sign of an active and curious mind.

"Will he be able to have a normal life?" Bessie asked when I had finished.

"I think so," I said. It was difficult to say what constituted 'normal' for lakers. Likely Bessie's concern was still primarily for Trevor's survival. "You say he's physically healthy, other than his difficulty swimming?"

"He is," Bessie said slowly. "His size is normal for his age, and he is strong, though clumsy."

"Then you have nothing to worry about," I said. "And neither does Trevor."

"I don't know about that," Bessie said, glancing out at the open lake.

Erie's broad expanse stretched away to the horizon and past it, an unbroken line of gray water beneath the clear blue morning sky. No matter how many times I beheld that vast expanse, I couldn't help but wonder at the sheer size of it, its distance and depth. Like her sisters, Erie was a lake only in name. In truth she was an inland sea, a world unto herself.

A world into which Trevor would be thrust in time, to journey through the secret channels and explore the distant tides on his own. Little wonder that his mother was so concerned for him.

It was hard to read the expression on Bessie's flat reptilian face, but I could guess the thoughts beneath. A mother's concern for her child lay deeper than any lakebed, ranged farther than all the waterways in the world.

"He'll be fine," I assured her. "Really."

"It's not that," Bessie said, shaking her great head. "If you say that Trevor will still have a healthy life, I believe you. I just...he tells me of these things that fascinate him. These mountains."

She turned, gold-ringed eyes glinting. "I have never seen a mountain, Dr. Spyros. I do not share his interest. I wish he had someone in his life who did, is all."

"Actually," I smiled, "I have someone in mind."

I came to visit Trevor again a week later. I did not come alone.

My companion would not set foot in even the shallows, fearing the water as he did. We approached Trevor's cove overland, trekking over fallen branches and dead leaves. Even through the thick foliage I could catch glimpses of the gray Erie beyond the trees. Every now and again my companion would stop and sniff the air, then look uneasily at the hint of open water. But still he came with me, and I was grateful.

Trevor was where I had left him a week prior, playing on the muddy shore. His mountain range had grown substantially.

"Hello, Trevor," I said.

His head shot up on its long neck. His deep eyes lit with excitement. "Dr. Spyros! You're back!"

“I am.” I smiled and bowed to him.

Trevor did likewise, then swung his head towards my companion. I watched as the young laker took in the new arrival: his towering height, his broad chest and huge hands. The long hair that covered him from crown to heel, and the kind brown eyes that held all the wisdom of the mountains.

“Is this your friend?” Trevor asked. “The one you told me about, from the mountains?”

“I am,” he said, his voice a rumble like a rockslide. “It’s a pleasure to meet you, Trevor. My name is Roger.”

Trevor looked from Roger to me, and back again.

“You’re not a walker,” he said slowly. “At least, not the same kind of walker.”

Roger’s laugh was like the scrape of flint over granite.

“No,” he said. He smiled, revealing even white teeth. “I’m a sasquatch.”

Mysterious Travelers

DOMINICK CANCILLA

"Mysterious Travelers. This is Cadell."

"Is this Mysterious Travelers?"

"Yes. How can I help you?"

"The travel agency?"

"That's correct. What can I do for you today?"

"You make travel arrangements for people with unusual needs?"

"Yes, we do."

"Very unusual needs?"

"That's correct."

"*Very* unusual needs?"

"We are happy to have you as a client no matter who you are."

"What if it's not who I am, it's what I am?"

"Every traveler is a 'who' at Mysterious Travelers."

"Really?"

"Really. Can I get your name, please?"

"Quagjam."

"With a Q or a K?"

"No idea."

"That's fine. How can I help you?"

"I don't know if you can."

"I assume you're calling about making travel arrangements. Perhaps if you could give me a little more information on what you are looking for?"

"I've never gone anywhere before."

"How exciting! Mysterious Travelers would love to assist you with making your first trip."

"I can't do it on my own. I've tried, and it's too difficult. I recently came into some money, so I thought you could help me."

"We handle that type of situation all the time. I assure you that there's no type of person we are unable to assist with any reasonable request."

"You say that, but I don't know. People don't generally get along with me so well."

"Let's see if I can reassure you. To help me start putting together a travel proposal, can you tell me what kind of person you are?"

"What do you mean 'what kind of person am I'? What kind of person are you?"

"I'm a Southern California lupus-filiae."

"So you're a – a what? A werewolf?"

"No, I'm fully human. I was just raised by wolves. And yourself?"

"Okay. Don't mock me, though, all right?"

"I promise not to mock you."

"Fine. I'm a Carolina swamp jelly."

"I'm familiar with Florida bog oozelings. Is that similar?"

"What the – no, you racist piece of shit! Might as well just ask if a bird of paradise is like a pile of rancid garbage that someone took a shit on with a rotting mountain troll's blistered asshole."

"I apologize for the comparison and meant no disrespect. I was just wondering if you were similar to an oozeling in size and body structure, not in moral or cultural value."

"Oh, well, yeah. That's similar, if you'd say that a human is about the same as a gorilla."

"For our purposes, I would, thank you."

"I hear they fornicate with crocodiles, by the way."

"Gorillas?"

"Oozelings. Completely disgusting."

"Moving on, can you tell me how large you are?"

"How is that any of your business?"

"It's for arranging travel. We can accommodate anyone from amoebakin to lake monsters, but I need to know what we are working with."

"That's offensive right there. Monster. It's offensive."

"Actually, lake monster is that species' preferred term."

"I didn't know that."

"Then I'm pleased that you turned to us for expert advice. You were going to tell me how large you are?"

"Volume and density, or height and width?"

"Whatever you have is fine."

"I don't know either. Not even sure why I asked. I'd say I'm about twice the size of a frog."

"Can you be more specific? I once saw a frogdingnagian in Texas eat a small camper van."

"What's a camper van?"

"A large vehicle. The point is that I'll need a comparison to something with a smaller ranger of sizes. For example, do you live in a Carolina swamp?"

"I'm a Carolina swamp jelly. I said that."

"One never knows, so I like to ask. A few years back I met a Florida bog oozeling that lived in a Mexican septic tank."

"Yeah, it would."

"Have you ever seen humans visit your swamp?"

"Yeah. Just this morning, as luck would have it. In fan boats, mostly. They fish or hunt reptiles, or they do this thing where two of them take off their–"

"That's sufficient. You mentioned fan boats. Could you ride in one of those?"

"Sure. Easy. A hundred times over."

"That gives me a better idea. Have you ever seen one of these humans in a fan boat wearing a hat?"

"All the time."

"Do you think you could fit under one of those hats without being seen?"

"Not with a head in it, but if it was on the back of a log or something, sure. With room to spare."

"Perfect! That gives you a lot of options."

"It does?"

"Yes. We can definitely help you make arrangements for your first trip outside the swamp. Have you given any thought to where you'd like to go?"

"Disneyland."

"Disneyland?"

"Have you heard of Disneyland?"

"I certainly have. In fact, I recently made Disneyland arrangements for a sentient housefly swarm."

"Then why did you sound so surprised? A Carolina swamp jelly isn't good enough for Disneyland?"

"Not at all. I'm just surprised that you chose Disneyland when Walt Disney World is so much closer to Carolina."

"Forget that. Too much of the wrong element in Florida. If I ran into a skunk ape, I think I'd spontaneously invert. Disgusting."

"Disneyland it is."

"That's the original park, did you know that?"

"I believe I'd heard that, yes."

"I found a 1955 *Life* magazine in a box in an old shack and read an article about Disneyland on some of the pages that hadn't rotted."

"I see."

"They have a castle there. And a train."

"That they do."

"And a robot hippopotamus."

"Have you thought about how you'd like to travel?"

"I want to go on that train."

"I meant how you'd like to travel to California."

"Do you think they'll let me on the train? Is there a height limit or something?"

"We can help you work all of that out a little later in the process. In the meantime, have you considered travel arrangements?"

"I thought I'd swim. Can you give me directions?"

"It's more than twenty-five hundred miles from where you are."

"Is that a long way?"

"Yes."

"Farther than Pittsboro?"

"Much farther, and there aren't any direct waterways. You'd have to travel on roads."

"I'm not good out of water for long. I'd be a puck in no time."

"I assumed as much, but that's okay. We can still help you."

"How?"

"We have associates all over the country who are happy to assist. Are you comfortable being in an enclosed space for a long period of time?"

"I once rode out a hurricane in a tree hollow for two weeks."

"Good enough. Then what I propose is that we set you up with a cooler."

"What's a cooler?"

"It's a small, insulated box with a locking top so that nobody will be able to bother you. It will have the words 'Donor Organ' on the lid so that they won't even be tempted to open it and will treat you with the utmost care and respect. We fill the cooler with nutritive swamp water and whatever you best like to absorb."

"Rat carcass?"

"We can do a rat carcass, certainly. Once you're settled, we send you across the country by air in complete comfort. You'll be in a hotel room at Disneyland in less than a day."

"That's amazing."

"It's what we do."

"But what happens at the hotel? Can someone help me with tickets and directions?"

"It's more complicated than that, I'm afraid. Humans don't react well to sentient non-humans, so you're going to need to remain out of sight."

"Racist!"

"Speciesist, but yes, very much so. Too many scales, not enough bones, necroambulatory, xeno-origined, sentient-mechanical, invisible, hovering, winged, glowing – almost anything will set them off. It's an unfortunate truth of American society, but one that Mysterious Travelers is very experienced at mitigating."

"It's disgusting that I even have to worry about that."

"It is, but here we are."

"If humans are that intolerant, what am I supposed to do? Sit in a hotel room all day? I'll be a dried-out puck by nightfall. How about I stay in that Disneyland jungle river instead?"

"Those rivers are heavily trafficked and you wouldn't find them pleasant – too much petroleum runoff and not enough rotten nutrients. Instead, we will arrange to have the bathtub in your hotel room filled with artisanal swamp water."

"Can you put a couple dead rats in there?"

"New ones every day. Mice, too, if you'd like to try something local."

"That does sound nice."

"It is! But you will want to see more of the resort than just your room."

"That *is* kind of the point."

"Exactly. We will be teaming you up with a tour guide who can help you visit the theme parks and shopping areas."

"What do you mean, 'tour guide'? I don't like the sound of that. I'm not very social."

"I completely understand. That's why I'm going to pair you with Acacia – I think she's available."

"No way. No. I don't want to be treated like a pet by some human for the whole trip. I know I'm going to have to be around the things, but I don't want to be around the racist bastards more than necessary. No offense."

"None taken. You don't need to worry, though. Acacia is a Nevada saguaro Jack and is as happy to avoid humans as you are. She trims her needles and wears a human disguise to blend in, but she's cactus at heart."

"A cactus woman? Isn't she going to have a problem with a swamp jelly?"

"Not at all. Acacia has worked with all kinds of clients, including gatorlings and naiads. A few years back she even accompanied the Honey Island swamp monster to a train museum and circus performance without incident. You and she will get along fine so long as you remember to call her Acacia and not Jack."

"Like I would do that."

"Of course not. Acacia has a specially designed case that looks like a camera bag but is expertly designed for you to ride in while you tour the parks. It also has certain features that will allow you to pass through park security in peace."

"Hang on – you want to put me in a bag?"

"Think of it more like a sedan chair than a bag. You'll have access to swamp water and there are ports that allow you to see out in any direction. Wireless communication is available so you can let Acacia know where you want to go and she can make suggestions. There's a concealed hatch so Acacia can pass you souvenirs and snacks at your request."

"Snacks? I like snacks. What kind of snacks?"

"There is a wide variety of food available at Disneyland."

"Rats?"

"Not so much rats in the parks themselves. I'd suggest a turkey leg."

"Ooh, that does sound good."

"Doesn't it? You will ride in comfort all day, going anywhere you like, seeing anything you want to see, so long as it's within the venue's limits."

"Limits?"

"You can't go in the river."

"Right. You mentioned that. What about the hotel pool? The magazine article showed a pool."

"Full of chlorine."

"Ouch! Scratch that. Well, this all sounds good to me. Let's set me up."

"Wonderful! I just need to confirm with you a few things for both of our protection. First, do you understand that in order to secure this vacation there will be a non-refundable deposit?"

"Okay."

"You will also need to agree to obey any instructions any Mysterious Travelers personnel give you."

"What kind of instructions?"

"Be quiet if there's a dog in the area. Stop trying to go in the river. That kind of thing. It's for everyone's protection."

"I guess I can do that."

"Acacia will also help you avoid situations that you might find unpleasant."

"Like direct sunlight?"

"Like that. It can be more subtle things, too. For example, pretzels in the shape of mouse heads are available at Disneyland."

"Nice!"

"But they're covered in salt."

"Ouch! Count me out."

"Exactly. And finally, we will be giving you a list of behaviors that, although you may feel they are perfectly natural, you will need to avoid during the trip. You will have to agree to avoid these behaviors at all times."

"What kind of behaviors?"

"For example, as a swamp jelly, when you see a human do you get the urge to leap into their face?"

"That is so racist! I'm an individual, not some collection of jelly stereotypes. I demand an immediate apology."

"Then you don't get that urge?"

"Well, sure I do, *sometimes.* Who doesn't?"

"You will need to resist during your trip or your visit will be immediately canceled and you may be subject to repercussions under human law."

"It's ridiculous that you would even think I'd do such a thing."

"I'm sorry, but that warning is a required part of my script."

"Leap at someone's face. Really."

"Again, I apologize. I do know where you're coming from, though. Considering my upbringing, I had a terrible time not rooting around in garbage cans the first time I went to a theme park."

"I can see that. Sorry for flying off the handle."

"Not at all. Now, let's discuss payment. I'm sure you understand that arrangements like this are a little on the expensive side."

"Don't worry. I'm ready to pay."

"Will this be precious metals, swamp gems..."

"No, not that. I don't have any of that. What I do have is, well, there was this human in a fan boat this morning, and he had these two suitcases. One is full of stacks of human money, and one is full of plastic bags of white powder. He also had a cell phone, which is how I'm calling you. I'm down to half battery, by the way."

"That sounds acceptable. Is it okay with this human if you use his items as payment?"

"He's not going to complain. He sort of had an accident."

"Do you mean he's dead?"

"Definitely dead."

"You're sure he's not just unconscious? We are not interested in payment that might be contested."

"No problem there. Definitely dead."

"You're sure?"

"Yeah, his face is completely missing."

"Because of an accident?"

"He stuck his face near my log; I got startled; things happened. Don't judge me."

"Wouldn't dream of it. Text me your location and I'll have someone there in an hour to collect payment and make further arrangements."

"I'll do that now."

"I'll watch for your text. Thank you for considering Mysterious Travelers. I hope you have a wonderful Disneyland vacation."

"Thank you! I will!"

Love Song of the Wendigo

BRIAN TRENT

The time had come to hunt an enemy of the tribe, Wendigo thought. The time had come to eat someone's heart.

He knew the sensation by now. For most of eternity, Wendigo dwelt in the gray woodlands of the Forest of Ghosts, where spirit animals dwelt among the soupy miasma of fog and brush and tree. Such entities scampered and played and hunted in dim memory of former lives.

The summoning took hold of him like a slow invasion of ants in his fur. Wendigo stirred from his half-slumber. The pins-and-needles sensation crawled across his powerful legs, each like a tree sunk in thick, ropy muscle. The summoning spread to his furry neck and face, his wild hair like shaggy moss, the yellowed tusks around his mouth like spear-points, and his eyes of molten flame. He felt it throughout his chipped, iron-black antlers.

Wendigo stood, as tall as an apple tree. Spirit bunnies, unaware they had been munching so close to the terrifying predator, dashed into the nearest brush.

"Wrath of Tribes!" a voice cried. *"Cannibal spirit of the Forest of Ghosts! Step forth to our hunting grounds!"*

He nodded wearily at the voice and stretched until his joints popped. It was time to hunt an enemy of the tribe, only *this* time he would not fail.

Must *not* fail.

And then the Forest of Ghosts faded into the purest white and Wendigo found himself standing by a waterfall in the land of the living.

"About time!" yelled Eddie Blackhawk, owner and operator of

Aztec Casino and Resort. "I closed off this entire wing and it's costing me $347,222 an hour!"

Wendigo blinked his flaming eyes in confusion. He was facing a cabal of oddly-dressed men and a shriveled, dancing old woman in the strangest forest he had ever seen. The floor was hard and shiny like volcanic rock. The trees didn't smell like trees, and surrounding each not-tree were glass tables. There was a waterfall, but it seemed to be coming from (and going to) nowhere – the frothy foam washed rubbery-smelling rocks above a frosted, roofless tavern bar lit by magical, heatless lamps.

"Are you listening, Wendigo?" Eddie snapped, clenching his hands in frustration. Rings glittered on every finger, as if he'd dipped them into a treasure chest.

Wendigo didn't reply. He regarded the night sky. The stars were out, but they were strangely flat, like images on tent-flaps. And the shadows of the moon were wrong.

"Hey! Wendigo! Pay attention! I need you to…um…" Eddie looked expectantly to the shriveled old woman.

"Bring the Wrath of Tribes to our enemies," she said helpfully.

"Right! Bring the Wrath of Tribes to our enemies, yeah."

At last, Wendigo turned his attention to his summoner.

There was no question who the summoner was. The protective Aura of Summoning flared around Eddie Blackhawk like flame-colored peacock feathers, and Wendigo could feel their dangerous heat. Sometimes people forgot to conjure the protective Aura of Summoning; Wendigo liked when that happened, because it meant he could rend his summoner to pieces and return quickly to the Forest of Ghosts before a mission was assigned to him. Once a mission was assigned, he had to complete it. Those were the rules, damn them.

Eddie Blackhawk was thirtyish, his black hair styled flat against his head, his lean body in a tailored black suit with a red tie. He regarded Wendigo with sharp, impatient eyes. "By Earth Mother and Father Sky, I assign you a target." He handed Wendigo a photograph.

Wendigo had never seen a photograph; it reminded him of a leaf-pressing in soft earth. He took the glossy image wonderingly in his talons.

"His name is Jimmy Tapahe," Eddie spat. "He's an enemy to the tribe. I told him what would happen if he came back. I warned him!"

Wendigo returned the photograph.

"This pressing is remarkable," he said in his low, unexpectedly-articulate voice, "But it does not bear the target's scent."

"Oh, right!" Eddie dug into his suit jacket and retrieved a plastic bag. Inside was a folded sheet of paper.

Wendigo dipped his snout into the bag and sniffed.

"A woman handled this parchment," Wendigo observed, wrinkling his nose at the perfume. "Is she my prey?"

"What? No!" Eddie turned ashen. "That's a letter Jimmy wrote to my wife, professing his goddam love for her!"

Wendigo shook his head. "I need something more. A lock of his hair, perhaps. A few drops of his blood on your hunting knife. One of his arrows from the carcass of a buffalo."

Eddie stomped his foot. "I don't have anything like that!" A realization hatched in Eddie's aggravated gaze. "Wait, here." He dug in his pockets and retrieved a jingling key ring. One of the keys was radically unlike the others; old, scratched, dented along its length, and with teeth that were as worn smooth as river stones. "Try this old thing! Lord knows we both used it enough."

Wendigo sniffed the key. He nodded.

"Tonight's Friday," Eddie said softly, "and Jimmy usually goes to Dominick's on Friday after work. That's one exit southbound off the Interstate. Every other night and he's here, in my casino, haunting my wife's steps!"

Wendigo didn't know what a casino was, but he was starting to realize it was some kind of deranged longhouse. "Then perhaps," he suggested, "I should wait for the nights when he prowls here, and I can pounce on him as he enters the territory."

The incendiary outrage on Eddie's face was enough to tell Wendigo that his suggestion was a bad one.

"You can't kill him in my casino! Jesus, why would I need to summon *you* if I could just kill him myself! Go to Dominick's! His comings and goings are as regular as the tides! Tear his balls off!"

"I do not tear balls off. Perhaps you meant to summon a thunderbird or skin-walker. They do that sort of thing."

Eddie seized the old woman's arm and shook her. With her yellow hide-skin tunic, waist-length gray hair, and shriveled countenance, she resembled a dried-out Corn Husk doll. Eddie screamed into her face, "We went through that six-hour ritual of chanting and smoke and goddam rattles and you summoned the wrong monster?"

"If you wish this enemy dead," Wendigo growled, narrowing his molten eyes in displeasure at seeing a tribal shaman treated so rudely, "I can do that. I will track him down, corner him, and pluck out his heart while still he lives."

Eddie released the woman. He fixed his tie and grinned; Wendigo had never seen teeth so white – even the moon couldn't compete. "That's great! Bring me his heart on a plate!"

"I eat the hearts."

"You bring me this one!"

Wendigo's eyes flared. "I eat the hearts," he repeated.

Eddie looked almost relieved. "Okay, okay! Do what you want with it! Just kill him. You've got his scent now! Get Jimmy out of my life!"

Wendigo was relieved to get out of the casino.

The world beyond made sense, even if the asphalt roads were strange and the streetlamps and traffic lights and white-eyed herds of automobiles were shocking. When Wendigo glanced up, he saw real stars and a real moon above him, and the potted hydrangeas and red cedar and lavender plants soothed him. He sighed and wished there was a pond nearby. Ponds had frogs.

He sniffed the air, pulling great torrents of scent into his puckering nostrils. The scent from the old car key was there, and so acute was his sense of smell that he could almost *see* it like an aurora borealis in the night sky, ribboning a mile upwind.

Wendigo went hunting.

He galloped along the breakdown lane, unseen by passing cars, his hooves trampling broken bottles, discarded coffee cups, and shredded blown-out tires. He bolted down a highway off-ramp as a car blasted by him.

The ribbon of scent curled down to a small longhouse with the word DOMINICK'S glowing above its painted red door.

Wendigo went in.

Taverns had changed radically since last he had been summoned, and yet somehow, they had not changed at all. He squinted through dusky tobacco smoke. This late at night, the tavern was mostly deserted. Two drunks slumped in a corner booth. An older woman who was desperately trying to look twenty years younger was applying makeup in her pocket mirror. The bartender glanced up as the tavern door jingled, but didn't see Wendigo, because Wendigo did not wish to be seen.

Wendigo sniffed the air once more. He regarded the man sitting alone at the bar on a cherry-red barstool.

The man was dressed in a tan suit jacket and blue jeans. His shoulders were slouched, the posture of the defeated. A shot glass sat in a ring of spilled vodka.

Wendigo sighed in disappointment. *This* forlorn vagrant was worth summoning the Wrath of Tribes? Where were the days when he was tasked with hunting a ferocious brave? Wendigo shook his antlered head and approached the man. He drew back his talons, fixing his sights on the man's back, between his scapulae, from where he could most easily wrench out the beating heart. He sighed again.

The man turned around on the barstool and squinted at him.

"Figures," the man said. He turned back, listlessly pushing his drink across the vodka puddle.

The ancient hunter frowned. "What figures? "

"That he'd send a Wendigo after me." His prey lifted the shot glass and poured its clear contents down his throat.

Wendigo stared, slack-jawed, for half a minute. Finally, eager to break the awkward silence, he stammered, "You're not going to… resist? Scream?"

The man turned his hollow gaze on him. Wendigo looked away, abashed and somewhat unnerved by the hopelessness in those brown eyes.

"I guess not," Wendigo muttered.

Jimmy Tapahe unbuttoned his shirt and exposed a smooth, hairless chest. "Go ahead."

The bartender glanced up from wiping down the counter and scowled at Jimmy. "You okay, Jimmy?"

Wendigo gave an awkward scratch at the flesh around one of his antlers. "How is it that you can see me?"

Jimmy Tapahe said, "I grew up on the reservation. My Nan always told tales of our heritage. Earthdiver Turtle. Thunderbird." Jimmy sighed. "Wendigo. I know Eddie Blackhawk summoned you from the Forest of Ghosts to eat my heart. Here you go. Dig in." When Wendigo didn't reply, Jimmy waved the bartender over. "Hey Tino, pour me a last shot, okay?"

Tino, wearing his usual blue bandana and beaded turquoise necklace, drummed the countertop, looking cross. "Jimmy, don't you think you've had enough? I mean, you're talking to yourself, man!"

"This is the final one, I promise."

Tino reluctantly filled the shot but withheld the glass. "Your keys, Jimmy. Hand 'em over."

Jimmy obliged, and the bandana-wearing man moved off, shaking his head and putting the keys in a little gray box on a high shelf.

Wendigo didn't know *what* to make of that exchange.

Jimmy looked into the ancient hunter's tusked face. "Are you going to eat my heart?"

"It's what I do," Wendigo replied, almost apologetically. He stared at Jimmy's chest, seeing the heart's spiritual analog in the near-umbra.

Then he frowned.

"What's *wrong* with your heart?" Wendigo asked suddenly. "It's all twisted and aflame."

"It's broken," explained Jimmy.

"What's broken, Jimmy?" asked Tino from the bar.

"My heart."

Tino shook his head. "Everyone knows that. You need to get over her, man!"

Wendigo grumbled. He had heard of this problem – men who beat drums and danced for days in a fruitless attempt to petition *kachinas* for their help in winning an unrequited love. Women who wailed and tore at their hair to beg for the return of a dead husband or son. Wendigo neither felt nor understood such human traits. The men he was sent after were typically the type whose hearts were only big enough to hold themselves. A wicked Skokomish chieftain. A rapist Sioux. A bearded conquistador. A sadistic Civil War doctor who liked to sew tribal people's eyes and mouths shut. Whatever their crimes were in the opinion of the tribe, Wendigo only cared that their hearts were good enough to eat. Strong, healthy, unbroken.

Wendigo licked one of his tusks with a black, forked tongue. "So Jimmy…how did you, um, break your heart?" *And how can we fix this*, he wondered.

"The woman I love was taken from me," Jimmy replied.

"Who took her?"

"Eddie. He grew up with us, you know. He and I were best friends! We tore around in the shittiest rez car you've ever seen – wheels practically falling off, engine roaring like a sick animal; when you stuck it in neutral and revved the gas, it would erupt a black smokescreen like something you'd see in a Bond flick." Jimmy chuckled quietly, remembering a happier, lost era. "When I met Vicky, everything changed."

Jimmy took out his mobile phone and conjured a picture of a woman. Wendigo squinted to see the tiny image.

"See? She's beautiful! That's a pic of us at Shelton Farms. We were dirt poor, you know, but Vicky knew how to find beauty in anything. We didn't need money, man, when we had each other! Do you understand what I'm saying?"

"No."

"No one believes in love at first sight anymore, but I'm telling you, it happened to Vicky and me! You'd think my best friend, Eddie, would be happy for me."

"He wasn't?"

A blush of anger spread across Jimmy's cheeks and he lifted his shot glass and slammed it on the bar. "He took one look at her – I remember when I introduced them – and you could see it in his eyes. He wanted her. Wanted her as a trophy. As a merit badge with a pulse! Wanted to have her on his arm so he could prove to the world that Eddie Blackhawk was *not* a failure, that he was somebody important! That he no longer drove that crappy car. Understand?"

"Again. No."

"People 'round here like to say that when the Blackhawk family started the casino, that's what changed him, but that's bullshit." Jimmy dipped his fingers in the spilled vodka and drew a listless circle. "Vicky's family had lots of debts. Her mother had a long sickness and racked up medical bills. I couldn't help them… I was taking a bus every day to a minimum wage job. By then, Eddie's family had built their casino. The *Aztec!* Ha! *He isn't even an Aztec!*" Jimmy shook his head bitterly. "He offered to pay for everything and buy up the debts. As long as she married him. And still she refused until she had no other recourse, until her mother's medical bills were killing the family. That was a year ago."

Tino strode to him. "Jimmy, I've heard this story a hundred times. I'm driving you home now." He rounded the bar. One of the drunks at the back abruptly vomited onto the floor. Tino cursed and ran over to prevent the man from tumbling into his own puke.

Unperturbed, Jimmy said to Wendigo, "Even then, Vicky made Eddie promise on our ancestors that he would never harm me or have anyone in his employ harm me. I'll say this about my old pal: he always keeps his oaths. He's superstitious. His oath is as strong as oak. He swore that neither he nor any person at his behest –

person! – would bring harm to me. That's why he summoned *you* to do his dirty work. You're not a person."

"Of course I'm not a *person,"* Wendigo said, deeply offended.

Jimmy sighed and for a moment, hope flickered in his eyes. "Vicky and I are in love still. Eddie's bodyguards don't allow me to get close to her, but we sneak notes to each other by slot machines or beneath drinks. Eddie hates it. Hates me because I remind him of the days when he was nothing. Hates it enough that he summoned a Wendigo." For a moment, Jimmy rubbed his chin. "Couldn't you kill *him* instead?"

"You have been declared as my target."

"But Eddie is wicked!"

"I care not for your human emotions! Since the ice retreated and the great beasts died, I have failed but once! It shall *never* happen again!" He pounded the bar with a taloned fist. The bottles shivered in their racks; two wine glasses, hanging like bats from the rack, kissed and hummed out a lonesome note.

Tino glared up from his mopping work. "Take it easy, Jimmy!"

"You failed once?" Jimmy asked, with such innocent and genuine astonishment that Wendigo felt his resolve quaver. "How? What target could possibly evade something like you?"

"It was a long time ago," the ancient hunter said, lowering his talons and slumping onto the barstool beside Jimmy. "A medicine man summoned me to kill a tracker of the Ojibwe. I…" Wendigo hesitated. "I failed. It was embarrassing."

"How?"

"I don't know! The tracker ducked off into the wilderness. I followed his tracks across the snow, until he lost me at the river. I followed his scent on the air until one day it was gone! I went into villages hoping to catch word of his whereabouts, but no one knew! I'd been *thwarted!* By the next new moon, I had no choice: I returned to my summoner and ate his heart."

"You have a time-limit to succeed?"

Wendigo nodded, slumped in his barstool, and longingly eyed the bottles of liquor. He needed a drink.

Jimmy thought for a moment. "Could you…let the time run out for me? Could you let me go?"

"*Let* you go? I never *let* anyone go! The Ojibwe tracker escaped me!"

"But this is about love! Why can't you make one exception?"

"Because I'm the hunter," Wendigo said, as if burdened with the incredulous task of having to explain that the sky was above the trees, or that fish lived in water, or that the steam from a sweat lodge was the physical manifestation of manitous of healing.

"Hunters aren't *always* successful," his prey protested.

"I'm not *a* hunter, I'm *the* hunter. The Wrath of Tribes. The Cannibal Spirit!"

"And I love Vicky with all of my heart! Don't you love anything? Isn't there something that you desire so much you'd do anything to attain it?"

Wendigo stood. He rounded the bar and grabbed a bottle – tequila, as it happened. He unscrewed the top and took a gulp.

What *did* he desire? His first thought was for the waters of time to run upstream and allow him to go back to that fateful winter when the Ojibwe tracker had evaded him, and *this time*, catch the sneaky bastard!

But slowly, Wendigo realized that he truly wanted only one thing. He wanted to retire to the Forest of Ghosts. Wanted to lay down on the soft grass of a riverbank, and watch the frogs. He liked frogs.

"I can't let you go," Wendigo said at last.

"But you also can't eat my heart when it's in this condition," Jimmy reminded him. "It's broken, remember?"

Wendigo licked his lips. "You must fix it!"

"I can't!"

"You must!"

"No!"

Wendigo roared.

It was a roar out of time, a gushing eruption like a hundred waterfalls colliding in thunderous cacophony. The sound of earthquakes, of landslides, of tornados carving up the plains, of buffalo herds shaking the world as they sought better grazing. Bottles jumped and committed frothy suicide on the floor.

Wendigo slammed the tequila bottle on the counter. "You *must* heal! You can't let me fail again!" Frogs don't fail, he thought. They sit like little stones, patient and perfect.

Jimmy slid out of his barstool and started to collapse. Wendigo caught him and walked him out of the bar, the man's legs dragging on the floor and his arms hanging free, neck tilted backwards, so that it seemed to the drunks at the back that he was gliding on a clothesline out through the front door.

Tino gaped in astonishment. "Jimmy, what the *hell*, man?"

Wendigo paced anxiously in the posh executive office of the Aztec Casino and Resort. He had to hunch to avoid striking the ceiling, and he didn't like the feel of the carpet on his hooved feet, and the wooden paneling was bothering him; it resembled wood, but it was so highly polished it gleamed like crystal and smelled of pine but was not quite pine…

The door swung open. Eddie, wreathed in the scorching light of the Aura of Protection, arrived at the head of a retinue of bodyguards.

"It's done?" he demanded.

"No."

"Why the hell not?"

Wendigo said, "I need to borrow your wife."

Eddie Blackhawk froze in place, not so much like a petrified deer but rather like a haughty bear unused to being challenged by a creature infinitely his inferior. "Borrow my wife," he repeated slowly. "What, in the holy hell, for?"

"Jimmy wants to meet her."

"I don't care what that sniveling little loser wants! I swore an oath that I'd never let them be together again and I *always* keep my oaths! Why haven't you killed him yet? What kind of Wendigo are you, anyway?"

Wendigo grumbled. "I have my reasons."

"You're not supposed to have reasons! You're supposed to be a killer! I don't want your paws on my wife, and I don't want that goddamn failure to come within spitting distance of her, so no! Go do your fucking job!"

"Are you telling me," the ancient hunter snarled, "that you are *thwarting* my mission?"

Eddie's first instinct was to get right in the creature's face and remind him who had the power. But Wendigo's tone seemed to lift a haze from his eyes. He suddenly remembered that he was facing a ten-foot tall bipedal antlered abomination with yellow tusks and livid scarlet eyes and talons that looked capable of gutting an Abrams tank like a trout (and in fact, they were capable of this).

But Eddie Blackhawk was not the kind of man to show his fear – he had sworn an oath to himself years ago that he would never show fear to anyone or anything – so he quickly converted his expression to mild annoyance and said, "Fine, whatever. She's in Room 611."

Wendigo went up to Room 611.

Vicky was sitting at her room's desk when he stooped to enter. She glanced to the mirror as the door opened behind her. Her pretty, freckled face frowned.

"A Wendigo?" she asked doubtfully. "He summoned a Wendigo?"

Wendigo sighed.

"You can't eat my heart," she said, turning and clutching a diary as if it had talismanic powers of protection. "It's broken… "

"Don't I know it? Come along, damn you. Jimmy wants to meet you."

With the striking exception of that Ojibwe tracker's peerless wilderness skills, humans had little to recommend them. Wendigo sometimes wished that his targets were more challenging, or interesting, or powerful.

But there were times when he was reminded that they were capable of things he did not comprehend.

This was one of those times.

The reunion between Jimmy and Vicky occurred by the casino's waterfall at 9:41 a.m. The casino wing was closed down once again for the occasion (at a cost of $347,222 per hour). Jimmy had arrived early, waiting by the foaming torrent, when Vicky came down the stairs. By herself. Unescorted.

Of course, the wing was stationed with Eddie's bodyguards in their blue and black and gray suits, and Eddie himself sat hunched at the bar like a singularly well-dressed species of gargoyle, glaring at Jimmy over his gin-and-tonic while angrily fingering his red tie.

Wendigo did not concern himself with this tense standoff.

His molten eyes remained fixed on his target.

Jimmy had cleaned up from his drunken stupor the night before. He now simply wore jeans and a T-shirt. He stood proud, shoulders back, and as he turned from the waterfall to take in his first sight of Vicky that morning, his heart flared like a volcanic eruption.

Vicky dashed across the gaming floor. Jimmy hurried to meet her.

Wendigo flexed his talons.

The two humans entwined like eagles on their timeless lovers' plummet. Jimmy's broken heart radiated like the sun-piercing storm clouds; it nearly reflected in the hideous casino machines and the glass tables all around them.

How foolish, Wendigo thought. *Doesn't he know that I've done this just to kill him?*

They kissed. Eddie made a strangled sound of protest from the bar and turned his furious scowl on Wendigo.

But Wendigo waited. The broken heart radiated and changed. Wendigo had to shield his eyes. Vicky's heart brightened as well. It was a radiance only he could see.

"I love you forever Jimmy! I don't care what tries to keep us apart!" Vicky stared over his shoulder to Eddie at the bar. She shouted at the top of her lungs, "I love you, Jimmy, forever!"

Jimmy rotated to fix his old friend with an equally defiant gaze. "Ed-boy, you're the master of nothing! You don't own her heart, and *that's* what matters!"

Eddie staggered off the barstool and took a lurching, drunken step towards them. He halted alongside Wendigo, but his hateful glare was only for his old pal. "I own her debts, her clothes, her car, and her body! That's enough, James."

Vicky gave a blistering, scornful laugh. "A body that I've never given you!"

A blush of color spread across Eddie's face like a crimson shadow.

Wendigo was barely listening to the petty human squawking. In the scintillating light, Jimmy's wounded heart had healed! Like a gash on a riverbank suddenly melting away by the rise of water and the gentle tumble of silt. He began to salivate.

Watch this, Ojibwe tracker, wherever you are!

"You're the man who has nothing, Eddie," Vicky called out, her voice resonating in the airy casino hall. "My true love always occupies my mind and heart, while you, you're just another lifeless piece of brass in this artificial nightmare. The man who wants everything, who drools for the world, but who will always be that poor kid with the shitty car and–"

Eddie jerked something from his suit jacket. The gunshot was so loud in the airy casino that even Wendigo jumped.

His surprise turned to pure disbelief as he saw the red stain on Jimmy Tapahe's shirt. The air reeked of cordite.

"Let him occupy your mind and heart like *that!*" Eddie snarled, and then he slapped Wendigo's arm. "*That's* how you do it! Who needs a totem creature when you've got a .40 caliber bullet, huh?"

"You shot him," Wendigo muttered.

"Damn right I shot him! Oath or no oath, it's ended." Eddie detached the old rez car key from his key-ring and flicked it at Jimmy's sprawled-out, bleeding body. "Who's the failure now, Jimmy? Who's just failed at *life itself?*"

Wendigo crossed to Jimmy in two strides. Vicky held him, pale, and sobbed against his ruptured chest.

"His heart is all yours!" Eddie said, turning aside. "Eat up, Wendigo!"

"I can't," Wendigo said. "Because you shot it."

Eddie walked on another two paces and then halted, the implications settling over him.

"You thwarted my mission, Eddie Blackhawk." Wendigo rose and flexed his talons. The Aura of Protection vanished like the loss of moonlight on a cloudy night.

There were thirteen more rounds in Eddie's gun, and a hundred more from his bodyguards, but every bullet ever made couldn't have stopped a rampaging Wendigo.

Their hearts were most delicious.

Jimmy Tapahe died on the main gaming floor of the Aztec Casino and Resort at 9:52 a.m. while the love of his life held him in her arms and wept.

At 10:02 a.m., Wendigo brought him back to life after a skillful heart transplant.

"How?" Jimmy asked, as he weakly sat up.

"I know a thing or two about hearts," the timeless hunter said, tightening the last of the bandages across Jimmy's bloodied chest. "You can't help but pick up a few things when you've been plucking hearts as long as I have." He sniffed the wound, gave a satisfied nod. "You just get plenty of rest and avoid heavy lifting for a few weeks, and you'll be just fine."

Jimmy blinked. "Whose heart do I have now?"

"One of the bodyguards. It's just a muscle, and his was in fine shape. Looked mighty delicious…" He licked his lips, glancing at the bandaged chest in sudden longing.

Vicky interposed herself. "The deli on Blue River Square stocks cow hearts. I could buy you a whole package!"

The timeless hunter shook his massive, antlered head. "The lesser aurochs make poor eating! Besides, I must be getting back."

Jimmy winced as he tried to stand. "What do you get back to? What's the Forest of Ghosts like? Wendigo?"

The creature was already gone.

It was another gray, misty dawn in the Forest of Ghosts, like a lost world perched forever on autumn. Wendigo found his favorite oak and happily sat against it, stretching his legs out and staring at the creek, listening to the quiet babble around jutting stones. He glanced hopefully to the bordering rocks and smiled.

The frogs were there, sitting in stoic attentiveness.

Patient and perfect.

PG at the Park

AMY LYNWANDER

"Let's face it, a carousel, a couple of rides, and carnie games on the edge of the woods can't compete with a sports plex by the mall." Ginny's accountant delivered this pronouncement from his musty office, which hung off the back of his ramshackle house like it was waiting for the right moment to escape.

Ginny huffed at the mention of her ex-boyfriend Tyler's place, and fell back into her seat. "I can't be the one to fail Goatman's," she said, "my grandfather would turn in his grave."

Unmoved, the accountant snapped shut the ledger. "If you close now, you can still pay your staff and might be able to sell off the equipment. Aren't there collectors for this kind of thing?"

Ginny made a face as he continued. "That land is valuable. I know that Tyler's been sniffing around. You'd be a fool not to sell. Your grandfather wouldn't want you to starve because of pride."

Ginny's grandfather created Goatman's after a fateful meeting with the Maryland cryptid, the night his truck spun out during a rainstorm and went into a ditch. No revving of the engine could propel it out of the muck, and her grandfather resigned himself to sleeping out there, when a creature slapped an axe against the window. Grandpa jumped and hit his head on the ceiling as he took in his visitor. Upright like a man, but covered in fur with a distinctly goat-like face, his unlikely savior jammed the axe head underneath the tire and rocked the truck until Grandpa could pull it to the road.

"Good thing I wasn't a couple of teenagers," Grandpa joked, referring to the Goatman's dicey reputation on lover's lane.

An unusual friendship developed from there, with Grandpa leaving prime cuts of raw meat out for the Goatman, and culminating in the creation of this monument/theme park that featured regularly on 'off the beaten track' and 'quirky landmark' lists, a flight of fancy constrained by cash and formal training.

Murderous failed experiment and kids' amusement park wouldn't seem to be an obvious match, but Grandpa had faith in the creature's goodness. Not homicidal, just cranky. That dog probably looked like a wild boar, and who didn't find teenagers annoying? Plus, carrying an axe when you lived in the woods was only practical. Grandpa swore to Ginny that after the park closed, the creature would step from the forest and sit with him while he whittled wood.

When her grandfather passed, Ginny heard a heartbroken bleating in a copse of trees outside the cemetery. In *that* they were united, and when Ginny found she'd inherited the theme park, she continued the meat tradition, although she suspected wild animals were the recipients of the bloody Wagyu (only the best for Goatman), since she'd never encountered the creature.

Now she sat on the big plastic Chessie, Nessie's Chesapeake Bay cousin, as the carousel turned slowly. Snallygasters and jackalopes cycled up and down nearby. Only the Goatman was missing; he would have had to be bent over for his saddle, and her grandfather didn't find it dignified. She gazed at the archway to the park with a majestic and muscular Goatman statue next to one column, his horns twisting out of a narrow face and his arms outstretched in welcome. To the left, the garish Lover's Lane stood, all pink hearts and yellow wood siding. Ginny knew that an animatronic Goatman would slash at the riders on their way out of the ride. Their screams still made her smile.

As the carousel slowed, Katy, a high school girl, aka Ginny's 'staff,' approached. She'd taken off her Goatman vest and handed Ginny the cashbox.

"Tyler's here."

She found him standing by the edge of the woods. "Did you see that?" he asked.

"What? An aging jock trespassing on my property? Yeah, I saw that." Ginny answered.

Tyler laughed, twisting his Rolex watch, making sure she'd seen it. "You always were a funny one. Why drag this out? You know I want your land for a hunting lodge. Do you really want to spend your life running this place? You can't possibly believe in the old hoax. The Goatman. BAAAAAAAAA!"

Ginny caught a flash of something in the distance. Tyler followed her gaze. "You saw it too. Something big out there, but not a goat. You better let me bring in my hunters so it doesn't eat your customers." He gestured at Lover's Lane. "Want to for old time's sake?"

"I'd rather eat glass, thanks."

"Like I said, funny. Just think about it." He gave her the double finger-point and ambled back to the parking lot.

Mulling the fact that she once dated someone who used finger guns, Ginny drifted back to the carousel and flicked it on, hopping on the ride as it slowly started back up. She wound through the various steeds moving towards her favorite, Chessie, but it was already taken.

The creature had a narrow goat's face and his shrewd eyes were fixed on Ginny. Short black fur covered his muscular body, and human-seeming hands held a dangling axe. Her heart sped up.

"Goatman?" she whispered, stupidly. Who else could it be?

He nodded once and glanced at the Snallygaster next to him. She walked over on jelly legs and took a seat. They rode in silence while Ginny's brain stuttered over what to say.

Finally, she blurted out, "I'm sorry I'm losing the park. It's just that people want more excitement these days, like the sports plex." Tears blinded her eyes. "I really tried." She covered her face with her hands and felt a furry mitt touch the nape of her neck. Ginny was not surprised when she opened her eyes to find an empty Chessie.

The next day, Ginny heard high-pitched screams coming from the balloon dart booth. She ran over to find the measly three children in the park clinging to their teenaged babysitter.

"We saw him! The Goatman!" The girl showed Ginny the blurry photo she'd posted on social media.

That night, the park was livelier than Ginny could remember, with teenagers jostling each other, taking pictures by the Goatman statue, and stuffing themselves with cotton candy. As the park thinned out, a girl ran to the middle shaking a large stuffed panda split open belly to stern, white fuzz flying everywhere.

"He got him with his axe! He got him!" she cried.

Ginny walked quickly to the first aid tent for Pepto Bismol for herself; it was too late for the bear.

The next night, Ginny had to call her back-up high school staff to run the rides because she couldn't keep up with all of the activity. Her accountant was thrilled. She wandered into the woods at one point and stood quietly. The Goatman stepped out from behind a tree.

"I want to thank you," Ginny looked into his dark eyes, picking her words carefully, "I appreciate you keeping it PG-13." He cocked his head questioningly. "I mean, not actually hurting anyone."

He snorted and moved back into the woods. Ginny tried to parse if it was a mocking snort or one of agreement.

She kept busy pitching in at the rides and the booths until people left the park. Only a couple of cars sat in the parking lot when Tyler pulled in. He strode over in a pressed polo and khakis.

"What are you doing here?" she asked.

"The sports plex is pretty quiet tonight. Thought I'd stop by." He looked past her to the woods. "You got the Goatman in there? Wouldn't mind shooting him."

The forest stilled as Ginny tried to pull Tyler away from the trees. "Don't talk like that."

He pulled away. "You actually believe it. Come on, Ginny, you're as bad as the old man. Don't feed people this BS. Listen, I know these woods and if there was some kind of freak living in them, I would have seen it and would have the head on my wall."

With an angry snort, the Goatman stepped from the trees and into the light.

Tyler's mouth dropped open and he rushed back to his truck, pulling his rifle from under his front seat.

"Tyler, no!" Ginny shouted.

The Goatman slipped back into the woods, Tyler at his heels. Ginny ran after them, barely feeling the branches scratching at her arms as she careened blindly through the forest.

A gunshot rung out and then a scream. Ginny tripped, falling down hard on her wrist. Another scream. She dragged herself to the parking lot and limped to the carousel. Sitting on Chessie, Ginny wondered what would happen to the park with no Goatman. She would never sell to Tyler.

She felt the carousel dip as someone else climbed on. Ginny looked up to see the Goatman next to her.

"You didn't keep it PG-13, did you?" He shook his head. "R?" she asked hopefully.

The light glinted off the Rolex on his wrist and caught the dark patches on his axe.

Tyler always did resemble a wild boar.

Landlocked

ALI HABASHI

It was not the violent quaking of the mountain that drove the Bolter towards the surface, but rather the thundering moan that beat through the layers of stone with each new explosion. The soundwaves shook the Bolter to her stone core, rattled each pebble of her body until they threatened to jar loose from her.

The men were back, returned for the silver. She had hoped that they would stay away after the last time she appeared. Their high-pitched screams that day had certainly been promising. It was a human sound, a fearful sound. Comfortably familiar by now.

The Bolter breached the surface of her mountain and joined the rocks as they cascaded towards lower elevations. She loosened the hard boulder of her form so as not to harm the roots of the trees when she broke the surface, taking lessons from the shifting sands she had met when she'd first come ashore. Although in this case, her care may have been futile. The avalanche was already mowing down everything before it, the greenery bowing before the weight of the sudden onslaught. As the mountain's latest scar took form before her, one of many since the mining had begun, the Bolter peered through the dust and chaos.

Looking for the men who had woken her up.

The Bolter did not really recall her life before she'd met the land. There were only vague impressions. The peace of the deep dark water, the quick snap of her jaws around a squid, breaching the surface for a fresh breath of air. Most of all there was the comfort of company as the other sperm whales in her pod pressed close, their clicking conversation echoing around her.

She wished that this particular impression wasn't so clear, if only so that she would no longer understand how sharply loneliness stung.

The stone whale supposed she must have been warned at some point about the dangers of the shallows. Being alone all this time, she'd come to understand that her ilk, those who had broken through the foamy border between land and sea, did not usually make it past the beach.

Nuzzling her way into the sands was her first real memory. It was rough on her skin, and the heat that beat down on her from above was – different. So unlike the numbness of before. She'd shoved forward, tipped over, and did not stop even when the safe shroud of the water fell away completely.

She'd been utterly fascinated by the land, even as every instinct urgently clicked at her to turn back. Next to her, a crab in coral-colored armor strode from sea to shore, a judgmental eye upon her. Her fluke beat the air, the bulk of her head rocking. The sand coated the gray-blue of her soft skin. She opened her mouth, and the sand fell over her tongue. The crab still watched her, warily now.

The Bolter had clicked feebly, but the sound was all wrong, too quiet. Her voice did not carry, did not fan out and echo back to her. She needed to dive, she needed…

She'd nosed deeper into the sand. Each grain was so small, but together, they were solid, even as they dipped and crested under her movements. If she were only smaller, able to shapeshift like the earth beneath her, then she could swim. The Bolter thrashed weakly as the sand roughly scraped the last moisture from her body until finally, she stopped moving altogether.

A cold splash over her nose had jarred her awake. A human calf, clutching a small pail, watched her worriedly. He dashed off, back to the waterline, only to return and pour another splash over her. The Bolter shifted uncomfortably. She did not want the water. When the sand was wet, it did not move as easily.

And she needed to move.

The boy had woken her up, and now she had to go.

With one last heave of her body, the Bolter fractured, and dove. She breathed the sand as she once did the water, clicked in celebration as she dove deeper, although her voice was a grainy whisper now. She broke the surface for a blow, sand spouting into the air, startling the crab so terribly that it scuttled straight back into the ocean. She heard the high-pitched giggle of the boy just before she dove into her new element.

"The Slide-Rock Bolter!"

They shouted her name, always in that tone. She opened her jaws so the gneiss rock of her teeth were on full display. She did not plan to eat the men, as stone had no need for that, but it did make them stop gaping at her. They fled, on foot and on horseback, until their camp was abandoned. The Bolter plowed through it, guiding their avalanche where she wanted it to go. The rock and dirt swallowed what the men had left behind.

The Bolter slammed her tail into the ground, slowing to a standstill. The dust settled around her, and she peered in the direction of the town – Rico. Humans had been her neighbors since she had settled here among the sandstone and granite and shale. They had never bothered her until they had built the town, though.

Now, the explosions that shook her mountain were beginning to mark her terrain in ways that felt permanent. The rock slides were splintering the trees that held the topsoil together, and she felt each crack in the stone as though it were happening to her. Which, in a way, it was.

Adapting to the earth around her had become her way of traveling. Her body was made of whatever surrounded it, whether it be layered sandstone, dark limestone, or soft clay. She was quartz, iron, and lead. She was the silver that the men wanted.

She stared at the town of Rico, the base of operations for the miners that spoke her name with such fear. As though she were the one attempting to flatten a mountain.

The bustle of the mining town died down as the light faded, and gently, the Bolter slid back into the earth. The familiar comfort of her mountain's embrace lifted as she dove beneath the sleeping

Rico. This disturbed slice of land felt less organic, more difficult to move through, as though the humans had poisoned the very dirt beneath their feet. The Bolter's rocky clicking voice rattled in irritation.

From the dirt path that shot between the ramshackle buildings, the Bolter rose, her glare leveled at the squat structures on either side of her. Somewhere within their nests, the humans had hidden the noisy fire that they were using to level her mountain.

The humans of Rico had built their nests of stone. The Bolter couldn't fault the humans for using the materials she herself had assumed into her being in order to survive landfall. She nosed closer to one of the stonefront buildings, the call of the neatly stacked rock too much of a curiosity to resist. She nestled close, and a shiver quaked through her as she changed to match the new material. The scraping sound of her transformation was punctuated by a sharp intake of breath from behind her.

A man wearing a fine layer of dust over his clothes stood frozen, only a stone's throw away. The patch of hair below his nose twitched in fright even as his twiggy frame stayed perfectly still under her scrutiny.

Sandstone, she thought. And then, Trouble.

The Slide-Rock Bolter was not used to panicking. And yet as soon as the man opened his mouth, no doubt to alert his fellows to her presence, she pushed through the dirt path that divided them and opened her maw around his thin frame. As she closed her jaws around him, she dove into the earth and buried them both.

She could feel the echoes of his shouts as they bounced around inside of her head, his small hands as they attempted to clutch at the soft bed of soil in her mouth. She flipped her fluke through the layers of stone as she swam back towards the mountain, maintaining only enough of a form to keep the man sealed within the cave of her body.

The Bolter was slightly mortified at herself. She'd never before felt the need to do much more than scare the men away. But back in Rico, where the dirt tasted wrong and the nests were made of sandstone, the disbelieving eyes of one man had made her forget she was not the invader there.

She was not the monster.

She breached the surface of the mountain, near the weakened crust where that morning's avalanche had stirred the earth. Unclenching her teeth, she dropped the man onto the ground, where he landed in a sprawling heap. She watched as he stood, listed to the side and fell back down again.

The moon was full that night, and the bright white of its face was lighting up the mountain. After the pitch dark of her mouth, the man probably saw her all too well as she settled her bulk into the rocky surface and waited. She considered vanishing back belowground, but something made her pause. She wasn't sure why instinct had made her take him, but she didn't want an injured human on the mountain, especially if the others were to continue attacking the landscape around him. If the trees could not withstand the rockslides, then this meager animal would surely be flattened.

He scrambled backwards as his eyes landed upon hers, choked sounds of fright escaping his throat.

"Get back!" he said. Finding a loose stone next to one of his hands, he gripped it and flung it towards the Bolter. It bounced off of her, and she blinked. The man flinched back as her form twisted into a mottled gray.

Granite, she thought absently.

The man scanned her body, his chest heaving slightly less now as she failed to attack him. Hesitantly, he fumbled for another stone and flung it her way. This toss was decidedly less violent.

Sandstone again. The Bolter shifted once more, body pink-tan with a new terra cotta warmth.

"Huh." The man pushed slowly to his feet, holding his hands splayed in front of him, as though to push her back should she charge.

He didn't seem injured, which meant leaving him here should be fine. They weren't at a very high elevation, so he should be able to find his way back, especially with the generous moonlight tracing the path. Once he began to run away from her, she would return to the comfortable core of her mountain. She would investigate Rico another night, and find the fire they were using to dismantle her home.

Hesitantly, the man took a step towards her. She stayed very still.

That's not right.

Humans did not approach her. Not on purpose.

The first and only human to have approached her had been the little boy on the beach. The one that had splashed the last of the ocean's cold kisses on her nose before she had left the water behind for good. The man took another step and she blew dust in a warning cloud above her. His eyelids fluttered as it swirled around them in a dirty mist. After a pause, he started forward once again.

Did he have some of the fire with him? she thought. She had seen what the thundering sound had done to the rocks around it, how they had scattered. She did not know if her consciousness would survive a cacophonous violence like that. She thought back to when she had first begun to learn about the different species of earth. Just beyond the beach, she had met the sandstone, which was much less flexible than its wet neighbor. She had not yet known how to properly transform to accommodate, beyond spreading herself too thin and too far. When she had finally come back together, she'd lost some of herself to the stone. The Bolter had never managed to recover it.

Perhaps that was where her memories of the water had gone.

The man's hands were still spread before him, handfuls of blisters on his palms and nothing besides. He trod lightly, even in his heavy boots, and the clothes hung loosely on his narrow frame.

"Hi," he said. "It's okay."

And then one of his palms was on her nose, patting it gently.

The Bolter's cautious focus was broken by the shock of the

touch. It was a ghost of a thing on her armored skin, but the slight pressure from his hand was warm like the sun had been that very first day on the sand.

Spending most of her time below ground had made her a near-stranger to mammalian touch in any form, to the point where a white-crowned sparrow landing on her back, or an oblivious ground squirrel scrabbling along a fin, had become a welcome sensation.

This, however, was deliberate. A trick. But his other hand was on her nose now as well, and the grin on his face had turned his eyes into sparkling crescents.

"My mother used to scold me for trying to make friends with wild animals. Can you imagine the whooping I'd get if she could see me petting the Bolter? You aren't so bad though, are you, old girl?"

The Bolter clicked, the small tic tic sounding, as always, so small without water to amplify it.

"I'll tell you what. Let's you and I be friends. Lord knows I need one right now. Between work and dealing with Stanley, I was just about ready to walk right on back home to Missouri."

The Bolter clicked in response and puffed dust into the air. He nodded as though he understood.

"A friend certainly is a rarity out here, isn't it?"

The man called himself Louis, and despite the continuation of the work on her mountain, she began to eagerly anticipate her new companion's visits. He came sparingly at first, wandering towards the mountain every few days or so. She would feel the light pattern of his steps as they approached, and she would announce her presence by sending a light tremor his way. A grinning Louis would greet her more comfortably each time, and she would press herself closer to his outstretched arms, careful not to bowl him over with her weight (after the third time she nearly crushed him). Eventually he began to appear more frequently, and on more pleasant nights would sometimes bring something to sleep on if their visits went too late.

Louis took to leaning up against her side and chatting endlessly, responding to every slight budge or click she made as though they spoke the same language. She appreciated the gesture, even if she did not fully understand his reasoning behind it.

His one-sided conversation consisted of three main topics: his parents, his work, and Stanley. The latter most of all.

"I just don't know what he wants from me. Whenever we're in a group, he turns into a different person. Why, just the other day, we two were chewing the fat, and William and James show up and that lunkhead just goes quiet in the middle of a sentence. Then suddenly he's talking to them, and I'm just…in the way."

The Bolter clicked in sympathy.

"I tried!" Louis responded, tossing his head back into her. "But I can't get in a word edgewise when those two are around. They don't much care for me. Think I'm a pantywaist, probably. The only reason they tolerate me is because Stanley is there and he likes me just fine."

The Bolter huffed, quartz teeth clattering together. Louis' head turned so that his eyes met one of hers.

"No, I'm sure he likes me." His face softened. "When we're alone, that man has said some of the sweetest things that any person has ever said to me. He might seem rough on the surface, but underneath all of the loudmouth bravado, Stanley is…soft."

Louis nudged her gently. "Just like you, Bolter."

Warmth filled her. Her vague impressions of life before dry land were easier to face now, the barely-recalled camaraderie of her pod as they brushed against each other in the deep and the cold. Despite her great love for land, the Bolter nevertheless could not deny the empty hollow left behind by her missing family. To have this now, to have Louis, felt like a triumph that she hadn't felt since first discovering her mountain.

Which made it particularly heartbreaking when she was forced to ruin it.

The explosion was closer this time. She awoke to the fire and the sound searing through her in waves, the earth roaring around her. As she pushed through the injured rock and emerged in the midst of an avalanche, all she could feel was a shocked fury. Louis' company had deadened her instincts, made her forget why she had gone into Rico in the first place.

Silver made up such a small amount of the mountain, and these men were willing to shatter everything for a chance at it. Their heavy boots skittered all over her home, ants on the wrong hill. She could feel them as they marched into the hollow they had built for themselves, feel their tools scrape and prod and chip away.

Well, if the men wanted silver, then she would oblige them. Furiously clicking, the Slide-Rock Bolter dove through the waves of cascading dirt and stone, into her mountain, and swam until she felt the mixed ore flow hot within her.

Molten metal burst through the surface of the earth in a writhing mass of copper, silver, and gold. The gagging choke of sulfur accompanied her arrival, and men's screams filled the air as she assumed her form. A far cry from the smooth shine of an ingot, the Bolter's cooling skin was the ore of her mountain, and ore was a tangled thing. The thrash of her tail guided the avalanche close to the fleeing bodies, enough so that they would feel the danger at their backs. The glowing orange veins of the cooling ore and the ghost-trail of white steam in her wake was driving them to greater panic than usual.

"Monster!"

"Demon!"

"Slide-Rock Bolter!"

She gnashed her teeth for good measure, herding the humans back towards Rico. To dive into the rock and stone around the mine itself would destabilize the already precarious mine, so instead she smacked her fin into the stone behind her and hooked into the mountain face. To properly grip the rock, she needed to bend her fluke unnaturally, so that it more mimicked the talons of a bird than a fanning tail.

Even for her, ascending the mountain using her tail proved to be a slow and arduous task. When she finally reached the mine, she continued past it, the rhythmic thunk-scrape of her body's movements naturally driving the last of the humans from their man-made cave. Once she had positioned herself above the mine, she no longer needed to purposefully intimidate the men to have them fleeing. She simply hung there and observed them as they clambered away from their posts and scattered.

The only one that did not run was, of course, Louis.

Looking haggard and more dirt-encrusted than usual, he stared at her until another man took his hand and pulled him away.

He did not visit her for six days.

When she finally felt his familiar echoes through the rock, she sent a small, excited tremor to him and emerged so quickly that he stumbled backwards. Louis crossed his arms and glared through his eyebrows at her, pushing her back when she tried to nuzzle closer.

"No!" he said. "You don't get to do that anymore."

She clicked frantically, and hated that he could not understand her.

"Do you have any idea what you did? People are calling you a demon. They say you came out of the mountain, breathing fire like some kind of hell beast. You almost caused a cave-in in the mine when you dragged yourself back up. I thought that you were actually going to start eating people for a moment, like everyone says you do. What were you thinking?"

The look of furious indignation on Louis' face intensified when, for the second time since they had met, the Bolter snapped him up in her jaws and dove beneath the surface. She spat him out higher up the mountain, where he instantly rolled away from her. After standing up and brushing off, he folded his arms and aimed a glare in her general direction.

"We are not friends anymore," he groused. "Take me back down."

She nestled gently into his side.

"No. I'm mad at you." A more insistent nudge and he stumbled heavily into a felled tree with a small "Oof." Finally, he turned in the direction of the latest scar that ran the length of the mountain.

"Oh," he breathed. They stood in silence for a time, and the Bolter watched as his tense shoulders slumped and his tight expression fell into one of extreme weariness.

"They don't mean anything by it, you know," he said. "The miners. It's just another job to them. A hard one at that. Not much choice for men like us."

He looked bitterly at his boots, and slowly reached out to place one palm flat against the Bolter's side.

"Not much choice."

She puffed dust in response, and was delighted to hear him snicker quietly.

"Would you take me back down now, you brute? I haven't been sleeping much so I can't be chewing the fat all night with you."

She carried him back down the mountain on her back, moving slowly across the abrasion from the avalanche so that she would not crush any more of the vegetation. Despite his obvious exhaustion, Louis was talking to her like he had been saving up his words for the entire six days he'd been away.

"You've got everyone well and truly spooked, Bolter, I'll tell you what. James left Rico altogether a few days after your trick with the fire. Not too sad to see the back of him. Always got the sense that he wanted to fight me. Not sure why. I must've said five words total to the man since I met him, great windbag that he is–"

"…Louis?"

Louis clamped his mouth shut and the Bolter stilled. The stranger before them was large for a human, to the point where his broad shoulders strained through his worn clothing. He had the same mustache as Louis, but his hair was lighter, and his face was freckle-flecked like granite.

The Bolter could feel Louis tense up again.

"What are you doing here, Stanley?"

"I saw the Slide-Rock Bolter eat you. I thought maybe I could catch you two up."

Stanley wasn't looking at Louis. Instead his eyes bore down on her, cautious and confused and very, very nervous. Her companion slid off of her back and took a hesitant step towards Stanley.

"You came to rescue me?"

"I...don't really know. I just went after you. I wasn't thinking."

Louis seemed pleased. The Bolter couldn't imagine why, considering the discomfort of the other man.

"It's all right," said Louis gently. He approached Stanley rather like he had her the first time they met. Another skittish animal. His eyes only left hers when Louis clasped one of his hands and tugged slightly. The Bolter recognized him suddenly as the man who had pulled Louis away from the mine as she was hanging by her tail.

"She's friendly."

"Friendly?" Stanley snatched his hand away and stepped back. "Feeding the birds is one thing, Louis, but this is an honest-to-goodness monster. One wrong move and you're food yourself. That thing is a demon. Have a little sense. Come away from it."

Louis crossed his arms, then turned around and strode back towards her.

"Louis, goddammit."

"You know, I heard you and the boys talking about me. They all think I'm the softest thing in the mine. Think I have bones like those birds I feed. I was grateful that you had nothing to add, but I sure didn't hear you defending me either."

Louis leaned his back against the Bolter's side and stared at him.

"But here's the thing, Stanley," he said. "I don't think I'm the soft one."

Stanley looked back at him like a man lost in the dark. Louis patted her side.

"So how about you come over here," he continued. "Don't worry, I'll protect you."

There was a stalemate for a moment, before Stanley started

forward with stuttering steps. Slowly, he reached out and placed his hand on her as well.

"See? Isn't she pleasant when she's not on fire?"

Stanley yanked his hand back quickly, as though the memory itself had burned him. Louis laughed as the other man glared.

"It's just instinct," he said. "She's defending her home."

He gestured to the path they were on, plowed down by their own instruments of destruction.

"I think the explosives scare her. Maybe even hurt her. Either way, we can't blame her for chasing us off when we're digging into her stone."

"I…suppose that makes sense." Stanley pressed his palm back into her side. "Well, she'll be happy to know that this whole operation probably won't last much longer."

"What are you talking about?"

"I've been hearing rumors lately. The mine's not profitable enough to last, especially with the Bolter messing around, driving people off. Miners are already hot footing it out of here after her last stunt, and I don't blame them."

Despite his words, Stanley had both hands patting her sides now, and she rocked back and forth happily, just enough to stir Louis.

"I really think I should tell you something, Louis."

"Yes?" Louis grinned.

"I think the boys are going to try and blow up the Bolter."

"What?" Louis pushed off of her side and faced him fully.

"They've been talking about it since last week. They've got this whole plan to stuff a dummy miner with dynamite. They think the Bolter will eat him and they can–" he mimicked an explosion with his hands, splayed fingers pointing in all directions.

"She doesn't even eat people!"

"She ate you earlier."

"That doesn't count. Besides, she's a solid rock, they can't just blow her up."

"Solid rock hasn't stopped any of us before. Besides, a few of them are thinking that if this plan doesn't work, they'll just go hunting for her. Some of the bigwigs are even getting involved, hoping to squeeze some profit out of the mine before it all goes belly up. Talk is that they're putting a price on her."

The Bolter felt Louis› weight sink heavily against her.

"I'm sorry, Louis."

The Slide-Rock Bolter hung from the mountain by her tail, waiting for the screaming to start. Stanley and Louis had been visiting her every night since their meeting on the mountain, discussing the state of the mine and the men and the ever-evolving plan to kill her. Her two companions sat side by side, leaning against each other and her.

The night before, they'd warned her that the false miner with the explosive core would appear among the men the next day. Louis told her, in no uncertain terms, to stay hidden.

She didn't listen, of course.

The Bolter knew that, even if the men failed to trick her into eating dynamite, her mere presence on the mountain would bring them back. The mine may not be profitable anymore, but it didn't mean that the men would leave the mountain be. Especially if she remained there. The rumors of her attacks would travel well beyond Rico, until people returned.

For her.

So, she would end it. Give them a new story to tell – that of her defeat.

But first she needed them to see her.

A shout echoed towards her, and she shifted in anticipation, watched them skitter away. Until only one remained. She stared at it, unmoving, helpless below.

And then, like a good monster, she attacked.

Her belly cut through the dirt, and as she slid, she scattered herself. She kept the few memories she had of the sea, of her pod and the comfort that she had felt with them. She kept the wisdom of how to shift between each type of sand and stone and alloy. She kept the love she had for Louis and Stanley.

And everything else – the long loneliness especially – she left behind.

And it was that great bulk of her that she let slide down the mountain, maw open, towards the trap.

The Bolter felt the familiar trod of her friends' boots that evening. She had worried that they wouldn't come, with the rumors of her demise.

She was no longer large enough to send a tremor towards them as warning, so instead she nosed through the soil and slid towards them. When Louis' tear-stained cheeks appeared before her, she leapt from the ground and into his arms, bowling him over.

"Bolter!" he cried, clasping her to him. "I love you but you're still heavy."

She rolled off of him and onto the ground, the glittering white quartz of her body thunking in a dusty cloud.

"She's so small," laughed Stanley.

"More than appropriate for traveling with me once the mine shuts down, don't you think?" said Louis, running a hand over her nose.

"Where are you thinking of going?"

Louis cleared his throat slightly. "Well, where are you going?"

"Depends," Stanley said after a moment, eyes traveling over him.

Louis looked immeasurably pleased at that, before turning back to the Bolter. He placed his forehead against hers and hugged her to him.

No mountain's embrace could ever compare.

The Development

ALISON AKIKO MCBAIN

"My name is Kami," she said.

Paul hadn't asked. He had barely glanced at her as he walked by the bus stop. She was sitting on a dirty bench under the straight arch of clear plastic, with graffiti covering the walls and bisecting the scene at her back.

Behind the bench was a huge hole in the ground, the detritus of roots poking the empty air, feeling with shaggy fingers for the dirt they had lost. The start of construction for the new library, it looked like they'd gotten stalled with the sudden downpour. A group of men loitered under a neighboring overhang, smoking and talking in that particular cadence men get when there are no women around. They obviously hadn't seen the girl outside the chain-link fence.

There was no time to stop and chat with her, but he had already met her eyes, so he couldn't just ignore her. Maybe some people could, but his mother's voice was in his head, lecturing him about respect. So, "Hi, Kami," he said. "Kami – pretty name."

"Thank you." She smiled. When she didn't say anything else, he gave a half-wave and walked on. A little way down the block, he turned back to look at her. She was still sitting at the bus stop, staring after him.

He thought about her all through the class he was teaching. Students asked questions that he didn't hear. At the end of the lecture, one boy stopped by Paul's desk. "Professor Watanabe, you all right?"

"Sure." He waved the boy on his way.

But the girl and her heart-shaped face lingered. He didn't know why.

He passed by the construction site on his way home, but no one was there, of course. She had probably caught her bus to wherever she needed to go.

Still, the next day walking to the university, he looked out for her thin face, her dark eyes. But it was a different day and a different time – the bench was empty.

Tuesday again, and he was running late. From far away, he could see the orange and black diggers doing something at the edges of the hole they had made. They'd brought a crane in, although the workers seemed to be watching it sit there, rather than using it. Perhaps this time of day was always their break, he thought – smoke ran in furls up into the air, the thick scent of tobacco blown through the chain-link fence.

He almost missed her, he was concentrating so hard on looking at the progress of the construction. When he spotted the black bob of hair and stick-thin frame on the bench, he felt shock for a moment, as if seeing someone he had thought long dead. She smiled at him, and after a moment, he smiled back.

"Hello, Kami," he said, pausing by the bus stop. Part of his brain was counting the seconds he was tardy, and the ticking in his head sounded as if it were saying *too late, too late, too late, too late…*

"Hello, Paul," she replied.

"How are…" He stopped. Held her black gaze. "How did you know my name?" he asked quietly.

"I know many things," she told him matter-of-factly.

The workers were looking over at him through the wide-open fence. A quick glance, and then away again. He wondered if they could hear them speaking, could eavesdrop on this bizarre conversation. Probably they were too far away.

"Okay," he said. He wondered if she had looked him up on the university's website, Googled him and come up with the articles listed under his name in obscure physics journals. Placed name to face.

Maybe. But there was no time to ask, and there seemed little point to pursue it. What harm could she do to him, this slight stick of a girl? "I'm running behind." As he turned away, "Have a nice day."

"Thank you," she said, but his back was already towards her and he didn't glance back.

He flubbed three formulas that day. Two of them, his students caught, and he corrected the third one before they discovered it. After class, he went to his office and sat in his chair, staring at nothing. Was Kami a previous student of his? Was that why she seemed so familiar? Why could he not remember her?

Finally, he went home past the construction site. He knew she wouldn't be there. Not at night. Not until the next week.

Paul set off for the university a whole hour earlier the next Tuesday. He could have made the excuse to himself that he had work to catch up on, which he did. But he was a night owl, preferring to stay later after his classes rather than get up when the air was moist from the passing night and the sun still deciding whether to turn the day blue or gray.

Today, it was gray – clouds hovered overhead in the middle distance, not quite threatening rain. As he hurried towards the university, with one eye on the developing weather overhead, he could see the large machines at the construction site from far away. They reminded him of when he was a boy in Naha, in Okinawa Prefecture, and he'd had a complete Tonka Toy set, bright yellow and black. He'd played with them for hours, digging, filling up the dump truck, winching the crane until the string broke from too much use. There was still that latent fascination with big toys, that quickening of his pulse as he saw the machines.

Or maybe it was anticipation. The men were by the fence, filling the air with the incense of rolled tobacco. And there, on the bench – there she was. An hour early, like him.

"You don't have to be afraid," were the first words she said to him.

There wasn't really any way to reply to that, so he didn't try. He had stopped walking – what was the point in ignoring her? His mother's voice again: *Good boys always respect women.*

"I'm disappearing. You might say I'm dying," she said.

It made him look at her, truly look at her. Other than the thinness of her figure, she looked healthy. But looks could be deceiving. "I'm sorry," he finally said after realizing the pause had gone on too long.

"There is always sorrow when things pass on. But change can't stop."

"That's a very mature outlook to take on it."

"No," she said sadly. "I have lost many friends. Some cried and some threatened. But they all disappeared. So I am who I have always been."

He nodded his head to her. "I see," he said. Attempt at consolation.

But he didn't.

She smiled when she saw him next. He noticed her teeth were slightly crooked, and it made her look like a child.

"How are you feeling today?" he asked politely.

She waved a hand around her, as if to say, *As well as to be expected.* Behind her, the workmen talked with each other in their corner of the fence. The steel skeleton of the structure was reaching for the sky, but it was all jagged edges, incomplete. Around it, the dirt humped up in brown waves, exploding outward from the rising building.

"It was beautiful once," she said, following his gaze. "A long time ago, there was a forest here. The trees spoke, and their conversations could take a season or more. Rabbits and badgers and foxes lived here. Deer and unicorns."

He would have laughed at her whimsy, until she turned her serious black eyes on him. "Unicorns?" he asked instead. She nodded.

"Among others."

"Were you here then?" He didn't remember a forest at this spot. In fact, he didn't remember what had been here before. He had lived in the Senbaru neighborhood in Nishihara for ten years, and he suddenly realized that this space had always been a blank to him. Perhaps an empty lot? That didn't seem right.

"I hid it," she told him. "After the trees were cut down and the animals died. I hid this place from those on the outside, but I was weak and couldn't hide forever."

"What do you mean?"

"No, that's a lie," she corrected herself. "Perhaps I could have continued hiding. But I was lonely."

He half-smiled. "You're a lovely girl. Don't you have parents? Friends? A…a boyfriend?" The questions felt inappropriate.

She shook her head.

"I'm sorry."

After a hesitation, she said, "Thank you for speaking with me. All these times when others would not – thank you."

He had so come to expect her there every week that, when the next Tuesday came, he paused at the bench automatically even though he had seen from some distance off that it was empty. For once, the men were working rather than taking a break. They'd filled in the structure and were putting in drywall with spaces cut out for windows.

"Sorry," he heard behind him, and he turned to see her coming up the sidewalk. She seemed out of breath, even though she was moving slowly. She sank down onto the bench and her chest rose and fell too quickly. For the first time, he sat beside her. Put his hand on her arm. She was so small, so skinny.

"Are you okay? Can I help you? Do you have medicine?" He looked for a purse – every woman had one, didn't they? – and was stumped to see she carried nothing. Come to think of it, he'd never seen her with a bag.

"There is no medicine I could take," she finally said. Her cheeks were flushed and her face shiny with sweat. "Not much longer now."

At her words, he found there was a thickness in his throat. He swallowed past it and glanced behind her. Unnoticed by him, the men had paused in their work while he'd watched Kami walk up, and now they were eyeing him through the fence, smoke curling out of their mouths and noses. At his glance, they turned their backs, deliberately. But they didn't speak, just smoked until their cigarettes became small stubs, and then lit fresh sticks from the old embers.

"Don't worry about them," she said. "They'll be all right. None of them will die from cancer."

Paul turned back to her. He'd never seen anyone with eyes so dark, so black, that he couldn't distinguish the pupil from the iris. On this Japanese island of dark-eyed, dark-haired people, he had never once seen eyes consume the light like hers did. Never seen eyes with so much history.

"Is that what you have? Cancer?" he asked.

Her mouth moved, but it was not quite a smile. "No."

"What can I do?" he said. "I *need* to be able to help you."

"Remember me," she said. Then, "Remember unicorns. Trees talking. Rabbits." She laughed.

He laughed with her, but when he took her hand, it was light as air. It was as if it wasn't there anymore, even though he could feel her bones through the thin skin of her wrist and fingers. After a moment, she took her hand back and he stood up and walked away.

It was weeks later that it happened. What he had been dreading. Weeks later when they took away the bulldozers, the diggers, the cranes, the machines. When the building was finished and sat empty, waiting to be filled. The ribbon-cutting ceremony would be next weekend, but everything else was done. The workmen were gone, their smoke was gone, the hole in the ground was gone.

And so was she – gone. He never saw Kami again.

Later, he went to the ribbon-cutting ceremony. Entered the building that had taken the place of the forest of whispering trees, the unicorns he'd never seen, the many small lives of the wild places – the badgers and the rabbits and the long-lost spirits who protected them.

He remembered Kami's stories. He remembered her black, black eyes. He remembered her.

He remembered.

Skrunch

R L MEZA

At the sound of Timothy's scream, the dinner plate slipped from Bonnie's hands and shattered, spraying glass across the yellowed linoleum. In the ten years of his life, she'd never heard her little brother scream like that, not even when the boys at school had held Timothy down and pinched his nose shut, trying to force through his clenched teeth a dead, squashed up snake they'd found in the road. Timothy cried out again – a reedy, panicked shriek – and Bonnie rushed for the back door. Her soap-slicked rubber gloves fumbled with the knob, squeezing a fistful of bubbles from the sponge still clutched in her right hand. She tore off her gloves, wrenched the knob, and the back door opened a rectangle of light into the night.

"Tim?" Bonnie's voice was faint, choked with anxiety. Their mother wasn't due home from work for hours, and despite her brother's screams, the windows in the neighboring houses remained dark, staring back at her like flat, lifeless eyes, reflecting the moon.

Beyond the reach of the doorway's light, a black shape was hunched over in the grass. Bonnie snatched the broom from beside the back door and choked up on the handle, brandishing the wooden stick at the shape in the yard. She waded forward into the knee-high grass.

"*Timothy!*"

The shape rose, stumbled toward her. "B-Bonnie?"

Tim's soft stutter drifted through the darkness, followed by the pale moon of his face. Beneath a tangled nest of dirty blonde curls, his blue eyes were wide and shining with fear. Bonnie seized Tim by the shoulders and hauled him toward the back door. Once they were inside, the back door slammed behind them, she shot the deadbolt into place. A pungent odor filled Bonnie's nostrils.

As Tim twisted from her grasp and backed through the kitchen, Bonnie saw the soaked crotch of his pants, the stain spreading down both legs to his–

"Tim, what happened to your shoes?" Her tone was sharper than she'd intended, and Tim cringed. "There's s-something out there, Bon. A m-m-monster."

Bonnie shook her head. Two years of after-school speech classes, and still Tim's stutter persisted, emerging only at the worst of times – like when the boys were closing in on him, their fingers ready to pinch and twist and make T-tiny T-talking T-timmy squeal. With their mother working long hours, and their father lost to the war in Vietnam, Tim's care had fallen to Bonnie; but there were only so many times a fourteen-year-old sister could chase the bullies off before the ambushes became more clever, the insults more cruel. Whatever Tim had seen in their yard, it must have been worse than all the bullies combined. All those beatings, and Tim had never wet his pants, not once.

"I t-t-took the garbage out like you s-said, and i-it was digging through the bin, r-r-ripping the b-bags open…" Tim shuddered, rubbed his eyes as if to erase the image from his mind. "It s-s-saw me, and it r-r-r – came r-right at me, clawed my shh – my sh-shoes, and–"

A thump from the front porch silenced Tim. Bonnie crossed the room in four quick steps, listening for the jingle of their mother's keys at the front door. "Mom?"

Snuffling, through the crack at the bottom of the door.

Bonnie reached for the curtain covering the front window. The wet snuffling turned to panting, heated blasts of breath that Bonnie felt on her bare ankles. Ignoring Tim's frantic hand signals, Bonnie peeked out.

Below the sill, she saw a blur of gray – not clothing, like she'd been hoping, but rough, leathery skin stippled with coarse hairs. Bonnie gasped, and the shape below the window jumped, straightened.

"Bonnie, call the police," Tim squeaked. "Please, they'll have guns and they can–"

Bonnie couldn't help it, she needed to see the rest of thing, had to, a glimpse just wasn't enough. She tore the curtain aside. The porch light illuminated a gray face and two pink eyes like saucers, each larger than her fist, and Bonnie screamed. The creature on the porch recoiled, echoing her scream with a hissing screech. Slivers of teeth poked out from its open mouth. Three strong legs tensed beneath it, muscles bunching under gray skin, and then the creature was gone from their porch in a single bound, leaping into the night.

"Y-y-yes, a m-m-monster." Tim peered out at Bonnie from the kitchen, cord trailing from the receiver pressed to his ear. "It's t-trying to get in. P-p-p – hurry!"

Tim's call didn't bring the authorities, but the four shots fired from the McDaniel house did. In the silence that followed, Tim whispered, "D-did he get it, you think? The m-m-monster?"

"I don't know." Bonnie ordered Tim to stay in bed and donned her mother's housecoat, venturing onto the porch just as a state trooper's car pulled up next door. A flashlight beam moved through the field behind the McDaniel house, panning over the wavering grass, and the trunks of the trees that bordered the property. Beyond the trees lay the railroad tracks. Bonnie used to dream of jumping a train, riding it out of Enfield to the mountains and forests of Washington, where her aunt lived. But there was Tim to think about now; defenseless Tim, and she'd never be able to leave him.

"Miss, you okay?" The trooper's flashlight struck her in the eyes, and Bonnie raised a hand to shield her vision.

"Blind, but otherwise fine," Bonnie said. "You here about the monster?"

"I hit it!" McDaniel strode through his back field, rounding the house toward the trooper.

Bonnie eyed the .22 pistol in McDaniel's hand with caution. McDaniel raised two fingers, red and glistening, and said, "There's a trail of blood leading off into the trees. If we hurry, get a party together–"

The trooper motioned for him to lower the firearm. "Mister McDaniel, is anyone hurt?"

"No, sir, nothing human, anyway," McDaniel said. "Come have a look at these claw marks."

Bonnie trailed along behind them. Neither man seemed to notice her presence as McDaniel traced the ragged scratches that marred the house's siding.

"There are tracks here," the trooper said, kneeling to inspect the dirt. "Some kind of animal. Stray dog, maybe a coyote. Probably just trying to get at the garbage in your bins."

McDaniel snorted. "Trying to get *in my house*, more like. It got the bins open just fine, there's garbage everywhere, so why's the siding all clawed up? Because that monster wanted my children. They said it tried to get through the front door. What kind of coyote has six toes, can you tell me that?"

"And three feet." At the sound of Bonnie's voice, the trooper's flashlight beam came up to stab at her eyes again. Bonnie pointed at a pair of tracks four inches wide, then a third, smaller track just behind the first two.

"Fifty feet," McDaniel breathed. "The damn thing covered fifty feet in three bounds. I've never seen anything like it."

The next morning, Bonnie and Tim waited until McDaniel's truck had turned the corner at the end of the road before sneaking next door. They moved quickly, ducking low to cross the open field that stretched between the McDaniel house and the tree line beyond. Beneath the shelter of the trees, Bonnie hunkered down to inspect a bed of leaf litter dappled with droplets dried to reddish brown.

"You think Mister McDaniel found it already?" Tim said.

"I think if he found anything, we'd have heard about it." Bonnie discovered more blood ahead, spaced fifteen feet from the first traces.

They reached the railroad tracks ten minutes later. Either the monster's fear had diminished, or its strength had, because now the trail was easy to follow, the droplets closely grouped along the ties. Bonnie pointed at a dark smear on the metal track to their left, and whispered, "This way."

She pushed through the brush into an overgrown clearing, circled the dilapidated house at its center. The house was abandoned, had to be. No one would live in a house with half the roof caved in, although there was enough garbage to suggest that more than a few people had spent the night.

"You're not going in there, are you?" Tim squinted at the door hanging ajar, a gaping black maw that made Bonnie shiver. She said, "I'm going in, and you're going to wait here. If anything happens, you run back and–"

"No." Tim lifted his chin, puffed out his chest. "I'm coming with you."

Impressed by his uncharacteristic display of courage, Bonnie snatched up a thick branch and passed it to Tim. "Okay. But keep this ready, just in case. And be careful, if you hit me by accident, I'll make sure you don't sit right for a year."

Bonnie crept into the darkened house, wrinkling her nose at the musty odor. "Hello? Anyone here?"

Nothing but the sound of their breathing, and then–

Something crashed to the floor in the next room. A vibration passed through the floorboards, the drumming of feet on wood. Bonnie seized Tim's wrist, towed him into the adjoining room, a kitchen, where the cupboard doors hung open – all of them empty, except for one. Beside a rusted antique stove, a gray mass shifted, stuffed its bulk deeper into the bottom cupboard. Clawed feet knocked back the swinging door with a bang. The creature's rough hide jumped and quivered as it redoubled its frantic efforts to fit inside the cramped hiding space.

"It's scared," Bonnie whispered, heart pounding in her chest. "See how it's shaking? I don't think it means to hurt us."

Tim nodded, but he was swaying on his feet, glassy-eyed, like he might faint. Bonnie snapped her fingers in his face. "Tim, give me one of your candy bars."

Some color returned to Tim's cheeks; his lower lip pooched out, as it always did when he was trying to slip a lie past her. "I don't have any."

Bonnie rolled her eyes. "You always have one. Give it here."

"Fine." Tim sucked in his lower lip and removed a candy bar from his pocket. The wrapper crinkled in his fist as he took a step toward the cupboard. "But I get to feed it."

Bonnie blinked at her brother's furrowed brow, the grim set of his jaw. Bemused, she said, "Snap it in two, and we'll do it together."

Tim broke the candy bar in half and passed a piece to Bonnie. They crept forward, left their offerings on the floor, and retreated to the doorway to watch, breathless. A short limb emerged from the cabinet, six digits splayed and patting the floor. Seeking. Wet, muffled crunching issued from the cupboard, and the arm appeared a second time. But Tim's piece of candy was beyond the creature's reach. It poked its head out. Saucer eyes caught the sunlight slanting through the holes in the roof and glittered like pink tourmaline. The creature emerged from the cupboard, and Bonnie saw the wound in its rear flank, still leaking blood.

The creature found the second piece of candy and devoured it in a single bite, smacking its lips and scouring the floor for more, limping closer to their position in the doorway. Muscular, but no taller than four and a half feet, the creature was far less frightening in the light of day. Its nose was a smooth bump below its enlarged eyes; a pair of nostrils twitched as the creature scented the room, looked up. Locked eyes with Bonnie. It released a startled shriek, and Bonnie's mouth dropped open. This was the cry she had heard the night before – not Tim, but this wretched, terrified creature.

Tim rushed forward, ducked under Bonnie's arm, and she had time to think, *Two – he had two candy bars, the little sneak*, before Tim knelt on the floorboards with his hand outstretched. The creature's arms were pulled up to cover its chest, its head shaking side to side. But there was nothing to fear, no weapon in Tim's hand, just the candy bar pieces, the chocolate slowly melting from the heat of his palm.

The creature's tongue slid over its lips. Bonnie and Tim remained frozen in place, neither daring to speak. Then, the creature spoke – at least, that's what Bonnie thought the sounds were meant to be – throaty gurgles and chirps spaced like words, wet burbling, baby noises. Curious. Hopeful. Its hand darted out, lightning-quick. Gnashing the candy between its teeth, the creature settled back onto the floorboards with a heavy sigh.

"You're hurt," Bonnie said, pointing to her hip, then the creature's rear flank. "Can I look?"

The creature tilted its head to one side, but made no move to flee when Bonnie approached. From a pocket in her dress, Bonnie removed the small bottle of rubbing alcohol she'd pinched from the medicine cabinet back home, along with a handful of cotton balls. There were two holes where the bullet had passed clean through. Bonnie cleaned the wounds, and though the creature hissed, it did not flee from her touch.

"Stay here, okay?" Bonnie patted the air with her open palms, pointed at the floor. "We'll come back, bring more food for you, but you have to wait here."

On the walk back, Tim lagged behind. He kicked at the ground, used the branch she'd given him to stir up leaves and smack the bushes. After the third unexpected stop, Bonnie snapped, "*Tim*, we have to get home. Mom will be awake by now."

"I'm covering the tracks," Tim said, shrugging.

Together, they erased the evidence of the creature's passage, scuttling across the field to with only minutes to spare before McDaniel's truck rumbled into the driveway.

When the boys ambushed Tim, the creature came for them.

In the two weeks since they'd discovered the creature at the abandoned house, Bonnie and Tim had visited at every opportunity, cleaning its wounds and feeding it, toting armfuls of books and toys and games. The creature rolled on the floor with Tim, grasping at plastic soldiers, running off to hide while Tim covered his eyes and counted to ten. Bonnie taught it how to play checkers; it often greeted her with a favorite book cradled in its short arms. It was still an 'it,' for they could not determine its gender by looking at it, but after much debate, Bonnie and Tim had settled on a name: Skrunch, after the creature's favorite Wonka candy bar, the peanut butter kind that it liked to chew with its mouth open, seemingly delighted by the sound of the crispy rice. Bonnie thought it was a silly name, one she couldn't say without smiling and rolling her eyes, but it had been Tim's idea, and she hadn't had the heart to discourage him.

Bonnie was alone, searching the house for Skrunch and Tim, when she heard the commotion: shouting, a loud hiss. Screams of fright. She burst through the trees to find the warring parties divided by the railroad tracks. On the right, her brother wrestled with a snarling Skrunch, pleading. Tim's eye was puffy, his shirt torn and filthy. A trio of boys cowered on the left side of the tracks. Bonnie recognized the bullies immediately.

The oldest and largest of the three, Ricky, had just turned thirteen. Ricky was sprawled on the ground, greasy ginger hair clinging to his forehead; blood poured from his crooked nose. The tall boy to Ricky's left scrabbled backwards in the dirt at the sight of her, perhaps remembering the time Bonnie had swatted him off his bike with a two-by-four for spraining Tim's wrist. The third boy huddled behind Ricky. Bonnie narrowed her eyes at them and advanced, predatory. She saw the blood-spattered branch lying on the tracks, heard Tim yelling, "Stop! Skrunch – *Bonnie* – both of you, stop!"

And so she did, chest heaving, her breath coming fast and hot. Bonnie opened and closed her fists, said, "What happened here?"

The tall boy stabbed a finger at Tim. "Your crazy brother hit Ricky with a branch, and then that – that *thing*–"

Bonnie hefted the branch and leveled it at him. "And what did you do?"

"W-what?"

Bonnie's voice lowered to a growl. She repeated the question, slower, punctuating each word with a jab from the branch. "What did you do?"

"We jumped him," the other boy squeaked from the ground.

"Lewis!" The tall boy paled.

"What, Mark? He's going to tell her anyways."

"Both of you, shut up." Ricky stood and wiped his bloody hand on his shirt. To Tim, he said, "You've got one hell of a swing. You ever play baseball?"

Tim shook his head.

"We could use you on the team this summer. You got a mitt?"

Again, Tim shook his head. Skrunch had ceased struggling and was watching the exchange. Bonnie couldn't help but think the creature looked as baffled as she felt by the sudden shift in mood.

"That's all right. My kid brother's got one, but he can't play worth a damn. You can have his." Then, casting a wary glance at Skrunch, Ricky said, "I don't know how you're holding that thing back like that. I'd be pissing myself. It really listens to you?"

Tim shrugged. "Skrunch is cool."

"Can you, uh, keep it from ripping my head off, if I want to get a little closer? Just to talk?"

Tim murmured something into the recessed hole of Skrunch's ear. Snorting, Skrunch curled a lip at the boys. "It's okay, Skrunch. *I'm okay*, really."

Skrunch huffed and sat back on its haunches, glaring at the bullies. Its hooked claws tapped the metal rail – a steady *tick-tick-tick* that made Mark and Lewis exchange nervous glances.

"Come on over," Tim said. "Skrunch won't do anything."

Stunned, Bonnie realized that – despite the bullies, the swollen eye, the conflict on the tracks – Tim wasn't stuttering. Standing there with his spine straight, his shoulders squared, Tim looked just like their father. Calm, courageous. And in that moment, Bonnie experienced an intense combination of sorrow and pride.

"So this is it, huh?" Ricky crossed the tracks, hands shoved in his pockets, and said, "This is the monster that McDaniel's been telling everyone about? He's not the only one who's seen it, you know. Some radio guy and his friends said they spotted it out near an old house the other day. That's why we came out here, before..."

"You tried to beat up my brother?" Bonnie's rage was still simmering beneath the surface. Skrunch uttered a soft hiss in agreement.

"I'm sorry about that," Ricky said. He extended a hand to Tim and, after a moment's consideration, Tim shook it. "Sorry for all of it. Really."

"Us too," said Lewis, elbowing Mark in the ribs. "Yeah. We're sorry."

Bonnie dropped the branch, and everyone appeared to relax.

Ricky said, "You know, there's a lot of reporters in town from all over, hoping to catch a picture, a story. My dad's talking about joining up with one of the hunting parties, said they're all coming out here, early as tomorrow. Been hearing rumors about some kind of reward for whoever can get proof of the thing – dead or alive, you know?"

The thought of hunters made Bonnie's stomach knot. "The sheriff can't be happy about that."

Ricky raised an eyebrow. "Bunch of drunk old men, beating the bushes, shooting everything that moves? What could go wrong?"

Skrunch leaned past Tim to sniff at Ricky's pocket, and Ricky said, "Can you really leap a hundred feet at a time?"

"More like fifty feet," Bonnie said.

Ricky rolled his eyes. "You see? Drunk old men and their rumors. They're saying it can climb trees and fly, that it tried to eat McDaniel's kids."

"Skrunch would never!" Bonnie scowled in the direction of the McDaniel house. Ricky removed a half-eaten packet of crackers from his pocket. Skrunch nosed Ricky's hand, inhaled a dusting of crumbs, and sneezed. The boys laughed. Ricky bent down and offered Skrunch a cracker.

"I have an idea." Tim was pacing the tracks, his blue eyes alight. "But we'll need your help."

Bonnie dragged their mother's travel trunk into the bedroom and flipped back the lid, trying to appear casual in her inspection of the interior. From the doorway, Bonnie and Tim's mother said, "I really think it's a bit much. You're just visiting for the summer."

"Yeah, but I'll need my clothes, a couple pairs of shoes – boots – and Aunt Ida said to bring a coat for the rain. Oh! I'll have to bring my books, my drawing supplies…"

Bonnie continued packing things into the trunk until their mother relented with a sigh, kissed their foreheads, and left for work. Tim watched through the window as their mother turned the corner at the end of the street, then ran into the yard, forking his fingers between his lips, the way Ricky had taught him, to whistle the signal. Between the five of them, they were able to empty the trunk and carry all of Bonnie's things out to the abandoned house in a single trip. As they moved through the trees, Ricky peered over an armload of Bonnie's clothes at the furry gray bundle slung over Tim's shoulder, and said, "What the hell is that?"

Tim grinned. "A wolf pelt."

"I didn't think we had wolves around here," said Lewis, eyeing the underbrush.

"We don't." Bonnie stooped to pick up a fallen sock. "Our dad shot it. It's been hanging on our wall at home since before I was born."

The old house came into view through the trees, and Tim said, "Really? Nobody's going to ask me what the wolf pelt's for?"

"Guessing Bonnie likes to wear it when she's beating up boys."

Bonnie smacked the back of Ricky's head, but she was smiling.

As the sun fell below the horizon, Bonnie's excitement turned to anxiety. Tim pulled the wolf pelt on, and she used shoelaces to secure the pelt in place. When she was satisfied that Tim would still be able to run, Bonnie hugged him close, whispered, "Remember, *only* come out if we're spotted. And be careful. If anything ever happened to you– Please, can't we just have Ricky do it?"

Tim shook his head. "I want to do it."

No stutter. That look of hard determination was back.

There was no way they could wait inside the abandoned house, not after the man from the radio station had spread the news of his sighting there. The hunters had been out since noon, weaving through the trees with their rifles in hand, making it impossible for the children to sneak Skrunch back to Bonnie and Tim's without being seen. But under the cover of darkness, there was a chance. Crouched beneath the porch with Skrunch between them, the children waited.

Raucous laughter signaled the hunters' arrival. From the amount of noise they were making, Bonnie guessed that Ricky had been right about the drinking. When she heard the front door of the old house bang open, the thump of boots on the floorboards overhead, she signaled that it was time to move. Ricky crawled out into the darkness and waved them through. As they crept into the underbrush surrounding the house, Bonnie saw the flashlight beams bouncing off the walls inside, heard something fall with a clatter. She gave the boys a push in their backs to hurry them along.

Skrunch was frightened, whimpering low in its throat. Bonnie folded one of the creature's six-fingered hands into her own and squeezed. "We won't let anything happen to you, I promise."

They were almost to the tracks when Mark stumbled, twisted his ankle with a pained screech that sent birds flapping up from the nearby bushes. "Idiot," Ricky hissed, hauling Mark upright and ducking under his arm. "Help me with him, Lewis."

A shot rang out, freezing them in place. The trees at their backs came alive with shouts, loud whooping. The hunters crashed through the underbrush, headed right for them.

"We have to split up," Bonnie said. Jerking on Skrunch's arms, Bonnie managed to convince the creature to let Tim go. They hunkered down behind a fallen log to wait, while Tim and the boys moved out onto the tracks.

"Wait until we see them," Ricky said to Tim, "then run as fast as you can, down the tracks and into the trees. Don't stop until you hit the Davidson place–"

"And hide in their back shed," Tim finished. "I know. It was my plan."

"Once you're far enough along, we'll draw them off of you." Ricky hefted a pair of knapsacks filled with rocks and passed one to Lewis, who said, "What about Mark?"

"You can still throw rocks, can't you, Mark?"

With Mark between them, Ricky and Lewis moved into the trees. Twigs snapped, leaves crunched underfoot, and Bonnie saw the barrel of a rifle glint in the moonlight. As the first of the hunters emerged from the tree line, Tim let out a fierce hiss and sprinted down the tracks. Bonnie held her breath. Drunken hollering between the hunter and his lagging companions – "It's here! Quick, I've got the monster!" – and Bonnie's stomach knotted.

She heard the metallic click of a rifle being cocked and tried to stand, no longer willing to follow Tim's plan, because it was foolish, stupid – he was going to get himself killed – but strong hands were pulling her back down, holding her tight; the gray body pressed against her was trembling with fear and desperation. Skrunch didn't want to be left behind, and if they discovered the creature now… Bonnie shut her eyes, tried to breathe. Tim was a gray blur on the distant tracks, veering toward the shelter of the trees.

Bang!

And the gray blur that was her brother went down. Bonnie stifled a scream. *Up again* – Tim was up again, moving more slowly, and then she could no longer see him. He'd made it into the trees. Five hunters pursued him down the tracks. The frontrunner paused to fire off another shot, then ducked and bellowed at his companions as they fired off their guns behind him.

"You could've hit me!"

"Don't let it get away! Go, go!"

Ricky and the boys unleashed a volley of stones from the bushes. The hunters threw up their arms, shouting in confusion, rocks striking their backs as they retreated. Bonnie bit her lip, and the pain focused her. She grabbed Skrunch by the arm, and together they barreled through the trees toward home.

"I still can't believe it," Bonnie said, tears in her eyes. She didn't want to cry – not with the room packed with kids from their school, the reporters vying for position outside the open door of the hospital room – but the tears came faster than she could wipe them away. "I can't believe you're alive."

Tim flashed a grin, set aside a homemade card signed by all the girls in his class, and whipped back the sheet that covered his bandaged leg. A collective gasp rose from the other children. "I bet that hurt like a son-of-a-bitch," said Ricky.

Bonnie and Tim's mother pursed her lips. "Richard Livingston, mind your language. Bonnie, say goodbye to your brother. You've got a train to catch."

Leaning in, Bonnie kissed her brother's cheek. Tim blushed and whispered in her ear, "You'll say goodbye for me? Find Skrunch a safe place in Washington – a home?"

"Yes and yes," said Bonnie.

In the hall, Bonnie's mother gave the sheriff a withering glare, then spun on her heel, shoes clacking on the tile as Bonnie rushed along in her wake. She supposed that after the merciless reaming their mother had given the group of hunters, the bars of a jail cell would come as a relief. Given her role in the ill-fated caper, Bonnie had expected her trip to be cancelled. But, after Ricky and his friends had called the sheriff to report the shooting, Tim had saved Bonnie with a lie, claiming that he'd sneaked out after dark to meet the other boys, to see the monster for themselves.

An hour later, Bonnie stood on the platform with the trunk beside her. She cracked the lid open an inch and wormed a finger through the gap, smiled as the creature pinched her fingertip – their agreed-upon signal that Skrunch was okay. "Tim says goodbye," she whispered.

Skrunch made a soft rumbling sound that resembled a purr. "Shh. You have to stay quiet until we've arrived, okay? I'll open the lid when it's time."

The train pulled up to the station, and Bonnie shut the lid, locked it.

"Young lady, do you need help with that?" An older man approached, smiling.

"Yes, sir. Thank you."

"Oof, awfully heavy. Got everything but the kitchen sink in here, feels like."

"Just what matters," Bonnie said, taking a last look around before she climbed aboard the train. As Enfield, Illinois receded into the distance, Bonnie stared out the window, determined to stay awake for the entire trip, to see everything that she could. The west coast and Washington lay ahead, and if it was anything like the picture books, Bonnie thought that she and Skrunch would be very happy there, indeed.

Leviathan

MARLAINA COCKCROFT

"You don't want to eat me," said the fish, in a surprisingly deep voice.

"Sure I don't," I said, lifting the line higher. I'd hooked him under a rib, looked like, and he wriggled unhappily. "Why, you going to grant me some wishes?"

Normally I'd question this conversation. But I'd finished off the rest of the wine last night, and my cousin Shelly's little beach condo only had decaf coffee left, and I couldn't tell whether my headache was hangover or caffeine withdrawal or some glorious combination of both. So the talking fish was clearly a hallucination. I should've gotten properly awake before walking down to the water, but you're supposed to go fishing early in the morning, right? I'd read that somewhere.

The fish puffed up around the hook. "Grant *what*? You dare? I'm not some silly fairytale fish. I am Leviathan."

I laughed so hard I almost fell off the dock, then winced as my head throbbed. "No, I know these stories. Leviathan is a giant sea monster, king of the ocean. You're barely big enough to keep."

He was a pretty fish, though, the silver scales turning iridescent as the sun hit. Wasn't there a book about a rainbow fish?

He stopped wriggling. One round eye stared down at the waves beneath us. "I was bigger then. Or the world was smaller. Yes, the world was smaller."

"You sure you didn't just devolve?" I was making Darwin jokes to a fish, what was in that wine? But he ignored me and kept talking, his unfishlike voice broken into little pieces.

"I am Leviathan. I am mightier than the fiercest wave and colder than the bleakest depths. I–" His eye slid upward. "I don't remember getting smaller. I don't know what happened to me."

Now the fish sounded like me.

I stumbled, like the dock had shifted with the tide, except it hadn't. The fish swayed on my line, watching me.

Years of eating seafood, and I was going to cry for an imaginary fish? Yes, yes I might. I blew out a soft breath. "Can you prove it? Prove you're Leviathan?"

The fish sputtered. "You think being king of the ocean is some silly magic trick?"

No, I thought the last month and a half had finally gotten to me and I'd snapped. Just another loopy tourist talking to her fish. And ludicrously, I was looking for the words to explain all that, to the fish, when I heard heavy footsteps coming down the dock. I quickly drew the hook out. "Good luck," I whispered as I dropped him in the ocean.

"Morning." The man ambled up beside me – a fellow fisherman, looked like, except he had real gear instead of the dented old pole I'd found in Shelly's front closet. Sensible boots, instead of my sockless sneakers. "What'd you do that for? It looked big enough."

"Because . . ." I had no good answer, so I shrugged. "He begged me for mercy." My face was already flaming, so I hurried up to the road. Coffee. Somewhere in this tiny town, there had to be coffee.

Lots of people lose their jobs. I still wasn't sure why losing mine had upended me so much.

I poked at the pancakes I'd decided to get along with the coffee, to treat myself, forgetting that pancakes usually sat like a rock in my stomach and that a diner this small wouldn't have turkey sausage, just the regular kind. Did I get special dispensation for pork if my life was upended?

First came the divorce, but most of my friends were already on their second marriages anyway. Then I lost my job. I planned fundraisers; I helped people. But the company's cash flow dried up, so they fired me to save on my salary. Yes, I am so helpful.

Now I didn't know what to do next, or where to go once my rent money ran out in a few months. "Go use my beach condo,"

Shelly said when she called to check on me. "Take a break, you need it."

"I can't impose," I said, meaning, I can't accept your pity vacation.

"No, seriously, it's just going to sit there empty. I'm leaving for France in two days. Can you believe it?"

Well, in *that* case.

I huddled over the plastic booth table and chewed the sausage, savoring the mix of fried meat and maple syrup. There were worse places to hide from the world, really. Leviathan and me, both hiding at the beach.

The waitress, bless her, bustled over and refilled my coffee cup before I could ask. Definitely awake now, and still I was sure the fish had talked to me.

Leviathan was the original sea monster in Judaism. All-powerful, nearly indestructible. So overwhelming that the Lord destroyed its mate, so that it could never breed. Possibly involved with that whole swallowing-Jonah business.

I speared a bit of pancake with my fork. That little thing, Leviathan? I'd seen salmon fillets in the freezer aisle that were bigger.

"Give up on fishing?" The man from the dock tipped his baseball cap to me as he stopped at my booth. He was closer to my age than I'd realized, and his face had a friendly sun-worn look.

"I guess I'd rather buy my food than catch it," I admitted.

He laughed, his whole body leaning into it. "Well, if you're looking to relax a little, I run a whale-watching tour. We've got a few seats left on the afternoon run, the storm's supposed to miss us."

I blinked up at him. "Whale-watching, here?"

"Hey, it's the ocean. You never know what's out there." He pulled a business card and a pen out from somewhere, scribbled something on the card, and left it next to my plate. "Let me know if you're interested. Enjoy your breakfast."

I watched him ease his bulky body down the crowded aisle, calling hello to the waitress, the cook in the back, and half the customers. I knew, without looking, that his own number would be on the back of the card. It was a little charming.

I drained the coffee. Wasting time with people seemed more appealing than wasting it alone.

Or offering sympathy to hallucinatory magic talking fish.

For twenty minutes, it was perfect. The waves gently rocked us along. Timothy – my new whale-watching friend – chatted to us as we sat in a semicircle on benches ringing the rear of the boat, about the history of the town, the type of boat we were on, the different types of whales, the right way to spot a whale. If I was the only member of the tour group listening, while the two teenagers across from me rolled their eyes at their parents and the couple next to me took selfies, he didn't seem to mind. The breeze tugged at my hair again and I gave up on it, pulling the curls into a scrunchie.

I closed my eyes and let the sun warm my face. Out here, my life wasn't a wreck. Out here, none of it mattered.

"When are we gonna see a whale, huh?" One-half of the couple next to me, her arms folded, while her giant-brimmed straw hat whacked me in the ear again.

"Yeah, what is this, false advertising?" Her husband, who had much less hair but no head covering, smiled in that thin-lipped way that says *just joking* but also *I'm not joking at all, you schmuck*. "We could've looked at the waves from the beach."

Timothy didn't answer right away, studying the sky, then lifting his mirrored sunglasses to check his phone. I caught his eyes, just before he dropped the sunglasses back in place. They were wide and…scared? He stood to swing the boat back around, and a chill sliced down my neck.

"Sorry, folks," he said, somehow keeping that friendly tone in place, "looks like that storm decided to come our way after all, so we'll have to cut this short." He gunned the motor. The couple next to me started in on refunds and bad reviews.

"No," I said to them. "*Stop.*" Because I could feel it now, too, the air heavy on my shoulders. The sky, just like that, went from blue to gray. Timothy gripped the wheel like he could will the boat to go faster. And the storm was on us.

I couldn't see past the rain, couldn't breathe past the wind. My neighbor's hat went sailing off, along with my scrunchie, and a wave swallowed them both. I gripped the railing and huddled into my life jacket. Waterspout? Derecho? Whatever it was, it was going to capsize us. The boat spun. *Going down the drain*, I thought. My stomach lurched and I clenched my teeth, hoping the pancakes would stay down.

How long would it take the Coast Guard to find us, after we were reported missing? A day? A week?

Leviathan didn't grant wishes. But maybe he returned favors.

I twisted around, toward the terrifyingly large waves, and leaned over the railing. "Leviathan!"

"What are you *doing,"* yelled the man next to me, grabbing at my arm, but I shook him off. My hair whipped into my eyes as I shouted my throat raw.

"Leviathan. You're mightier than this storm. You rule here. Prove it. *Prove it.*"

The salt stung my eyes, my hands slipped, I was sure I was going overboard and underwater. Behind me, Timothy yelled something. Several other people screamed.

A flash in the water. A streak of iridescence. A dark shape rose up, rocking the boat backward, and kept rising until it blotted out what remained of the sky.

"Is that a whale?" someone gasped. Maybe Jonah had thought that, too. But no whale was ever the size of the ocean. Whales don't have shining silver scales.

His sheer mass blocked the winds. One round eye fixed on us for the longest, scariest second of my life. Without warning, his giant fin flipped up and flicked the back of the boat. Everyone screamed again, falling to the deck as the boat shot forward. Timothy croaked out, "Hold on to something." I managed to lift my head enough to see him. His knuckles were scraped and bloody, but he still kept the wheel steady.

I could've cheered when the dock appeared in the distance. It got closer. And closer. I realized Leviathan didn't care about anchors, or brakes.

We crunched into the dock, the engine screeching before dropping to a sickly sputter. Timothy bounced up and grabbed whatever arms and shoulders were in reach, pushing everyone off the boat as it listed to the side, already half full of water.

I was last, still clinging to the rail until Timothy clamped a hand on my wrist. I scrambled up over the broken boards of the dock, wondering distantly whether I was getting splinters. I had to use both hands to lift my hair up and see.

Everyone huddled at the far end of the dock, spilling back into the parking lot, clutching each other and crying. One of the parents, arms wrapped around her teenaged son, was screeching that her phone was still on the boat. Too late, then, because the boat slipped fully underwater with an almost audible sigh. Timothy stared down at where it had been, and I hoped this wasn't going to get him fired. And that the boat was insured.

The storm slowly dissipated, lightening into a more regular sort of rain. A little ways off, a flash of silver in the waves. "Thank you," I called. And if the others gave me funny looks, I didn't care to notice.

Police tape lined the dock entrance the next morning, along with a handwritten DO NOT ENTER sign, but I ducked under it, as much as I didn't want to be near the ocean right now. I crept out as far as I dared, up to the ripped-off ends of the wood. He had to be out there.

"Hey," I heard from behind. Timothy. He smiled, but he still looked as pale as he had yesterday. "Inspecting the scene of the crime?"

I winced. "It's not really a crime scene, right? No one's blaming you?"

"No, no no. Weather is weather. That one lady wants to sue me over her phone, but–" he shrugged. "We did get to see a whale, anyway. At least I *think* it was a whale."

I didn't bother to correct him. He didn't look like he believed himself, either.

"I feel terrible about the whole thing. Especially since I talked you into coming in the first place." He ducked his head, oddly shy. "Can I make it up to you somehow?"

I couldn't help grinning. "You mean with dinner?"

"Well–"

"I'm heading home soon, actually. But thanks for the offer."

"Oh." His voice dropped a note or two. "I'm sorry to hear that. You ever come back this way, let me know? I'll give you a disaster-free tour."

"Can you really promise that?" I asked, my eyes back on the waves. He was silent. A minute later, he clomped back up the dock.

I had a long drive ahead, and any second I was going to get hauled off for trespassing. "Well?" I said to the waves, and then his snub nose poked out.

"I heard you yesterday," he said stiffly. "You did not need to thank me again."

"Did you know?" I asked. "That you could still do that?"

His eye darted around. "I'd dreamed of it. Many times. I suppose I should thank you for your encouragement." The small mouth flattened into a scowl. "It was *extremely* tiring, though."

"I bet." I tried not to laugh. At this size, his scowl was kind of cute. "You inspired me, actually. I wanted to tell you that. I think I'm ready to fix things now." Or at least to update my résumé.

"Yes, yes. How nice." I was boring him, clearly. He nodded to me, then vanished underwater.

I turned to leave. "Honestly, though," I added over my shoulder, "you *really* should know better than to go after a baited hook."

A wave smacked me across the back. "Hey!" I whirled, but no iridescence anywhere.

Shaking myself off, I headed for my car, briefly fantasizing about rainbow fish fillet.

Post Card from Roswell, New Mexico, USA

CARMAN C CURTON

Dear Ma and Mary Sue,

Well, they're real. I seen 'em myself. Thing is they're tall and they ain't gray, but they got long fingers and they have to touch you when they talk. A lot.

They don't want our water or our cows, like in those movies, and they don't want to probe nothing neither. They're lonely and they like games. Hide and seek is their favorite. But when you got stellar drive, you always win. So sometimes they come down and play by our rules. They been traveling a long time. Seems like they need to have some fun. Will tell you more when I get back. Gotta go. I'm gonna teach 'em Patty Cake and Thumb Wrestling next.

Love,

Earl

When Death Comes to Find You

YVETTE LISA NDLOVU

Marange Diamond Fields, Rhodesveld

Takura sifts through the sand. Not even the groan in his belly or the dirt lodged under his fingernails will stop him. His faded yellow hat does a poor job of shielding his face from the sun so he brings his prosthetic arm to his face. It's only been a month since the local blacksmith attached the auto-appendage, after he'd lost his right hand to the Grootslang in an abandoned mine.

He doesn't have time to grieve the loss. Besides, he isn't the only makorokoza with an auto-appendage or who had incurred the Grootslang's wrath. All around him the other makorokoza, there must be a hundred or maybe two hundred of them, are also digging holes in the ground searching for the treasure.

At least we still have lives, Takura thinks.

The sound of the makorokoza's shovels fills the once-quiet savanna grassland. Female traders carry baskets over their heads. They move from makorokoza to makorokoza, selling protection charms that promise to ward off the Grootslang. They sell other things too – bananas blackened by the sun, red freezeits for shaved ice – anything to attract a sale from one of the wretched young men who might happen to dig up something worthwhile.

Takura checks his sieve expectantly. More worthless rocks and dirt. Being an artisanal miner is thankless work, but he does it anyway. One never knows when the god of luck will sit on your shoulders and you'll strike it big. Every korokoza knew the tale of one such man who'd dug up one of the biggest diamonds to be discovered in the area. It had changed his entire life. He was now a big-wig politician enjoying his riches.

I will find something too.

Takura doubles down on his efforts, putting more earth into

the sieve. He whistles to distract himself from the sound that won't go away. It's not the ceaseless digging that bothers him. It's something else, something beneath the soil, as if a million people are trapped down there. The weeping sickens him. The other makorokoza call it the makorokoza's curse. They say the sound goes away after you pay the Grootslang's toll. Most makorokozas cannot afford the toll, so drowning the sound down with a drink usually does the trick temporarily. Takura can't even afford a can of beer to do that.

Takura wants to scream at the voices beneath the ground to shut up, but he doesn't want to look unhinged in front of the other makorokoza, so he whistles louder. Takura thinks back to the day he lost his hand and counts himself lucky. He'd narrowly escaped with his life. The Grootslang, the guardian spirit of diamonds, does not take kindly to those who take precious gems from the earth without paying the toll. If he hadn't been quick on his feet, perhaps he would be one of the unfortunates underground.

Takura is so troubled by the wailing that, at first, he doesn't notice the sparkle in between the sand.

A diamond!

He inhales sharply when he picks up the gem, rubbing away the dirt around it.

He drops the sieve as he inspects the find, the euphoria dizzying as he tries to calculate how much he could get for this. Takura is about to put it away, when he hears the distant whir of an airship. Everyone stops their work to look up as the ship closes in.

The balloon-like craft blocks the sun as it hovers overhead, putting everything beneath it in shadow. Takura notices too late that the airship has the Rhodesveld army's seal emblazoned on its side. Noticing the seal too, the other makorokoza panic and make a run for it. Takura stuffs the diamond into his pockets and scrambles out of the hole he's dug. Before he can retrieve his sieve, the airship fires, the bullets ripping into the backs of ten makorokozas near him. Takura's insides turn to mush as he runs in the same direction as the other survivors, but this is a fatal mistake.

The makorokoza and traders ahead of him scream in horror as they are intercepted by a group of soldiers with auto-dogs. The dogs' mechanical bodies are a polished silver.

Takura flees in the opposite direction, the auto-dogs giving chase. He scampers past a protective charm trader, a round woman who struggles to run with a tray of unsold beaded necklaces. It's not long after he passes her that he hears her scream as the auto-dogs tear into her.

Takura reaches an abandoned mine shaft and dives inside. He listens for the approach of military boots, heart hammering. He reminds himself that he has a diamond, that he will be okay. Surely the gods wouldn't be so cruel as to end his life when all he's ever wanted is in his pocket?

Suddenly, a teargas canister nosedives down the shaft, and gas clouds rise around him. He crawls toward the surface, chest and eyes burning. Takura reaches into his pocket and clutches the diamond as if it is the only solid thing in this world. When he reaches the surface, his vision is too blurry to see the soldier who lifts his shotgun as Takura emerges from the shaft. Takura is still clutching the gem when he hits the ground, a bullet between his eyes.

The Wondergat

When death finds you, may it find you alive.

The last thing Takura remembers is being shot, darkness, and then waking up here. The air reeks with the sulphur smell of rotten eggs. He can't tell where exactly here is, but he knows it's underground. He brings his hand to his forehead. There is a hole there big enough for a bullet to fit.

No. No. No, he screams. A makorokoza should never die before paying off the Grootslang's toll.

It is unbearably hot and he is chained to the earth and chained to all the people who'd been shot dead in front of him. A whip cracks from somewhere. He doesn't see it, but he feels it licking his taut back. Around him, everyone is wailing, wildly scratching at the earth for an escape. Takura picks up a fistful of soil and it turns to diamonds in his hands. It is only then when he fully accepts where he is. *Fuck! The makorokoza curse.*

He's been so overwhelmed by the wails of the other makorokoza, that he's failed to pick up on another sound. A low, rumbling noise like something large breathing.

"Who dares enter the Wondergat?" a voice booms, echoing as if a thousand voices were layered on top of each other.

In the dark a pair of red eyes glint. The speaker is a gray-skinned elephant with four tusks and a giant serpent's body, forty feet long. Takura wants to scream at the sight of the monstrous being before him, but the creature opens its mouth to speak again, and reveals a pair of fangs glimmering in the dark. Its open mouth resembles that of a Venus fly trap.

"You are charged with stealing gems from the earth without paying the toll, korokoza," the Grootslang says, its hot breath hitting Takura like a furnace.

The creature sits atop a stockpile of gemstones and polishes a large diamond with its trunk. It's the same trunk that wrapped around his arm and snapped it off that fateful day he went too deep into the abandoned mine shaft. Takura wants to run away but he is chained to the ground. He remembers that the legends say one can bargain for their freedom with the Grootslang by offering her a gem. Takura reaches into his pocket and pulls out the diamond he found before he died.

"Please take this as an offering," Takura says with a shaky voice.

The Grootslang laughs, her laugh something between a vuvuzela, a hiss, and an elephant's trumpet.

"That would work if you were an ordinary human who'd stumbled into the Wondergat by mistake," the Grootslang says. "But you aren't an ordinary human. You are a korokoza. One measly gemstone won't be enough to repay all that you have stolen from the earth."

"But I didn't have a choice but to become a korokoza," Takura says. "What options does an orphan–"

"I'm as old as time itself, boy. I've heard every sob story you can think of," the creature says. "None of them move me."

The Grootslang drops the diamond she was polishing onto her mountain of jewels.

"I the Grootslang, guardian spirit of earth's gems, sentence you to grow diamonds until you've made enough to pay off the unpaid toll you've incurred," she says. "Only then can you have your freedom. Only then can you move on to the afterlife."

Takura remembers an older makorokoza told him it is a well-known secret that diamonds are grown by dead makorokoza. Takura dismissed it as a superstition meant to scare poor orphan boys like him from becoming makorokoza.

"I would have paid the toll, I swear," Takura says, desperately. "I just died before I could–"

"Silence!" the Grootslang says. "I care not for the ramblings of thieving humans. Now get to work. The more diamonds you grow, the faster you can pass on. From the looks of it, you're going to be here a long, long time."

THE KIMBERLEY PROCESS REPORT TO THE LEAGUE OF NATIONS

SUMMARY

Twenty years ago, a group of diamond-producing states, diamond industry executives, and activists against blood diamonds met in Kimberley, South Africa, and vowed to keep the trade in rough diamonds conflict-free. Ever since, only member states of the Kimberley Process can legitimately sell diamonds across the globe.

THE PROCESS

In order for a country to be a member, it must:

i) ensure that any diamond originating from the country does not finance a rebel group or other entity seeking to overthrow a League of Nations-recognized government,

ii) that all diamond companies operating in its territory pay a toll to the Grootslang,

iii) and that the country's makorokozas are protected. The

willful murder of makorokozas to increase the number of diamond growers bonded to the Grootslang is strictly forbidden.

This three-step process has rid the world of blood diamonds.

The Kimberley Process Annual Summit, South Africa

The politician reaches into his suit pocket, pulls out his whiskey flask and takes a quick sip. He looks out the window at the stunning view of the vineyard. He is here to represent his country. The president and the minister of defense gave him strict instructions to get results on this trip.

In the elevator down to the conference room, he recites his speech in his head. His palms are sweating when he shakes hands with diamond industry executives, government officials, and even makorokoza rights activists. He takes his place at the conference table to listen to a robot standing by a podium. She is the leader of a task force sent to investigate the alleged human-rights abuses at Marange Diamond Fields.

"The nation of Rhodesveld is accused of engineering mass executions of makorokozas to increase the amount of diamond growers indentured to the Grootslang, thus increasing their profits," the robot says. "When I interviewed the survivors of the Marange Massacre, my human colleagues were so appalled by what they heard that they had to leave the room. I present the facts here today."

She fixes her eyes on the politician as she narrates every detail, every murder, every data point she'd collected. She narrates how, after shooting artisanal miners dead, the Rhodesveld army brought in prison labor to dig the mass graves. She talks about how each dead makorokoza meant more diamond outputs for the big companies. She talks about how Rhodesveld's army is the owner of one of the biggest diamond companies in the country. The politician's face does not change, does not betray any emotion.

"The crimes committed by the Rhodesveld army must

be acknowledged and must stop," she says. "Until they do, I recommend that the Nation of Rhodesveld be suspended from the Kimberley Process on the basis that marange diamonds are blood diamonds."

The politician curses inside. He wishes he could smash the robot into pieces, maybe sell off its limbs as auto-appendages. He doesn't betray his rage as he goes to the podium to speak. The politician is a heavy-set man, which many people in the room find ironic, because he is one of the leaders of a nation on the brink of starvation. He scratches his mustache before he begins his rebuttal, sweat licking his brow as he remembers the minister of defense's thinly-veiled threat about the consequences if he failed. He is the minister of mines, a cushy position he isn't willing to lose just because a few dirty makorokoza had been killed to ensure business ran smoothly.

"Your data is wrong. All those testimonies are false, lies meant to discredit and undermine Rhodesveld. Two hundred people didn't die in Marange, only two died and that's because they trampled each other during a stampede. The army had nothing to do with that," he begins. "The makorokoza are illegal miners who trespass on government property. As soon as security caught them, they fled and trampled each other in a stampede. Rhodesveld complies with all the demands of the Kimberley Process. If the Kimberley Process wants to impede on a sovereign nation's business, then we don't need you. We will sell our diamonds no matter what you say."

The European and American delegations shift uncomfortably at the threat. They can't have all the diamonds go to their enemies. Diamonds power airships, robots, and everything else in this goddamn world. If they need to placate a troublesome little African country to get enough diamonds to keep their countries running, then so be it.

"Yes, the mining industry in Rhodesveld is controlled by the army," the politician says. "This robot, which I need not remind you is powered by diamonds mined at Marange, wants to suspend

Rhodesveld on the basis that our diamonds are conflict diamonds, but the Kimberley Process defines blood diamonds as 'diamonds mined by a rebel group or other entity seeking to overthrow a League of Nations-recognized government.' Last time I checked, the Rhodesveld army wasn't a rebel group. The Rhodesveld army is part of a democratically-elected government, a League of Nations-recognized government. Marange diamonds cannot possibly be blood diamonds."

When it is time to vote on whether Rhodesveld should be suspended from the Kimberley Process, the vote is unanimous. Marange diamonds are not blood diamonds.

The politician exits the meeting with a huge smile. He can relax now. His position is secure. He is about to get into the elevator when the wailing starts, louder than he has ever heard before. It's as if underneath the floor there are millions of people pounding with all their might, screaming to be let onto the surface. He curses and takes another swig of whiskey from his flask. The noise ceases.

The politician hasn't always been minister of mines. Most people don't know that he was once a makorokoza but, unlike the others, he managed to crawl out of the dirt.

Cambridge, Massachusetts

The alchemist opens the door in his kitchen and descends the moldy stairs leading to his basement lab. He changes into a white coat, gloves, and goggles. He can't do this kind of work at the lab at Harvard, because he doesn't want his faculty advisor taking credit for his research.

At the center of the lab is a strange cylindrical contraption that, if it were hovering in the sky, people would call a UFO. A lavender glow emanates from it.

Everything's coming together quite nicely, he thinks. *I won't even need Harvard anymore when I share this with the world.*

He calls the device a diamond grower. He can't think of anything more creative than that. The device mimics the high pressure and high temperatures of the earth's mantle, where diamonds naturally form over millions of years. That's what the science says about how diamonds came to be in this world, but everyone in the diamond industry knows the real truth. The best diamonds grow in Africa because some sort of demon overseer called the Grootslang enchants the process. It is dead humans down there who make the diamonds, until they can pay off their toll to the Grootslang.

If the alchemist succeeds, he will be a true alchemist. He can almost taste the Nobel Prize. He would have single-handedly rid the world of blood diamonds. His diamonds would be ethically and morally pure. No makorokoza would have to be indentured to a demon spirit for diamonds to exist in the world.

An alarm sounds and the alchemist inspects the device closely, picking up what lies at the bottom with tweezers. He grins and marvels at the little gem he has just grown.

The World Diamond Council Headquarters, New York

A small group of diamond mining executives gather around a conference table. The window has a view of Central Park. They've all had a terrible morning, jetting in on their private airships from all corners of the earth for this emergency meeting.

"Airlines across the world are canceling their contracts with us and opting to use these synthetic diamonds for their airships," a British member of the council says, unable to stand the silence around the table. "That's half our target market gone. Who would have thought that some nerd tinkering in his basement would disrupt the diamond industry?"

"Have you heard what they are calling him?" an American asks. "The alchemist."

"There is no need to panic just yet," the council president says, standing before a hologram of a young couple, a large diamond on the woman's ring finger.

"This is who we should reach," he says, pointing to the hologram. "18 to 30 year olds. The millennials."

"Who are we kidding," the Brit says. "The two things that

could destroy us all are synthetic diamonds and marriage-adverse millennials. Both are already here!"

"She's right," the French council member says. "When baby boomers were 25 to 30 years old, 80 percent of them were already married. Millennials aren't even interested in love, let alone marriage."

"Another thing we're forgetting is that the millennials are broke!" the Brit shouts across the table. "They can't buy diamonds when they can't even afford their rent."

"Indeed millennials earn less than baby boomers did at their age," the president says, trying to restore calm to the room, "but our research shows that millennials buy luxury items like iPhones, pet auto-dogs, and don't hesitate to drop thousands of dollars to travel to another country just for good Instagram photos. So money isn't the problem. We just need to convince them that the money they would have spent on other things. Just as smartphones are status symbols, we should make wearing a diamond necklace, watch, and ring status symbols again."

"And how are we going to do that?" the Brit snorts. "The millennials think diamonds are evil."

"And this synthetic diamond-growing alchemist hipster is marketing his diamonds as conflict-free," another executive whines. "That will surely attract all the millennials. They care about such foolish things, ever since that movie with that blonde actor, what's his name again?"

"We need to take back the narrative about mined-diamonds," the president says. "My team of researchers have learned that synthetic diamonds take a lot of energy to make and, as a result, the process emits a lot of greenhouse gases. If we release this information, people will be up in arms. They care more about the environment than some poor makorokozas in Africa. The issue of the makorokozas will soon be forgotten."

All the executives around the table nodded. Even the Brit doesn't have any snide remarks.

"We need to market mined diamonds as natural, from the earth," the president says. "People will buy a tomato for a hundred bucks if you slap the label organic on it. Why not do that with diamonds? Where synthetic diamonds ruin the environment, natural diamonds are from the very earth we need to conserve. That's why we pay the hefty toll to the Grootslang, the spirit caretaker of the gems, to preserve the earth. That's our message."

"And what about all this Marange Massacre nonsense?" the Brit asks, skeptical.

"Again, we flip the narrative," the president says. "By buying natural earth diamonds, you are helping a poor miner in Rhodesveld. Diamonds uplift communities."

The executives put their billions where their mouths are, and greenlight the new marketing campaign.

Los Angeles, California

Hailey walks into Tiffany & Co, the blue of the building transforming her bad mood instantly. One of her sorority sisters had shot down her suggestion this morning that everyone in the house switch to cruelty-free makeup brands. *What a bitch,* Hailey thinks, *what kind of a monster is against cruelty-free products?* But Hailey knows just the right thing to make her feel better. A marange diamond necklace. They're all the rage these days, plus buying one supports a whole African village or whatever. She's gotten rid of all her synthetic diamond jewelry as soon as the awful news came out that synthetic diamonds killed the environment. Marange diamonds were natural, earth diamonds, given freely by the Grootslang, a benevolent creature that looked after the diamonds underground. Lily-Grace, the influencer she follows, did an informative YouTube video about the history of the Grootslang while unboxing her marange diamond necklace. Hailey had fallen in love instantly.

"From our newest collection," the shop assistant says when she notices Hailey eyeing a seven-strand necklace. "Natural, earth diamonds from Marange."

"That name is so cute," Hailey says. "It kinda sounds like Meringue."

When Hailey leaves the store, she has new earrings and a necklace.

The Wondergat

There are two things Takura knows to be true. One: life is unfair. Two: death is even more unfair.

"When death finds you, may it find you alive," Takura says to the korokoza who works next to him, an old man named Sekuru Bob, who'd been killed at Marange too.

"Reciting old proverbs are we?" The korokoza chuckles. "Anything to make the work go faster so we can pass on."

"What makes you so sure?" Takura says.

"What do you mean?" Sekuru Bob asks.

"What makes you so sure that what comes after this will be any better?" Takura says. "Our lives were shit. Our deaths are shit. You think our afterlife will be any better?" Takura snorts. "When death finds you, may it find you alive. What a joke. I've never understood what that means until now. We've never lived, Sekuru. When death came for us, we'd never lived. Do you know who gets to live? Rich people. Those diamond executives, those politicians. The afterlife will probably be nice and cushy for them. We will probably be their servants in the afterlife, polishing their fucking shoes for eternity."

"Come on now, don't talk like that," Sekuru says, patting Takura on the shoulder. "There is hope for a better–"

"The makorokoza are punished for being poor!" Takura says, unable to contain his rage. "We are punished because we are unable to pay the toll to mine the Grootslang's diamonds while we are alive. Big diamond companies can pay the toll without blinking an eye. When an exec dies, they won't be stuck in this stinking hole. Even the afterlife is made for the rich."

The other makorokoza perk up to listen as Takura speaks. Takura recognizes every makorokoza down here. Some are older men who died years ago. They sing a work song in a call-and-response style as they dig in time with the rhythm. Takura's outburst is drowned out by:

Shosholoza!
Shosholoza
Kulezo ntaba
Stimela siphume Rhodesveld.

Shosholoza!
Shosholoza
Kulezo ntaba
Stimela siphume Rhodesveld.

Wen' uyabaleka
Kulezo ntaba
Stimela siphume Rhodesveld.

To pass the time, sometimes the makorokoza argue about the origins of the work song. Some say it's South Africa's second national anthem, but the older makorokoza point out that the song was sung by Ndebele miners from Rhodesveld, who worked in South African mines and travelled back and forth between Rhodesveld and South Africa.

Takura loses track of time. This place is outside of time. He doesn't remember how long he has been here or how much longer he has to grow diamonds until he is allowed to rest.

Shosholoza!
Shosholoza
Kulezo ntaba
Stimela siphume Rhodesveld.

Sometimes Takura passes time by talking to the Grootslang. The Grootslang is surprisingly chatty as long as the work is being done.

"How did you come to be?" Takura asks her.

"I am as old as the world itself," the Grootslang says, proudly. "I was created when the gods were young, immature and inexperienced in the art of creation. After creating my kind, the young gods realized they had made something monstrous. My kind was too much, they said. Too smart, too cunning, too strong."

The Grootslang snatches a diamond in her trunk and squeezes until it shatters into a million pieces.

"The gods liked some parts of our design, they didn't want to completely get rid of us. So they decided to split my kind into two separate creatures. That's how the first elephants and snakes were born."

"Where did the rest of your kind go?" Takura asks.

"The gods killed my sisters off in a rain of fire. They said we were too monstrous to roam the earth," the Grootslang says, a tear pouring out of her red eyes that look so much like rubies. "I am the only one that survived. I hide in the Wondergat. I've been here ever since."

"You are not a mistake," Takura says. "My father did not want me, so my mother dumped me in a trash can. My whole life I thought I was a mistake, but I am not. I was just abandoned by my parents. Now both you and me are trapped here in this dark place. We are more alike than you think."

The other makorokoza continue to sing shosoloza.

"It is this world that makes monsters of us all," Takura says. "Maybe we should show them how monstrous they've really made us."

"What are you suggesting, boy?" the Grootslang asks, eyes narrowing.

"Why should we live in the darkness?" The words tumble out of Takura's mouth before he even realizes what he is suggesting.

The Grootslang flings her massive tail, wrapping it around him like thick vines, and lifts him off the ground.

"You think you can trick me, boy?"

"No...trick," Takura says, gasping for air. "There is a saying abandoned orphans like me used to say whenever people would pass us on the street without offering any help. 'When a needle falls into a deep well, many people will look into the well, but few will be ready to go down after it.' I've been waiting my whole life for my parents to love me, to finally give a damn about me and come find me. When I realized they were never coming, I waited for some kind stranger to come help me, adopt me, anything to put me out of my misery. Nobody came. Then I waited for the government to do something to help the street kids, to give a damn about us. I've been the little needle stuck at the bottom of the well waiting for someone to give damn, waiting for someone to stop watching my pain and actually do something to end it. But I know now that no one is going to do that, so today I choose to get out of the fucking well myself."

The other makorokoza chime in and a revolutionary fervor sweeps across the Wondergat.

"There is an entire world on the surface," Takura says. "Why should you be down here and everyone and everything else up there? You are the first creation, so smart and so strong that the gods feared you. The gods called you a monster but what of the army, the diamond companies and the politicians who murder to fill their pockets? The real monsters are up there."

Suddenly, the Grootslang drops Takura and breaks his chains. She breaks every indentured makorokoza's chains. Everyone in the Wondergat falls silent, staring at the Grootslang.

"Is this a trick?" one of the makorokoza asks.

"No trick," the Grootslang says. "You can pass on to the ancestral realm. Or you can come to the surface with me and we will show the world and the gods who the real monsters are."

Every makorokoza stays put, nobody passes onto the ancestral realm. The Grootslang picks up Takura and carries him on her back.

"To the surface, monsters!" the Grootslang bellows.

"To the surface!" the makorokoza yell, their fists in the air.

> Shosholoza!
> Shosholoza
> Kulezo ntaba
> Stimela siphume Rhodesveld.

The Grootslang charges towards the opening of an abandoned mine shaft. The Grootslang sees sunlight for the first time since her sisters were exterminated, the light almost blinding her ruby eyes. One by one an army of ghosts breaks the surface.

When death comes to find you, may it find you alive.

Original Activist

FRANCES PAULI

Harold slides hairy fingers through the six-pack's plastic rings. He pulls the cold beer from the case, closes the foggy glass door, and shuffles toward the counter to pay. The convenience store is close to his trailer, a short walk and a few bucks and he'll be set for the next few days.

Behind the counter, the norm who runs the joint keeps one eye on him. It's not personal. The guy knows him, just can't help himself. When an eight-foot sasquatch is navigating around your too-narrow aisles, you tend to get twitchy.

At least if you're a norm.

Harold likes the guy well enough, likes that he minds his own business, only asks ordinary, polite sorts of questions. Still, he takes his time on the way to the front, veering into a side aisle for a stick of overly dry pepperoni wrapped in plastic. Part of him enjoys the way the norm cringes as he side-steps between the displays.

The front door opens as he grabs a chocolate bar to chase down the meat stick. An artificial chime announces the next customer, and Harold watches the norm's attention shift. This newcomer, the guy doesn't know. He's not sure, suddenly, and Harold sees his hands fidget, flutter over the button hidden just below his counter.

Even though the kid coming in is clearly harmless.

He's young, for one, barely out of puberty, and not much taller than the norm. For a crypt, that's pretty short. This kid is no Squatch either, his head is vaguely equine, and a pair of useless, fluttering bat's wings fold neatly against the back of his jacket. His hooves ring on the tiles, and he gives the counter guy a quick jerk of his head before focusing on Harold.

Crap. The kid recognizes him. He's almost certain of it. Just as sure that this crypt isn't from around here. Clothes are too nice, too custom made. When Harold was a kid, Jersey's had to cut wing slits into their jackets with scissors. This guy's coat is made for a crypt, which means he's got more money than Harold has seen since... Since longer than he wants to remember.

Harold makes a beeline for the counter. He sets the beer and the junk food down long enough to fish his wallet out of a rear pocket. He wears jeans with the hems torn away. They reach to his calves, end in shreds and strings that didn't bother him until the kid showed up.

"Nice day," the norm says, but his eyes never leave the other crypt.

Harold can tell where the kid is just from this guy's face. He can tell he's being shadowed, that the Jersey Devil has shuffled up behind him, long before he hears the kid knock over a rack full of chips.

"Yeah." Harold pays while the norm frowns at the Jersey and the sound of the kid scrambling to clean up his mess fills the store. "Thanks."

He makes a quick exit while they sort out the damage. It *is* a nice day, actually. Sunny, even before noon, clear skies, and the warm scent of drying-out asphalt filling the air. Harold heads down the sidewalk, lets his stride lengthen, and prays the Jersey is smart enough not to follow him.

This part of town can get a kid into trouble, especially a kid who's not from around here. Harold lives in the same trailer he always has, but new buildings have taken root around it, replaced fields with storefronts, and parking lots that smell all right when the sun bakes them.

He's always liked that greasy, artificial scent.

Footsteps behind him say the kid is not half as smart as Harold hoped. He's being tailed for real, and that hasn't happened since he fired his agent, changed his name, and stopped answering his phone. He doesn't want it anymore, doesn't want this bright-eyed kid chasing after him. Doesn't want to talk about it all over again.

Worse, this part of town isn't safe for a slick, citified Jersey kid. The last thing Harold needs is for his only remaining fan to end up in the hospital on his account. Bad press, he has learned, is not better than no press. And no press is the best thing he has going for him these days.

He walks faster, hoping to lose the kid before they reach the edge of town. It's been too long. He's forgotten how tenacious fans can be, how determined, how brazen.

"Hey!" The Jersey shouts at him.

Harold ignores it and shuffles faster.

"Hang on," the kid calls out. His hooves bang a trotting rhythm on the asphalt. "Wait a minute."

He's not going to give up. Harold knows that tone, the sharp cadence of a crypt on a mission. He's not as fast as he used to be, either, and this kid literally has wings. Still, Harold strides on, makes his shadow work for it and is out of breath when the Jersey finally catches up.

How many years since he's tried to ditch a fan?

"Hi!" The Jersey's voice is too bright, too loud for the alleys between these buildings. "I'm Jim."

"Jim the Jersey?" Harold shakes his head. "You'd think they'd have gotten tired of that trick by now."

"What?" Jim asks.

"Integration office," Harold mutters. "Not important."

For three steps the kid's quiet. Pondering Harold's mystery perhaps. Maybe he hasn't noticed the alliteration before. Maybe Harold has disappointed him. If he's lucky, the kid will pout and give up on the idea of harassing him.

He hasn't been lucky in a long time.

"Anyway." Jim stresses the 'any,' makes the word a statement of significance. "I'm on the committee for cryptid citizenship."

"No." Harold cuts him off. It's worse than he thought. The kid isn't a fan. He's an activist, someone hoping to leverage Harold for whatever cause he's currently chasing. "No endorsements, sorry."

"But we're trying to get the vote." Jim makes it sound like Harold is crazy, like every crypt alive should be on his side. "We have rights just like anyone."

"We don't," Harold says. "Or you'd be out of a job."

"I'm a volunteer." Jim pouts, kicks at a stone, and lets Harold get a few steps ahead again.

The buildings are already thinning. There's a hardware store on their left, a cracked parking lot, and a row of meters on the street. Beyond that the used car lots start, and if he can't lose the kid before they pass those, he's screwed.

His trailer is too close. Too obvious on its scrubby lot surrounded by industry.

"They have to let us vote." Jim the Jersey finds his voice again. "And once we can, we'll have the power to make things better for all crypts."

"Which is why they don't want us voting." Harold engages despite himself. The kid's idealism scratches like a sticker in his pelt. Ironically, this Jersey already looks like he has it better than a lot of crypts. He looks spoiled in his fancy jacket. "Listen, kid. You want an autograph or something, fine. But I'm not joining your crusade. No endorsements. Period."

Jim stops walking. Harold continues on, passes the car lot without the ringing of hooves in his shadow. Good. He thinks it's for the best. Harold has beer to drink, a trailer to pack up, and the norms are never going to give crypts the right to vote.

Not that he cares.

He has his own problems, and his idealism died in another life.

Harold sips from his can and watches the kid through a rip in his curtains. He's already eaten the pepperoni, chased it with beer and the chocolate, and ended up with a stomachache. His single-wide is a maze of cardboard cartons, a minefield of empties. His laundry needs to be washed, and he hasn't replaced the rubber hose on the machine yet.

Outside, the kid paces at the end of the gravel driveway. He looks toward the trailer every few steps, but so far, he hasn't braved the approach. The 'No Trespassing' signs may be holding him back, but Harold thinks he will risk them soon.

His kitchen table is built into the wall. Harold shoves aside a pile of old mail and sets down his beer. Jim takes a step up the gravel, pauses, reads the signs again. Harold can see the light in his eyes even at a distance. Suddenly, he doesn't want to look.

The front door is locked. He can sit here and pretend not to hear. He can shuffle down his too-narrow hall and collapse on his sagging mattress. Pretend not to be home.

Even if the kid saw him come inside.

His fingers tap at an envelope on the table, the one he's supposed to be ignoring. It's open, tattered at the edge and filthy from being read again and again. He gives it a little shove and thinks about going to bed early. Thinks about not packing, about leaving it all behind and just wandering off again.

In his yard, the Jersey kid makes up his mind. Harold sees it, in the way his spine straightens. His tiny wings flutter, ridiculous. He marches up the driveway, and Harold cringes behind curtains so thin they are threadbare.

He won't open the door. It'll be easier on them both if he just slips down the hall and takes a good long nap. He's already pushing his chair back when the kid yelps.

Harold pries at the rip and leans his hairy face closer to the window. Jim the Jersey is bouncing around on one leg now, holding the other hoof in both hands. His long face is angled down, but the rubbery lips twist in pain. Probably a sharp bit of gravel wedged in his hoof.

Probably serves him right.

Harold sighs and stands. He lifts his eyes, once, to the ceiling and shakes his head.

"No endorsements," he reminds himself before shuffling to the door. "Never again."

The kid sits at his kitchen table with one of his legs resting across the other. His hoof is bleeding, but it's just a trickle. There will likely be a bruise. He might limp for a little while. Harold has pried the stone free and set it atop his letter. He squats beside Jim and eyeballs the wound.

"Not deep," he grunts. "Just a scratch."

"Is that a photo of you and the president?" Jim points at the dining room wall as if he can't feel a thing anymore.

"Maybe." Harold grunts. "I have some iodine in the bathroom."

The kid ignores him, looks around the trashed trailer as if he's in an art gallery…or a museum. His ears swivel constantly, and he actually sniffs the air. Big mistake, kid. It's laundry day.

"I'll get the–"

"I can't believe it's really you," Jim says. "I mean, I'm really here…with you."

So much for activism. That's a fan talking, a fan's awe-touched voice. Harold finds it less annoying than he expected. He softens despite himself.

"No big thing," he mumbles.

"It is." Jim's declaration fills the trailer. He's bouncing again, even sitting down. "You're the one, you know. The first crypt to show themself. The *original*."

The way Harold remembers it, he had little choice. The world had been shrinking for too long, the forest dwindling. It might even have been an accident, but he's never told anyone as much.

"It was a long time ago," he says. "Things were different, then."

"Do you ever regret it?" Jim leans forward, placing his elbows on his thighs and resting his chin in his palms. "Ever wish we didn't let them know about us?"

Does he? Harold thinks about it. His eyes drift to the letter, but he still can't quite believe he's homeless. He should probably read it again.

"Did you ever wipe your ass with a pinecone, kid?"

Jim blinks. His ears lay flat against the back of his neck.

"Ever fight a bear for your breakfast?"

"N-no." The equine head shakes back and forth.

"I have," Harold says. "I don't regret a thing."

"You'd make the difference," Jim says.

It takes Harold a long moment to follow, to get that they've changed gears again, that the activist is back on deck.

"If you signed off on it, if you spoke out, they'd give us the vote."

Harold shakes his head, but he's too slow, his hesitation too obvious.

"You know!" Jim shouts. "It's true, isn't it?"

No endorsements. He has promised himself, hasn't he? Harold has given up his past. He has given up.

"I'll grab you that iodine," he says.

The bathroom is trashed. Harold spends too many minutes staring into the mirror, looking through a haze of dried-on toothpaste, at his own hairy face. His sash hangs from the corner of the medicine cabinet behind him, its words backwards in the reflection. Maybe, they've always been backwards.

Kid would like to see that, he thinks. Everyone remembers the sash.

He pulls it down and drapes it over one arm before opening the cabinet, snatching the iodine and a box of cotton just in case the cut is deeper than he thinks. He carries it all down the hallway, but when he gets back, the kid is gone.

Harold stands in his dining room and looks at his boxes and his dirty clothes. He kicks an empty can aside and slumps toward the kitchen. The sash slides off his arm, falls to the floor. He puts the iodine and cotton on the table and stares at the letter. It has been opened. It has been read.

The kid knows.

Jim the Jersey is a snoop. He's poked his long nose into the wrong envelope, and now Harold's shame is free. He can feel it, racing down his driveway, flying on ridiculous bat's wings straight for the public eye.

No hiding from it now. No more pretending.

Harold grabs the rest of his sixpack. He stomps down the narrow hall and goes back to bed.

There is too much noise when he wakes. At first he thinks he's gotten the date wrong, that the foreclosure is underway. Panic drives him upright in bed, tosses his covers to one side before his brain registers the sound is too big. There are too many voices. Many people shouting outside his trailer.

Jim the Jersey.

"Crap." Harold drags his bones out of bed and shakes from his head to his toes. The bedroom fills with shed hair, and he sneezes.

He pulls on his shredded pants, digs for a t-shirt without stains while the crowd outside his trailer begins to chant something too low to make out. Only the murmur of it reaches him, the cadence and rhythm like drums around a campfire.

Harold stumbles down the hall, crosses to the kitchen table, and peeks through the curtain slash. "Stupid kid."

The first thing he sees are the signs, the waving boards on makeshift stakes. Protesters. Harold growls until the table rattles. He balls his fists and stares at the demonstration on his front lawn. The crowd mills all the way down his long driveway.

He grinds his teeth together and lets the rumble build. He doesn't want this, doesn't *do* this anymore. The floorboards complain as he staggers to the front door. His empties tinkle against one another.

The kid is waiting on his doorstep. He spins around when Harold opens the door, spins, and has the good sense to look sheepish. Jim the Jersey, a lot more trouble than Harold ever guessed.

"Get them out of here," he snarls at the kid. "Go away and leave me alone."

It's too late. Someone in the crowd sees him. They press forward, shouting and waving their signs. Harold reads the hastily painted letters: *Housing Equality Now, Repeal 1072, Save Bigfoot.* They don't get it. Harold hasn't paid his bill. He's not a cause to rally around, and he's had enough of this already.

There are other Squatch in the crowd, more Jerseys, and a handful of other crypt species. Harold hasn't seen a Howler in ages, but Jim has brought three. The kid has dredged the depths of crypt hell and delivered its outcasts to Harold's lawn.

He needs to get rid of them, but when he pushes past Jim, a pack of humans in matching t-shirts surge forward. They squeal. They wave a different sort of sign.

Harold snarls and grabs the kid by his shoulder. "You called the fan club?"

Jim cringes, nods apologetically.

"I ought to eat you," Harold says.

At the street, a white van pulls up. There are huge letters painted along its side, letters Harold will never forgive.

"The press is here." He moans and releases Jim. "What did I ever do to you, kid?"

"We…" Jim shakes himself, flutters, and shifts from hoof to hoof. Not limping after all. "They just want to help."

"Tell them to go home." Harold tries, but the press is already pushing through the mob. The camera rests on the big shoulder of a Lizardman in blue coveralls. The chick with the microphone is all norm. Harold recognizes her, but only from the TV.

She is young, too new to remember him.

"Excuse me." She is tiny, but her voice manages to carry, to reach over the chanting and silence it. An aisle forms to let her pass, a special kind of magic known only to reporters.

Harold braces himself, widens his stance, and rolls his eyes.

"Excuse me," she repeats when she reaches the doorstep. "Are you the landowner here?"

"What of it?" Harold shrugs and uses his own magic, leans out just enough to remind her how big he is, how much he towers above any norm.

She is unmoved by him, unphased. "This property is scheduled for foreclosure," she says. "For lack of payment."

"Yeah." Harold looks sideways, glares at the kid. "So?"

Jim beams back at him. His tiny wings stretch to the sides. His long nose lifts and he fixes Harold in a shining gaze.

"So," the reporter infuses her words with the drama of her art. "Who are you to demand special treatment? There's no violation of rights here. What makes you above the law? This city is full of integrated crypts, crypts who get up every day and go to work beside their human counterparts. Crypts who *participate* in our society. Who are you to deserve all this attention? Who are you to–"

Who is he?

Harold roars. He opens his mouth, and it thunders free. The sound is not as loud as he remembers, but it has been decades since he made it. It still shakes the trailer, rattles the signs, and sends the crowd shuffling a step backwards. Even the reporter cringes from him. A flight of blackbirds explodes from the car lot as the echoes spread. The reverberation lingers long after Harold has closed his mouth again.

Then, a moment of silence. An intake of breath during which Harold makes the mistake of looking at the kid. Jim the Jersey has stars in his eyes.

The fan club breaks into a communal squeal. The mob howls with them, claps, and stamps, and chants his name.

"Harry! Harry, Harry!" The refrain is nearly as loud as his outburst.

The camera swings in an arc to capture it all. The reporter plays with her mic, but there is no use in speaking. Her magic is not strong enough to be heard now.

The mob sings Harry's name, and he turns his back on them. He opens the trailer door, steps inside. Jim calls for him to wait, but Harry tunes him out. He bends to his ratty carpet and picks up his sash. He holds the satin in hairy fingers. He reads the words.

When he emerges again, they are confused, milling about, unsure of him. The sash brings them back. It rests across his chest at an angle, lays against his shaggy pelt with the words clear and in the right direction.

"Original Bigfoot."

This time, when the cheering starts, Harry rides above it. He hears them, hears his name on their lips, and lets the sound carry him. He waves, and he winks. His fan club swoons.

Jim is jumping up and down now, leaping into the air and flapping as if his wings might actually carry him. Harold puts a big hand on his shoulder, holds him still long enough for the crowd to settle.

The reporter seizes her moment, shoving her mic up. It only reaches his chest.

"It *is* you," she says. "Isn't it?"

"Yeah," Harry shrugs. "I guess it is."

"Do you plan on using your celebrity to stop the foreclosure?" she asks. The mic wavers, hovers between them, trying to reach him, trying to trap him again.

Harry leans down so that his lips are close to the thing. He looks sideways at the kid, at the fan club, and the mob carrying the wrong signs after all.

"Screw the foreclosure," Harry says. "This is about the vote."

Jim shouts, "Yes!"

The crowd howls. Applause thunders. Even the reporter cracks a thin smile, nods approval.

"Is it?" she asks.

"It is." Harry raises his voice, makes his endorsement a declaration. "And it's about time."

"You heard that, folks." The norm takes her microphone back, turns to her camera, and grins. "Straight from the Original Bigfoot himself. Votes for crypts, and what then, Harry?"

She turns back, thrusts her mic like a sword.

"Will there be a Squatch on the next ballot? You got your eye on an office in the big city?"

"Not me," Harry says.

He looks at Jim, looks into those shining eyes and smiles.

"But *when* we get the vote," he says. "I'm sure we'll talk about it."

He is old. He is tired, and politics is a young crypt's game. Harry might have big feet, the original big feet, but he likes to take very small steps.

The Beauty in the Unexpected

EUAN LIM

Sawyer finally found the cambion at sunset, lying on the rocky bank by the lakeshore next to a spiky green-and-orange bush. For someone that was currently so badly hidden, their brick-red skin standing out against the pale rocks, the cambion had been frustratingly difficult to track over the past two days.

Sawyer stepped off the path, picking his way over to the prone kid – he could barely be older than twenty, two lanky adolescent horns curling out of his forehead, his face boyish and lax in unconsciousness. His legs drooped in the shallows, one of them surrounded by pinkened water, the steel jaws of a leg-hold trap clamped just above his ankle, biting into torn skin.

The cambion jolted when Sawyer touched him, screaming and scrambling into the bush, his clothes sticking to twigs. The heavy trap smacked Sawyer in the shin, making him swear and hop back.

"I'm *helping*; look, ranger's patch! I *work* here!"

The cambion froze, fists and tail clenched, knuckles split and bleeding.

"Do you mind letting go of the creeping juniper?" Sawyer asked sourly. "If you tear it up, the bank'll erode."

The cambion released the bush.

"Help?" the kid asked, voice raspy.

"Yes," Sawyer said, kneeling down, reaching for the trap. It wasn't rusty, but Sawyer figured that since the cambion was bleeding, a tetanus shot should be piled on top of everything else – antiseptic and bandages, an X-ray, a potential cast – just to be safe.

"I can't get it off," the cambion sniffed, tensing as Sawyer lifted his leg gently. "I don't know how it works."

"That's fine," Sawyer said, instead of rebuking him on being stupid enough to step in the thing in the first place. If he was anything like the others, blind panic had sent him into the park, and people generally didn't look where they were running when they were being chased. "It's not your fault. Where are you from?"

"Calgary," the cambion said quietly, while Sawyer depressed the levers of the trap, letting the jaws fall open limply. The kid whimpered, pulling his leg away from the cruel metal. "They drove me out. I was doing fine, before that!" he said defiantly, then ruined his cocky act by flinching, hard, when Sawyer let go of the levers, sending the trap snapping shut on empty air.

Sawyer straightened and cast an eye over the cambion's muddy clothing: white shorts and a god-awful black sweater with 'FENDI' in bright gold letters slapped across the chest and what looked like overblown leopard spots down the arms.

"Dad left me with so much stuff before he went away," he said, looking down, his hands knotting together and his voice cracking.

Lifting the trap, Sawyer looked away awkwardly, unsure of how to comfort a sad half-demon. "Come on, get up. You can't stay here, this is federally-owned public property."

The cambion's mouth downturned into a perfect upside-down U, tears welling in his yellow eyes. Horrified, Sawyer looked away, the sound of vigorous sniffing making it to his ears.

"I didn't *want* to leave!" the cambion said indignantly. "I *like* Calgary! We had a house on Briar Hill and the view was really pretty even if Dad never let me go outside."

"Okay," Sawyer said desperately, looking around for someone to save him, but the cambion wasn't done.

"And then Dad left, and he's been gone for ages!" The cambion collapsed in on himself, pulling his injured leg closer, face twisting in pain. "People came to the house 'cause I couldn't work the lawnmower and everything was getting dirty and overgrown, but Dad said if the police ever got me, they'd hurt me, so I ran away and I came here, 'cause I've always wanted to see the mountains."

Sawyer nodded anxiously. "How about you get up and tell me more on the way to Banff?"

The cambion looked up at him, sulking. "I don't *want* to."

"You can't stay here."

"I don't care, I'm not listening to you! I *hate* humans! You're all terrible!"

"Even me, after I helped you?" Sawyer asked flatly, twining the trap's chain around his hand. To his surprise, the cambion cringed, looking away guiltily.

Sawyer stood there gauchely, not knowing how to coerce this cambion into listening to him. All the others had listened, putting up minimal fuss, letting him sneak them into Banff and patch them up, then drive them to the nearest demon-friendly cities, smaller places dotted in the mountains or in the countryside where others like them already resided.

"My name's Bradford Tseng," the cambion said eventually, in a very small voice.

"Okay," he sighed. "Bradford. Can we get up?"

"I'm not going to Banff," said Bradford stubbornly. "I don't need help! I can figure everything out by myself. Alone."

Sawyer stared at him: literally the skinniest thing he had ever seen, who would probably stand no taller than five-foot-six. "Fine." Sawyer turned around.

"Hey!" came the immediate yell. "Wait! Where are you going?"

"Back to my cabin. I'm tired and it's almost night. I'm going to eat and go to sleep."

"What about me?" the cambion's voice trailed pitifully through the air. "You can't just leave me here! I'm in – this is the middle of nowhere!"

"Thought you said you could figure it out on your own."

He heard some rather magnificent spluttering. "Well – well, why can't I just come with you? You seem okay, I guess."

Sawyer glanced over his shoulder: Bradford was frowning, gentle shadows slipping over his angular face and the horns that peeked out of his matted hair.

"You have to carry me," he ordered. "I can't walk. My leg hurts. I'm dying."

Sawyer sighed, turning around, and heading back toward the cambion.

"No, not over your shoulder!" Bradford shrieked as Sawyer leaned down to pick him up. "What am I, a sack of rice?"

"Fine. Hold this, then." Sawyer nestled the sprung trap against Bradford's stomach, and the cambion flinched away before settling, his thin fingers wrapping tentatively around the metal. Sawyer set his arms under Bradford's knees and back and hoisted him up with a grunt.

"You're manhandling me!"

"A tragedy."

"You're all fat with muscle and you don't know how to use it?"

Sawyer glared at the cambion flatly and Bradford shut up, biting his lip and looking away, his hand gripping Sawyer's shirt so tightly his red skin went light pink at the knuckles as Sawyer carried him back toward his truck.

"My leg really hurts."

"Advil's in the car."

"I'm really hungry. I haven't eaten in forever. I stole some stuff from a Tim Horton's a couple days ago, but I felt so bad about it that I threw up. Do you have food?"

"In the car."

Bradford was silent for a bit, the quiet accentuating the crunch of Sawyer's boots against the gravel path. It was mostly out of the way, this little trail; it came from a picnic area where most people preferred to linger.

"Was someone trying to hurt me?" the cambion asked quietly, readjusting his hand, his sharp little fingernails pricking through the cloth of Sawyer's green shirt. "Are you going to hurt me? Why are you doing this?"

Sawyer's grip tightened. "Because I know how it feels to be tossed out, and if I can't stop it, at least I can be there for others, since nobody was there for me."

There was an unexpected silence.

"Oh." The cambion's hand moved unexpectedly over his chest,

pressing down slightly. When Sawyer looked at him, Bradford's face was furrowed into an unbecoming frown. "I'm sorry. Are you okay?"

"I'm fine," Sawyer said, and perhaps the tone of his voice was too sharp, because the cambion quailed and looked away, changing the subject.

"Who were the traps for? Were they for me?"

"No. Wolves and bobcats."

"Well, that's stupid!" Bradford snapped. "You shouldn't allow anyone to kill the animals, this should be their safe space, shouldn't it?" He sounded, for the first time, actually angry, his voice raw with pain.

Sawyer grunted, not telling him that this wasn't how it worked: Bradford seemed like the kind of person who would argue with him endlessly, and Sawyer didn't like arguing. He wanted to patch this guy up, set up his health records, and send him packing. It would be a win-win situation: Bradford said he liked to be alone, and Sawyer liked to be alone. He lived out here so he didn't have to deal with people; he supposed the nature was all right, he just didn't pay attention to it all that often anymore.

Thankfully, the cambion was quiet all the way back to Sawyer's truck. Sawyer settled him inside, plucking the trap from his lap to toss it in the back and then dropping the remains of his lunch in Bradford's lap.

"What's this?"

"Sandwich. Muffin." He slammed the door shut and rounded the hood as Bradford tore into the lunchbox with the desperation of a starving man.

"'M I gonna get gangrene?" the cambion mumbled as Sawyer got in the driver's seat and started the engine, his mouth so full of bread that his cheeks were pouched out.

"No," said Sawyer, pulling out of the parking space.

"My leg hurts. It's going to fall off. Can I have painkillers?"

"Finish eating."

"Water?"

Sawyer hesitated for a moment at the stop sign leading out to the main road, his turn signal clicking, then reached into the back to grab his water bottle and shove it at the cambion.

At least Bradford couldn't talk while he was eating, even if he ate voraciously fast, and then shook so many ibuprofen tablets into his hand that Sawyer had to lunge for him and pry the bottle away, swearing as he nearly swerved the truck into the ditch.

"Look at the sunset!" Bradford said, undiscouraged, pointing and crunching. "Isn't it pretty?"

Sawyer glanced up. Above, the sky was light blue, gilded at the edges with clouds that turned blood red and deep violet, the setting sun streaking orange and pink across the horizon. It wasn't something he would have otherwise paid attention to, and melancholy swept through him.

"Don't chew the Advil."

"Okay, *Dad*."

Sawyer slowed as the road became bumpier, several thin branches brushing the side of the truck. The cambion pulled his tail into his lap, pushing his nose up against the window, his horns clanking against the glass.

"Is that your place?"

"Yes." He pulled up and killed the engine.

"I like it! Hey, look, there's a magpie on your porch! I love birds."

"This is Alberta," said Sawyer dryly as he climbed out of the car, getting Bradford and carrying him over to the porch, the bird fleeing as they came closer, and Sawyer's eyes caught on the iridescence of their feathers, probably just because he'd thought it would be something Bradford would like. "There are magpies everywhere."

"Don't you have keys?"

"Door's unlocked," said Sawyer, and it took Bradford several seconds of blinking before he realized he needed to reach out and open it.

"That's a really easy way for you to get stolen from, you know. Someone could walk right in here and make off with your stuff. Where would you be then?"

"In an empty house." Sawyer carried him to the bathroom, intending to sit him on the toilet and fix up his leg, but it seemed Bradford had other ideas: he squirmed hard, like a recalcitrant cat, and Sawyer was forced to drop him.

"Go away," Bradford commanded from the doorway, like he had suddenly made himself emperor of the house. "I want a shower." He twisted around, taking in the small room: the sink right behind him and the toilet next to it; the shower on the other side with its neat cluster of toiletries in the caddy; the shelf above the small cabinet across from the toilet that had towels stacked on it.

"Your leg," Sawyer said, and Bradford balked.

"It'll be fine," he decided after a moment. "I'll, like, stick it outside the water. And then you have to come back and fix it. You promised." He pushed at Sawyer's chest, surprisingly strong, forcing him back a step, and then slammed the door in Sawyer's face before he could respond.

He stood there, staring at wood, listening to the rustle in the bathroom, not entirely sure that Bradford wasn't going to keel over dramatically and then demand for Sawyer to come in and bathe him, considering his behavior so far. When several minutes had passed and he heard the shower starting up followed by a not-insignificant amount of swearing, he sighed and left the cambion to his own devices, making his way down the hall.

His bedroom was small, too; the bed, across from the door, fit perfectly between two walls, a cabinet by the head half-obscuring the window there, leaving barely enough room to walk back and forth. Sawyer liked it. It was cozy, and just one person could fill the space, making it easier to forget he lived unaccompanied.

He changed, tossing his uniform over the footboard and pulling out an old pair of jeans and a T-shirt for the cambion.

When he turned around, Bradford was in the doorway, a towel clutched to his throat like the ghost of a Victorian dame, and Sawyer leapt backwards in alarm.

"How long have you been there?" he demanded, pressing a hand to his chest, trying to calm his racing heart. "Hell. Here. Clothes."

Bradford went, "Clothes?" as if he had fully intended on waltzing around naked, and hopped clumsily forward in the narrow space, blocking Sawyer's way out. Sawyer nearly jumped when Bradford's tail curled up to wrap around the bundle, brushing against his fingers.

With absolutely zero hesitation, Bradford dropped his towel, and Sawyer got a glimpse of a skinny chest, ribs showing through, before he yanked his eyes up to the ceiling, horrified.

"Thanks," said the cambion, putting a hand out on Sawyer's chest to balance, gingerly at first, then harder when he realized Sawyer could take his weight, hopping closer so that his every other move seemed to brush against Sawyer's skin, and Sawyer squirmed with awkwardness. "The painkillers finally kicked in. I'm feeling better now! Whoa. These are huge, are they yours? Hey, am I ever going to get your name?"

"Sawyer."

"What's your Chinese name?" Bradford's hand was replaced by his tail momentarily curling around Sawyer's wrist, making him inhale sharply, jerking in surprise. Bradford didn't seem to notice. "Mine's Nianzhen. My dad was Chinese. He was foreign-born in Malaysia – and descended from this ancient warlord, isn't that cool? – and he immigrated here for college and became an interior designer, and then he got rich, though I don't understand *how*, 'cause he sold couches that looked like they were made of spaghetti."

Sawyer hesitated, attempting to pluck out the question that had been buried somewhere amidst all those words. "Don't have a Chinese name." Not a masculine one, anyway; after he'd come out, his family had stopped talking to him, so he couldn't exactly ask them for a new name. They didn't want anything to do with him anymore, so he lived out here. Alone.

"Ugh, that's terrible!" Sawyer's bed creaked as Bradford fell onto it to pull on the pants. At least it meant he wasn't pressed so close to Sawyer anymore, and Sawyer could make a wheezy attempt at breathing. "Well, I really like 'Xing-fu'; Dad almost named me that.

It means 'happiness,' so if you want, you should use it! Yo, you can look now, Mr. Prude, my dick's all covered up now."

When Sawyer looked down, an odd feeling squirming in his chest, Bradford was glancing around the room with jerky little movements of his head, like a little bird.

"Do you have more food? I'm still hungry."

Bradford subsequently demanded to be carried out of the bedroom, then wanted a couch pillow on his chair because his ass hurt, then picked out every single bit of ham from the navy bean soup Sawyer reheated for him: not because he was vegetarian, but because he didn't like ham.

"I smell funky now, by the way," he said as Sawyer knelt by his chair, laboriously rolling up his pant legs, alcohol and cotton swabs and gauze on a dish on the floor. "You know, like fake watermelon? I can smell it every time I breathe in. I think it's your lotion–"

"Why were you using my lotion," Sawyer asked flatly.

"I wanted to be moisturized!" Bradford said defensively. "Do you know how dry my skin gets? Look at me, I'm not a man that can be chapped and ashy! Do you want to be able to see my *pores*? From *space*? Ow, *ow!*"

Bradford's wounds looked less terrible now that they were clean: there weren't any big gashes like Sawyer had expected: mostly bruising, and some cuts that Sawyer expected had come from the cambion's claws as he'd tried to tear the trap off.

"It hurts," Bradford gritted, adjusting his leg, making Sawyer push his pants up again as they fell.

"I know."

"Can I take the pants off?"

"No."

"But look, you keep shoving at them anyway! You wouldn't have to look at my dick, you know, I can keep it out of the way."

"What's your fascination with your crotch?"

"What, I can't talk about it? What's wrong with talking about penises and vaginas? I didn't know people were so squeamish. I took a bunch of sex health courses online, you know, Dad made me. I did this one on gender identity, too, it was funky. It said I didn't have to be a man even though I had a penis, though Dad said differently."

"You don't," Sawyer said. "You can be anything, if you want. Man. Woman. Not a woman or a man. Whatever."

Bradford frowned, tilting his head. "I guess," he said eventually. "I don't know. I don't feel like a woman, you know? I don't think. What does it feel like to be a woman?"

"I wouldn't know," Sawyer said. "I've never been one."

"You don't have a penis, though," Bradford pointed out, too loudly, really, and Sawyer flushed red, abruptly furious.

"How the fuck do you know that?"

"I saw you just now. Changing. You're really hairy: you've even got hair on your butt cheeks. Is that 'cause of the testosterone? I'll admit, I did a little snooping around in your bathroom, and I saw the teeny hormone bottles in your cabinet."

"That's private!" Sawyer's voice was raised, but the cambion didn't even flinch.

"I think it's fine!" he said defensively. "I'm not *shaming* you over it or anything! Like, you're a dude, so what if you don't have a wiener? You just *said* you can be whatever you want, so what's the big deal? You're a man. Cool. I'm a man too. We can have a gay time together. Bro." He slapped Sawyer heartily on the shoulder.

Sawyer stared at him, anger flushed away by the confusing fizz of faint pleasure for it not to be...a big deal, even if he hadn't wanted anyone – he hadn't wanted *strangers* – to know.

He eventually settled for scowling. "Don't go through my stuff again."

"Okay, daddy."

"Shut up with that, too."

"Do you think my dad loved me?" Bradford said, changing the topic so quickly Sawyer got whiplash. "'Cause, he made me take those courses, and then he said I wasn't allowed to have sex with anyone ever 'cause he didn't want more cambion babies. That's why I'm gay now," Bradford tried to joke, but his voice cracked a little bit. "And, y'know, he *probably* loved me, but, like, how much do you think he loved me if he doesn't love cambions? Like, he only loved me 'cause I was his son, not 'cause of…'cause of me being me? He said demons are all supposed to be evil and horrible, but I don't feel evil and horrible. I just feel like…like a person. Kinda lonely. Y'know? Do you get lonely?"

Unable to answer this without choking, Sawyer said, "I'm sure he loved you," as he unwound a spool of gauze.

"He said Mom just dumped me outside the summoning circle one day," Bradford said miserably. "What if he just wanted a hot succubus hookup and I was an accident?"

"Not worth getting caught up over, is it?" Sawyer asked. "You said your dad's gone."

He heard the silverware clatter back into the soup bowl, and a moment later, Bradford's hand came down on his head with a hefty smack.

"You're making it *worse*!" Bradford cried, his eyes shining with unshed tears.

Sawyer looked away uncomfortably. "I don't know how to comfort people," he said, finishing the bandage on Bradford's ankle.

"Well, figure it out, you beefy fuck! 'Cause I'm sitting here and I'm *not comforted!*" His voice was wobbling as he jerked his gaze away to the window over the sink, his Adam's apple bobbing as he tried not to cry.

Sawyer stood and patted Bradford clumsily on the back before moving away, returning the first aid supplies to the cupboard.

"I don't know if I like you that much anymore," came the very quiet voice from the table.

"That's okay," said Sawyer, slightly disappointed, which was ridiculous. "You won't have to deal with me after today. I'll drive you to Banff tomorrow morning and settle all your medical records, then get you over the border to one of the towns on Highway 95." Bradford would like it there, since he liked the mountains; it would be better for him than one of the farming hamlets to the east.

Overwhelming silence forced him to glance over his shoulder.

Bradford sat despondently at the table – that was the only way Sawyer could describe it: he seemed to droop, his tail limp on the floor, his eyes glassy with defeat.

"Whatever," he said, softly – dully – and went back to eating.

He was quiet the rest of the night, as Sawyer did dishes, then when Sawyer gave him a toothbrush, then the bed, Sawyer himself taking a blanket to retire on the couch, staring up at the ceiling in the dark and telling himself he was imagining the sniffling that came from the bedroom.

It took a long time for him to fall asleep.

The next morning, Bradford seemed to have recovered completely, considering he'd barricaded himself in Sawyer's room and was yelling that he didn't *want* to leave, he'd changed his mind.

"Bradford, open the door!" Sawyer said, shoving at it.

It didn't budge.

"I can't!"

"You can't stay in there forever!"

"Well, I should think not! I'm starving to death already, and my leg hurts again."

"Open the door!"

"Are you *deaf*? I can't! Your chest of drawers is in the way! You think I can move that?"

"You *put* it there!"

"Fairies did! In the night! Clearly I'm supposed to stay here with you, not get carted off to some weird hick town where people chew grass like cows!"

"You don't want to be around me, you like being alone!"

There was silence inside the room, and Sawyer shoved at the door again.

"I've changed my mind on that, too," came Bradford's supercilious voice. "I've been alone for so long. Dad never talked to me, 'cause he was so busy working, and I've never had any friends. I've never wanted to be alone, Sy! I want a friend. I've spent my whole life talking to *bookshelves*. Have you seen *Frozen*? I'm like Anna in *Frozen* after her parents die and she gets locked in the castle! You need to be my Kristoff!"

"I've known you for three waking hours!"

"We can know each other for longer if you let me stay!"

Sawyer swore under his breath and took a step back.

"Sy?"

There was quiet, for a couple of seconds, and Sawyer was worried Bradford had done something stupid – like fallen off the bed and snapped his neck – and he nearly slammed the door again in panic when the cambion's voice started up again.

"Did you see the sunrise? I did. I woke up 'cause the birds were *so loud*, and it was really pretty! You have a great view from your window, by the way. Hey! Also! You have a tree right outside here that's growing into your wall, and there are birds nesting in there. Little ruby-crowned kinglets, they're so cute, you better check them out before they leave, their nestling period is only sixteen days, you know that, right?"

Sawyer had not known about the birds, but he wasn't going to admit this.

The window – he could go around to the window.

He left Bradford talking to the hallway, going outside and dragging out the ladder from under the porch, rounding the house. It was true he'd been ignoring the spruce tree outside his room for quite some time now: it was bigger than he remembered, nearly reaching his roof. It made it horribly difficult to set up the ladder, especially with the way the hill sloped down precariously.

As soon as his gaze was in line with the glass, Bradford's head popped up scarily fast, making him clutch, white-knuckled, at the window frame.

"What are you *doing*?" Bradford yelled, muffled, one hand buried in his fluffy hair, the other clenched around his horn in distress.

Sawyer rapped on the glass. "Open the window!"

"Sy!"

He banged on the window again, and Bradford glanced around

the edges of it, flustered, before he noticed the lock and struggled through the motions of getting it open.

"Listen–"

"Sy, the birds, are you *mad?* You're going to scare them away!" He grabbed Sawyer's hair and Sawyer wobbled, hauling himself half through the window in panic so that the frame dug into his armpits.

Bradford's hand tightened until Sawyer hissed, but the cambion wasn't looking at him, his gaze fixed off in the distance. "Don't move. Don't move, Sy, the dad's right there!"

Sawyer froze, staring at Bradford's eyes, round with wonder, like this was his first time seeing something like this. Maybe it was, being trapped in a city house all day, never allowed out to touch the leaves or the grass, to see the elk and deer sauntering by, to catch a glimpse of a lynx's yellow eyes in the darkness after sunset. Sawyer glanced at his camera, hanging from the far bedpost, dusty after being left untouched for several years. Would Bradford like photos of that kind of stuff? He had some: old ones, that he'd never shown anyone after his parents had said his hobby was foolish and pointless.

Before he could open his mouth, the two-part scold of the kinglet broke the still morning air, and Sawyer felt the tiniest prick of claws on his shoulder, through the thin fabric of his shirt. Bradford's eyes went even wider, if possible, glittering with stars.

Sawyer didn't dare breathe.

The bird hopped a little down his arm, chattering angrily, then flitted away with a brush of their wings, disappearing into the depths of the spruce, loud peeping starting up as the chicks begged for food.

Bradford's face melted into a smile, his eyes darting as he watched what Sawyer could not, relaxing when the chicks quieted down, the father having left, his cheeks flushed with excitement.

Laughing breathlessly, he let go of Sawyer's hair, making Sawyer's scalp sting. "That was so cool! Bet you'd never have seen that if I hadn't blocked the door and made you go outside. You're a park ranger who lives in the park, and you don't even pay attention to this stuff, do you? I have to point it out for you. Hence: I am useful, and you need to keep me around."

"You can't stay here. This house is too small."

"It's too late: I've adopted you. You look so sad all the time, Xing-fu, I bet you need a friend, out here all alone. I'm friend-sized! Also, how are you even going to get me out? You can't fit through this window, what were you were thinking? I'm stuck in this room until my leg gets better and I can move the cabinet again. A tragedy. You should go get me some food. I'm hungry."

Sawyer stared at him.

Eventually: "You're not eating in my bed."

"I'll eat on the floor next to your bed."

"Come out of my room, and you can have food."

"If I come out, you have to promise not to send me away. I don't want to be scared anymore. I don't want to hide. Y'know? I wanna be who I really am, without people threatening to take that away from me."

"Fine," Sawyer snapped, because this cambion was *impossible*, and wasn't that what Sawyer had wanted, too, when he came out here? Who was he to take that away from Bradford? "Come out of the room, and you can stay until your leg heals." It would be a few days at most; it wouldn't be...horrible.

"No, I can stay *forever*."

"You can stay until your leg heals, and then we'll renegotiate as necessary."

Bradford's face split into a grin of delight. "Okay!"

"Now move the cabinet."

"Can you bring me a granola bar or something first? I'm wasting away, I have no muscles!"

"Fine. One."

Bradford stuck his head out of the window, watching Sawyer with bright eyes as he descended the ladder. "You won't regret this!" he called. "I promise!"

Sawyer sighed as he rounded the cabin, trying to convince himself this was a foolish idea.

The problem was, part of him didn't think it was awful at all. He propped open the storm door, moving to rifle through his kitchen cabinets, his ears catching on the warbling birdsong outside.

"*I can hear the kinglet again!*" Bradford yelled from the bedroom, and Sawyer couldn't keep his lips from twitching in a faint smile.

The Water Horse

SHAWNA BORMAN

Once upon a time, near this very river, there lived a girl about Nat's age. She had hair dark as ravens' feathers and eyes bright as amethysts...purple, dear. People most certainly do have purple eyes. Well, it's my story and I say they do. Now, where was I? Oh, yes. Her skin was the kind of golden bronze the sun makes when it hits the water just right at sunset. Yes, like that.

Every month, she would follow that road over there into town. Back then, it was nothing more than a dirt trail the locals used when collecting water. Anyway, she would go to the town and everyone would stare. No one spoke to her, none dared. No one could match her ethereal beauty. It means otherworldly. No one in this world was as beautiful as she. She would walk to the far end of town, turn around, and walk back. Her only stop would be to buy an apple or whatever happened to be in season.

It was late September when she made her final trek with a red apple, nestled in her palm. At the edge of the trees blocking the river from view, she took her first bite. By the time she reached the water, the core was ready to be discarded.

No one knew where exactly she came from. There were no homes that close to the river, and whenever anyone was near, she would loiter by the water until they were gone. Loiter? It means to hang around like you have nothing to do and nowhere to go.

That day, a boy a little older than her followed her to the edge of the river, even though he wasn't supposed to. It was an unspoken rule in the town that if you found yourself in this young lady's path, you were to quickly remove yourself, and you were never to follow her. But he did.

When she stopped by the water's edge, he sat on a log to wait. Not once did he hide himself from her. The sun passed slowly behind the trees. Her eyes never left the rippling stream. Hours passed. He didn't move. Neither did she. It was midnight when she finally turned to him.

"Why do you follow me?" she asked.

Her voice flowed like the water. Clear, strong, playful.

"I only wished to see you a little longer."

"You have seen. Now, you can go."

The boy stood. He moved closer to her. She stood her ground.

"You first," he said.

Her eyes sparkled in the moonlight. The air was cool on her exposed skin. She assessed the boy from top to bottom. He was handsome, in a plain sort of way.

"Do you not have someone waiting for you?" she asked.

"No one I wish to return to."

The wind gusted, blowing her hair across her face, the hint of a smile creasing the corners of her eyes. She took a step toward the water. Her feet sinking into the moist ground of the bank.

"Would you like to join me?"

Silence. Her eyes drifted to the water.

"Where are you going?"

She held her hand out. He waited.

"Come with me," she said.

He touched her hand, her fingers wrapping around his. She stepped into the running water. It parted around her ankles, as if welcoming her home.

"What are you doing? We'll drown."

The boy tried to pull away, but his hand was stuck to hers. She spun toward him. Her legs had changed. Lengthened. They looked almost like those of a horse.

"Trust me."

Her voice mingled with the whispers of the water bouncing off the rocks, the bank, the roots reaching deep into the riverbed. It was music. It was nature. It soothed the boy. He took one step, then two. When he was waist deep, it happened.

The girl let go of his hand. Her fingers merged into bronze

hooves, but they were backwards. She didn't seem to care. She was no longer girl, but horse. The eyes, though. They were the same. They urged the boy to trust her. He did. He touched her mane, black as ink, and climbed onto her back. They dove into the depths of the river, melting into the shadows that danced on the riverbed.

The next day, people from town found hoof-prints in the mud of the bank. The next month, the girl didn't come back. That was when they knew the water horse had found her mate.

To this day, there are rumors that if you look deep enough, and the sun catches the ripples just right, you can see the water horse and her ghostly rider. Yes, love. They lived happily ever after.

The Goat-Boy Paradigm

RICK HODGES

Marty Abel was under The Spell again.

This time it was the afternoon sun that warmed the brick walls along Water Street. The warmth made the wall glow and vibrate, inserting bits of each brick's history into the best parts of Marty's mind, like the most distant and precious memories of his time as a young boy. The hole in the Earth that produced the wet clay, the hands of long-dead men who had names and thoughts and childhoods too, who had formed the bricks and set them in the mortar, the wall that stood firm for 200 years as people coughed and ate and laughed and schemed and cried and cut each other with knives on either side while the wall remained exactly in its place, even as it whirled through space millions of miles per hour anchored to its mother planet – all these things Marty wondered on, but all at once, as the sunlight on the bricks slowly and pleasantly blew his mind.

"Are you listening, Marty? Is this our stop? Marty, is this our stop is this our stop is this our stop?"

"Uh, no, not yet."

Ilena turned back around and let her arm fall from the pull chain. The heavy diesel engine shook Marty in his seat. Ilena's lab partner Tim sat next to her, his long leg stuck way out into the aisle of the bus, the better not to touch his seat mate even a little. Tim rode the school bus that way too.

Nobody was sitting next to Marty. His lab partner had been some kid from India or somewhere, who left the country in the middle of the school year.

Marty felt the nervous pull in his gut that urged him to pay attention long enough to catch the bus stop. He caught a glimpse of sunshine on ancient brick again. He knew that it took four minutes for the light from the sun to reach that tiny brick, and then bounce to his eye. It meant something.

"This is the stop, right?"

Marty reached up fast for the chain and yanked, even though Ilena had already done it. "Yeah, this one."

Marty led them around the corner to the coffee shop. Tim shuffled his big feet, trying to slow his long legs to match Marty and Ilena's shorter gait.

"Mr. Barker flunks you if you don't clean up your lab station every day," said Tim.

"No he doesn't, he only deducts 10 points," Ilena said it with a hint of disdain, like she said almost everything.

"That could flunk somebody."

"Maybe you, but not me."

Marty had chosen this place. Like every place, he chose it for the ambiance, the feeling, the waves it radiated down to him from the shape and color and the trailing wisps of energy left by the people who worked there, like their breath. He chose a table he hadn't sat at before but had wanted to. Marty dumped his backpack full of textbooks in the chair positioned with a view of the window and the entrance, all the better to affirm the unique time and place each moment offered, from the spot each person occupied and the thoughts that occupied their head to the rings in the trees lining the street outside, each moment never before and never again to exist exactly like another, time and space forever stretching as he surfed his tiny slice of the Big Bang.

Tim eased into the chair across from Marty's. Ilena dropped her backpack in the third seat and went to get in line, with Marty behind her. He studied the delicate, lovely blonde hairs on the back of her neck, the last hairs before scalp yielded to skin, the hairs that made every woman beautiful and precious. Marty didn't care for those shiny porcelain packages in cheerleader skirts who commanded all the attention. He liked Ilena's neck hairs.

Ilena had stepped aside and she was nudging him with her elbow. "Your turn, space cadet."

Marty ordered his drink and paid. He watched the guy making the drinks struggle to pull three containers of milk and cream from the refrigerator with one hand. White cold air poured from the bottom of the open refrigerator door like a waterfall.

"Why are you always looking out into space?"

"Huh?" Marty hadn't heard her, he was too busy looking out into space.

"You always look like you're daydreaming. What are you thinking about?"

"I don't know. Everything."

"You're a total space case."

"I just…see things."

"Whatever." She paid for her decaf with room for cream. "Marty, do you think Tim likes me?"

"Sure."

"No, I mean, does he like me, like does he want to hook up."

"Oh, like romantically like."

"Yeah." A strand of hair that always fell over her eyes fell over her eyes. She bit her lower lip and waited for his opinion.

"I can't tell. Want me to ask him?"

"No! Don't you dare!"

So she liked Tim. Marty had once thought she was interested in him, but it must have been wishful thinking.

"Guys are clueless when a girl likes them," she sighed.

As they labored over molecular weights and ionic bonds, Marty saw atoms spinning and swirling, connecting and popping apart, hugging and shearing, forming great chains and melting into small strips.

Tim slapped his book shut with a loud pop. "That's it, my brain is fried for today."

"Me too," said Ilena.

"Me too," said Marty.

"Your brain is always fried." But she smiled at Marty when she said it.

Tim shut another book forcefully and dropped it on the table, making two loud pops. "Okay, so today is Halloween, right?"

"Duh."

"So tonight when it gets dark, me and Jay Ishikawa, that Chinese dude from French class, we're going to go over to the graveyard."

"Japanese."

"Japanese what, Marty?"

"Jay Ishikawa. He's Japanese."

"Oh. Okay, me and Jay are going to go to the graveyard and wait until dark."

Ilena pushed her hair out of her eyes and back over her ear. The hair framed a chunky adolescent face struggling to stretch into a graceful adult bone structure, like a chick pecking out of its eggshell. "What are you idiots going to do at the graveyard, make out with each other?"

"We're not going to do anything because we're not idiots."

"Oh, sorry, so what are you two geniuses going to do in the graveyard?"

"We're going to look for the Goat-Boy."

For a moment, nobody spoke.

"That's stupid." Ilena broke the silence. "There ain't any Goat-Boy."

"It's an urban legend," said Marty.

"But it's a true urban legend," Tim insisted. "Jay's older brother's friend saw him once."

"Where?"

"Where do you think? In the graveyard, on Halloween night! That's where the Goat-Boy comes to look for little kids. Sometimes trick-or-treaters cut through the graveyard, and Goat-Boy catches them and eats them."

"Yeah right." Marty smirked. But he had heard the stories too. He pulled his coat tighter. Why was he so cold?

"They found a kid's skeleton down by the creek once. They said he had been eaten."

"He probably drowned," said Ilena.

"And got eaten by dogs or something after he died."

Tim wouldn't yield. "But they tested the tooth marks on the

bones. They couldn't tell if they were goat or human. Because they were both!"

"You guys are stupid." Ilena drained the last of her coffee and stood up to leave.

"You two should come with us to the graveyard."

"No way," said Ilena as she pivoted toward the door.

"Goat-Boy just caught another kid today," said Tim.

Ilena pivoted back around.

"That third-grade kid with the really red hair and freckles who we used to ride the bus with."

Marty stood up. "Hey, I know that kid! Tommy Reilly! He lives down the street from us!"

"He disappeared this morning. He never got on the bus. It was all over the news."

"I used to play with him and his brothers," said Marty. "It wasn't Goat-Boy, it was some kidnapper."

"Maybe he fell on his head and he has amnesia and he's wandering around truck stops," offered Ilena.

"Goat-Boy got him. You know he did. And me and Jay are going to go find the kid's carcass in the graveyard."

"You are so sick. Good luck on the test." Ilena pushed the door open. "I'm walking home, and it's perfectly safe to walk home, by the way."

Marty jumped up and headed for the open door. "Are you going to walk me home, Marty?" But he rushed past her and raced down the street.

Marty went through the schoolyard, using the spot in the chain link fence that was cut open. He slid down the shorter, steeper trail through the woods, past the old refrigerator that had once been castle, fort, and spaceship to his playmates a few years ago. Emerging from the woods onto his street, Marty saw the first of the trick-or-treaters. They were the youngest children, trickling down the sidewalks in their tiny costumes, their parents egging them into approaching strangers at their front doors.

Marty didn't stop to catch his breath until he got to Tommy Reilly's house. Two police cars filled the driveway, and a small crowd was gathered on the curb. Tommy really was gone. Tommy, the little kid who was braver than all his older friends, the kid who was the first to cross a rickety log over the creek or throw dirt clods at cars from behind the fence. Tommy was the fifth of five brothers, and he had all the bravado of the older boys, but little of the sense. All his brothers had moved on to high school with Marty, leaving Tommy to ride the bus without them. Now all the brothers surely were out combing his friend's houses and ravines and crawl spaces under porches, hoping to find Tommy, yet hoping they didn't find him if it meant finding a body instead of a runaway or a sleepyhead or a truant.

"You here to volunteer?"

The man was somebody's dad from the neighborhood, but Marty couldn't remember whose. It wasn't Tommy's redheaded father. Tommy's dad was the kind of man who loved being a dad. He stocked his refrigerator full of soda for all the neighborhood kids, even the ones whose parents didn't want them drinking too much soda.

"Volunteer?"

"To search for Tommy. Do you know Tommy?"

"Yes."

"Good, then you can help find him. Go to that policeman over there and tell him your name and they'll tell you where to look and what to do if you find Tommy or…anything."

The policeman sent Marty to look in the spots where they once played. Marty looked around trees, behind the transformer box, and called into drainage pipes. He tried to look in places other people wouldn't think of, like the policeman told him to do. But the light was fading, and though it was spring his heavy winter coat still couldn't quite keep him warm. He would need to go back to get a flashlight, and to tell his parents that he was helping with the search. He headed back home, a different way than he had come, still on the lookout for Tommy.

He pushed through a dark tangle of brush and vines, a little jungle he would never bother to penetrate except to search for a lost kid. The creek ran through here. He chose a stone in the middle and stepped across. He tried not to imagine Tommy's half-gnawed bones on the shore. He pushed through the brush on the other side; his street was somewhere just beyond.

But it came out at the graveyard instead.

Marty had cut through the graveyard before. He and the Reilly boys had ventured there, reading a few headstones and telling ill-informed stories about the embalming process to gross each other out. But this was the first time Marty had visited the graveyard after dark, on Halloween night, while searching for a lost boy that may or may not have been snatched and eaten by a half-boy, half-goat monster that everyone said inhabited this very same graveyard. There was a first time for everything.

The moon had taken over for the night shift. Marty felt considerably colder now, like he was huddled in a refrigerator. He had emerged directly behind a huge white marble monument, taller twice than he was, that glowed in the moonlight. Marty thought he saw frigid white air pouring over it like the mist from the fridge in the coffee shop. He squinted and looked again, and it was gone.

He swallowed his trepidation and circled around the monument, catching a glimpse of the inscription: 'Carolyn something' and 'wife of' and '1903.' It wasn't the fear of a mythical half-goat creature that made his knees feel rubbery as he walked. It was the likely presence of idiots like Tim and Jay Ishikawa who did things like dress up as mythical half-goat creatures and hide behind monuments to scare the hell out of the other idiots who came looking for cheap thrills on Halloween night.

Marty knew that his street was not far across the graveyard, just behind the three huge oaks. In the daytime, he would see it from where he stood. But it was not daytime, and the oaks cast their shadows in moonlight over the crumbling stones. Over the path he would need to take to the street.

He listened carefully for the sound of howling or giggling or hushed conversation. Sneaky footsteps would suffice. Save a few furtive crickets, there was no sound.

Marty froze. Somebody was crouched behind one of the oaks. He saw blue jeans, and above them he could see part of the furry costume. He couldn't have had better luck – he had spotted them before they jumped out at him.

"Got ya! You can come out now, Tim or Jay. Nice try."

Tim came out from behind in the tree. Marty knew it was Tim from his height. His costume was quite a work of art. He was covered from the waist up with fine white fur, and he had glued strands of fur all over his face, or maybe over a rubber mask. It was hard to tell in the moon shadow. A thin goat's beard hung from the tip of his chin, and large curly horns protruded from his skull, with the string or strap that held them on hidden expertly in his hair. He even wore cloven hooves over his hands.

"Okay, you got me-e-e-e," said Tim. He said it in a warbly goat voice. Tim put his hooves on his hips. Marty was so relieved he was spared the embarrassment of jumping up in terror while his friends rolled with laughter, that he forgot about the cold.

"Nice costume, man. You really went all out."

"Think so?" The goat-voice, still. Denied the thrill of scaring the bejesus out of someone, Tim was going to stay in character for a while.

"Where's everyone else?"

"There's nobody here but you and me and lots of dead people."

Something wasn't right. The voice was too high, and Tim was a little taller than this.

"You're not Tim, are you?"

"Why, no."

"Jay?"

"Don't know a Jay. I know you've hear-r-r-rd of me. I'm the famous Goat-Boy."

"Who are you?"

"Goat-boy. G-O-A-T-B-O-Y. Here, pull on my horns." He leaned his head forward.

Marty took the opportunity to pull the mask off and reveal the would-be terrorizer. He grabbed a horn and pulled.

The Goat-Boy's skull pulled with it. His neck bent further forward. The horn was firmly attached to bone.

Marty let go and fell backward to the ground. His pants got suddenly warm; he remembered it later when he discovered they were wet.

"Now, relax, Marty. Take it easy. I haven't eaten you, have I?"

Marty felt dizzy and clung to the ground for support.

"Are you okay, Marty? I'm not going to hurt you. All that crap about eating children is just stories."

Marty woke up with his back leaning against a cold stone. Goat-Boy was sitting across from him, ankles crossed. Marty saw that he had hooves for feet too.

"You passed out. I elevated your feet for a while to get the blood back to your head. I have to revive people a lot in this business, so I know what to do."

Marty got up and ran, but then he felt Goat-Boy's weight on his back. He fell to the ground and his arms were pinned by a pair of hooves. Goat-Boy's breath warmed his neck.

"Marty, listen car-r-r-refully, and say everything I say. Goat-Boy is real, and he is my friend and he won't hurt me. Say it."

"Goat-Boy is…"

"Real, and he is my friend."

"And he's my friend."

"And he won't hurt me."

"And he won't…hurt me."

"Good. Now say I won't ru-u-u-n away, I will sit and talk for a while." His beard tickled the back of Marty's neck. His breath smelled sour but green, like hay.

"I won't run away, I will sit and talk for a while."

"Now, when you're ready, say so and I'll get up."

"I'm ready."

"No you're not."

"I'm ready. I won't run, I swear."

"Okay." And Goat-Boy planted his hooves on the ground and lifted himself up. Marty stayed down, in case he felt the urge to run again when he got up. Plus he was still dizzy.

"I know this is weird for you, Marty, but there's not many like you so I have to take the opportunity when I get it."

"Like me?"

"Yeah, people like you who can see me."

Marty's arms and legs took over, and he started to crawl away. Goat-Boy leaped around to face him, crouched and ready to pounce again to counter his next move. Marty could see the tiny hairs that radiated out from his burning yellow eyes.

"Dude, snap out of it. We don't have much time. I'm not going to hurt you. I'm here to help. I'm a good monster. Me gooood monster." He laughed a little goat-chortle.

Marty backed up into a sitting position and pulled his coat tighter. Goat-Boy relaxed his stance.

"Look, I know I have a reputation as a mean guy," the creature said. "But it's just bad publicity. It comes from jokers like your friends. By the way, don't worry about them. I scared them off an hour ago. They couldn't see me, but they sure as heck can hear me banging rocks on gravestones. Your buddy Tim peed his pants too while he was ru-u-unning away like a chicken-baby."

The image made Marty laugh, and laughing made him remember to breathe, and breathing made him relax. He summoned his courage, turned over, and looked at the monster again. He was still just as real. Marty could see, just barely, the follicles that anchored the coarse hair in his skin. No glue, no rubber mask.

"So not everyone can see you?"

"Nope. That's how I get around without getting caught by animal control."

"And you don't eat kids?"

"Negatory on that one too. Though when I'm seen, it's usually around the time and place that some kid disappears. That's guaranteed to get you a bad rep sooner or later. That and looking like a freak."

Goat-Boy sat on the ground, like a dog sitting up to beg. His yellow eyes seemed to pin Marty to the ground. He used a horn to scratch the back of his hand.

"You're not a freak."

"Oh, Marty, you don't need to be polite to a half-man, half-goat you meet in a graveyard. I'm a freak, and I'm proud of it. You're a bit of a freak too."

"I'm a freak? What do you mean?"

"You're differ-r-r-rent. You see things nobody else does. Me, for instance. But that's not all. You see the beauty in everyday things, the vibrations of every moment. You see the past and the future in the present. You see possibility and wonder where others just see a rock, or tree, or a girl. It's hard to know that you're different in your brain, since you've never been inside someone else's brain. But you are, and you're starting to notice. Am I right?"

"Yeah, I guess." Marty sat up. He wasn't going to get eaten, or suffer the worse fate of being laughed at for weeks at school. He heard someone in the distance yelling for Tommy Reilly. "How do you know all this about me? How do you know my name?"

"Well, Marty, you're not the first freak who can see me who I've talked to out here. And I could see you long before you saw me. Say, do you mind if I have a snack?" Goat-Boy dropped to all fours, his beard grazing the ground, and nibbled on the short grass.

He was right. Marty could see things other people couldn't seem to understand or notice. He could never quite put his finger on them either, as if they appeared in the corner of his eye but vanished before he could focus on them. He called the feeling 'The Spell' but had never stopped to wonder why he was different.

"Speaking of names," Goat-Boy added after a long chew, "why does everyone have to still call me Goat-Boy?" He stroked his beard between his hooves. "I've got a full beard, see. I should be Goat-*Man.*"

He let out a warbling goat giggle at his own joke.

"Why can I see things other people don't?" Marty asked.

Goat-Boy munched as he pondered the question. Wads of grass

filled each furry white cheek. "See, there's a part of your brain that's turned off, has been since you were bor-r-r-n. Sounds weird, I know. You would think having part of your brain turned off would be bad, but it's the part that's supposed to keep you from seeing everything out there. Other people have it turned on, and they miss a lot because of it. They get more done, but their lives are boring."

"Why would we need that in our brains?"

"Because most people would go insane if they could see everything. They couldn't concentrate, or they couldn't tell the difference between what they see and what everyone else sees. In fact, most of them do go insane, or at least everyone thinks that's what they are."

Goat-Boy raised his yellow eyes up from his midnight snack and pointed a hoof at Marty. "You, on the other hand, have had this skill a long time. You are handling it well so far. I wasn't positive it was safe to come out, but there wasn't time. You have something very important to do."

"This doesn't make any…it doesn't make sense."

"You're right. It doesn't make any sense. Talking to a goat doesn't make sense either. But here you are. You should try some of this grass, it's really sweet. Do you know what a paradigm is?" he said through a wad of green.

"A paradiggum?" Marty purposely mispronounced it, for fun, like he always did.

"Yeah, a 'paradiggum.' Smart boy, you can spell. But do you know what it means? It's how you look at everything. It's the filter you see the world through. And it can change. If somebody told you the Earth is flat, you'd laugh, but a couple thousand years ago most people would laugh if you told them the Earth is round. Different paradigm. There are invisible waves in the air you can talk over, called radio waves? That's crazy! Oops, different paradigm."

"So I have a different paradigm?"

"Not yet, but you could if you want it."

Goat-Boy stopped talking and let Marty think about it all.

He turned his horns down low and gently butted against a tall headstone, like a golfer practicing his swing with an imaginary club.

"They've proved this brain stuff scientifically, you know. Doctors. They measured the brain activity of people having spiritual experiences. A certain part of their brain was shut down. The part that gets in the way."

"How do you know that?"

"Oh, I read a lot. I like the Sunday *New York Times.* Nobody can see me, so I can walk right into the library. I don't even need a library card."

Marty yawned. It was late. Maybe he was asleep and dreaming all this? He rubbed his eyes and looked again. Goat-Boy was still there, his head tilted to the ground as he munched away at the grass, but with his eyes lifted to Marty.

"You're wondering if I'm just a dream, right."

"How'd you know that?"

"The eye-rubbing always gives it away. I am a dream, sort of. When you're asleep and really dreaming, it's just part of your brain getting up and sneaking out while the rest of it is still snoring. You are one of those types who dream a little all the time, even when you're awake."

Wow, he really understands me, Marty thought. Maybe he's right.

Goat-Boy took one more bite, and stood up on his hind legs, as tall and straight as a human. "You've got a lot of time to learn all about this stuff. But now you've got a job to do. There isn't much time left."

"A job to do?" Marty thought for a moment. "Tommy?"

"Yes, Tommy. You're catching on. You can find him. You just need to trust yourself a little more. People call it instinct, but that's just another way of saying your brain is letting you see."

Tommy! The moonlight was gone, and the sky was just beginning to brighten. It was morning already. Marty jumped up. He had the power to find Tommy. But how?

"You help find lost kids, don't you? That's what you meant when you said you are around them a lot."

"Yes. I don't always succeed, I'm afrai-ai-aid. Sometimes they just find bodies, or nothing at all. I can't find Tommy. But you could."

"So how do I find him?"

"I told you how. That's all I can do. I can't exactly call the cops and say, 'Hi, I'm Goat-Boy and I want to join the search party.' Trust yourself."

"Why can't you just tell me where he is?"

"Like I said, I don't know where he is. My goat-power doesn't work that way. You're the one who can see things, not me. I'm just a friggin' goat, remember?"

"Why do you do this?"

Goat-Boy's beard jiggled as he sighed. "Let's just say I was a lost boy myself once. Now go!" He waved Marty off with his hooves and turned away. Marty ran past the oaks to the street, and looked back, but all he could see was the edge of the rising sun. It seemed like such a short time, but he had spent all night in the graveyard.

Trust yourself. Instinct.

It was too much pressure. Even in the sun, he was cold again. Cold. Marty ran back toward the ridge that led up to the wooded playground where Tommy and his brothers had played so many times. Every inch of the place – big trees and young ones, the two-by-fours nailed to the side of the largest tree to form a crude ladder to a cruder tree house, the pile of rocks in the far side of the clearing, the holes dug and filled with water and slowly obliterated by the rain, the old tire dragged in by one of the Reilly brothers with a broken rope tied to it, the other end of the broken rope hanging from a tree branch, the ever-present but always changing sky – all were part of Marty and he of them, as if his memories were hands that could build things out of clay and his imagination could bend the trees and stir the sky around. And he felt it now, the vision that bypassed his eyes, the spell, the power that let him gather everything around him and all the passage of time into his arms and feel their weight and their warmth. And he shivered again, still cold, and hungered for milk on cereal, and turned toward the old refrigerator lying against a tree.

Refrigerator.

Tommy was not dead. He was scared, and tired, and hoarse from yelling for help in vain behind the thick walls of the old fridge. Though there was no door, Tommy had somehow pulled it over himself. The boy couldn't move it or dig his way out, but he had managed to dig just enough space to breathe.

Marty led Tommy home, sometimes half-dragging him on his tired feet, sometimes carrying him. Mr. Reilly, the jovial redheaded boy in a man's body, saw him first. He almost tackled them both with joy. Marty's mom saw Tommy and burst into tears, and Marty realized that he, himself, had gone missing last night, too.

He knew what everyone at school would ask. Did the Goat-Boy get him? Did he pull Tommy from Goat-Boy's jaws just in time? Which half was goat and which was boy? Things like that. Marty had time to come up with some clever responses, but he couldn't bring himself to play the game. He settled on, "Goat-Boy wouldn't want me to say," which actually was kind of true.

Adopt A Human

CARMAN C CURTON

Adoption: The Program for Improving Cryptid-Human Relations
Humans are ~~delicious~~ friendly, with ~~no fangs~~ sweet smiles, and ~~short claws~~ an energetic playfulness.

May require relocation – few humans enjoy living in swamps, lakes, caves, trees, or haunted forests.

Click here for more info: https://cryptid-human-beneficial-integration-society

Approved for Twitter and Instagram **WITH CORRECTIONS**
–K.R. ACKEN XCVII

The Kyivan Song

ERIC SHLAYFER

Natalka is five, and her world is small and tight, monochrome, and square-shaped. She's growing up, trapped in the dull, bleak concrete cages of urban Kyiv when her mother takes her one day out of the city to a little settlement called Pushcha-Voditsa, famous for its massive forest and clearwater lakes. She plans a weekend of lying in the sun and splashing in the water, a little reprieve for her sad-eyed child.

Except that Natalka doesn't like water, doesn't want to get wet, doesn't know how to swim, so she sits at the edge of the lake and watches the flat surface glisten under the sun. She digs her toes into the hot sand and wraps her little arms around her knees, and she stares into the distance, seeing things that her mother doesn't.

A girl sits down next to Natalka. She looks like she's also five years old, and her face is blank and a little lost, as if she's just appeared out of nowhere and isn't sure what she's supposed to do, now that she exists. She looks thin and brittle, her skin almost transparent in the bright sunlight.

She has green hair and Natalka thinks it's the most beautiful thing she's ever seen.

"What's your name?" she asks the girl.

The girl turns to look at her with her huge bog-green eyes. She doesn't reply.

"I'm Natalka."

The girl nods and turns away, keeping her gaze fixed on the water.

They sit together and watch the lake.

It's the best weekend of Natalka's short, little life.

Natalka is eight and her world is expanding, filling with new doubts and rife with questions, when her mother takes her and her little brother to the lakes for a family day in the country, an affair of rosy cheeks and sunburnt ears.

They book a gazebo overlooking one of the lakes, and Natalka's mother grills meat and hot dogs for the children, which they devour with glee, smearing grease and ketchup everywhere.

People around them dive into the lake, swimming, playing, their limbs loose and golden and made of solid things like sports and good meals. Natalka's mother takes her little brother into the water, teaching him how to swim, holding him afloat at the surface as they laugh together, shrill and brilliant. Natalka watches them and shouts that she's all right where she is, although they are too far and don't hear her.

She still doesn't like water.

While she sits alone, her world shimmering at the edges, the girl with the green hair comes up to her again, dropping down on the bench to sit next to her. Her hands are folded in her lap, and her fingers look frail, but her nails look sharp. She doesn't say a word, and Natalka doesn't ask.

"I like hot dogs," she tells the girl because it seems important at the moment.

The girl nods but doesn't say anything in response. Natalka thinks that she doesn't know if the girl even eats at all.

Somehow, it doesn't matter.

"They look like they're having fun," Natalka says, pointing at her family in the lake. The girl looks in their direction and shrugs, a pensive look settling on her face, making her ageless. "We're having fun too, right?"

The girl nods again, her head bobbing up and down like it's on some kind of spring.

Satisfied, Natalka settles into her spot on the bench, leaning just a bit closer to the girl with the green hair.

The green hair smells like morning and fresh water.

Natalka is fifteen and her world is getting too large for her, an unwieldy bubble of ragged dreams and distressing truths. Her new boyfriend takes her to Pushcha-Voditsa to spend a day walking around the forest and lakes, away from the city's vices. It's the most romantic thing anyone has ever done for her, and she does her best to appreciate it.

She likes the forest and she likes her boyfriend, and the day passes by quicker than she cares to notice, full of pine needles and pretty rocks.

"How about a quick swim?" her boyfriend asks, when they come out of the forest beside one of the lakes.

"Go for it," Natalka tells him, eager to please. "I'll wait here."

Her boyfriend takes off his clothes and splashes into the lake, giddy and excited like an overgrown puppy. He frolics in the water, shouting that the water feels good and warm, makes little fountains with his mouth, and exudes so much life that Natalka has to shield her eyes when looking at him.

She watches him with a twisted knot of tenderness and regret in her chest. He's a good boyfriend, open and honest, cocky but attentive. It's not his fault that Natalka will probably break up with him this very day.

She just doesn't love him, that's all. He's too vibrant, a vivacious bundle of hand-waving, teeth-baring mirth, and Natalka can't help but be overwhelmed.

Sitting on the bank, she waits for the girl with the green hair and smiles wide when the girl settles down by her side.

"I knew you'd come," Natalka tells her.

Like always, the girl doesn't answer. She looks fifteen, just like Natalka, her face longer, with a sharp jawline and even sharper cheekbones. Her eyes are still bright, making Natalka feel like the girl is looking straight through her, perceiving secrets hidden so deep that Natalka doesn't know about them herself. Whatever she sees, she must like it, since she stays, and Natalka takes solace in that thought.

"I like sitting with you," she says, not expecting an answer.

The girl looks at her and nods. This, Natalka decides, is answer enough.

Natalka is twenty and her world is collapsing because her life doesn't exactly go as planned, so she takes a day off and boards a tram to Pushcha-Voditsa to spend some time in the forest, sitting by a lake.

She's tired of Kyiv; the hustle and bustle of the metropolitan city exhausts her, and she longs for the simplicity of water and trees, the sky above her head and the grass under her feet.

She also dreams about the girl with the green hair every long, stifling night.

Studying is boring and so is work and whatever else she's trying to do to fill the time ticking its way past her. Her closest – only – friend has stopped talking to her, drifting away into the land of carefully-set priorities and neat to-do lists. Then there's her family, but they just don't understand. Her future stares at her like a black void that threatens to suck her in, cheerless and hopeless, and the only thing that she still has to look forward to is that girl, and she doesn't even know her name.

She walks through the autumn forest, feeling leaves crunch under her boots, taking what joy she can from being surrounded by nature that doesn't judge. It's nice, refreshing not to be evaluated for every move she makes. The air smells like freedom here, and that's one reason she likes this place.

When she reaches the lake, her heart does a little flip in her chest. The water is a mix between dirty green and slate gray, the surface smooth and reflecting the gloomy sky. It's chilly, but Natalka is wrapped in enough layers to stave off the cold.

Gathering her skirt around her, she drops onto the beach, settling on the pale sand.

The girl with the green hair doesn't make her wait long.

"How are you doing?" Natalka asks her, even though she knows the girl won't speak to her.

The girl turns her head slowly, pinning Natalka with her bog-green eyes. "All right," she says, and her voice sounds rough, but with an underlying melody to it, like she's an instrument that hasn't been played in a long time.

For a moment, Natalka is speechless. She'd never thought she'd hear the girl's voice, and now it feels like her life has snapped into place, the missing piece finally uncovered.

"What's your name?" she asks, hoping she'll get an answer this time.

The girl turns away, looking at the water. She's dressed in a simple sleeveless white dress, a flimsy thing holding onto her shoulders by two thin straps. Her skin has a pale greenish tint to it. She must be cold, but she doesn't shiver.

"Aren't you cold?" Natalka asks, reaching out to touch the girl's shoulder. The girl's skin is smooth and deathly chill under her hand.

"No," the girl says, her voice low and hollow, as if she's speaking from the bottom of a deep well.

Natalka wraps an arm around her shoulders anyway and pulls her close, settling her chin on top of the green hair that she dreams about at night.

They sit like that and slowly, Natalka's life starts to feel whole again.

Natalka is twenty-four and everything is falling apart around her, so she does what she does best: she takes her bag and runs away, to Pushcha-Voditsa, to the lakes and the forest.

To the girl with the green hair.

When she arrives, she doesn't waste time wandering around the forest and walks straight to the lake, its surface hidden under the thick cover of ice. A family of ducks trudges across the lake, undeterred by the cold snow under their delicate webbed feet.

Natalka sits down on the snow, her long fur coat keeping her warm and dry. She inhales the stark winter air and waits, her fingers worrying the tassels of her woolen scarf, her soul attached to her body by the thinnest of threads.

She doesn't hear any footsteps before the girl with the green hair lowers herself onto the snow next to her. It's as if the girl walks on air or weighs nothing at all.

"Hi," Natalka says, watching the girl closely, counting the

folds of the unchanging white dress that ends around her knees, exposing her pale, thin legs. She's barefoot, and her feet are milky white, almost the same color as the snow around her.

"Hi," the girl echoes, and her voice rings in Natalka's ears, like the music of a distant star.

She reaches out to take the girl's hand in hers. It's cold and limp, but the contact fills Natalka with unfamiliar warmth, spreading from her fingers up her arms into her shoulders, then down her chest, all the way over her belly to the tips of her toes. It's like nothing she's ever felt, and she finds it's the best feeling in the world.

The girl looks at their joined hands and says nothing. She lifts her bog-green eyes at Natalka, and there's a bottomless depth in them, inviting Natalka to plunge right in and never worry about anything else in her life.

"You're a *mavka*, aren't you?" Natalka asks, and the girl nods.

A water spirit, a forest spirit. A creature of death and darkness, a poor soul, a restless soul. A mean spirit, a vengeful spirit, a *mavka* is so many things at once. She's evil, she's beautiful, she's merciless, and she's Natalka's best friend in this and any other world.

"You drowned in this lake, didn't you?" Natalka asks, and the girl nods again, her face like a wave-polished stone.

"Is it true that you have no back and I can see your insides?" Natalka asks, remembering the old folk tales.

Wordlessly, the girl turns around, and Natalka gasps when she sees her unbeating heart, trapped in the cage of her ribs, so small and fragile. She wants to cradle it in her hands and treasure it forever.

When the girl turns back, her brow is furrowed and her eyes are shining. She looks at Natalka expectantly, and Natalka realizes she's waiting for judgement, for the mortal to pass a sentence on the dead, for the order of life to restore itself.

Natalka takes the girl's face into her hands and kisses her on the lips. The kiss tastes moist and mildewy, with a hint of afterlife staleness that makes Natalka's head spin. Incongruously, she likes it, likes everything about it, and her tongue probes at the girl's lips timidly, wanting more. The girl opens her mouth for her, and for a few glorious moments, they sit in the snow, kissing each other, like there's nothing else in the entire universe.

"I've been waiting for this all my life," Natalka says against the girl's lips. "Will you tickle me to death now?" she asks playfully because that's what *mavkas* are supposed to do, cunning and cruel as they are.

"No," the girl says and leans her head against Natalka's shoulder.

Natalka hugs her close and they sit like that for a long time until it gets dark and Natalka has to leave to catch the last tram into the city.

"I'll come back to you," she promises, and the girl nods, her lips curling up just slightly.

Natalka is thirty and she has to admit that she's losing at life. Her aborted attempt at a marriage crashed even quicker than she had expected, and she's stuck in an ungrateful job that neither fulfills her nor brings her enough money to tolerate it. Her family might as well be aliens from a different solar system, and her friends have all forgotten about her.

So, she flees. Again to Pushcha-Voditsa, to the world from a fairy-tale, a glimmering illusion of what life could be if miracles still existed.

It's summer with its hot days, dog days, and the beach is crowded. People are chatting joyfully, basking in the sun, renting boats to row around the lake, slathering each other with sunscreen. Everything is too bright, and Natalka squints. There's life everywhere, but what she longs for is a whiff of death.

When her *mavka* appears at her side, it's like everyone else ceases to exist. The beach is suddenly very quiet, and Natalka can hear her own breathing. The colors dull, as if some benevolent spirit took a green glass and put it between Natalka and the rest of the world. She likes it. Her eyes don't hurt anymore.

"I'm glad you came," she says. "I missed you."

Her *mavka* looks at her and nods, a small, grateful smile on her thin, bluish lips.

"I've decided," Natalka tells her, and the clarity of her decision hits her again. Her head feels pleasantly empty and light. "I won't leave you again."

The *mavka* blinks at her, uncomprehending. "But you're alive," she says, her voice like a tolling bell.

"I only feel alive when I'm with you," Natalka says, and it's true, even if it may be wrong. "What do I need to do so I can stay?"

The *mavka* bites her lip, then takes Natalka's hand and stands up, tugging Natalka with her. She nods at the water and gives Natalka a long, searching look.

Mavkas are vile, implacable spirits who deceive their victims, luring them underwater and keeping them there until the life seeps out of them. They're crafty and charming, ensnaring gullible humans with their wiles, their otherworldly beauty, their sweet singing voices. They're devious, unholy enemies of humanity, or so the tales go.

Natalka doesn't believe in the tales that the living tell each other anymore. They're all lies, imagined for the sake of keeping the children in check. It's the living who are dishonest, for they are the ones who have something to lose.

The dead have nothing, and so, they have no reason to lie.

Natalka has nothing, too.

She follows her *mavka* to the edge of the lake. It was bustling with activity just a few minutes before, but now it's empty, it's surface level and blue. Everyone else has disappeared. There's only Natalka and her *mavka* left in the world.

The *mavka* drops Natalka's hand and turns to face her, walking backwards into the lake. She stops when the water reaches her knees, lapping at the hem of her dress. Silently, she reaches out and beckons for Natalka to join her.

Natalka shucks off her flip-flops, the air thick in her throat. All the times she's been to these lakes, and she has never touched any of them before. It scared her, the soft plinking of the water, the unknown depth of it, its irresistible pull.

She isn't scared anymore.

She takes a step forward and lets the water take the tips of her toes. Her *mavka* smiles at her, sweet and luminous.

The water feels warm and welcoming.

She walks on.

The Beast in the Deep

NORA BAILEY

One lone cloud on the horizon caught the glow of the setting sun, until it looked like a bonfire in the western sky. Adriaen had been a sailor long enough to know that foretold danger overnight – and a first mate long enough to dismiss it as poppycock. He just hoped none of the crewmen would see it and raise a ruckus. All the more reason to keep them busy. Besides, yelling at people was one of the few bright spots in the drudgery of being at sea.

Adriaen had perfected the art of using his lung as bellows, and now he inhaled and barked out, "Bert!"

The young sailor jumped from where he'd been lounging against the railing. It was his first voyage sailing with the *Unity*. Savvy enough to know the first mate was the captain's brother, but hadn't yet realized how little sway that held. The alacrity of his, "Yes, mate," made the corners of Adriaen's mouth curve up of their own will.

"Check the lines in the forward locker. I expect they'll need coiling."

Bert's nod was so sharp his chin almost knocked onto his chest, and he scampered away over the salt-rimed deck. Add swabbing to the list of chores for tomorrow, then. Not that Adriaen much cared, but Captain Dirchs didn't tolerate a dirty deck. And if Henricus wasn't happy, God help his first mate. Only an inkling of familial obligation had put Adriaen on the *Unity* in the first place, and he didn't dare put any weight on it for fear it would snap, cutting through his fragile stability as easily as a parted line through a man's arm. Henricus had a counting ledger in place of a heart.

Adriaen scowled once more at the blazing cloud. He was glad it was Frans up in the nest this evening. The lad had a solid head on his shoulders, more than could be said of most of the crew. Sailors were a superstitious lot, and between the ones that longed to be enslaved as the first leviathan rider in a generation – as if that was a thing to *want*, to link the mind of a beast and die of madness – those that fell in love with imagined mermaids beneath the waves, and the ones terrified of every beast ever rumored to swim the seas, it was hard to find one that could actually keep an eye out for *real* dangers. But Adriaen would have laid good odds against Frans stirring up a panic. Was putting good odds against it, in fact, because with one last glance around the deck for any loose articles, Adriaen retired below to the cramped cabin that was his privilege as first mate.

It had been a long day, up before first light to see to the crew's roster, and hear any complaints before they grew severe enough to warrant Henricus' attention. Pitching in here and there to help the sailors, sitting through an infernally pointless meeting in the captain's cabin, taking a turn on the wheel, and God even knew what else. Adriaen's whole body ached, from the tensed muscles in the back of his neck down to the throbbing pain that plagued his heels. Sleep should have been a welcome friend.

Instead, he stared up at the rough wooden planks that made the ceiling of his cabin. As the ship rocked over the gentle swell, the planks shifted and creaked. Some sailors swore they couldn't sleep without the noise, and probably they meant it, but the damned racket made Adriaen's head ache. The rocking of his bunk was more nauseating than comforting, and his wool blanket scratched against his skin and stunk of stale sweat and other less definable but no less unpleasant smells.

He'd been advised to try counting fish, to imagine them swimming through his mind one by one until the number grew so high that he fell into the fuzzy state that preceded sleep. But whenever he tried, the fish would start to swim faster and faster until they were an uncountable swarm, and the only numbers that he could think of at all were the debts that he owed Henricus. And no matter how high those numbers got – and they went quite high, quite high indeed – they never brought any sort of sleepiness at all, only an intense anxiety that made his chest start to ache to match his head.

He thought about getting his lap desk and writing a letter, but he didn't want to bother with a candle, and he didn't have anyone to write to besides. He had a stack of such aimless letters already cluttering up his less-than-ample drawer; adding more was an exercise in futility. And a waste of ink, the price of which had increased murderously the last time the *Unity* was in port.

So Adriaen just lay in his bed, trying to think of nothing and therefore thinking of everything, until his chest ached so badly that there might have been a whale lying on it, except that the cabin was very small and a whale would never fit. When he squeezed his eyes shut he was surprised to realize he was crying.

At first the increased noise was part of Adriaen's dream. He was running down a long passage that was both the upstairs hallway from his childhood home and a rainy alley in Ghenaut. Someone was pursuing him, their footsteps clattering against the shifting wood-stone surface, but he wasn't sure if it was Henricus howling about a broken toy or an innkeeper hollering murder. Adriaen wanted to stop and plead with them, but one of them, at least, was right about what he had done, and so he ran ran ran until all he could hear was their footsteps in his ears.

"Please, Henri!" he shouted, as if they were still the children who had gotten along quite well and not the half-estranged adults forced together at sea, the vicissitudes of life and coin and business revealing them to be very different people indeed. But it was not Henricus now, it was the innkeeper, and Adriaen could only keep running.

He awoke in a sweat, the wool blanket tangled in his feet and his exposed nipples hard in the chill. His heart was still galloping in his chest, and he sucked down gulps of cool air. *Just a dream, just a stupid dream.* Except the noise hadn't faded with sleep. The boards above him fairly shrieked, and his cabin was being tossed from side to side. A gale, then, though he couldn't discern the sound of the wind.

Adriaen shoved his head into his blouse and pulled the striped fabric down even as he was lacing up his breeches. Someone should have woken him if there was a storm coming through, especially when it was so unexpected. They'd paid a handsome wage to a weathermage back in Asterdelm, who had sworn they'd see naught but clear skies and calm seas for weeks.

"Damned hokester." Adriaen had tried to warn Henricus at the time, but as usual his opinion had been worth less than horse shit.

He darted up the narrow stairs two at a time on his way up to deck. The ship itself seemed to be shaking, now, and while the last remnants of sleepiness tore away from Adriaen, the terror of the dream lingered and mingled with the terror of what he would find above deck.

The first thing he noticed when he popped out of the hatch, was the bright swathe of stars across the sky, the Hunter's Bow emblazoned to the north. No storm, then. The second thing he noticed was that Verner had replaced Frans on watch. He wished he hadn't learned this from running head-on into the man, but Adriaen had the feeling this wasn't the sort of night that was going to go his way.

He picked himself up off the deck and held out a hand to Verner, who was still splayed on his back. "Report, Verner."

The other man was breathing heavily, and rather than speaking he gestured towards the starboard flank. Adriaen turned and his own breath was stolen right from his lungs.

The head was a triangular wedge of darkness against the backdrop of the stars. Light from the ship's lamps glimmered dimly in the creature's eyes, and the shadowy ambiguity was worse than anything that might have been revealed with more light.

"Go." His whisper was hoarse, nearly lost in the ship's protests. The beast must have a hold somewhere – how was his brother sleeping through this? "Wake Captain Dirchs."

Verner scrambled towards the hatch without ever fully rising to his feet, cowering underneath the looming bulk of the creature. *The leviathan.* Adriaen tried to push the thought away, bury it underneath the panic and disbelief crowding his mind. Leviathans had always been rare, but in recent decades they had vanished. The last leviathan rider had died before Adriaen had even been born, and a wild leviathan was the thing of drunken sailors trying to boast another round out of the more gullible listeners.

And yet. The beast that loomed was more real than anything Adriaen had ever seen before. He found himself looking for a rider, desperate, as if they could stop what was happening.

Adriaen shook his head to clear away the thoughts. Not the time for rumination, and he recognized it as the second level of panic. Next would come the shaking and a blank mind, which would hopefully pass quickly into purposeful action. Preferably before his little brother arrived on deck and demanded to know why his useless first mate had done nothing while a leviathan – a *leviathan* – had the ship in its grip.

The shakes robbed Adriaen of his feet, and he fell onto his knees and stared agape up at the leviathan. That was how Henricus found him when he stumbled up on deck, half-supported by Verner.

"Adriaen, what is the meaning–"

His gaze followed Adriaen's, and his jaw fell slack. Firmness returned to Adriaen's limbs as quickly as it had left them, and he jumped back on to his feet. His mind was a whirl of confusion, trying to piece together the slur of Henricus' voice and the deck canting to starboard and the rest of the crew pouring up from below, and above it all the unlidded eyes of the leviathan reflecting the soft glow of the lanterns.

"Verner, stay with the captain. Frans! Eduard! With me." He didn't wait to see if they would follow, didn't give them the chance to cower as he strode across the sliding deck to the weapons locker.

The keys were down in his cabin with his shoes and his belt and most of his wits. He grabbed a marlinspike and began to hammer at the lock. It fell apart on the third blow, and he made a note to tell Henricus to invest in better locks. Frans and Eduard gave him a strange look when he laughed.

He shoved a musketoon into Eduard's hands and a boarding pike into Frans'. Would they be of any use against a leviathan? God only knew, but better for them all to at least try. Go down fighting. He grabbed a musketoon for himself but then cast it aside in favor of a sword and a boarding axe. They fit into his palms with a reassuring weight.

Adriaen didn't issue any commands, didn't wait for the sailors, didn't come up with a plan. He hefted his weapons and charged towards where the starboard railing was splintering into kindling. Someone had lit another lantern, the light dancing off the leviathan's scaled skin, revealing a light blue color banded with black.

It was only the smell of smoke that made him realize there were no extra lanterns after all.

He roared a wordless shout and his arm came crashing down, axe blade shining, and then rebounded with a jarring ache. The leviathan's skin wasn't even marked, but its attention was on him now. He could feel the force of the monster's glare, the head swiveling towards him and screaming open to reveal teeth. *Fangs*, he corrected himself, even as he was stumbling backwards. More of the ship's starboard flank fell away into the sea.

Eduard fired at the leviathan, but whether he hit or missed was impossible to tell. It was unaffected either way, and Eduard fumbled the musketoon when he tried to reload. Frans ran past, brandishing his pike, but Adriaen grabbed his arm and spun the lad around.

"Stop," he shouted, but Frans only shook his head. Between the churn of the water, the roar of the growing fire, and the chaos of the crew, it was impossible to be heard. Adriaen hauled on Frans' arm until they were far enough back to speak at a shout.

"We can't fight this thing. That's folly. We need to get the crew to safety."

Frans stared at him with round eyes. "No! The cargo!"

It was like hearing Henricus' voice coming out of another's

mouth. As if the goods for the southern colonies mattered more than their own lives, as if the loss of one small ship would be more than a tiny note in the stories of the Hollanthe Empire.

Adriaen left Frans and lurched across the unsteady deck to where the ship's bell glinted in firelight. He unhooked the clapper and rang it frantically, then stilled it and rapped three short bongs. He repeated the abandon ship pattern until his arm ached.

He was making his own way towards the ship's lifeboat – the port lifeboat, as the starboard one had been an early victim of the leviathan's attack – when Henricus accosted him.

"How dare you?" Henricus' pupils were so dilated that his eyes looked like black pits. "This is my ship. My life. We abandon when I say we abandon!"

"Then start saying it." Adriaen didn't stop walking. "The ship is gone, Henri. What that damned leviathan doesn't rip into splinters is going to burn. All that's left to save is our lives."

"Don't call me that!"

Adriaen stopped and gripped his brother's upper arms, forcing him to maintain eye contact. "*Captain Dirchs*, are you going to do the right thing by your crew or by your pride?"

Henricus' eyes bulged, but before he could start shouting, they were interrupted by a frightful silence. Adriaen's mind raced to take stock. The fire was still crackling merrily at midships. The crew was abuzz with noise as they gathered at the lifeboat and began to prep it. The leviathan, then. He released Henricus and dashed back towards the starboard railing.

The beast had released the *Unity* and was retreating into open water, but Adriaen felt no relief. He could see the thing's eyes still, and somehow he read the desperation there. It would no more leave them in peace than Henricus would abandon his precious cargo.

The end of its tail broke free of the waves and reared into the night sky, trailing sheets of water. It was thicker around than a wagon, slightly flattened in shape and rippling with muscle. There was no hesitation as it paused, lifted, only a breath to realize what was about to happen. No time to react. Adriaen could only watch, helpless, as the tail came crashing down, tearing into the damaged *Unity* like a beggar into a loaf of bread. Adriaen was thrown, tumbling through the air in a sickening whirl of images, until he came crashing down into blackness and the relief of nothingness.

Reality came back to Adriaen in the form of a foul taste in his mouth. His tongue was furry and twice as heavy as normal, and his eyelids were crusted shut. They ripped open as he forced them, letting in a flood of too-bright sunlight and a ripple of pain that was subsumed into his larger pain.

Everything hurt. His head ached where he must have hit it, his shoulders throbbed, his skin seemed to sting all over. He could not shake the certainty that he ought to be dead, and it unsettled him to have to take measure of his sure-to-be-short life.

Adriaen couldn't swim, but luck had brought him onto a large piece of wreckage that buoyed him out of the water. Only his left foot dangled in it, the toes wrinkled and waterlogged as he wiggled them with a wince. Thirsty, so thirsty, but for all the water around him there was none to drink. He would have laughed if it didn't hurt too badly.

The sun was out, just short of its zenith. A good long while since the attack. He looked around but there was nothing to see except endless sea and the occasional bit of wreckage. The leviathan, so fierce and desperate, was nowhere to be seen. Had it gone down with the ship? Been satisfied with the wreckage and paid no mind to a lone man, stranded, and destined to die?

A bottle of wine drifted past, no doubt part of the cargo shipment. Henricus didn't give anything so nice to the crew. He reached out and snagged it. Salvage rights. Not that there was anyone to justify himself to. The rest of the *Unity*'s crew was likely dead, and Adriaen would follow them soon enough. He was alone, adrift, miles from land or help.

"Sorry, Henri," he muttered through chapped lips. He broke the top of the wine bottle and poured a sip into his mouth, careful to avoid the jagged edge. It was a mellow red that tasted like a miracle.

He had just decided he would try to sleep away the rest of his life when his frail, serendipitous raft was hit from beneath, bobbled hard, and nearly tipped him into the sea. Adriaen clutched the wine bottle in his right hand and the edge of the raft with his left. A familiar banded, triangular head loomed up from the water, and his heart almost failed him entirely.

But a few heartbeats later, he was still alive. Now he realized that this head was much, much smaller than the one that had spelled doom for his brother and his ship. The unlidded eyes peered at him curiously, the head tilting to the side.

"Oh good, you're awake! Play with me?" The voice echoed in Adriaen's head. He tried to clap his hands over his ears, the wine bottle bruising his cheek, but it didn't help. The voice was *inside* his head. Oh no. No no no.

"Please?"

Adriaen remembered the desperate look that he'd seen on the other, larger leviathan. A mother, protecting her nest. No. That was madness. He was already going crazy from exposure and thirst. The last leviathan rider was dead and gone, and surely even God in all her capriciousness would not consign Adriaen to that fate. Always linked, never to set foot on land, becoming more and more like a beast himself every passing day. Some said that eventually the leviathan riders died by plunging themselves into the sea, thinking themselves leviathans in truth.

He shut his eyes, but it didn't help. He could feel her, not just her gaze and her voice, but her very essence settling into his mind. *Azazili.* That was her name. She hadn't said it, but he knew all the same. Adriaen sighed and poured a generous amount of the red wine into his mouth. She trilled, a physical sound this time.

"You *will* play!"

She sounded so pleased that Adriaen couldn't help but smile.

Whatever games the leviathan had in mind, Adriaen did not understand them. After she had borne him away from the lingering bits of the *Unity*'s wreckage, she dove away beneath him with a delighted gasp that echoed in his mind, leaving him to flounder on the surface.

"I can't swim, Azazili!" he shouted, but his mouth was too full of water to say the words out loud. Somehow he had used his *mind*, just like she had to him. It felt deeply uncanny. What would Henricus say about it? Except Henricus was dead. He would never chide Adriaen about his lackadaisical indifference to responsibility, about his wasted adolescence, about anything at all.

The leviathan resurfaced, and he gasped and choked upon her back. She said nothing, but he could feel the apology rolling off her. She did not want him to drown. A hopeful sign. Perhaps he wouldn't go mad and dive into the sea after all.

Except he was talking with a sea creature in his mind, and still had nothing to eat or drink or protect him from harsh salt and sun. Mad didn't seem like a strong enough description.

"I need to eat," he told her. She twisted her head to gaze back at him, confused.

"I need to eat," he tried again. "Fresh water. Shore. Land."

She seemed to understand now, though a pang of her sadness echoed through Adriaen's chest as if it were his own. As the sun sank off to their left, she swam fast and true through the water.

Azazili bore Adriaen as easily as if he were the child and not she. Her powerful tail and lithe form cut through the water faster than any ship that had ever sailed. Adriaen, hungry and thirsty and full of pain and misery and grief, laughed at the way the wind whipped his hair.

Then, blessed land appeared on the horizon. A faint smudge of green, no more substantial than smoke, until it grew larger and taller and then reared up out of the water in front of them. Tree-topped cliffs plunged directly into the sea along the coast, but there was a small stretch of sandy beach at the foot of one cliff, and Azazili headed that direction as soon as Adriaen thought of it. He shivered, and not from the cooling evening air.

"Wait here," he told her, sliding off her scaled back and into the waist-high water. The beach was small, but the cliffs weren't insurmountable – he spotted a small game trail that might lead to a spring and perhaps some form of civilization. Some escape from this madness.

Azazili watched him wade through the water with distress, her body writhing in the shallows and her eyes bright. Adriaen gritted his teeth and continued. But when he reached the shoreline, where the gentle waves lapped softly against the wet sand, a swell of pain ripped through his entire body.

It was pain such as he had never known. Next to it, the pains from the shipwreck faded to nothing. The time he had been shot in a misunderstanding about some weighted dice in Ghenaut was but a ghostly memory in comparison. And it was not just a physical pain, but it scoured out his soul like the purest form of grief.

"Don't leave the water!" Azazili cried.

He could not tell if it was warning or plea. Adriaen looked at the beach. One more step, and he would be on the dry sand. One more step. One small, impossible step.

Gasping with the pain and sorrow, he stumbled back into deeper water. The pain eased. The salt water lapped at his legs like a welcoming embrace. Azazili's fear was still palpable in him, but entwined with a budding relief that warmed his insides.

Her emotions warred with his own. Fear and loathing and desperation that clawed at his throat. Never to step foot on dry land again. Never to live among people, his family and friends.

Although, come to that, he didn't have much of those. Henricus had been the last of his family and – the grief was a fresh wave. And a string of women of varying levels of seriousness who probably never gave him much thought at all. What friends he'd once had seemed to vanish in proportion with his gambling debts.

"How will I eat?" he asked Azazili, leaning his head against her smooth skin.

"I will take care of you," she said. "And you will play with me. The world will be right."

"The world will be right," he murmured. With her help, he clumsily boarded her back again. The sun was setting now, sending beams of light along the surface of the water that made a shimmering, ephemeral road. Azazili carried him along it.

From the Ashes

MERINDA BRAYFIELD

Henry carefully drove his truck up the winding road towards his cabin. While the blast hadn't flattened trees quite this far, there was still evidence of the all-too-recent eruption in the ashen trees and dusty road.

He pulled up to his cabin and turned off the truck, feeling the quiet settle around him. Too quiet, really, for this stretch of backwoods. But hopefully the animals would start coming back now that the mountain had, seemingly, begun to calm.

Henry knew he should check his cabin, but first he had to see for himself. There had been plenty of pictures on television and in the newspapers, of course, but it was something entirely different to take the trail behind his cabin and climb up to the ridge top and look towards Mount St. Helens.

For nearly ten years, Henry had made this cabin his home, and he'd often come up here to look out at the view. And for a decade Mount St. Helens had stood proud against the sky.

Now it was broken and Henry felt an ache in the broken parts of himself. Though he'd left before he could blow his own top, he felt a kinship with the ragged gray rocks and downed trees. The entire top of the mountain was gone, leaving only devastation. At least he'd been able to come home. At least there had been a home to come back to this time.

Turning away from the view, Henry made his way back down the path. The little cabin looked much the same as when he'd left it, except for a broken window on one side. Frowning, Henry went back to his truck to get his gun, just in case, then headed for the front door.

Taking a breath, Henry yanked open the door, ready to fire if he needed to. But the place seemed empty, at least the main room.

The door leading to the bedroom was partially closed, unlike how he usually left it, and it looked as though something had gone through the kitchen cabinets.

Frowning, Henry pushed open the bedroom door. At first he thought it was a bear sleeping in his bed, but as the creature stirred, he realized it was something much more man-like.

The creature reminded Henry of stories about Sasquatch in these woods, but as it sat up he could see this being also had bat-like wings. Their short, silver-blue fur and wings were singed and burned. They cowered away from him, fear plain on their face.

"I won't hurt you," said Henry, lowering his gun. "Did you come from the mountain?"

The creature watched the gun warily. "The mountain?"

Henry gestured in that direction, "Mount St. Helens. Mountain. Volcano."

"Ah, yes. Home," sighed the creature, bowing their head and covering themselves with their wings.

There didn't seem to be any threat from the creature and they were obviously intelligent, so Henry figured he should introduce himself. "My name is Henry."

The creature peeked out at him as if weighing whether Henry was worthy of their name. "Bren," they said at last.

"Nice to meet you," said Henry. "You're hungry, I take it, and injured. Let me help you." He turned and went towards his kitchen, putting his gun aside. If he was hallucinating, it was like nothing he'd ever experienced before. Besides, he'd always suspected there was more in these woods than folks knew, and the eruption would have disturbed anything and everything living in the area.

He got a pot boiling on the stove, turning as Bren stepped out of the bedroom. Bren looked even taller now, head nearly bumping the ceiling. And Bren was definitely male, Henry couldn't help but notice. He held his wings close to his body, as if afraid of taking up too much space.

"It's all right," said Henry, nodding at him. "You speak English."

"I have watched," said Bren. "I was away from home when the deadly cloud came. I ran. I saw this place. I took shelter."

Apparently he spoke better English than Henry had expected. "I'll have to replace that window, but I understand," he said. "This place is shelter for me, too."

"Window was broken when I found it," said Bren, perching on the edge of a sofa that was almost comically small for him.

"Well, I'm sure lots of animals were trying to run from the blast," said Henry. "The government told me to evacuate, so I did. I've survived this long, wasn't going to let a volcano get me after everything."

Bren nodded, watching him. Henry finished fixing them both some lunch and brought a bowl over, handing it to Bren. "Do you want me to look at your wings?" he asked.

"They hurt," admitted Bren. "But they will heal."

"I can at least give you something for the pain," said Henry. "But go ahead and eat, first."

Bren nodded, watching Henry and then copying the way he ate. Logically Henry knew he should be afraid, but he wasn't. Maybe after everything he'd seen there was just little left that could phase him. Besides, if Bren meant him harm, he would have attacked right away. As they finished eating, Bren seemed to relax, wings not held so close to his body.

"Not sure if they'll work for you, but I've got some strong pain meds from the VA," said Henry, getting up to fetch them.

"You are trying to help me."

"Yep, we need to watch out for each other out here."

Bren accepted the pills and water Henry offered, watching as he covered the broken window with newspaper and set about putting his kitchen to rights.

By the time he finished, Henry found Bren snoozing on his battered sofa. There was something endearing about the way the large creature contorted himself to fit on the narrow furniture.

Henry lit two lanterns, leaving one inside the cabin and carrying the other outside to look for damage.

Overall, considering the nearness of the blast, he was in good shape. The volcano hadn't exploded in this direction, so while there was ash carried by the wind, things were in decent shape. There was even the sound of birds starting to return.

He swept ash off the roofs of his greenhouse and cabin and tidied up a few more things, then once more took the trail up to the ridge.

The sun was beginning to set behind him as he looked towards the shattered mountain. It was still hard to reconcile the devastation with memories of the green and living land that had been there before. It reminded him too much of some of his worst days in the war. Land scrubbed clean of all that was good. Taking a breath, he turned away, running a hand through his hair, before heading back for the cabin.

Bren was still asleep, so he did a little more work before going into the bedroom. Probably he should change the sheets, but frankly he was just too tired to worry about it. Instead he climbed into bed and closed his eyes.

Henry startled awake a short time later, the echoes of nightmares ringing in his mind. He sat up, breathing heavily, scrubbing his face in his hands.

There was a noise and he looked up to find Bren standing in the doorway. "You are hurt?" he asked.

Henry shook his head. "Not anymore. It's in my head."

"You are hurt," said Bren, coming into the room and sitting next to him. "Head hurt is still hurt."

"I guess you're right," shrugged Henry. "But nothing anyone can do about it."

"I will stay," said Bren.

"If you do, you'll be the first."

Bren put a wing carefully around him. It made Henry feel safe, in a strange sort of way. After all, he didn't even know Bren. But there was something familiar in him, something that told Henry he might understand his bad dreams, something that made him want Bren to be telling the truth. Maybe it was so many years alone, maybe it was that Bren truly seemed to care. Maybe they could help one another.

He leaned against Bren, finding his furry body to be warm. His scent reminded Henry of the reasons why he'd come to the woods in the first place. He closed his eyes and fell asleep again, feeling safe in a way he hadn't in a very long time.

Over the next few days, they fell into something of a routine, the two of them taking care of the cabin and each other. Bren was a bit large for the house and the furniture, so Henry modified a chair for him. Henry couldn't always reach high things, but that wasn't a problem for Bren. And after that first night, Bren would lay down with him when Henry went to sleep, holding him through his nightmares.

Bren's singed wings did start to heal, and he went into the woods from time to time, always coming back by dusk, sometimes carrying meat or other things he'd found in the forest. Henry didn't question it too much, but at least Bren didn't seem to mind when he cooked it.

For the first time in a very long time, Henry didn't dread closing his eyes at night, and when he did wake up, he didn't immediately reach for a bottle. He didn't need to.

The bad memories and thoughts still haunted him, though, and one afternoon Bren caught him staring off into the woods, not looking at anything.

"Are you all right?" asked Bren gently.

Henry shook himself. "Yeah," he said, out of habit more than anything else, turning away.

Bren put a large hand on his shoulder. "You carry a heavy weight."

Nodding, Henry scrubbed his face in his hands. "I was in a war," he said. "Do you know what that is?"

"I've watched your kind for a long time, I've heard of such things. We fight sometimes among ourselves, but not like you humans do."

"We're almost always in a war somewhere," agreed Henry. "I saw and did a lot of things. When I came home, well, who I thought was waiting for me, wasn't. And the city was too noisy. So I came here."

"I'm glad," said Bren, putting an around him. "And I am glad that I sought shelter here."

"Me, too."

Henry looked up at his face for a moment, then looked away. "Come on, I need to tend these crops."

Bren held him for a moment longer, then let go. Henry felt his heart skip at the loss of contact, but said nothing else.

A few days later, Henry went to the ridge near sunset to find Bren looking out at the view. He silently reached out for Henry's hand as he approached. Henry gave it to him.

"It's a lot different. I'm sorry about your home."

"My people will survive. They've made it this long with you humans filling up the empty spaces." He sighed. "I haven't felt like I belong with them for a very long time."

Henry squeezed his hand, noticing how his silver-blue fur caught the rising moonlight.

Bren glanced at him. "Come with me," he said, starting down the far side of the ridge.

Ordinarily Henry wouldn't venture into the woods after dark, especially not unarmed, but it was different with Bren.

They walked without speaking, Bren especially quiet, considering his size. Henry wondered just where they were going as Bren kept him from stumbling in the gathering darkness.

Suddenly they reached the edge of the trees. They shouldn't have been able to walk this far this quickly, but perhaps it was one of Bren's gifts. And there was no denying the taste of ash on his tongue or the way the rising moon lit the barren landscape. Henry raised his gaze to look at the broken mountain standing against the stars.

Bren silently sheltered Henry with his wings as the moon rose higher. There was something peaceful, despite the destruction.

"I grew up in the shadow of this mountain," said Bren. "I played in the pools and hid in the shadows."

"It must be very hard for you to see it this way."

"The goddess does what she will," said Bren, wistfully. "But she sent me somewhere safe."

"She did," said Henry, hugging him.

Bren wrapped Henry in his arms and the great wings started to move. Henry held on, eyes closed as he felt his feet leave the ground.

He should perhaps be afraid, but he was certain Bren would not drop him as they moved swiftly through the air. Henry opened his eyes again as his feet touched down. Bren ran a hand through his hair as he opened his eyes, finding himself again on the ridge. If not for the lingering taste of ash he might have thought they hadn't moved. He smiled. "Let's go to bed."

Three weeks after Henry returned home, he heard a car approaching as they worked in the garden.

Bren met his eyes and then hurried into the shelter of the trees. Henry held his hoe like a weapon as he cautiously moved towards the front of his cabin to meet his visitor.

To his surprise, it was his brother, Andy. "What are you doing here?" he asked, lowering the hoe as Andy got out of the car.

"I can't want to come check on you?" he asked, leaving space between the two of them.

"I'm fine," said Henry, leaning the hoe against the porch and going into the house, knowing Andy would follow.

"You left as soon as they said it was clear." Andy paused in the doorway. "You know you can stay with me and Jocie as long as you need."

"I don't need to, though," said Henry, pouring a drink for each of them and gesturing for Andy to join him on the sofa. "This is home."

"You don't have a telephone, or running water, or anything up here."

"I'm fine."

Andy ran a hand through his hair. "Look, I know things weren't good when you got back. But it's been nearly ten years. I can get you a job. We can find you an apartment…"

"No." Henry's voice was firm. "I appreciate your worry, and thank you for letting me sleep at your house when I had to leave here. But I'm not going back. That's not my life. This is."

Andy opened his mouth and then closed it again, clearly understanding that this was an argument he wasn't going to win. "All right. Jocie said I was wasting my time coming up here."

"She was right."

"I worry about you," Andy admitted quietly.

Henry studied his brother's face for a few long moments. "I promise you. This is the best place for me. I wouldn't be alive now if I'd stayed in the city."

Andy's shoulders sagged. "Okay. Just be safe…all right?"

"I will." Henry got to his feet again and walked Andy out to his car. "And you be careful driving home."

Andy hesitated. "Can you see the mountain from here?"

"Well, you can up the trail. You want to see it?"

"Might as well."

"This way, then." Henry led the way around his cabin, hoping Andy wouldn't notice any signs that he'd had anyone here but himself.

Andy was out of breath by the time they reached the top of the ridge. "Oh. Wow," he managed, looking out at what remained of Mount St. Helens and all the damage around it.

"I guess I got lucky it didn't blow up this way," said Henry. "Hardly had any damage at all."

"Well, I'm glad you came down and stayed with us." Andy put a hand on Henry's shoulder.

Henry resisted wincing away from the touch. He knew Andy meant well. He always did. "Let's get you home," he said instead, turning and leading the way back down the trail.

Henry was on the porch watching the woods when Bren came back at dusk. "It's safe?" he asked.

"Yeah, he's gone." Henry reached for Bren's hand. "I was worried you might not come back."

"I will always return," promised Bren, pulling him into a gentle hug.

Henry relaxed and raised his head to kiss Bren, the movement as natural as breathing. Bren made a soft noise and held Henry a little tighter before gradually letting go.

"This is home now," said Bren.

"Yes, it is, with you here," answered Henry.

They went inside the little cabin, safe with one another. Birds swooped through the trees, already starting the process of bringing healing to the land beyond the ridge. Henry had certainly never expected a creature like Bren in his life, let alone that anyone would make him feel whole again. It felt strange to be grateful for nature's wrath, but the eruption had bequeathed him a blessing.

Pics or It Didn't Happen

ELIZABETH WALKER

Nate removed the camera from the shipping box and a grin bloomed on his face. "Cassie, come look."

"What?" Nate's wife wandered over and made appropriate *oohs* and *aahs* when he handed her his new camera. "It's heavy."

"Good cameras always are. I got a fancy panoramic lens to take shots of the lake."

Cassie tucked back a strand of his hair. "Babe, you know I'm excited about this trip?"

"Well, yeah. Why wouldn't you be?"

"We are going to do *something* besides look for the Loch Ness Monster, right?"

"Of course." Nate turned his new toy over to inspect the digital screen. The camera was heavier than he'd thought, and he nearly fumbled it as the weight shifted in his hands.

"Careful, Nate. You don't want to drop it."

"*Oh my goodness.* Cassie, do you see this?" Water splashed all around, rocking their rowboat as the giant plesiosaur – Nessie herself – surfaced right next to them.

"That chum we bought at the bait shop really works."

"*Pictures.*" Nate leapt across their boat to snag his camera bag. He jerked the zipper open and scooped his shiny new camera into his hands.

Nessie shifted, their boat rocking in her wake. The camera bobbled in his hand. Even as his mouth opened, forming a voiceless *no,* the camera slipped out of his hand and into the black waters of the lake.

Nate blinked, shock reverberating through his body.

Cassie cleared her throat. "You want me to get one with my phone?"

Before he could answer, the boat rocked again as Nessie dove under the water.

Cassie squeezed his hand. "Oh, Nate."

Next year, when they took their vacation at a little B&B in England, he learned his lesson: not only had Nate bought the best camera money could buy, he bought a camera strap to go with it.

They'd left milk outside their door where it faced the woods, hoping to attract some fairies. Unfortunately, there was no sign yet, and their vacation in Cottingley was almost over. Nate had worn his camera for a necklace all weekend with nothing to show for it.

"Honey," Cassie said one morning after he complained of neck pain. "I have a camera phone. So do you." They were eating breakfast on the porch of their B&B. The air was crisply cool, the view of the forest lovely. The food was so-so.

Nate used his toast to mop the egg yolk from his plate. "Camera phones aren't good enough. I need high resolution, close up, or no one will believe me."

Cassie shrugged and crunched her toast, shooting him a fond, if mildly-exasperated, smile.

Behind her, little sparks of light began to dance in the foliage. Nate jerked in his seat as he realized the lights were shaped like small people. One creature fluttered closer, landing on a flower just over Cassie's shoulder. The fairy was a beautiful woman in miniature. *"Cassie."*

She turned ever so slightly and gasped. "How pretty."

At the sound of her voice, the fairies froze but did not fly away. Yet. Ever so slowly, Nate lifted the camera. He didn't even look through the view finder – he was scared any big movement might frighten the skittish little things off.

"Nate–"

"Sssh."

Click.

The moment the shutter whirred the fairies scattered, disappearing into the forest.

That didn't matter. He had his picture. Smiling, Nate let his camera fall against his chest, a satisfying weight, and no longer a burden.

Cassie's gaze flicked from his camera to his face, and her eyes pinched. "Oh, Nate."

"What?"

"The lens cap, honey. You left the lens cap on."

The next year they went hiking in the hills of British Columbia. Nate didn't even bother bringing his fancy camera.

Cassie sent him an incredulous look as she laced her boots for their first hike of the trip. "No camera? But this is Bigfoot country."

Nate dug into their trail mix, picking out the M&Ms. "Something will go wrong. It's just not meant to be."

She dropped a kiss on his cheek. "I'll have my cell phone with me. Just in case."

"It's a bear." Cassie gripped his arm as they huddled together behind the tree, waiting for the giant animal they had heard, but not seen, to pass them by.

As the brush crunched on the path, Nate pressed her hand. The sounds of heavy animal breathing filled the air. *Maybe it* is *a bear?* Nate wiped a bead of sweat away. He ducked his head around their tree trunk, trying to see if the animal had moved away yet.

What Nate saw instead made him freeze, his heart racing.

"Is it a bear, Nate?"

"No." He swallowed. "It's Bigfoot."

"What?"

"Gimme your phone. *Your phone, your phone, your phone.*"

They scrambled, her trying to hand it over, him trying to grab it. Their arms bumped and tangled together. Then at last, *at last*, Nate had the phone in his hand, the camera app open. He eased around the tree…ready to take his shot…*almost there…almost…*

"Excuse me?" Bigfoot said, turning to look at Nate over his heavily-furred shoulder. "That's kind of rude, man."

Cassie squeaked in surprise. "Wh-what?"

"People run through this forest all the time trying to take my picture, but does it occur to any of you to *ask?*" Bigfoot folded his massive arms across his chest and leaned against a tree, looking very much like a moody teenager pouting in front of his locker.

"Um…" Nate exchanged an incredulous stare with Cassie. She gave him an encouraging smile, motioning for him to go for it. Drawing himself up, Nate stepped forward. The phone shook in his hand. "Excuse me, would it be all right if I took a picture, Mr., um, Sir?"

"Please?" Cassie added.

"Well, sure." Bigfoot grinned, showing a lot of very large, very yellow, very sharp teeth. "How about a selfie? I've never taken one." Bigfoot snatched the camera out of Nate's hands and threw his burly arm around Nate's shoulders. The monster of the forest smelled a lot like wet dog, and Nate became uncomfortably aware how large the creature was. At least nine feet tall. Cassie still clung to the tree, her eyes wide.

"Say 'cheese,'" Bigfoot caroled out. The camera made its shutter noise, then Bigfoot shoved the phone back into Nate's hand. Bigfoot gave him a friendly, stinging slap on the back. "That was fun, guys. Enjoy your vacation. Watch out for the poison oak." Bigfoot lumbered away into the forest.

"Nate." Cassie rushed forward, her face lit with delight. Nate was still too shocked to feel much of anything. Although the *smell* of Bigfoot certainly lingered.

"The picture. Show me the picture." Cassie bounced with excitement.

He unlocked the phone and pulled the picture up…and his heart sank. He *had* managed to get a picture of Bigfoot – a picture of his head. The top of it. Just Bigfoot's hair really. Hair that could have belonged to any hippy in the Pacific Northwest.

Cassie's face fell. "Oh, Nate." She reached up to pat his shoulder.

He caught her hand and pressed a kiss to the palm. "Cass, I don't care about Nessie or the fairies or Bigfoot. I'm on vacation with my wonderful wife, and I want to enjoy it. Let's you and me take a picture for once."

"Really?"

"Yeah."

"Okay." She smiled.

He swiped open the camera app and raised the phone to take the picture.

She stopped him with a gentle touch on his arm. "Honey, how about I take the picture?"

With a laugh, he kissed her cheek. "Good idea."

New Song for the Old Canary

EVADARE VOLNEY

Alice fidgeted inside her itchy mask. She wore heavy boots and poked with her stick at the ground as she walked. This was prime copperhead habitat.

This was the easy part. Her friends from the research lab were up above her, around the overgrown hole in the ground. The day was bright and sunny, with a fresh nip in the air, a perfect Appalachian spring day.

But that viney, twisty opening into the earth was opaque black inside. She knew the lay of it pretty well in theory – it had been digitally mapped out by her coding team, and students had made a lot of cautious incursions to the outer rungs. Her backpack was heavy with sensors for all the important factors, to determine if this was a suitable reclamation site. She'd have to study air quality, stability of the earthen overlayer, and not take any crazy risks.

Environmental restoration of old mining sites was a risky business. Nowhere near to being an actual miner, of course. Still, there was also a body count of explorers and spelunkers who'd misjudged, and gotten overwhelmed and lost, which was ridiculously easy to do, and stumbled into a terrible slow death. And everyone in this line of work in the old coal fields remembered poor Centralia, its underground fires still burning after sixty years.

Still, she liked this old mine in particular. It had a vibe that called to her, and she just sensed that with funding, it could be a good museum candidate if the air quality was redeemable.

She gave the sky one last look, just in case it was her last, because you just never know. Deep blue, fading to gray in the west where clouds were beginning to darken. Probably rain later.

"I'm ready," she said, fastening the carabiner of the rope to her wide leather belt as she prepared to go in.

At first, it was a gentle slope. Further down into darkness, the light faded fast, but she expected that. The old-time miners had it right; she turned on the headlight on her helmet as she walked. She kept checking the fastness of the attachment to her heavy belt: so far so good. There were old tracks here for the carts hauling up the heavy black coal. As Alice went down and down, the sunlight got more and more remote.

She was from the hills and hollers herself, about a three hour drive away from the mine. When she had been at college, when she was on the campus, she felt safe to be openly herself – but when she came back out back of beyond, she toned it down and reluctantly took the Pride pins off her denim jacket. There were good people here, lots of them. But it only took one bad one to ruin a day or a whole life. Alice wanted to build up some community and help her land survive – oh, it would never go back to what it had been long before she was born. But at least she could help the water be cleaner, and help stop people being driven off their land over mineral rights.

And she could help spread the possibility of another way of life, one that cherished the earth and gave the people a way to make a living that wouldn't ruin the hills and their lungs.

Down and down she went. The incline got steeper, and she was now grateful for the mask – what air was coming into her lungs was thin and gritty. She carried a tank of mountain climber's oxygen just in case.

She shined the flashlight around. Her bodycam was working for once, and she started to narrate.

"Terrain is walkable. The tracks are in disrepair but I've seen worse. The ceiling seems solid for now, although the timbers are aged. Recommend serious reinforcement for possible museum use. I'm getting a sore throat even with a mask on, so we definitely need some medical professionals to assess air quality – but I'm not dead yet, so it's not a deal-breaker. My little joke. I'm the canary and I say so far, so good."

She stumbled and then caught herself. "We do need a better

path down. Maybe a cable car? I know that's a big demand, but I want it to be accessible."

She heard a knocking sound, and let it pass even though a shiver ran down her spine. "You guys need to see this. It's actually kind of beautiful down here."

The knocking came again, and she said, "Did you hear that? That's the planet talking. I consent to post this on Instagram."

The signal on her phone was very low.

She had lowered herself down to what looked like a massive room with multiple chambers branching away. Her light, as she raised it and lowered it, showed a very high ceiling.

Her phone now showed no bars. Walkie-talkie then.

Although this cave was man-made, Alice felt an awe similar to the one she'd felt in Mammoth Cave in Kentucky once. An underground room that never saw sunlight.

"Floor quality seems good here. Give me a little more rope, I want to take a look into some of these passageways. Don't worry, I won't go too far."

Like Theseus following Ariadne's thread, she thought. No, actually, more like Ariadne leaving the thread in the first place. What must she have felt, going into territory left empty for so long?

She took a deep breath, and let her Gift reach out. Deep sense of abandonment, as expected. No one had been here in decades. Some other old mines, she'd found beer cans from the 1970s, and occasionally animal bones, and once, memorably, human. Cold case solved by accident.

The sense of absence down here was nearly complete. The mountain itself seemed to have completely forgotten this hole in its gut.

But then the knocking came again. Closer this time.

A shiver ran down her spine. Instinctively she looked up at the old timbers. A knocking could be the earliest signs of a crack that could lead to a collapse. She could never allow herself to forget that there was an entire breached mountain full of weight over her head.

They seemed to hold steady. *Silly*, she thought. *They've been here for almost a hundred years. The odds of them coming down on any given day are miniscule. Never zero of course, but there's no reason to think they're out to kill you in particular.*

The knocking seemed further off. She wondered if there was a pattern to it. Knock knock. Knock knock.

"Do you hear that?" she asked her team up on the surface.

"Hear what?" Sean asked. "If there's something weird, get out of there!"

"You don't hear it?"

"Naw but if you do, get out."

"Walls and ceiling seem secure. I want to know what it is."

"You don't wanna run into a mama bear and cubs, do you?"

"It's not a bear." Determined now, Alice ventured across the main room. Steadying herself on the chipped black walls, she shone her halogen light down the tunnel where she thought she heard the sound.

"What are you doing?" Sean demanded. "Don't make me come down there!"

"Shh," Alice said impatiently. "Don't talk. I'm listening."

She was doing more than that. Her Gift was a risky talent to use in an old coal mine, because there was a lot of bad energy here. A lot of abuse and oppression, sickness and injury, bodies slowly absorbing poison with their labor. Death.

But if she could manage to get beyond that, into the very soul of the mountain itself, there was a different kind of sadness. Did the mountain actually miss the tons of black-pressed fossils that had been dug out of it? Did it miss its billions of years of unviolated wholeness, all gone in what, to it, would have been less than the blink of an eye?

Alice was shocked to find a pervasive sense of something like loneliness. It came out of a consciousness similar enough to be understandable...but different enough to be deeply weird, as if the floor of the mine had shifted under her feet and left her standing at a slight angle from where she had been.

Slowly she toggled off the volume on her body cam. She knew now that the sounds she was hearing weren't going to be captured on it anyway, and she couldn't bear any interruptions to the flow of her outreaching. Sean and Dwayne and the rest would be horrified, but she took her moments of precious quiet.

The knocking sound came again, quieter this time as if in retreat. She heard the word just as loud in her head as if it had been shouted in her face: *DON'T.*

And then all went silent, and the sense of not being completely alone was gone. She felt like a door had just been shut in her face.

"Alrighty then," she said. "Guess I'm going to go back up." She took a few more photos and set herself to the return journey. Up was always harder than down. The increasing light was far grayer and dimmer than it had been. Dusk came early in these hills, where the sun set behind the mountain ridges and cast the valleys into shadow by mid-afternoon.

"What do you think?" Sean asked when her eyes had adjusted to the daylight, and she'd struggled out of the most annoying of mask and climbing gear.

"I think it's the most promising site yet," she said. "Entrance is a little steep but we can smooth that out. Air quality isn't too bad, considering. And there's a lot of space down there. Considering it hasn't been an active site since the 60s, the tracks aren't even in too bad shape. They could probably run a little coal car still if they just fix it up a little."

"Sounds good," said Dwayne. "Hungry?"

"Hell yeah."

They had dinner at the little BBQ and brewery, set up down by the river for the fishing and white-water rafting crowds. In the off season, it wasn't too busy. Later they retreated to their own little rented cabins.

Alice lay down on the narrow camp bed and plugged in her phone to charge, feeling a bone-deep weariness. She'd meant to read, or to pull out her laptop and see if she could get some more research on the site, but that started to feel more and more like something that could wait.

Something urgent was tugging at her mind, and the heaviness of her limbs made her feel groggy. She'd been behind a desk too long, her body forgetting the rigor of field work. She barely had time to switch off the little bedside lamp before she began to dream.

She was in the mine again – she knew the contours of its walls intimately, as though she had been there for years. She saw miners, filing to and fro, chipping coal from the cut and filling up the train cars. She seemed to float through them, insubstantially. The noise of the chipping and scraping was deafening. Their chatter seemed far away and hard to understand.

She wondered if this was a dream or a true Seeing. She tried to calm her thoughts and empty her mind, to accept. She felt a sense of satisfaction, as of someone who enjoys their work, hard though it may be. Someone with a sense of purpose. Someone who had come on a long journey. Someone who had a realm to guard.

Knock knock came the sound. She saw miners following that sound to find new veins. She heard frantic knockings that came as a warning that gave miners time to get out before a wall collapsed – and saw what happened to those who did not heed the sound.

She saw that the miners understood these sounds. A code, older than Morse, old maybe as mining itself, transmitted itself into her mind, and hammered with a terrible urgency. Then she fell into darkness. Not a normal night-darkness, normal sleep-darkness – this was darkness like a tomb, deep in the roots of the mountains, never to be opened, and all the busy bustle of a working mine silenced forever.

She woke up with tears in her eyes and a terrible headache, and knowing that she *had* to go back down in that mine. If she went back in time and conjured up Mamaw's voice in her head, she'd hear something like, "Child it's not safe, not gonna tell you it is. But I know you, and you have the best luck when you push it a little. And if there's something out there trying to tell you somethin', it's usually a good idea to listen. You never know what you'll find out, or who you can help."

"Help?" she wondered aloud.

There was something very important there. Her work wasn't done, and a big part of it was going to be persuading her friends. Dwayne, she knew, would probably be receptive, there was a streak in him that loved weird shit, and this adventure promised even more of it than she'd thought. Sean, though – more of a feet on the floor sort of guy. And he really didn't care for risks.

She didn't know how to tell them that whatever was down there, she felt concern for it. That if she walked away and left others to do the work, she would be letting someone down. She'd never know the truth of what she'd felt, and it would haunt her to the end of her days.

On her second trip down, it was still dark as a sealed tomb. She thought about myths of the living descending to the underworld on missions. Inanna. Orpheus. This was nothing so grand as that, but she couldn't bring herself to believe that it was mundane.

On the ground, there was bat guano. Ordinary. In a corner, an abandoned, old-fashioned tin lunch box, dented to hell.

She heard things. Voices. The constant ring and chomp of pickaxes biting into the black gold. The roar of the coal cars on the little track. Prayers. The men would make rough jokes to ward off the fear – she could see their faces, stained and streaked. And the knocking. When the echoes of the sounds of a busy working mine had passed, the knocking remained. It was coming from the tunnel she had considered before and then decided to save for later. Well, now was the time. Knock knock. She checked her monitor. Air quality still decent. Headlamp and flashlight fully charged. Carabiners still firmly attached to the line.

Her heart floated like the ghosts of a hundred canaries.

Part of her was absolutely terrified and wanted nothing more than to run away from that knocking sound, and that part was screaming at the rest of her that was walking towards it, against all reason.

There there, steady now, she thought, in a burst of half-effective self-soothing. She had never been so certain of anything in her life…she was meant to keep going.

The further down she went, the clearer the air seemed. Weird. She didn't want to trust it. But honestly, she hated the feel of the mask on her face. If she could trust the readings, she'd be able to take it off.

No, don't listen to that. She understood that there were voices here that she could not necessarily trust, so she kept it on.

And then, she saw *her.*

Her, she knew instinctively, although she had opinions about pronouns.

The creature was knocking. Helplessly. As if that was all she could do.

She pounded on the rock wall in desperation, as if she didn't know she was being watched. Alice crept closer, and instinctively turned her light away. The creature beat on the coal with a little stone pickaxe, as black as the coal itself, but harder. She wore a rough work shirt and trousers and heavy leather boots. Something about her clothes was…early 20th century, Alice conjectured – menswear of course. But something whispering at the back of her mind said, it could very well be much older. It could have been handwoven, homespun. It could go back hundreds of years. Farther. It was impossible to place in time, in Alice's knowledge.

The creature was small, and a little bit hunched, with strange, long-pointed ears and leathery skin. There was a wiry strength to her, and her face was smeared with coal dust – and emanating a certain phosphorescence, an eerie otherworldly glow. It looked to Alice like her dirty face was streaked with something that could very well have been tears.

"Hey," she said gently. "Hey."

The creature – she – stopped abruptly, and turned to Alice with multifaceted diamond eyes. She looked like she was about halfway to speaking, and about halfway into fleeing back into the unfathomable darkness.

Alice repeated herself. "Hey. I'm not going to hurt you. Who are you?" *What* are you, she really wanted to ask, but she thought that might be rude. Rational brain was screaming, what is it, it's not human, it's nothing you've ever seen before, it's got to be dangerous. *She*, corrected that part of her mind.

The creature spoke, and none of what she said registered. She wasn't speaking English.

"I'm sorry," Alice said. "I don't understand you."

Something touched her mind then. *It's because you're not hearing me right. You're not a miner.*

"No," she said apologetically. "I'm not."

Why are you here if you're not a miner?

Alice didn't know how to answer that. She didn't know how to explain what she was.

There used to be miners here. Lots of them. All the time. My people – we worked with them. Sometimes for them, sometimes against them. But they knew us and we knew them. I knew all the faces of them, and there were so many of us. But they left. They stopped. And my people, most of us…we moved on. Or faded away. So many have faded away. I should have too, but I did not. I kept on. For so very long.

"Your people…" Alice asked. "Who are you?"

"We are the *coblynau*," she said. The word formed itself in Alice's mind as though telegraphed.

Well, let me help you, Alice said, in much the same way.

"Where have they gone?" she asked. Her voice was plaintive for all its roughness. "Why is there no one here anymore? Why is no one working?"

Alice felt her heart breaking for this strange creature – and also saw something in those luminous eyes, designed by something other than nature to be at home in the darkness.

"Coal is…" She didn't know where to begin. How to explain that coal was less profitable? How to explain that mining wasn't underground work anymore? That it was done by machines that ripped the very mountain apart, no tunnel work required, and nothing but gravelly devastation left behind?

She found she didn't have to explain it. The creature came forth, closer in the dim light of her headlamp. "You're not a miner," she said again

"No. I'm not. My great-granddaddy was, but that was a long time ago."

Not to me.

She'd been around then. How long had she loitered in darkness, knocking on the walls and waiting for an answer? "I'm here to assess this site. Preserve it, if possible. Clean up the water. And if it's not possible…we have to seal it. It's not safe."

"Seal it?"

Alice looked into those luminous eyes. The figure seemed to shrink, her strong wiry shoulders slumping in despair.

"Yeah. We don't want people stumbling in, getting hurt. Dying in the mine. You know. You've seen all the ways people can die down here, can't you?"

Part of her mind was just thinking, this is crazy, what am I doing talking to this – person – who seems to live down here, seems to have been here for decades, hasn't seen the sun in all that time and doesn't seem to want to. A dizzying sense of unreality had set in, and she found that her head spun less if she stopped resisting it. She'd sort it all out later when she had more time to process. But then she had to address that terrible fear and sorrow.

If we seal it, we entomb her forever, she realized.

"You can't just…leave, can you?" Alice said. If she was in a fairy tale, then she'd just have to rely on fairy tale logic. The coblyn, she'd called herself. Knockers. Were they bound to their mines forever? That hardly seemed fair. And they weren't native spirits, just like the mines weren't natural. They'd come to work alongside the peoples who had their legends, the Welsh and Irish and Cornish, and she was sure that everywhere in the world people dig for wealth beneath the earth, there was some type of creature just like this with them. It wasn't the coblyn's fault she was an invasive species.

As was she, for that matter. From a certain point of view.

The creature shook her head. "Don't you think I would have done by now?" She had a Celtic lilt to her scratchy voice, and she held her head high. She was sad and abandoned, but she still had a certain pride. Alice looked at her again – her lean, wiry muscles, her work boots and jeans and shirt from decades before, ragged and coal-dusted, but still oddly flattering.

Alice nodded. “Look, I can’t bring the miners back. But–” She wasn’t sure she wanted to get the coblyn’s hopes up. It would be cruel to do that and have the funding fall through. But this site really was perfect, and close enough to the tourist areas and far enough away from the other exhibition coal mine at Beckley…

In that moment, she was the most precious thing Alice had ever seen.

She came forward, blinking in Alice’s headlamp. “What do you do, if you’re not a miner?” She was wary, justifiably so, but her curiosity was sincere.

“I survey old mines…and I test the air and the water. The solidity of the walls. Whether they can be reclaimed for other purposes. My job is to return the sites to the land. To nature. To the earth.”

“Oh,” she said. She gave a strange, twisted little smile. “Nature, yes. I loved a dryad once.”

“A dryad?”

“Yes. Back in the old country. Long ago. You remind me of her. In your…mortal way.”

That struck a chord deep in Alice.

The fae looked away sadly. “I don’t know where she went. Her tree was cut down.”

“I’m very sorry.”

“All things must pass.” If the creature was waiting for Alice to blithely nod without wondering what exactly that meant, she would be disappointed.

“And you…do you just…pass?”

“I wait,” she said. “No one has ever told me what happens when we grow idle for too long. Not for certain. Some think we turn into coal ourselves. Blend into the walls of the mine, and never speak or move again. And when the crust of the earth moves and rumbles and crushes our hillside down or forces it upwards, and wears away the walls with wind or water, or presses down on us with irresistible force, we become dust or diamonds, according to our lot. If there is no work, then we must simply wait."

"Well that's just unacceptable," Alice blurted. She dared to step closer now. In the averted light, her black eyes glittered, light reflected in a hundred facets. She was, Alice thought, surprisingly beautiful. No. Not surprising at all. Perfectly natural in her supernatural way – Alice felt something sliding into place in her own mind. There was more in heaven and earth than had been dreamed of in her ecology. And she was sworn to improve the world for all life. "What is your name?" she asked.

The creature shivered for a moment. *Oh wait*, Alice thought. *Fae. Names are a sensitive subject.*

Finally, Alice asked instead, "What may I call you?"

"I'd like it if you called me Drysor. I haven't heard that word in too long."

Alice leaned in closer, and she shed all her protective equipment. None of that would help her now. All that mattered was connecting with this being. Drysor at last approached her without fear, and Alice was stunned by the intensity of her desire and the absoluteness of her commitment. She kissed Drysor and said, "I swear to you, I will make this better for you."

Drysor accepted her kiss, but backed away with her eyes full of tears. "It is a lovely promise. I would like to believe. But I will wait for the proof. All that I ask is that, if you fail me, I will be no worse off."

Alice wished that she could promise that. It was all her heart desired. "I'll fight for you and your home with everything that is in me," she said. "But if I fail, may I come back? And show you the way to a new place? I won't let anyone seal you in. I'll fight that with every fiber of my being."

"Why would you fight for me?"

"Because I love the land, and all the wild things that live in it. I chose this fight before I knew you existed, and you've renewed my commitment. You've made it personal. Please." She reached out her hand, and Drysor took it once again. "I need to spend more time with you. To know you. And to love you, if you'll have me." What had gotten into her, to say such things? The strangeness of the air? The lingering wildness of her dream?

Drysor leaned in close, and this time the kiss was longer and lingering. The faint hint of sulfur in her mouth was not repellent but erotic, a taste of who she truly was. Alice pulled back at last, and their foreheads touched as they gasped. Drysor placed a small object in her hand. It was coal, but it also glittered. In the process of becoming a diamond. Alice could feel the energy emanating from it with her sixth sense.

"For luck."

Alice already knew she would keep it close on her desk while she wrote the grant proposal.

She'd been skeptical of the stones – after all, everybody knew about fae treasure, how it dissolves in the light of the next day, turns to earth and dead leaves. But she'd put them to their intended purpose, and the mail started arriving, the biggest stream of good news she'd ever had in her life.

When Alice was hired as curator and supervisor and tour guide, and the little museum was built with its gift shop and cafe, when the old tunnels were restored to full working order, when school groups and tourists came for the rides in the coal carts and the glimpse of what life might had been like long ago, Alice worried a little bit if all this activity might be too much for Drysor. After hours, she made her way down further, past the chain gates that closed off the private bowels of the mine to visitors.

Drysor was, as always, positively glowing. She spent her days double-checking everything for safety and efficiency, and from time to time, causing a bout of eerie knocking that would give the schoolkids something to talk about for weeks after. As always, they kissed. And when the night was fair, Alice would drape a blanket over Drysor's shoulders and take her to the park maintenance pickup truck, which she kept lined with a thin layer of coal dust.

And they would ride together through the night, and Drysor would touch trees again, and feel the moonlight on her skin. Alice took her to the overlook with the dramatic oxbow curves of the New River below and the stars overhead.

And the water ran clear and the second-growth forest was thriving, and sometimes Alice saw Drysor looking at the memorial just within the walls, with the photos of the men who had died there long ago, and she would whisper words that Alice knew she did not need to understand.

And Alice wore a Pride pin beside her nametag, and sometimes she'd let people glimpse the elusive shadow of a girlfriend, and the best-selling book in the museum shop was a collection of mining folktales.

Road Trip

CARTER LAPPIN

Kai tapped his fingers on the windowsill, wondering if he should say anything.

Next to him, in the driver's seat, Bigfoot was tapping his fingers as well, mouthing along to the radio. A battered iPhone with a green cover was sitting in the cupholder between them, hooked up to the AUX cord. The scenery was rolling by the windows, mostly fields and billboards for car insurance. Bigfoot was wearing a t-shirt that said *I Ate a Ten Pound Sub at Sonny's Sandwich Shack!* It was too small for his massive frame, which he had to bend nearly in half to fit into the car. The air conditioning was cranked all the way up.

Finally, Kai decided he would just go for it. "Uh," he said, "do you think we could listen to something else for a while?"

Bigfoot looked over at him, expression unreadable behind the mountain of fur on his face. "No."

Kai shifted in his seat, pulling at the seatbelt across his chest. "Look, I like *Wicked* as much as the next guy, but we've listened to the entire soundtrack all the way through like fifteen times in a row. Even 'Defying Gravity' starts to get old after a while."

"No it doesn't," Bigfoot said.

"At this point, even *Phantom of the Opera* would be an acceptable substitute."

"No. I like Idina Menzel. She has a beautiful voice."

"She was in other stuff, too. Plays and movies," Kai said, somewhat desperately. "We could listen to the soundtrack of one of those instead."

Bigfoot looked him directly in the eye– "Hey, eyes on the road!" –and turned the volume on the radio up to the highest setting. The station wagon's outdated speakers vibrated with the effort of keeping up with the admittedly-impressive vocals.

Kai slumped back in his seat. "Now that's just rude."

Bigfoot shrugged. At least he wasn't singing along anymore. Kai was sure there were many things that Bigfoot was talented in, but hitting the high notes of a Broadway singer was not one of them.

"This is what I get for hitchhiking," Kai muttered to himself unhappily, crossing his arms over his chest. His mom had always told him not to get into cars with strangers. Though he doubted that this was the exact scenario she'd had in mind.

They sat in relative silence for a while longer. Bigfoot did eventually turn the music down a little, if only because the speaker was still having a hard time handling it. It was not a new car.

In fact–

"Where did you even get this car?" Kai asked.

Bigfoot looked over at him like he was stupid. His fur, which covered his entire body, was blowing slightly in the wind created by the A/C. "I bought it."

"You have a job?"

"Why wouldn't I?"

"You told me you lived in a cave."

"I have wifi," Bigfoot said.

Kai considered this. Then he sat and considered it a little more. There was a lot to consider. "Okay," he said eventually.

Bigfoot spotted a sign and perked up. "You want a burger?"

Kai shrugged. "I could eat."

Bigfoot put the turn signal on.

They ate at one of the tables next to the food truck. They were the only customers, and they sat at the farthest table, under the shade of one of those industrial umbrellas. It was striped, red and blue. Bigfoot was so tall his head brushed the side of it.

"So," Kai said, pointing a fry at Bigfoot. "What do I call you? Is Bigfoot actually your name, or is that offensive?"

Bigfoot shrugged. He had five burgers for Kai's one, along with a side of onion rings. He'd draped a napkin over his lap to keep ketchup from dripping onto his cargo shorts.

"Sure, you can call me Bigfoot," he said, "I don't mind."

"So that *is* your name?"

He shrugged again. "As much as anything else is."

Kai shook his head and ate the fry. "Eminently helpful, thanks."

The food here was only okay, but the girl behind the counter hadn't batted an eye at Bigfoot's hulking, fur-covered figure, nor the fifty dollar bill he'd peeled off of a crumpled wad of hundreds to pay with. Bigfoot, as it turned out, was an excellent tipper and had put the change she'd handed him directly into the tip jar by her elbow. She hadn't blinked at that either. Retail workers would truly ignore anything.

"What about you?" Bigfoot asked.

"Me?" Kai asked, surprised.

"Yeah. I picked you up a hundred miles ago. You never told me where you're headed."

Kai could have given an answer. Could have talked about home, about how it *wasn't* home anymore, about the little sister he'd had to leave behind. Instead, he just said, "South-ish. Or west. Which way are we going now?"

Bigfoot didn't look amused. Though, it was hard to tell – fur covered a lot of sins.

Kai picked tomato off of his burger. He offered it to Bigfoot, who opened up the top of one of his own and let Kai mash it into the lettuce before putting the bun back where it belonged. He then watched as Bigfoot crammed the entire burger into his mouth at once. Kai was pretty sure mouths weren't supposed to work that way, but he thought it might be rude to ask.

"Anyways," he said, watching Bigfoot chew with a sort of horrified fascination, "Whichever direction you're going, I'm okay with it. Where *are* you going anyways?"

Kai was aware of the hypocrisy of the question. He reached over and ate one of Bigfoot's onion rings off his plate.

Bigfoot eyed him warily. "Don't do that again."

"Okay." Kai stole another onion ring.

Bigfoot growled a little. He sounded kind of like a bear. On an unrelated note, Kai decided he wouldn't be stealing any more onion rings in the future. Bigfoot watched him for a while until this became clear.

"I'm on a road trip," Bigfoot said once he was satisfied. "To see humanity."

"Yeah?" Kai asked, "Is it like an annual thing? Oh, have you seen the world's biggest ball of twine yet?"

"No," said Bigfoot. "This is my first time. I've never actually left my cave that much."

"Yeah, I would be a little agoraphobic too if every time I walked outside there was somebody trying to take a blurry photo of me," Kai said. His milkshake was thick and he was having a hard time getting it through the straw without looking silly. He squished the sides of the cup a little, but all that happened was that some chocolate milkshake started leaking out between the seam of the cup and the lid. Kai mopped at it frantically with a napkin.

"You have no idea," Bigfoot said, sounding weary.

Giving up on the napkin, Kai licked the side of the cup clean. Bigfoot looked more than a little appalled at his manners.

"So, what, you're just wandering? Taking in the sights, wearing dad clothes?" Kai asked.

Bigfoot looked down at himself. He wasn't wearing shoes – there probably wasn't a company in the world that made them his size – but Kai thought that if he could he would have been wearing socks with sandals. "What's wrong with my clothes?"

"I thought you might be on the run. Like, from the government, or scientists. Or government scientists," Kai said, slightly disappointed.

"Why would government scientists be after me?"

"I dunno. 'Cause you're *Bigfoot*?" Kai ate a few more fries. "Anyways, I thought it would be something more exciting. Don't people look at you strange when you pull up to a tourist trap looking like actual literal Bigfoot?"

"You didn't," Bigfoot said. He was on his third burger. He was taking this one slower than the others. Maybe he was getting full, or maybe he just didn't want to run out of food that quickly.

"Yeah, but I'm weird," Kai said. "*Normal* people think that it's strange to see Bigfoot at a burger truck."

"Do they?" Bigfoot asked, like it was the first time he'd heard of such a thing. "Huh."

Kai reached for another onion ring, remembered, and changed direction mid-action to awkwardly grab his burger again, like a bird swooping in from above. He took a bite to cover up how strange the movements had looked. It was still only okay. The tomatoes had left behind an oily sort of flavor that he didn't like.

"Do you have a driver's license?" Kai asked.

"Yes."

"Seriously?"

Bigfoot dug in one of the zippered pockets of his cargo shorts. He passed over a small card. Kai looked at it. It was, indeed, a valid driver's license, made out to a *Foot, Big*. Bigfoot was wearing sunglasses over his furry face in his photo.

"How did you convince them to do that?" Kai asked.

In response, Bigfoot just smiled. Or maybe that *was* the answer – it was probably pretty difficult to say no when someone with teeth that size was asking you for something.

"Okay, sorry," Kai said, handing it back. "Just wanted to know if I was gonna get arrested for driving around with an unlicensed driver."

"Not for that, no," Bigfoot said.

"What's that supposed to mean?"

Bigfoot was silent.

"Bigfoot, did you commit a crime?"

Still, Bigfoot didn't answer.

"Bigfoot. Am I going to be arrested for aiding and abetting a wanted murderer?"

"I haven't killed anyone," Bigfoot said, consuming his last burger in a single bite. "You're a very paranoid person, you know that?"

"There are crimes other than murder. Did you rob a gas station? A bank?"

"Are you going to finish that milkshake?" Bigfoot asked.

Kai had only managed to drink half of it so far. He'd been considering just taking the lid off and chugging it to get around the problem. "No, go ahead," he sighed, pushing it across the table to Bigfoot.

Bigfoot popped the top and drained the lot. Show-off.

Kai crumpled up his burger wrapper. "So, where to next?" he asked. He tossed it toward the nearest trash can, and was pleasantly surprised to see it go straight in, nothing but net.

"That's assuming you're going with me," Bigfoot said.

Kai pouted. "You'll leave me here all alone to hitchhike with strangers? What if I get picked up by a murderer?" To demonstrate, he stuck out his thumb with a sad expression on his face. He might have been laying it a little thick.

Bigfoot sighed. It was a big, heavy sigh, full of feeling. "You mentioned something about a big ball of twine? What is that?"

Kai grinned widely. "Oh, Bigfoot, you're in for a treat, my friend."

"I doubt it," Bigfoot grumbled, but Kai thought he could see the hints of a smile forming on the ginormous creature's face. Again, it was somewhat hard to tell.

Kai just hoped that there weren't more showtunes in his future. Either way, though, he thought that this was going to be *fun.*

Grim Up North

PARKER FOYE

Morgan stank of stale espresso and overtime. He wanted to take off his shoes. He wanted the bliss of unconsciousness. He wanted to take the shortcut home.

He stood at the threshold of the cemetery and peered into the dark. The nearest streetlight had gone out again but light glowed from the terraced houses behind him, seeping through curtained windows and limning gravestones and scrubby grass in gray relief. Light beckoned at the other side of the cemetery, too, including from the house next to Morgan's, on the other side of the shortcut.

On the other side of the graves.

Morgan shifted his weight. He'd moved into the house a week ago, taking the ensuite room on the top floor of an end terrace, upgrading from a shared house of five to only him and one other. He'd expected more competition – a good price, with an easy walk into Durham town center, and even a parking spot for the car he didn't own – but all the windows of the bedroom faced a small cemetery, close enough he could make out the writing on the stones. That had put off other offers, the letting agent said, though the agent had promised there'd been no hauntings in a decade, and no reanimation ever recorded. Morgan had shrugged and signed the paperwork.

In the daytime, the little cemetery was cute. Atmospheric. It boasted a small chapel, the kind that looked good on postcards, and the outer edges were lined with heavy-headed trees thick with leaves. Grass tufted the path that snaked alongside Morgan's house and through the cemetery, ending at the top of the cobbled lane leading to town.

Yet in the night, as Morgan stood and shivered in his too-thin work shirt, thought processes slowed by overtime, his hindbrain saw faces in every shadow and hands grasping from every plot. The site hadn't been used for new burials for years, and he had his safety certificates from the letting agency, but standing at the threshold, reason mattered little.

Morgan glanced at the shuttered eye of his bedroom window again. He debated taking the longer way around but dismissed the thought. It would add half a mile onto his walk and his bed was *right there!*

Grumbling lowly, Morgan pulled out his phone and switched on the flashlight, then aimed the beam at his feet in an effort not to entirely destroy his night vision. He took a breath and blew it out. The route was short: straight ahead, follow the path when it curved, not too sharp a turn or he'd walk into the weeping angel, then through the snicket and home. Five minutes, maybe six. Three if he walked as fast as his nerves urged.

Another breath. Morgan stepped across the threshold of the cemetery and shined his phone's light on the ground as he walked briskly forward. Nothing to see here. What a lovely evening. Was that an owl? If his heart beat any harder it would break through his chest. Could hearts do that?

Did something move, there, in the shadow?

Morgan locked his gaze ahead. Even if something *had* moved, it was none of his business. The path curved ahead. He went right with it.

A shadow lunged to meet him.

Morgan yelped and stumbled backward, dropping his phone. His heart rabbited and his breath rasped as images of slough-faced zombies flickered behind his eyes even as his rational mind shrieked it would just be the *regular kind of murderer* – as if that might help. He landed hard on his ass and tried to scramble to his feet again, only for his hand to impact something…squishy…and warm…and provoking a deep and literal *woof* of pain.

Morgan froze. The textured shadow froze in turn. Hot breaths ruffled Morgan's sweaty hair. The breaths were tinny with meat. Slowly, Morgan lifted his hand, then shuffled to sit on his heels. He cleared his throat. Gray shapes formed as his vision adjusted, but not quickly enough to identify them in the dark.

"H-hello?" he ventured, like someone who would definitely be eaten in a film.

Another *woof.* Questioning. Impossible.

Morgan swallowed. "Hello, dog? Possibly a dog. Hopefully a dog." He glanced at the moon and found it half full. The sight was less comforting than it should have been; werewolves were a known quantity. "Okay, I'm just – I'm reaching for my phone."

His phone had landed light-down, the screen glowing around the edges. Something scuttled across his hand when Morgan retrieved it, and he shook his hand quickly, repulsed. He cupped his palm around the light, not wanting to lose the shapes his eyes had picked out of the gloom. Not wanting to see the whatever-it-was in its full and, undoubtedly terrible, glory.

Yet not knowing wouldn't prevent the creature from eating him. With trepidation, Morgan raised his phone and aimed the light at the ground.

Two paws – two *enormous* paws, the size of pasta bowls – flexed their clawed toes, the glossy fur black as tar. Morgan swallowed thickly and crept the light upward until he found teeth, which weren't bared in a snarl so much as incidentally exposed as the dog lolled its tongue while it panted. The flashlight made the dog's eyes seem red, like burning coals stuck in its shadowy face.

Morgan kept the light trained on the dog. "You seem friendly enough, but maybe don't leap out at everyone passing, hey? Humans can't see as well as you." The dog's tail whipped from side to side, responding to Morgan's tone. Morgan tugged sharply on the end of his hair in an effort to concentrate. "Think that's funny, do you? Fair enough. Right, I'm going to need to get by–"

The dog *woofed* and Morgan flinched at the noise. A whine followed, as if in apology, then the dog ducked its big head. When Morgan didn't react, the dog whined again, and its tail drooped.

"What is it? Do you want…" Morgan trailed off, not wanting to suggest the dog might be hungry. "What do you want?"

Wind nipped his fingers and Morgan pressed them into the edge of his phone. He shifted on the cold ground. The dog shifted in turn. When it moved from the light, it became shadow, the edges of its body diffusing into the night. Its tail wagged like a metronome.

Morgan was so *tired*. His brain felt like cottage cheese, badly strained. He tried to remember what you were supposed to do with dogs. Let them sniff you? Warily, he extended the fingers of his free hand.

"Pleased to meet you," Morgan said, because it seemed polite.

The dog sniffed Morgan's hand, then ducked its head again. Its ears flicked.

"Fine. Let's try this."

Tentatively, Morgan reached toward the dog's head, even as he resigned himself to losing his fingers. He watched from outside himself as exhaustion, defeat, a long day and not enough hours to dawn, all created distance between his mind and the fingers reaching toward the dog. The fire of the dog's eyes smoldered. Morgan made himself blink.

"You look like a good dog to me," Morgan ventured, his voice breaking on the last word. He cleared his throat, the noise a sharp crack in the quiet night. The dog's ears flicked and Morgan halted. But the dog only looked, some might say pointedly, at Morgan's outstretched fingers.

"Right." Morgan bent his fingers from where his knuckles had locked. The tips were going numb. "Rude to offer a scratching and not follow through, isn't it? Zero-star review. None of the other dogs will – oh!"

Tired of Morgan's babbling, the dog thrust its head beneath Morgan's fingers. Morgan's fingers sank through the dog's dense fur as he instinctively curled his fingers around the dog's head, to rub at the base of one floppy ear. The dog's eyes dropped and a rumble sounded in its chest.

"Listen to you!" Morgan grinned. The dog's size became less intimidating when coupled with a window-wiper tail and that welcoming rumble. "You smell like a bonfire. Gotta be safe around those fires, dog." Morgan glanced at the dog's throat. No collar, but people microchipped pets, didn't they? He'd never been allowed anything bigger than a hamster. "What a good–"

Suddenly the dog jerked back, ears going high and reddish eyes lighting like flares. The big head turned toward the town center. It took a moment for Morgan to realize the rumbling sound didn't come from the dog, but from thick clouds rolling in. Another bloody storm. When the dog didn't move, even its tail gone still, Morgan heaved to his feet and dusted off his jeans. The sky began to spit.

"Think it's time for me to be off, dog. Hope you catch that rabbit, or whatever it is you're listening to right now. Be careful of cats, hey? They'll be after your nose." The dog didn't look at him, though Morgan lingered for a moment, all the while knowing himself a fool. He hadn't been mauled. Take the win, Morgan. "Night, dog. Good hunting."

Though the walk home was short, by the time Morgan let himself into the quiet house, he was soaked through.

"Do you know anything about a stray dog?" he asked Carmel the next morning, waiting for the kettle to boil.

Carmel grunted, not looking up from whatever they were doing with their eyeshadow palette. Conjuring, maybe. "There's a terrier sometimes, nosing in the bins. I think it belongs to two doors down."

"No, not a terrier." Impatient, Morgan flicked off the kettle and filled his mug. He swirled the teabag around until the water turned murky. "A big black dog. Like a Labrador or, what's that other one? A mastiff. Except it could probably eat both of those."

He could feel Carmel looking at his back. He didn't turn around.

"You sleeping enough, Morgan?" they finally asked, hypocritically. Carmel spent most of their time in the university labs or library, finishing their PhD, and kept worse hours than Morgan.

Morgan slopped milk into his mug, then dumped in two spoons of sugar, and tried to drink the tea without removing the bag or the spoon. It tasted like shit. He finished the mug and let it clatter in the sink.

"I'll get that later," he said, and turned around. He smiled at Carmel. His throat hurt from gulping the too-hot tea. "I'm fine, yeah. Thanks. Anyway, I've got to go, got another shift."

Carmel grunted again, eyes on their reflection. Morgan left them to it.

Distracted as he opened the door, Morgan almost tripped over the enormous dog laid across the threshold. He startled back and nearly slammed the door closed on one giant paw.

"What the hell are you doing there?" he asked, once he'd collected himself.

The dog raised its head. Its tail wagged.

Morgan rubbed his face. He made a gentle shooing gesture toward the dog. "Can you move? Please? I haven't done enough stretching this morning to try climbing over you."

With a huff, the dog rose to its feet, tail still wagging, enough that it thumped gently against Morgan's leg. Then the dog pawed the ground and looked pointedly toward the path leading through the cemetery.

"Subtle, aren't you?" Morgan got an enthusiastic woof in answer and he grinned. "All right, you can join me on my commute this morning. If you can work out how to make tea with those paws of yours, let me know. This early shift is kicking my arse."

They walked together most mornings, after that, though the dog never did manage to bring a beverage. The dog was a good listener as Morgan talked about his shifts at the coffee shop, how he thought about maybe opening his own one of these days, about places he missed and those he'd never visited, all that. He asked about the dog's day too, of course, it would've been rude not to, and if anyone thought it strange to see him chatting away to the dog, no one said anything about it. Not to his face, anyway.

Despite being a huge creature, the dog never seemed bothered by any of the other animals they met on their walks; the mouthy gray squirrel that liked to scamper up gravestones to chatter as they passed elicited no more than a sneeze from the dog, while other dogs – from chihuahuas to golden retrievers – received only a wag of the tail. But a sad wag, it seemed to Morgan, like the small smiles he sometimes got from customers who'd had a hard day.

He started wondering if his manager would stock dog biscuits at the shop, so Morgan could use his staff discount to treat the dog. Buying them at full price was obliterating his tips.

As time passed, Morgan thought of asking his neighbors about the dog. One of them must own it; he'd found no collar in its shaggy ruff despite numerous scritches, but it seemed in too good a condition to be a stray. Besides, he'd never actually *seen* a stray dog before.

Maybe the dog had eaten them.

Morgan rubbed his face. Maybe he should drink more coffee. Less. Certainly one of those.

Two weeks after his first encounter with the dog, Morgan's old housemate Ingrid finally coaxed him from his work-sleep-more work cycle and into one of the coffee shops on Claypath, where the mugs were almost as big as the black dog's paws. They did much better hot chocolate than Morgan's place, and had a wider cake selection, which Ingrid knew to be Morgan's weakness. One bite into the fragrant lemon blondie and Morgan found himself telling the whole story about the dog and the cemetery.

At the end, Ingrid leveled an unreadable look at him. She hadn't finished her coffee cake.

"A big black dog. Are you sure?" she asked, poking at her cake with the little fork.

"'Big black dog' might be underselling things. Enormous hound the color of midnight. Gigantic beast with obsidian fur. Gargantuan–"

"Yes, yes, okay, you're fabulous at Scrabble–"

"–with burning red coals instead of eyes–"

"Wait what?" Ingrid's question took a moment for Morgan to parse, she spoke so quickly. She clenched her fork and leaned forward across the table, all amusement stripped from her, solemnity heavy on her sparrow-thin shoulders. "Morgan, what did you say about its eyes? Don't play words, just tell me."

Morgan raised his brows and lowered his hands from where he'd been signaling the comparative size of his canine visitor.

"The dog's eyes are red. A trick of the light, probably." A consistent trick. He scratched his jaw and looked away from Ingrid's intense stare. "Like embers, if you'll permit me the fancy."

Blowing out a hard breath, Ingrid sat back in her chair. In her silence, the chatter of the coffee shop, the clanking of cups, the hiss of the milk steamer, and the grumble of the espresso machine, they all seemed somehow fake, like ambient noise from a playlist. Morgan kept looking around as if he'd catch someone flickering. As if he'd been imagining the whole thing.

He pinched the skin on the back of his hand between his fingernails and it bloody *hurt*.

Shaking his hand beneath the table, Morgan waited for Ingrid to return from wherever her thoughts had taken her. In his coffee cup, foam dripped toward the center. Did people read coffee foam the way they did tea leaves? He squinted. The paw print inside was almost certainly a product of his imagination.

"It's a grim."

"What's a what?" Morgan asked, jerking his eyes to Ingrid.

She held her cup between her hands, like she'd gone cold and needed what heat lingered in the ceramic. "Your black dog. The churchyard, such as it is, they're a traditional place for grims. Barghests, as they're sometimes called. And with it waiting for you on the doorstep…" Ingrid's lips twisted, but she didn't look away from him. She'd always been the braver of the two of them. "They're death omens, Morgan. And this one's yours."

The whole thing could have gone better, really. Morgan wanted to dismiss Ingrid's observation as nonsense, but she'd been right about the brownies in their garden, and she always bought a phase of the moon calendar even though no one in her family was were. If anyone knew what they were talking about when it came to cryptid relations, it was Ingrid.

Grims, according to Ingrid and a visit to Wikipedia, were the spirits of dogs buried as foundation sacrifices in churchyards, tasked with guarding against whatever hijinks people thought might happen there. Body snatching. Grave robbing. Clumsy fools tripping over their own feet. Grims were portents, too. He'd read something about a church bell, and the devil, but Morgan focused more on the portent.

He didn't want to be portended.

He put a reminder on his phone to return his library books, just in case.

That night, thunder rolled close enough to shake Morgan's windows in the frames. Rain clattered against the panes. Leaning on his windowsill, Morgan watched the storm, and enjoyed the coziness of being adjacent to the power but safe from it. He drew a face on the inside of the glass, only to jerk and smear the smile when movement in the cemetery caught his eye. He peered into the textured shadows, scanning graves that had grown familiar. Something atavistic curdled in his brain despite his rational mind scoffing at the nonsense of fear. He was safe inside his house.

The shadows of the cemetery rippled.

It could be a bird. A rat. A branch, gesturing rudely to the storm.

The shocking red flare of a struck match boiled in the night. Two matches, smoldering in a dark face.

Morgan yanked the curtains closed. He laughed, thin and without feeling.

He didn't look out at the storm again.

The dog hadn't returned to Morgan's doorstep since the storm. Every morning, Morgan braced for it, for the portent to come for him, and every evening he dared himself to take the shortcut through the cemetery. Every evening, nothing happened.

On the plus side, *nothing happened.*

Yet it grew tiresome, waiting to die.

He asked Ingrid for advice, but only once, as she looked at him oddly and asked if he was disappointed she'd been wrong about the grim. Morgan didn't know how to explain. He'd returned his library books, checked the dates on the food in the fridge, even briefly investigated what would happen to his outstanding student loans in the event of his death, and then…nothing. Nearly a fortnight of nothing.

Which brought him to his current effort on this pale gray Tuesday afternoon: carrying dog-friendly treats and determination into the cemetery and perching on the edge of a bench. One of the trees drooped its spindly fingers into his hair with every sigh of wind, and fine drizzle misted over the gravestones like sea fret, though they were miles from the coast.

"I know you're here, dog," he said, the conviction primarily comprised of bullshit.

The tree ruffled his hair again. Morgan scanned the edges of the cemetery, pausing at the overgrown places between graves and the shadows puddled beneath the outstretched wings of statues. He glanced at his bedroom window, at the pebble-dashed houses studded with satellite dishes and solar energy panels, but that world faded in importance. The world within the bounds of a crumbling stone wall and the high fences at the back of the allotments – that mattered, in all its pale and rain-streaked glory.

He took a sip of his matcha latte and obnoxiously rustled the paper bag of treats with his other hand. "I brought you a present!"

The wind brought him the scent of bonfires. Morgan froze and stared as, between one breath and the next, the dog appeared like a reflection in a steamed-over mirror, sharpening into focus. Perhaps the dog had always been there, sitting on its haunches near Morgan's feet, red eyes afire.

Though he'd walked with the dog a dozen times or more, cold sweat prickled Morgan's nape as he allowed himself to see what he'd defensively skimmed on each prior occasion. The dog's red eyes were not a trick of the light, or a fancy of his memory, but captivating flames lit with human intelligence. Its fangs were as long as Morgan's fingers, and its claws were hooked, almost like a bird's. Morgan recalled, suddenly, the sound of those claws clacking over the cobblestones as they'd walked together into town.

The dog's tail wagged. It tilted its head at Morgan and gave an inquisitive whine.

Morgan swallowed. He set his takeaway cup by his feet. "Hello, dog. Are you a – well." He blew a breath through his nose, the way the internet claimed was calming. It wasn't.

Absently, Morgan wondered if his hair were curling. If that's how he'd be found, frizzy-haired and face down on a cooling puddle of his own blood, after the Hound of the Baskervilles ripped out his throat. He worked his thumb over the place on the bench where the wood had split, worrying a splinter with his thumb nail. The dog shuffled forward, ears low.

"I suppose there isn't any way to say this but straightforwardly, is there?" Morgan asked the dog. Then a thought occurred to him and he brightened. "If you don't understand me, it's not as if you can tease me about it, is it? You're just a dog."

The dog tilted its head the other way and made a low, scoffing sort of noise. Morgan's joy deflated and nerves rushed to fill the space. A splinter tore free from the bench and he flicked it away, then arranged his hands in his lap. The dog glanced at Morgan's hands, which had usually been keen to offer pets, and the fires of its eyes burned into Morgan's. Somewhere, thunder rumbled. The drizzle increased its efforts. Clouds thickened and the sun retreated behind them.

Wikipedia had said grims were associated with stormy weather.

Morgan swallowed. "Excuse my boldness, but are you a grim, dog?"

The dog's eyes flared so bright they left sunspots in Morgan's vision. He flinched, and again when the dog made a high, terrible sound, like the screech of metal against metal, like tinfoil between Morgan's fillings. An electric whine thrummed as the dog's body warped and contorted, its fur bristling to deadly spines like the winds of hell ruffled fingers through it.

Morgan heard whimpering and realized it came from his own throat. He slid off the bench and hunkered behind it, peering through the slats as the dog melted, the rain doing nothing against the heat rising from where the dog changed. Lightning flashed, sudden and blisteringly close. Morgan fell onto his ass and rubbed frantically at his eyes to clear them.

When he rose to his knees again, he blinked for a different reason.

A man stood where the dog had been. Rangy. Tall. Naked. Wild, curly hair the color of the dog's fur. Red eyes like banked fires. A wide smile showcasing his sharp – very sharp – teeth.

Morgan swallowed. He scanned the man from curly hair to muddy toes, lingering a little in the midsection, before dragging his eyes to the banked fires again. At Morgan's attention, the man's smile faltered and he scratched awkwardly behind his ear. Morgan made himself blink. He sat back on his heels.

"So…you *are* a grim, then. That feels like a solid 'yes'. Am I – am I going to die? How am I going to die? Will it hurt?" Morgan's stomach twisted. He clenched his hands to fists. "Please don't make it hurt."

"Fuck, no, this is awkward," the dog – the man – the grim said. He sounded like he was from Leeds.

While Morgan recalibrated his mental map, the grim loped forward, uncaring of his nudity, and knelt on the bench to face where Morgan sat behind it. The slats obscured Morgan's view of the grim's cock. Probably for the best, all told, considering Morgan's incipient descent into despair.

Why was Morgan thinking about the grim's cock when the grim was about to *kill him*?

Morgan briefly covered his eyes even as heat rose to his cheeks. "Awkward? You're not the one going to die!"

"I'm not – no." The grim flushed to the tips of his ears. It made his eyes seem somehow redder. "I mean, yes, I'm a grim, but…that first time, when you nearly tripped over me–"

"I did *not*–"

"–and I went to check you were okay, and you were really nice! You didn't need to be, but you were. And I kept meaning to say something, introduce meself, but I couldn't work out how to talk to you." The grim wrinkled his nose. "I suppose you'll think I'm daft."

Morgan blinked. He retrieved his cold drink and took a bracing sip. "I'm sorry, I think I might be confused about what's happening here."

The grim raked his fingers through his hair. The curls sprang instantly back into place. "I've been in the churchyard a long time and it's hard to get out and meet people, you know? In the community, everyone asks if I'm a werewolf, and outside of it…I don't want to scare anyone. I'm quite" – he gestured to himself and Morgan tried to squint through the bench slats again – "intimidating. But you spoke to me–"

"I spoke to *a dog*," Morgan stressed.

"Exactly! Me! You were nice, and you carried on being nice. Telling me about your day, asking me about mine. No one's ever asked about my day before."

Grasping for a way to lose some of the heat currently consuming him, Morgan shrugged off his coat and draped it over the bench. The rain had begun to let up, but the wind still teased its cold fingers. They were welcome on Morgan's flushed skin.

He pointed to his coat. "In case you're cold," he explained to the grim.

The grim grabbed the coat and pulled it on, adjusting the fabric to settle around his hips, then tugging the collar around his throat. He ducked his head into the collar and seemed to sniff it. His cheeks were pink with cold. Morgan wondered if he missed his fur.

If he missed his fur.

Morgan drained the rest of his matcha latte in one pull. He should've brought something stronger.

"So you like nice men, do you?" Morgan asked, inanely.

The grim nodded. He flashed his – sharp, extremely sharp –

teeth. "Very much. Handsome men, too. Which I think you are, in case that isn't clear. I haven't done this in a while. I've actually been trying to work out how to ask if you might want to go out sometime? With me? On a walk."

"…we've done a lot of walking."

The grim smiled wryly. "I'd be on two feet, this time."

"Let me get this straight. You *haven't* been lurking around because of my impending demise, and you're a biped as well as a grim, and you think I'm handsome? And want to walk with me? In a-a romantic capacity?" Morgan's voice crawled higher with each question, but that was okay. The grim would be able to hear.

The grim nodded. "That's about the shape of it."

Did Morgan want to go out with a supernatural death omen graveyard guardian? Who looked like *that*?

He beamed. "That sounds *wonderful.*"

They sat together on the bench. Grim, as he said he preferred to be called, rested his head on Morgan's shoulder, his hands wrapped around Morgan's arm. Clouds drifted over the sun and somewhere, thunder rumbled. Grim's hair smelled of smoke and his dirty fingernails left smears on Morgan's shirtsleeves. Morgan's ass was going numb on the bench.

It was perfect.

Loud Came the Rain

MADELINE V PINE

April 12th. Nadir's pen hovered by the logbook, body swaying in the gentle lull of the sea. Why was that date so imposing? He scowled in the wandering amber glow. "Markus, stay still for a sec."

The anglerfish skimming the ceiling paused, then swam over, lantern drooping.

Nadir's shadow ran wide over the log. His mother's birthday was two weeks ago, so that left no one on land he should need to congratulate. With a lick of dark fingers, he flipped the page, scanning empty lines for warnings.

April 15th: Tax Day.

"Shit," Nadir sighed, curling over his desk. He dragged his hands through oily hair. Markus nipped at his fingers.

Nadir pushed up and fetched the fish food from his little bookcase. Even sea spirits needed to eat. Leaning on the wall, he tossed bits to Markus and slowly drowned in his to-do list.

It wasn't as if he had wifi on this little ketch, not in the middle of the damn South Pacific. He hadn't planned to dock until Wellington, and that was just a day trip to restock, but New Zealand was weeks away.

What was he close to?

Nadir glanced at his nautical charts. He could just make the Tuamotu Archipelago if he caught the winds right. Did anyone live there?

While Markus chased herds of minnows across the ketch's floor, Nadir pried pilot books off the little shelves. Yes, one of the Tuamotu islands was inhabited: Rapa Iti. Between its six hundred villagers, someone might have a hotspot. He barged from the cabin and into the sea spray.

"Machi!" he shouted over the rails. "We're changing course!"

A lapis fishtail smacked the waves, big as a sailor's dream. White scales dove beneath the boat as Nadir turned the ketch to best catch the wind, then trimmed his sails. He stared into the endless water, culture-shocked. It'd been months since he'd thought of normal life, of governments and the electronics that gathered dust beneath his bed. Could he even use the outlets on Rapa Iti?

"Do you need a refill? You've been swearing up a storm." The lone café's waiter eyed Nadir's empty glass.

"What I need is to get back to my boat before it fucking rains." Nadir sat back and rubbed his stinging eyes. Three hours in this damned café, trying different websites to file his taxes for free because they all charged eighty dollars to rush his paperwork. The States wouldn't give him an extension without a permanent mailing address, as if he kept one when he spent all year on the open ocean.

It dawned on him what he said. His face heated. "Sorry…that was rude."

The young man shrugged. Not too young, Nadir corrected. Somewhere in his late twenties or early thirties, though it was hard to tell with that flawless smile. Flustered, Nadir glanced around the empty café, four bare tables in front of a house. Spare wood poles held up the thatch canopy, made from the same palm leaves that drooped right outside.

"The rain's a bit unpredictable around here." The waiter's dark eyes flicked to the rough tugboat docked at the lonely pier. "You lucked out, coming the one day we get another ship. Next one won't be in for months."

That boat was the only thing blessing Nadir with wifi. Half freight, half cruise ship, tourists to Easter Island lingered around its ivory base, unsure what to do with Rapa Iti's sharp hills or sparse trees. They feared the rough waters and rocks that had fought Nadir all the way here.

"I doubt they think anyone'd pirate 'em out here," Nadir darkly joked, frustrated. "Yeah, hell, get me that refill."

The waiter brought back some warm beer and smoked fish. He scooted out the other chair with his foot and let himself sit. "So. A sailor who doesn't like the rain." He smiled, wry, cheeks like apples and hair like basalt.

Shit. Nadir squashed his flipping stomach. He'd been at sea too long. He rubbed his collar, ducking his head toward the mind-numbing forms. "The rain doesn't like me."

"Nonsense."

"Then it likes me too much." He clicked the retired box. A popup demanded he confirm his age. "Goddammit, I know my own age. Sorry–"

The waiter waved him off. He leaned over and stared at the form. "What are you doing out here, American?"

"Nadir."

"Hm?"

Nadir's lips twitched up, "If you're going to peek at my social, at least catch my name."

The waiter laughed, a big, innocent sound. Nadir highly considered boarding that cruise ship for an hour. He couldn't waste time trying to replay that laugh.

"A'Hei." That easy smile returned. "And you've answered neither of my questions, Na… Nadir." A'Hei's lips pursed as he tried the name. He leaned forward, legs crossed. His collar drooped around his tan skin, revealing bits of tattoos. "Is it true Americans always rush? You're certainly secretive, coming all the way out here just to leave."

"You'd not like me here when it rains." Nadir clammed up, face heating. He clicked through a few forms as A'Hei waited him out. Nadir sighed. "The seas get wild when it rains."

"Then stay inland."

"No, the creatures. When it rains, they don't like to be near the surface. Makes 'em crazy."

A'Hei raised one brow.

"Surely you've noticed. They either dive deep or crawl inland. They don't dive down when I'm around." Nadir bent over his keys.

"How many fish are we talking? Enough for a feast?"

Nadir snorted. "You have no idea what you're asking. They warp. Hence why I don't stay on principle." He reminded himself. He scanned the numbers he'd entered and smacked his computer shut. He needed to scram before A'Hei claimed the sea drove him mad. "What do I owe you?"

"Bugger, come here!" Nadir chased a slugfish across the sand.

The translucent purple scales darted between coral shards and tidepools. Their big salamander tail swished, snaking meters in seconds. They taunted Nadir, fading in and out of solidity, like the dusk flickering between clouds. Nadir crept close. The slugfish burst for the trees.

An arrow shot through their bug eyes. The slugfish solidified with a jerk, dead. Nadir snatched it up by their salamander tail and hid them behind his back. He waved toward the seamless treeline.

"What in the seas is that?" A'Hei stepped out, carrying his curved bow. He'd left his shirt behind in the café, and intricate tattoos cascaded down his chest.

Nadir's ears burned. He'd purposely moved his boat to the other side of the tiny cove. Damn this one-street island. "Why are you here?"

"Because I couldn't tell if you lied. And you're not answering my questions again." He ambled up to Nadir, not quite as tall but near as broad, big feet pressing into the wet sand. "Don't steal another man's catch."

Nadir licked his lips, debating a snarky comment. He held the six-legged purple creature out. "They're the first signs I've stuck around too long."

A'Hei whistled as he brushed the seamless scales. "Looks like a mutated salamander."

"I didn't know what a salamander was as a kid. Named 'em after what I saw."

"And what did you name it?" A'Hei ripped his arrow out, cunning lids batting.

"Ah…slugfish," Nadir's mouth dried. God, why couldn't he have named it something beautiful? "And they don't follow me, they spawn. If water'n I are in the same place, these'll fade in, like ghosts."

A'Hei cocked his head, weighing the fish in his hands. They draped over both his palms, flopping for the sand. He grinned. "Can you eat a ghost?"

"Not if you want a normal life." Nadir turned to the ocean and cupped his mouth. "Machi! …*Machi!*"

That azure tailfin breached the cove, casting shadows over the sand. Nadir snatched the slugfish. With bulging arms, he shotput it over the waves. A mountainous snake surged from the surface, raining seafoam, and snapped the fish up in their white jaws. With a crash, the dragon plunged underwater, sleek body disappearing. A'Hei gaped.

Nadir rubbed his sticky, sweaty palms on his shirt. "If you eat 'em, you get more potent and then more of 'em appear. Figure it's why they've popped up more over the years."

A'Hei eased down, saucer eyes on the undulating waves. "Did the sea spirit…? The, the dragon…?"

"Dragon." Nadir nodded.

"Did it tell you its name?"

"Nah, I picked Machi up in Italy."

A'Hei stared at him.

"Machiavelli. Poor bastard was sulking in the depths of the Tyrrhenian Sea, trapped by all the shipping noise. For some reason, he's followed me round the globe a few times." He sat next to A'Hei, taking in the land vice at the end of the cove, which agitated the seas until they were too rough and unknown to try with the rising stars. He really needed to leave but…it was nice to be believed.

"Has it always been this way?"

"For Ma's family. Folks settled far away from any body of water, but I just went stir crazy."

"My brothers left home," A'Hei murmured, starstruck by the occasional gleam of white scales dancing in the cove. "Went searching for work on Tahiti. Don't you miss home?"

Nadir snorted. "You try being named Nadir in Oklahoma." He rubbed the back of his neck. "Plus, I don't bother anyone at sea."

"Mm, I miss them. But my brothers get two days off a month, and Tahiti's seas are too dirty to dive for my tastes, though tourists from dirtier parts of the world sing them praise."

Nadir couldn't remember Tahiti's waters. The coasts blended together. "There's more shores in the world than Tahiti's." The offer to show A'Hei died on his tongue. Stupid, only lonely fools offered like that. Or maybe he'd seem considerate? "You should go sometime."

"I can hear their afterimages from tourists." A'Hei stood and brushed off his shorts. "Are there more slugfish around?"

"I'll get 'em before I leave." Nadir slumped as A'Hei closed off.

"But then I'll never see such creatures again. And what if you miss a few? Teach me where they spawn, then I'll cook you something proper."

Nadir awoke to the pitter-patter of rain in the dark of night. Arm over his eyes, he lay in the unfamiliar bliss of a stranger's top sheet, warm from A'Hei slumbering beside him. A'Hei's tattoos had gone all the way down his back and across his legs. Hypnotizing. Nadir's stomach was still full of A'Hei's cooking, fish that had tasted oily and real.

Had he missed normal?

Wait.

Rain.

Nadir whipped up. He threw the sheet over A'Hei and stuffed himself into his clothes.

"Mm, what are you doing?" A'Hei mumbled as the rain beat the roof.

"I've stayed too long." Nadir yanked his laces tight. He glanced back and forced a smile. "Sorry." He ran out into the night and down the muddy path.

The road slipped beneath him and wet wild grass flanked him, batting at his face in the wind. The rain poured onto his clothes and splashed up his ankles. He shielded his eyes against the blurred neon pinks of gulper eels drifting through the air. Their mouths hung open like pelicans, brushing the overgrowth, searching for birds and silver sunfish.

"Where are you going!" A'Hei shouted from his doorstep, voice muffled by the rain.

Nadir jerked to a halt, heart pounding. The island rose up behind A'Hei's house, lit up like Christmas with what Nadir had brought in.

A roar echoed up from the coast.

"Shit, shit, shit." Nadir sprinted down the footpath to the main street, nothing more than a compacted footpath itself. In the distance, silver bucked across the black waves, wild.

Nadir's big chest heaved like the batting trees. His ship was on the other side of the damn cove.

Like a shock, A'Hei grabbed his shoulder, huffing, "What's going on? What was that?"

"Machi. The cove's too shallow. He can't escape the noise." Nadir jerked free and ran, cursing himself for thinking the weather would hold. At least the cruise ship had gone, but now all the locals would see Machi. What if they tried to catch him?

In his peripheral, Machiavelli flailed on the waves, a bucking bull. His grand tail slapped the cove, propelling whitecaps toward shore. Coral ripped from the rocks and piled against shivering huts.

"Dammit, the wind's blocking the way." It propelled right into the cove. If he sailed a close haul and then turned right at the mouth, he could get out, but would Machi follow him that close to the rocks? "Shit! Markus!"

"Who?" A'Hei chased, wiping rain off his face.

"Markus. She can't keep up while I'm sailing, so I let her out when I pick up supplies. *Markus!*"

"What does she look like?"

"She's an orange angler fish, about yae big." He held his hands a foot apart. "She glows amber. I can't leave without her. *Markus!*" Nadir called for her all the way to the dock.

His ketch rocked with the flailing seas. Machiavelli's bellows challenged the wind itself, echoing across the mountains and the clouds.

Nadir jumped on his ship and leaned over the rails at a sparse, orange glow. He dove over the side.

The warm water crashed in his ears. He bashed into rocks lined in amber, searching. For a moment, he dragged himself up for air and plunged back down. Distant, golden light flashed.

Markus quivered between jagged basalt, terrified of Machiavelli's roar.

Nadir scooped her up and kicked for the surface. His head broke water only to be swept over. Markus shook in his hold. He swam, one-armed to his ship.

A'Hei grabbed Nadir and hauled him up, staring at Markus' spiked teeth.

"Thanks," Nadir huffed and pushed past into the cabin. His muscles wouldn't stop trembling. He released Markus into the closed-off air, telling her, "Everything's going to be okay. We'll get your brother out of here." He burst out of the cabin.

A'Hei clutched the metal railing, caught between the spiritual lights and Machiavelli's agonized throws. "What can I do?"

"You can't stay here. I'm not coming back." Nadir started the engine.

A'Hei grabbed his arm. "Let me help–"

Machiavelli roared, a haunting, ear-numbing cry. The rain beat down on the men, pooling around their feet.

A'Hei glared. "I'm not a stowaway. You dove too deep too fast. Let me help."

Nadir struggled. A'Hei would be stranded on his boat– he couldn't return to the island, not if they knew about Machi–

"Hurry! That beautiful creature's hurting."

"Ack," Nadir pushed his wet hair back. "Fuck. Cast us off."

Nadir instructed while he steered them into a close haul, aiming as near as possible for Machiavelli. The wind fought him, whipping his sails. Machiavelli's writhing scales gleamed in the lights from his boat, undulating with the storm surges.

"Come on, Machi, follow," Nadir hissed as they approached. "Come on."

Machiavelli surged under the ketch and around it, back toward the dock.

"Shit, he's scared of the rocks. This cursed wind and rain. If either would let up…" He wiped his face on his wetter arm.

"Can we drag him to the open ocean?"

Nadir's gaped at the rope A'Hei held. He'd tied Nadir's dock and spring lines together.

"Is that a yes?"

"I can't lasso him!"

A'Hei wrapped the rope around his palm and handed the other end to Nadir. "Secure that." Then, with two fluid steps, he swung over the rails and into the black water.

"A'Hei!" Nadir struggled to spot the broad man's strokes. "Goddammit, you'll drown!"

Nadir tied down the other end and monitored the unfurling rope, useless, hoping, waiting. He retied the hasty knots A'Hei had made between the lines.

Meanwhile, A'Hei swam into rougher waves, pushing toward Machiavelli.

The black waves crested and fell, sucking A'Hei into their currents. A'Hei spat out seafoam as he rode the waves, tracking their swells and working with them. Machiavelli moved so much like a banded sea snake, A'Hei tracked his movements and predicted where he'd go. Gradually, A'Hei crept closer.

Machiavelli's yellow teeth were longer than A'Hei's arm. The dragon's flaring nostrils could encompass his head. Growling, Machiavelli thrust beneath the surface and flew across the rocks. He shot up into the rain, stories tall, and crashed into the churning waves.

A'Hei sucked in a freediving breath and ducked underwater. He chased those white scales down, down into the depths. Machiavelli surged across his rope head-first, long body shooting past. A'Hei swam up and around, then tied a slipknot as Machiavelli's tail approached. A'Hei pulled on the rope.

It snagged the base of Machiavelli's tail.

Machiavelli's roar cascaded over the seafloor, rattling A'Hei's bones. The man broke through the surface.

"Go!" he shouted at Nadir.

Nadir leaned over the railing, drenched. He yelled over the rain, "Grab the rope! I'll pull you in!"

"I'll swim back!"

He'd fucking drown.

"Go!"

Machiavelli hauled the rope, dragging the boat into the shifting wind. Nadir cursed. With a last look at A'Hei treading black water, he steered the boat toward the open sea.

In the creeping dawn, Nadir pressed his forehead to the boat's railing. His legs kicked over the side, arms folded on the cold metal. The easy sun painted the ocean pink and blue.

White scales slipped up to the surface, solemnly twinning the boat. Machi raised his head from the ocean.

"Feel better?" Nadir asked, exhausted.

Machi ducked just beneath the surface, big turquoise eyes apologetic.

"It's okay. I shouldn't have left you there."

Nadir glanced west at the smallest pinprick of Rapa Iti on the horizon. There was no port on the island's other side, where the ocean spread wide for Machi. Even if Nadir grounded his ship, he'd have to hike through the hills and forest to reach the cove.

"Dammit, I can't spend all my years wondering if he drowned. We're changing course." Nadir pushed himself up.

Machi puffed, throwing seafoam over the rails.

Nadir wiped his face on his salty sleeve. "Stop that. If nothing else, I shouldn't leave Rapa Iti covered in sea spirits."

Machi slipped back toward Rapa Iti, scales gleaming orange with the dawn.

"You'd best haul this ship off the sand when it's time to go!" Nadir scolded, unsure when that would be. Oddly, half a day's hike didn't sound so bad. "God, it'd be nice not to file taxes next year."

The Jackalope

ROBERT PIPKIN

There are many weird creatures in the world. Some are extremely hard to find and even harder to understand. Some people say the chupacabra is a blood-sucking pig-dog with no hair, but no one's ever seen one. Some people say the snipe is a flightless bird of the night that everybody hunts, but no one's ever caught one. Some people say there's a lake in Scotland with some gigantic thing living in it that's a cross between a dinosaur and a big log. Some people even claim to have seen this thing called a platypus that has a tail like a beaver and a bill like a duck and lays soft eggs. Some people say that the people that say these things are just nuts.

Then there's the jackalope. The jackalope looks like a giant jackrabbit with antlers. Their roar sounds like an old man sneezing, their purr sounds like kids misbehaving. The jackalope likes beer mixed with whiskey and leaves tracks that look like those of other animals. These scientific, indisputable, proven facts are all well-known and taught at all the finest American community colleges, but no one's ever told the story of how the jackalope came to be. This is that story.

The jackalope is like a recipe, just like baked beans, or barbecue, or s'mores, or Twinkies, and this is the part where we'll talk about the ingredients.

First, there was the jackrabbit. He lived on the Western edge of the Grand Canyon. Jackrabbits are big rabbits that live in the desert. Jackrabbits have fantastic vision. They're fast because of their big feet. They have excellent hearing because of their big ears, but they are terrible listeners. On that day, that jackrabbit was the fastest and most mischievous jackrabbit ever. He knew he was faster than all the other jackrabbits, and he believed he was probably faster than any other animal in the canyon. He was looking for a chance to prove it. For now, we'll set him aside and let him marinate in the next few parts of the story.

Then, there was the pronghorn antelope. She lived on the Eastern edge of the canyon. Pronghorn antelopes kinda look like deer, but they're smaller and much, much faster. Pronghorn antelopes have fantastic vision. They're fast because of their tiny hooves. They have excellent hearing thanks to their complex ears, but they are terrible listeners. On that day, that pronghorn antelope was the quickest and troublemakingest pronghorn antelope ever. She knew she was faster than all the other pronghorn antelopes, and she believed she was probably faster than any other animal in the canyon. She was looking for a chance to prove it. For now, we'll set her aside and let her marinate in the next few parts of the story.

Finally, there was the Havasupai medicine man. On a clear, hot, sunny afternoon, sometime between the day George Washington was born and yesterday, the man was at that spot that's located nine miles from both the Eastern and Western edges of the Grand Canyon. It's the spot precisely, specifically, and exactly halfway between the two sides that pretty much make up the widest point of the canyon. At that spot he was on a quest to become one with the universe and find all the answers to every question, since that's what medicine men did. He was dressed in the finest Havasupai feathers and pelts and was dancing magical dances and speaking magical spells and howling magical howls and tossing around things like bones and scales and claws for more magic. For now, we'll set him aside and let him marinate in the next few parts of the story.

This is when the jackrabbit and the pronghorn noticed each other. Despite the distance of eighteen miles, they both had fantastic vision and it was a very clear and sunny day. Just by looking at the pronghorn, the jackrabbit could tell that it was very fast. Just by looking at the jackrabbit, the pronghorn could tell that it was very fast. They both got the exact same idea at the exact same time:

"If we race, I will win, and it will prove that I am the fastest creature in the world ever!"

Just then, the Havasupai medicine man, in the middle of his dancing, yelled the word, "Hey!"

Both the jackrabbit and the pronghorn heard this, but since they're both terrible listeners they both thought he'd actually said, "Race!" The jackrabbit sneered across eighteen miles at the pronghorn, and the pronghorn scowled across eighteen miles at the jackrabbit.

Then the medicine man, in the middle of his dancing, yelled the word, "Hee!"

Both the pronghorn and the jackrabbit heard this, but since they're both terrible listeners they both thought he'd actually said, "Me!" which they both took to mean he wanted them to race to him. The pronghorn antelope arched its back and jumped a couple of times, sort of like an angry cat, to show the jackrabbit how big and scary it could be. The jackrabbit then drummed his left foot against the ground so fast it sounded like a ten-pound hornet, to show the pronghorn what it would sound like when the jackrabbit ran his race.

Then the medicine man, in the middle of his dancing, yelled the word, "Ho!"

Both the jackrabbit and the pronghorn heard this, but since they're both terrible listeners they both thought he'd actually said, "Go!" and they both leapt over their side of the canyon and took off for the medicine man.

The Havasupai medicine man saw none of this and kept on dancing.

In case you don't know, and based on what I know about you I'll bet my ring toe that you don't, the sides of the Grand Canyon at this widest point are several hundred feet straight down from top to bottom. This can make running difficult. The jackrabbit had launched himself into a smooth straight dive with his paws stretched before and behind him, but he didn't feel like he was going fast enough. He started running straight down the canyon wall. The pronghorn had somersaulted over the side into a beautiful headfirst nosedive, but she didn't feel like she was going fast enough. She started running straight down the canyon wall.

The Havasupai medicine man saw none of this and kept on singing.

The base of the canyon walls curved gently to slope down to the canyon floor. Both the pronghorn and the jackrabbit hit these slopes at exactly the same time. Like a bolt of lightning, the jackrabbit leveled off and tore up the ground beneath him he was moving so fast. Like a bullet, the pronghorn leveled off and turned the dirt to smoke beneath her she was moving so fast.

The Havasupai medicine man saw none of this and kept on throwing magic bits into the air.

For the next few seconds, the racers poured on the speed. The Grand Canyon shook and shuddered and rang like a bell beneath the onslaught of those eight feet. The dirt and rocks and sagebrush beneath those feet burned up like a wildfire in a twister. The Havasupai medicine man saw the jackrabbit, and he saw the pronghorn, and threw his hands up in the air.

They all crashed into the exact same spot at the exact same time.

For a moment just shy of the time it takes to crack an egg, there was a flash of light the color of sunrise. For a moment just shy of the time it takes to fall in love, there was a silence like the silence just after the rain stops. All was still.

There, at that spot precisely, specifically, and exactly halfway between the two sides that pretty much make up the widest point of the Grand Canyon, there was no jackrabbit, there was no pronghorn antelope, there was no Havasupai medicine man. There was a jackalope. It stood as tall as a horse. It shook its antlers. It looked around as though it didn't know where it was. Then the wind changed and its nose twitched with a whiff of whiskey from a poorly closed flask in New York City. The jackalope turned and hopped off to find the source of the smell, leaving behind footprints that looked like they came from a fish.

Healers' Song

ANGEL WHELAN

The man on the bridge was alone and afraid.

I could sense his fear, his reluctance to jump. He kept pacing back and forth, coughing hard and pulling his face mask down to his chin, drawing in great gulps of air between fits. I sat on the jetty below watching, waiting for him to find the courage within himself. As he stared into the icy black water I sang softly, letting the wind carry my mournful melody upwards. I saw him look around, aware of the music, but unable to place its source.

I sang of love, of family left bereft, of unfulfilled dreams. My song weaved a picture of a world without him, where only the jagged hole of his absence remained. His wife lying broken and sobbing on the bed that would forever more be too big. His mother's confusion as she waited in her retirement home for a weekly visit that never came. His daughter walking alone down the chapel aisle, tears in her eyes as she faced the congregation with only his picture in a locket to accompany her.

I saw how my song affected him; he stopped pacing and listened intently, his eyes glazed over as he let my words flow through him. But there was another song in his heart. I could hear that just as clearly as he heard mine, though it was a silent tune. His song spoke of unemployment, of lost medical insurance, of unpaid bills. It told of the virus that had stolen from him his best friend just weeks ago, and that now coursed through his own body bringing fever, pain, and terror. There was a desire in his song, a longing for the release from responsibilities. He didn't want to be a burden on his family. His death would be better than an expensive hospital visit.

I sang louder – of Thanksgivings and Christmases, of grandchildren yet to come, crowding around him for a bedtime story. I described tropical vacations, anniversary dinners, a promotion. But my song was too weak. Gone were the days when I could change a man's heart without breaking a sweat. The city was so much louder these days, with the constant wail of sirens and beeping of car horns. I still returned here each night, trying to bring hope and light to the world of humanity, but lately I felt my powers weaken.

The river grew more polluted and less able to nourish me. The fish dwindled in number. The sweet-tasting pickerel weed that had once been abundant was scarcer now, while the hardier algae choked the riverbanks. As the waterways suffered so my strength diminished, my voice weaker and less persuasive.

A splash broke the silence. Damn it, he jumped! I dove into the inky water, swimming as fast as I could upstream, the water a murky emerald green around me. In the past, I might have seen him from far away, my vision clear enough to guide me straight to him. But now there were too many discarded tires and garbage bags. Human detritus crowded my vision. I found him, but it took longer than it should have. He wasn't breathing as I hauled him towards the bank.

Dragging him onto the shore was quite a feat. On land I was slow and awkward, those features that made me so athletic in the water – chiefly my snake-like lower half – rendering me disabled here. It took all my strength to heave his bulky body onto the riverbank. He was blue around the eyes and nose, his skin as cold as death. I held his head on my lap, stroking the careworn wrinkles on his forehead. Bending forward, I lowered my mouth to his, gifting him my song. I let my words pour out, feeling them fill his lungs and spread throughout his body. I forced hope into him like an electric pump filling an airbed. His eyes fluttered open, and he turned to his side, spewing the tainted river water out in great gushes. I held him until he stopped choking. His eyelids drooped as I sang my farewell song; the one that told of forgotten encounters and secrets never told. Then I crawled back to my wheelchair, hoisted myself into it, and rolled away towards the busy streets of Philadelphia.

Almost a week had passed since the man on the bridge when I started to feel unwell. For the first few days it was not too bad, just a slight malaise and aching bones reminding me that I was not immortal. I grew weaker by the hour; unsure my body could fight this virus. So strange, I had long assumed I was immune to the diseases of the mortal realm, yet here I was, struck down and fighting for every breath. If Mother were still alive she would know what to do; it was her idea that I move to this condo with its refreshing saltwater pool in the basement.

But human lives are brief, and 80 years had passed since she took pity on that deformed, abandoned baby in the hospital. I don't regret our years together – all the wisdom she imparted and the love she gave so freely, never once making me feel less than or imperfect. These last ten years without her have been the hardest, and I would gladly have died alongside her in that hospice, or imparted some of my longevity into her failing body.

The thought of suicide crossed my mind often since that awful day when I let go of her hand forever and allowed grief to consume me. But she was as smart as she was kind; she extracted a promise from me as she lay dying, her breaths as ragged as my own are now.

She said, "Merin, when I'm gone, keep the hope alive. This world is so dark nowadays. They need you, sweetie, the people need you. Be their light. Do it for me."

And there is no way to refuse a request like that, is there? If I die, I fail her. I can't. I just can't. But it gets harder.

I fell asleep for a while, and when I awoke my skin was burning hot, and so dry I felt as though I might crack all over. I had to cool down, had to leave the stifling air in my 6th floor apartment. I somehow made it to the elevator through sheer force of will. Every movement felt like my last ounce of energy, over and over, with every push on the wheelchair tires.

I reached the basement level and panicked when I saw the sign on the gym door–

'Closed due to Covid Restrictions.'

Surely it would be locked…but the janitor must have forgotten to change the key code. Beyond the door, the intoxicating scent of brine called to me. I left the overhead strip lights off so nobody would come looking, but I could do nothing about the security cameras or the underwater lighting that gave the pool its mystical glow. I was fairly certain nobody would be monitoring the TV screens, since Barney the security guard was on a ventilator in Frankford hospital, unlikely to recover. I was fond of Barney; he always looked the other way when he saw me heading down to the gym in the night, despite the Condo Association rules. He called me Ariel and teasingly told all the residents I was a mermaid, because my adaptive swimwear has a large black flipper on the bottom. He did it to make me feel beautiful; special, rather than special needs. That kind of person is a rare creature indeed. He didn't deserve to die like this, with a tube jammed down his throat and no loved ones by his side. The pandemic stole everything from the people it touched, yet left others completely oblivious to their plight. I would never fully understand the human capacity for selfishness.

Tossing the blanket off my lap, I left my chair beside the shallow end. Here the Persian blue tiles sloped gently into the water. I slipped from the seat and hesitated a moment, before pulling my cotton nightdress over my head and discarding it with the towels. This was a crazy thing to do –I had never before swum naked in the pool. But I was not well enough to wriggle into my constrictive swimsuit, with its black mesh sides and plastic flipper. If I was dying it wouldn't matter who saw me, and my body thirsted for the healing salt.

The water engulfed me and I swam along the bottom, allowing it to flow like balm through my aching body. Filling my swim bladder, I breached the surface, my coughing reduced now, my gills no longer flaring wide with every strain of my ribcage. I floated for a minute, resting my aching arms and watching as my long hair rippled out around me. I tried to avoid looking at my body, but couldn't help it, even though it repulsed me just as much as it had in my teenage years. I hadn't changed much with the passing decades, though my breasts had swelled and my hips widened with the unfulfilled promise of fertility. I sometimes longed to be an amputee, to live life without my lower half. My gills could be explained away – as scars perhaps, from a surgery. There was no earthly explanation for the rest of my body. How my waistline changed abruptly from silky softness at the navel, becoming mottled and leathery and rough to the touch. The purplish tinge of that scaly skin as it stretched over my impossibly elongated spine, following each bumpy vertebra all the way to the end. The way there was only a single limb where two ought to be; snakelike, gradually narrowing until the bottom, where my horrific feet sprouted like a hellish plant taking root in the ground. My long, bony toes splayed outwards, the skin between each translucent, the delicate pink of a conch shell. If that weren't strange enough, each toe had an extra dorsal metatarsophalangeal joint, adding to the creepy way they undulated as I swam. I was a freak, and if any small child were to see me in the pool right now, the Little Mermaid would be the furthest thing from their mind.

I knew I shouldn't linger, but I felt some of my strength return to me, as it always did when I swam. The pool was no substitute for the river, where my heart yearned to be right now, but already my breathing was less painful. Maybe the virus was only ravaging my mammalian lungs, a small and unexpected mercy. I found myself hypnotized by the rippling of the tiles under the cloudy pool lights. My inner eyelids closed and things grew hazy, the water almost purple through the thin red membrane. I wanted to sleep; to sink down onto the smooth tiled floor and let the water embrace me. I let the sound of my muffled heartbeat lull me into a dreamlike state, feeling the pain leave my body in waves.

Suddenly, the darkness behind my eyes brightened to a light violet. The lights! Someone turned on the lights in the natatorium! I opened my eyes, swimming at speed for the deep end nearest the door, hoping the darker water would hide my body from whoever was there.

"Hello?" A friendly male voice called out, echoing slightly against the tiles. "Is somebody in here?"

"Go away!" I pleaded. "I…I didn't know anyone would come. I have Covid! Keep away!"

"That's okay" The voice replied, drawing nearer. "I'm a junior resident at Children's Hospital of Philadelphia – I'm already vaccinated, and besides, I had the damn thing back in September. So I'm double immune now."

"But I'm naked!" I yelped. I decided if the man entered the pool, I would drag him to the bottom and hold him under until he ran out of air. I had never done that before, but all the legends made it sound easy. He walked nearer, and I could tell he was tall, maybe 6ft 3, with black hair that coiled tightly. His eyes were open, but he didn't seem to be looking in my direction.

"Well, I'm blind, so you needn't be afraid. But if it makes you feel better, I can turn around until you get out and grab your clothes."

"Um, yes. Do that. Turn around. Thank you." I hesitated, reluctant to give up the safety of the water. The man turned his back, began humming to put me at my ease. I swam back for the shallow waters, pulling myself out and grabbing my nightdress. I struggled to get it over my head, but finally found the armholes and wriggled into it, still soaking wet. Adrenaline rushed through me and I was able to pull myself up into the chair without too much trouble, pulling the blanket around my body defensively. There, surely he wouldn't do anything to a disabled woman, especially one as sick as I was.

"Ok, I'm decent" I called out, and he turned towards my voice, smiling. I noticed he had dimples.

"I have a mask if you want me to wear it," he replied, pulling his top over his head with one hand in a way that was strangely mesmerizing. His skin was the rich warmth of clay.

"No, you're fine. Like I said, I already have the virus. And I'm so sorry for using the pool…I know I'm not meant to. I don't want to infect anyone. I was just so feverish and needed to cool down…"

"That's fine, nobody should be coming in here anyhow, I'm only here because I'm a lawless creature of the night." He smiled again, while still not looking at me directly.

It was so refreshing. Never before had I met someone who didn't see me as different. As Other. To this man I was not the poor disabled girl, pretty face, shame about the broken body. I was an exotic woman of mystery, seeking the excitement of a nighttime skinny dip. I was cold now, the wet fabric clinging to my skin.

"Why *are* you here?" I asked, wheeling as quietly as I could towards him.

"I just did a double shift at the hospital, and I ache all over. I felt like a half-hour in the hot tub, followed up with a cool off in the pool. I do it most nights since I started working the ICU – it's intense up there, so much death and sadness. I've been getting insomnia, but the water helps soothe me." He kicked off his flip-flops and walked forward carefully, as though counting his footsteps. He found the hot tub and grabbed the rail, feeling his way in. "Aaaah. That feels so good. I swear water is magical. Don't you think? Nothing a hot soak can't cure."

"Except Covid, it seems," I responded glumly, another coughing fit overcoming me.

"Well, I guess it has its limitations. But you must be cold after your swim…care to keep me company for a bit? It's lovely and warm. Might help loosen your airways. And if you get worse, there's a handsome young doctor here to help. Besides, too much isolation isn't good for your health, you know."

He was right. I had friends, or at least, acquaintances at work. But I had been alone for months, since the store I worked for closed during the first lockdown. Unemployment kept me alive, but I could go days without talking to a soul. And that hot, bubbling water looked so inviting.

"Fine, but scooch over to the far side. I have pepper spray," I warned.

He laughed but he moved around the large hot tub, far enough away that I felt safe. Besides, if he was lying, I could drown him as easily in here as I could in the pool. I put my brakes on and grasped the sturdy metal bar, heaving myself up the steps backwards. I kept my nightdress on – no way was I ever getting naked in here again. It billowed up around me as the air bubbles burst to the surface. The hot salty water was just what I needed, and I felt my gills expand and contract, taking the warmth deep within me. My throat felt less scratchy in the steam.

"There, just what the doctor ordered, am I right?" He asked.

I nodded. We sat in companionable silence for a few minutes, and I rested my pounding head on the tile ledge, realizing with a thrill that this was the first time I had ever been alone with a man. "Oh, by the way, I'm Antoine." He rolled his eyes. "I know, but my Mama is Haitian. I just moved into 6E." He held out a hand across the water, and I shook it.

"I'm Merin. 6C, so we're practically neighbors."

"Awesome! That makes you the official welcoming committee then, because I haven't spoken to another resident since I got here before Christmas."

"Yeah, it's a pretty quiet place really. Mostly older residents who moved in before the price hikes. I usually have the pool to myself." I stretched my body, allowing my feet to uncurl in the foam and float to the surface, being careful to keep to my own side. The tumultuous water thumped against my spine from the jet sprays, soothing my deep aches. I allowed myself to float to the surface, my body rising and falling in syncopation with the water.

"Well, I hope you won't mind sharing your sanctuary with me. I chose this place for the pool, I'm a swimmer. Got the letter jacket to prove it."

I laughed. It had been so long since anyone talked to me, truly with me, not at me. People say they don't see disabilities, but in reality I wonder, how many actually have disabled friends? Maybe if you are one of the 'lucky' ones; those born healthy and injured at some later stage, maybe then you can cling on to the old friendships from your previous life. But for those of us born different, life is hard from day one. Ever since my mother rescued me from the medical waste bin, where I had been discarded as 'incompatible with life' by a revolted midwife, my life had been tough. I don't think anyone had ever talked to me without an undertone of guilt, or at best an empathic gentleness that felt a lot like patronizing. This man made me feel like a normal person for the first time. It was exhilarating.

"Isn't it rather hard to stay in your lane, being blind?" I asked. "Or being a doctor, for that matter...I don't think I ever heard of a blind doctor before."

"I'm not completely blind, but I wasn't exactly lying, either. Without my glasses everything is just blurry shapes really." He looked up, staring directly into my green eyes with his hazel ones. "I'm really sorry Merin, I just didn't want you to be afraid of me. You know, being a tall black dude in Philly...I'm used to white women thinking I am some kind of drug-addicted rapist."

My heart pounded in my throat. I thrust my body down, back into the comforting cover of the foamy water. He could see! Of course he could see. How stupid of me, stupid to trust a human. Eighty years of hiding, of keeping my secret safe. I could feel the heat rise in my cheeks as I fumbled behind me, intent on escaping the hot tub.

"Please, Merin! You don't need to hide from me. I won't tell anyone!" He held up imploring hands.

I thought I would throw up, my stomach was churning and my swim bladder felt full of lava. I tried to drag myself away from this terrifying moment, but as I rose from the water black dots started to swirl around my head, growing larger, covering my vision. I passed out.

I awoke in my own bed. Opening my eyes, I could see bright sunlight streaming in through the tiffany blue drapes. My fever was gone, and my head no longer pounded. I reached a hand to my face, pulling away a plastic mask that covered my mouth and nose. My hand hurt, and I saw a tube taped in place, leading to a pole with several IV bags hanging from it. What on earth was going on? I tried to remember how I had got here. Nothing.

"Merin? You're safe." There was a man in my room! I struggled to sit up, suddenly wide awake.

"Seriously, I promise you it's all fine – I went through a lot of effort to steal this equipment from work to make sure of that." It was Antoine, the stranger at the poolside. I sat up, realizing I was in a pink nightgown, not the white one I remembered wearing when I collapsed. I fell back against the pillows, my mind reeling. This man, this doctor – he saw me. All of me, presumably. He knew my shameful secret.

"Why are you here? Why can't you leave me alone?" I felt hot tears forming at the corner of my eyes, and I blinked my inner eyelids to clear my vision. His eyes opened wider for a moment.

"I told you, I'm a doctor, Merin. It's my job to save people. When you collapsed in the hot tub, I figured you probably didn't want me to call an ambulance, so I brought you back to your condo." He took my hand, placing an oximeter on my index finger.

"You gave me quite a scare you know. I've never treated…well, I mean…you presented complications. Your oxygen saturation dropped into the 80s, that's why you blacked out. So I took a few days off work and liberated some oxygen and saline drips from the supply closet."

I tried to think. For 80 years I kept myself hidden, never seeking medical aid, never revealing so much as a crooked toe to anyone.

"Why?" I said finally.

"Why? You mean, why help you?" I nodded. "Well I could hardly leave you there in the hot tub with your stats dropping, could I? You were dying. I mean it, if I hadn't put you on oxygen when I did, you wouldn't be here now."

"Thank you. I…it's just a lot. You know? This is new for me."

"I mean, it's not exactly an everyday occurrence for me either," he joked. "Plus think about how I felt – you were completely out of it, unable to give me your medical history, and I kinda figured you might not have insurance coverage or anything. So there I am trying to treat you like I would any woman in her mid 20's with covid…except this woman has gills in her rib cage! Suddenly I'm up half the night researching fish anatomy online and trying to figure if I need to stick you in the bath or check you for fin rot." He could see the horror cross my face as I realized he really had seen my whole body. His gaze softened and he patted my hand. "Seriously, Merin, I don't care if you're not human. You can be a half fish, half unicorn swamp creature from Jupiter for all I care. I just think you're a nice person, and I'm guessing things have been rough for you."

I let the tears flow, unable to hold back any longer. I sobbed like a child, and he sat there and let me, rubbing my back without saying a word until I got it out of my system.

"Nobody knows. Nobody can ever know...please, promise you won't tell anyone about me."

"What do I look like, a Ringling brother? Think I'm going to cage you up and sell tickets?" He was grinning, and I began to realize he was genuine. This man really didn't care about my oddities.

"Well, I mean a lot of people would pay to see me. You could probably pay off your med school debts with the proceeds." I gave a weak smile.

"Nah, you're lucky. I was a scholarship brat. Swim team, remember?"

I looked at his broad shoulders and firm biceps admiringly.

"I'm something of a swimmer myself," I said with a giggle rather unbecoming for someone of my age. We laughed until it made me cough again, and I realized something was happening. I wasn't scared anymore, and I was no longer lonely.

Time moved strangely over the next few days, with many hours of sleep interspersed with brief moments of lucidity. Sometimes I woke alone in the night, watching shadows on my bedroom ceiling. During the daytime Antoine fed me vegetable broth, my head propped up with a pile of pillows as he deftly spooned the hearty soup into my mouth. In the afternoons, when I had more strength, we would sit and chat about his work at the hospital. I saw the faint lines where the PPE mask had bruised his cheeks, but they were almost gone now. Sometimes there was a sorrow in his eyes that made me yearn for the river and the healing water. I was too weak to sing hope into him, so I held his hand instead, and listened as he poured out his tales of misery in the ICU. He spoke of long hours without a moment to sit down, rushing from one patient to the next as they each followed the familiar yet terrifying pattern of plummeting stats, intubation, and death. Another loss, another person, and the beds refilled as soon as they had new linens.

"How do you keep doing it, Antoine? How can you go back, day after day, trying to heal, when you know that you are doomed to keep failing?"

"I don't have the answer to that. When you're a healer, you don't have a choice. You put yourself out there, knowing it's going to hurt, knowing you will be exhausted and frightened and that some days your heart will beg you to give it up. But you push through it, keep going, because sometimes you come out on top. The patient survives, the cancer goes into submission, the parents get to take their child back home again. Even if the losses outnumber the wins, like in the Covid wards of the ICU, it just makes the wins a little sweeter."

"But it's wearing you down. I can see it; you suffer inside. I wish I could help you."

He smiled. "You do help. Telling you this stuff, opening up like this…it's helping me. I'm actually sleeping better again now. And look, you're getting better too. I mean, it's pretty exciting, being the first doctor ever to save the life of a mermaid."

I pulled a face. "Ugh, I hate that term. Mermaid. Seriously, it makes me sound like an underwater housekeeper."

"Hmm, well, maybe you're something else. Maybe you're a water nymph."

"That's no better, makes me feel like I should be hanging around ponds trying to seduce people."

"Well, what do you call yourself? What did your mother call you?"

I thought for a while. "I guess we never really talked about it much. She just accepted I was different and helped me find ways to blend in. She did sometimes call me her little Hope Bringer. Or Light Healer."

"That's pretty. Why did she call you that? Do you have magic powers you're keeping from me?" He punched my leg lightly.

"Not exactly. Not magic. But...you've read the stories about traditional mermaids, haven't you? How they lure unwitting sailors to a watery grave with their hypnotizing songs?" He nodded. "Well, singing is a part of it. When I'm near the river I sing, and humans that hear me...they tend to do what I say."

He appeared intrigued. "So you can drown people with just your voice? That's crazy!"

"No! I would never do that! I sing to help people. If they feel sad or want to die, I sing and they realize their life isn't so bad."

"Wait a minute. A couple of weeks back we had a man brought into the ER, they found him on the riverbank after an anonymous call. He said he'd jumped from the bridge to kill himself, but he didn't know how he ended up on the opposite bank, no longer suicidal. Was that you?"

"Yes. I tried so hard, but his emotions were too strong. I couldn't stop him from jumping. My voice seems to be less powerful as the riverside gets more built up. Too much ambient noise."

"You saved his life, Merin! He's still in the hospital, but he's in the step-down unit. He'll be going home sometime this week. So you're a healer too, just like me."

We sat together for a while, enjoying the comfortable silence of longtime companions. I felt as though we had known each other for a lifetime, the connection we shared. My heart rejoiced. But I heard a muted singing, a tiny voice barely perceptible reaching out to me from deep within him. The song spoke of untold struggles, of the aching struggle to make it in a world that thought a young Black male could never amount to anything. It whispered to me about the fear of being stopped by cops, the way teachers graded him more harshly than his white peers, the sheer weight of carrying around the constant reminder that he should be grateful to live in a time of 'equality.' There was an inherited sadness from the generations of ancestors before him, and a desire not to wear his heritage on his sleeve.

It made me realize I was privileged. I could hide my ugly, misshapen feet with a well-placed blanket. I could wheel into any room and be assured of a friendly greeting, even if it came with pitying glances. The only doors closed to me were the ones without wheelchair access. Nobody ever expected me to be anything, there was no struggle to constantly be better than others, harder working, more conscientious, more polite. I had never in my life had to pretend to be blind simply to make someone else less afraid of me.

"Take me to the river. Please, I need you to take me to the river tonight."

He looked at me, searching for answers in my eyes. "If I do that, will you swim away from me forever?"

"No. I promise. I don't think I could go back to the loneliness I knew before I met you. But there is something we need to do, and we can only do it there."

Moonlight caressed the water, bathing it in a milky light. Antoine parked his beat-up old Toyota Camry near the entrance to the wooden dock, lifting me out of the backseat and into my waiting chair. He pushed me towards the end, stopping short and putting the brakes on. He carried me the last few steps, lowering me gently down and then sitting beside me, our feet dangling out over the water.

"Are you going to swim, Merin? Can I…can I watch you?" I nodded.

"I need to swim a little, the river brings me strength. It heals me like medicine heals you."

I hesitated, then removed my coat and dress, laying them on the splintered deck. My cheeks reddening with embarrassment, I dove into the frigid water. I felt truly alive, my gills opening up and making me one with the river. Sometimes I broke the surface, allowing my swim bladder to fill with oxygen and floating for a while. I felt Antoine's eyes on me, but it didn't feel wrong anymore, I trusted him. Finally I swam back, reaching my arms out towards him.

"You have to come in here with me now. Please."

He stood up, backing away. "Are you crazy? It's got to be freezing in there, it's January! No way Merin, uh-uh."

"Please, Antoine! I know it's cold, but you won't feel it when you are with me. Honestly. And I'm too weak to do this on the bank, it has to be in the river itself!"

He scratched his head, looking around nervously. "I don't know…how do I know you aren't just tricking me so you can drown me? You merfolk have a bad rep you know."

"You know me better than that. Come on, don't be afraid. Please."

He sighed and gave in, taking off his clothes until he was down to just his boxers. "I must be insane," he muttered, jumping in beside me.

He went under, then rose up, gasping from the shock of the icy water. I darted in close, taking his face in my hands, and I kissed him. His lips were warm and full, and my heart leapt as I felt him kiss me back, encircling my waist with his arm. I pulled back, and he looked at me in wonder.

"I'm not cold anymore! How did you…?"

"I don't know. It's just another weird thing about me."

I let him go, swimming away from him, not far, just out of reach. "I'm going to sing now, Antoine. I need you to listen carefully." He nodded solemnly, treading water.

I sang of his beauty and strength. I sang of his ancestors' pride and his patients' gratitude. I sang of mourning wives whose only comfort was the knowledge their husbands had not died alone. My voice rose like a wave of love, banishing his inner demons, taking his depression and smashing it against the rocky shore. I took his frustrations at the system that held him back, and I made him see that he was always more than, never less. Finally, I sang of my own heart, and how he had entered it so completely. My song complete, I swam into his arms, resting my head on his shoulder.

"You saved me," he murmured softly into my hair.

"You saved me first."

A Guide for the Lover of Jorogumo

SARINA DORIE

If you find yourself attracted to beautiful Japanese women into bondage, consider a jorogumo like I did. Legends tell that this itsy-bitsy spider isn't so itsy bitsy when she reaches puberty at 400 years old and develops some magic sexiness. With the upper body of a woman, and the lower body of a giant spider, she's not one to disappoint. After spending all those centuries eating insects and climbing up waterspouts, can you blame this demon spider for wanting to seduce virile young men? Contrary to popular belief, these multi-limbed, arachni-disiac women aren't hungry for your flesh – they're hungry for your love.

How do I know? I don't want to kiss and tell, but let's just say I am an experienced lover of all sorts of monster ladies. The real problem isn't convincing one to make you her love slave – it's finding one of these sexy recluses before someone else does.

All those dwerps on the internet say to stay away from large bodies of water when you're alone because a jorogumo might be there, and she'll snatch you up and bring you below. So what if drowning is the third leading cause of accidental deaths in Japan? I know better than to listen to those haters. In a jorogumo's mind, water + cute, nerdy businessman=extreme horniness. Sure, sometimes in the heat of the moment a jorogumo just doesn't know when to stop. I won't make the same mistakes as amateurs and get myself drowned. My lady and I are going to avoid large bodies of water and stick to hot tubs and showers for the horizontal tango.

Of course, a lake isn't how I met Kuroko anyway. As if I would have time to get away to the countryside and go to a lake when I work seventy hours a week! We met online.

Here's what to expect on a date with a jorogumo. She likes to start with some music. Usually she'll play a stringed lute called a biwa in a quiet, remote shack, free of distractions to set the mood. However, I had a feeling, from the piercings and Gothic Lolita attire in Kuriko's profile picture, she would want to try something a little less traditional. I suggested going to a little ramen shop and then karaoke for our first date.

Her text back to me demonstrated how thrilled she was: *Darwin, you should get an award for such a good idea. Or maybe just a reward…from me.*

After an evening of music and snacks, these feisty ladies are going to want more than just a kiss good night. This class of yokai demons aren't into taking things slow. Often times jorogumos are accused of using their venom to weaken a man so that he falls under her spell. This is just hooey. It's the wild sex all night long that weakens the man.

At least, that's what she said when we instant messaged each other.

Many jorogumos resent the connotation that they make a man their 'victim.' They prefer consensual encounters with submissive males who like being tied up with spider silk. The fun doesn't stop there. My jorogumo's wide range of sexual fetishes will make *Fifty Shades of Grey* look like Fifty Shades of Boring Wimp when she's done with me.

I haven't actually read the book, but she has. She's going to bring it on our date when we meet for the first time. We'll eat ramen and then sing karaoke in a private booth all alone. I can't stop thinking about all the kinky things she can do with eight arms all at once.

She said I'll never go on a first date with anyone else again after she's done with me. I can only hope it's true!

Fireflies and Thieves

NEETHU KRISHNAN

When the egg of mayhem cracked to life a ten-minute walk away from her grandmother's ancestral house, Naina had just settled down with rice and curry at the corridor table illuminated by the kerosene lamp.

There was no telling how long this power outage would last – a common occurrence here in Kerala – especially come India's monsoon season, so Naina wolfed down dinner while suicidal flies exploded in the lamp.

Picking out the light-dazed bugs crashing into her food was a minor annoyance compared to the agony of watching their winged flutters crackle in the tongue of the flame. She'd gently cup and fling the bigger ones into the front yard thickets, hoping they'd forget the luring lamp and fly to unburning solaces of light.

Cordoning off the majority of them from the death trap, however, was a lesson in futility. Her grandmother, stubborn as always, refused to have an inverter installed; she was the one who lived in the house after all, Naina and her parents lived in Bangalore and visited only briefly during vacations, so they had no choice but to let her be, with her candles and opaque-gray kerosene lamps.

The synchronized rhythm of the cymbals and cow-hide drums resounding from the nearby temple stuttered to stray beats, then stilled abruptly. Naina thought she heard a muffled galloping in the silence that followed, but it could have been an artifact of her imagination. The commotion that erupted a few pulses later, however, was an undoubted occurrence.

Cries of a crowd, either agitated or frightened, echoed in the distance, their impact strained through the obstacle course of two-storey houses with high walls and forested plots, before reaching her grandmother's house tucked away from the main road. Naina pictured the temple elephant transitioning from calm to raging without warning, triggering a stampede among the gathered devotees. While it wasn't uncommon for captive elephants to stamp their mahouts to death and wreak havoc until their cloud of sudden-onset madness passed, as she'd often seen on Malayalam news channels back home, it also didn't seem plausible at the moment. She heard no furious trumpets, or the loud bells on the elephant's neck, or the heavy thump of their chained foot racing the path. Her grandmother's comment from the dark bedroom plucked her from the carousel of her morbid hypotheticals, and grounded her back to the present. *Fireflies forewarn of thieves entering a house*, she prophesied from her stoop on the bed, betel box in lap, raising her chin to the few flecks of gold twinkling in the room.

Naina smiled at her from the dinner table, each seeing the other like a portrait margined by the black wooden frame of the bedroom door. Her grandmother smiled back and coasted to other topics as Naina rose to wash her steel plate in the kitchen sink, continuing to voice her bemused exclamations over the sound of running water.

Ever since childhood, Naina'd heard her grandmother matter-of-factly state claims similar to the fireflies, despite their ridiculous baselessness. It was only one of the many Keralite Hindu beliefs ranging from silly to morose that her grandmother fed Naina and her mother. Some of the rest went as follows:

Accidentally stepping on clipped fingernails was akin to inviting the darkest of sorceries onto oneself. Girls venturing out of their homes at night had to have iron on them – a key or a knife – to stop evil spirits from latching on. Pointing your finger at a partridge and calling its name would cause them to starve to death. An owl hooting or sitting vigil over a house meant imminent death for one of the residents. After a head bath, one ought to pat dry the upper back first before any other body part to rid oneself of *Moodevi*, the goddess of ill-temperament and bad luck, who mounted wet backs unless ritualistically prioritized first in the wiping.

These were only a topical few she could recite off the top of her head and in her sleep. At twenty-six, Naina still didn't have the heart to laugh at or challenge her sweet old grandmother's beliefs, so, done with the dishes, she asked instead if she should latch the front door shut for the night. Her grandmother, crushing a betel leaf triangle stuffed with areca nuts and lime in a mortar and pestle, nodded, her toothless mouth quivering with the movement, for she wore her dentures, unironically, for all purposes except chewing.

The bisected front door was always left ajar throughout the day, shut only at night, the norm in most Kerala houses. As Naina reached her arms out for the door panels, her gaze skimming the sickle moon on the blue-black easel of night, she froze. A prickle snaked along her spine, more electricity than fear, as a pair of orange-yellow circles about twice the size of her head blinked at her from up the wild jack tree in the front yard.

The tree was a good distance away, near the wall that separated their plot from the one facing the road, a two-minute walk from the house's threshold. The twin lights could have been anything, but Naina was sure it was a pair of eyes, their fiery circles shutting and opening synchronously, as if seeing, seeing *her*. But what creature had such huge orbs, like a colossal squid's? How big was the head then? And how was the abominously-proportioned creature so high in the tree? Their eyes were level with the clumps of coconuts on the adjacent, full-grown palms – it didn't make sense. Even if it was a bird anomaly or a terrestrial beast with extraordinary height-scaling skills, shouldn't they be massive enough that the boughs would buckle under their weight?

In the preternatural stillness, the harder Naina tried to concentrate, the more she sensed the eyes fading, like a trickery of light, until there was nothing to look at but dense, indigo air. She wondered if it was her imagination, after all. A loud clang of steel jolted her attention to the kitchen. Fearing her grandmother had fallen, as was common lately with her osteoporotic knees buckling without warning, Naina raced to the kitchen. She found it empty, the rack of steel plates tipped over on the floor the only thing out of place. She rushed to the bedroom to find her grandmother dozing upright, still stooped over the bed, back against the smoke-browned wall, her gray-streaked head like a heavy lotus bud drooped at the stem's neck.

Back in the kitchen, Naina looked about again. Something stirred in the fireplace, but before she could brace herself, a lithe white body dropped from the chimney, into the ash of the firewood stove. Her heart caught in her throat, then settled back in her ribcage just as quickly. Her relieved smile teetered on laughter at the unperturbed cat jumping off the platform, landing on all fours this time, and strutting past her without any acknowledgement, oblivious to the comical face mask of ash-gray on their precious little milk-white face. She'd forgotten all about the cats, despite them being permanent visitors in her grandmother's kitchen ever since she could remember. She resisted the strong urge to stroke the silken fur of their forehead; she didn't want to interrupt their meal, so Naina watched, her heart bursting with adoration as the tiny pink tongue darted in and out while the cat chewed dried fish, white-whiskered eyes shut in concentration as they maneuvered the crunchy fishbones in their little mouth. Her grandmother religiously purchased and stored dried fish solely for this purpose. Cats, both stray and familiar, knew the shaved coconut shells filled with fish-mixed rice were meant for them, so they snuck in, licked shells clean and either went their way or stayed, alternating between snuggling in the stash of firewood below the platform and melting over the extinguished, but still warm, firewood stove at night. It was nice, Naina thought, to be of use to these animals without claiming them as your own.

While she loved the idea of a pet, the thought of actualizing into a pet owner petrified her. Her friends from graduate college were already years into raising tiny human replicas of themselves, but Naina couldn't bring herself to even brave a cat. Not that she was irresponsible or selfish or lacking in the ability to love, on the contrary, she brimmed with the excesses of their opposites. She was so highly sensitive and empathetic that, whenever she hypothesized owning a pet, or more precisely, a dog, she choked at the thought of their too-soon departure, assuming, of course, that she outlived the dog by virtue of average lifespans. The terror of losing a love so primal and pure outweighed all the perks of having one in the first place. She understood in theory the paradigm of having loved and lost rather than never having loved at all, but it worked only for those who recovered in reasonable time frames and didn't carry the scars of their loved ones or the world, fresh and raw within them forever.

The lights all around the house hissed back to life and the cat sauntered to the still-open front door, where they snarled and almost flew backwards. Zooming past Naina into the kitchen like their tail was on fire, the cat dug themselves deep into the pile of firewood, the entire pile shivering from their fright. Confused, Naina padded to the door.

When she saw what was there, the ground suctioned her feet to the earth. So many jarring things grabbed for her attention, she felt her brain had been sizzled and she'd vacated her body without dying. The eyes from before, she realized to her horror, were very much real, and they weren't high up because a creature perched in a tree as she'd imagined; they were up there because they were attached to a beast resembling a long-necked dinosaur.

The terrifying monstrosity had been on the ground all along, peering at her from their eight-storey-high head.

Naina's first impression was of a peacock, because they had a fair-share of resembling features, albeit with colossal manipulations to the original archetype. Except for their head and wings and feet, they were the familiar electric blue of common Indian peacocks. Their variegated and sturdy feet, birdlike in their claws and talons, towered over the entire height of her; Naina could stand between them and still have plenty of space above and around her, not that she'd ever attempt anything of the sort.

The creature's tail of nine feathers fanned out in spokes, spaced out far apart, like a semicircle of poised arrows, the brilliant rainbow eyes at the tapering end of each feather softening nothing of their intimidating length and heft. From their bulky middle, also like a peafowl's, the creature's smooth-muscled neck snaked out rubbery, like a cross between a brachiosaurus' bendy length and the refined and graceful curvature of a peacock. Their wings folded to their sides, tawny and sinister, looking to be the kind that opened to a wide, gliding wingspan, like an eagle or an owl. Their distinctive head, with front-facing, uniform amber opacities for eyes, resembled an Indian eagle-owl's, complete with beige and black marks on their feathers, and a beak that mimicked an owl's. Though of elephantine proportions, and lacking a discernible black center like the average owl's, the eyes somehow fit reasonably against the acreage of their tawny face. Between the two characteristically-curled featherish horns, the owl head also had a crest of spatula-tipped electric blue shooting out the center, like the crown of a peacock. Magnificently huge and chimeric though they were, Naina couldn't help but be spellbound by the creature. They were beautiful and miraculous, like all towering entities of nature, but more than merely being humbled and terrified, Naina felt an unexplainable kinship with the giant.

Standing there, the creature kept stamping their left foot, flattening the plantain trees and shrubs and the carpet of wild jackfruits. The rest of their body was mostly still, their eyes trained on her. She didn't know what it meant, but she was sure the night must end with her being a paltry snack to the creature. There was nowhere to run, and even if there was, trying to outrun this dinosaur-owl-peacock hybrid was a laughably naive idea. Seeing no point in resisting, Naina accepted that there was only one thing she could do: keep her grandmother safe, away from the beast's preying gaze.

Stepping out of the house without trepidation, Naina latched the door shut behind her, careful not wake her peacefully-dozing grandmother, and paced towards the giant.

Watching her approach, the creature swayed like a playful elephant, raising one foot at a time, dangling it mid-air and then switching to the other. Every time they moved an inch, they toppled or squashed yet another young tree or hedge in the plot. She slapped her forehead at the noise, worried her grandmother might be roused and rattle the front door searching for her, panicking at her disappearance. The beast paused swaying, cocked their giant owl head to their right. A befuddled Naina met their gaze from across the distance, trying to read this curious animal/bird for any hint of understanding; the concentrating-puppy impersonation was impossible to ignore, and she felt her pull towards the creature only strengthen with something akin to tenderness. She raised both hands in the air, palms out, and picked up the aluminum bucket, emptied of the water her grandmother kept stored by the entrance to wash her sandy feet before stepping inside the house. Placing it before her in the soil, she gesticulated with exaggerated emphasis first to the bucket, to her, and then to the spot beyond. She raised her leg in slow motion, settling it to the other side of the bucket without touching it and repeated with the other leg, trying to prompt the creature into understanding the principal of circumvention. The creature bent their serpentine neck towards the ground, considering their own tree trunk-like feet. Steadying back, they locked eyes with her and raised their right leg and clapped it to the ground in a step narrowly missing a young papaya tree. The sudden cold didn't make sense until Naina touched her palm to her cheek and realized tears were streaking down her face.

Naina scaled the plot towards the creature and they met her halfway, continuing their careful, awkward strides. Up close, she felt an exhilaration throbbing through her and for some absurd reason the incoherent remnants of her mental chatter kept addressing the beast as 'pet,' despite them being an obviously-ferocious carnivore capable of inhaling her like dust and spitting out her bone shards in the blink of an eye. Empathic though she was, she wasn't the kind to utter words of endearment. She *was* the kind who giggled at those who used babyish voices with animals, not out of judgement, but because she somehow found it hilarious and absurd.

Her eyes roved the ridgy expanse of the creature's feet, the only thing in her direct line of sight, and she noticed the claws caked in the rust of blood. She bit down a shriek of concern, mustering instead the calmest voice she could summon.

"Is this your blood? Does it hurt? Do bird feet even bleed?" she mumbled, inching closer with each question. The glint of silver on the creature's left foot, the reason for their twitch, hadn't caught her eye until she was near. Fear stabbed her chest.

"Oh, poor you!" she said, closing the distance calmly. The creature inspected her, three-fourths of their neck length bent downward, head still hovering above and away from her. She couldn't read their blank, glassy-eyed face, but still she made no move to back off.

"I'm going to pull this out, okay? I mean absolutely no harm to you, pet," she soothed, almost clamping her mouth shut at the endearment that had slipped past. She didn't know if it was embarrassment, or a yet-to-be-named emotion; she'd stepped past her immutable idea of herself, in a silly word, and that was one way to sign-off from this life, she thought.

Assuming the knife to be deeply embedded, Naina clutched at it with the combined might of both hands. It was only lodged topically, like a splinter, so she fell backwards, knife in hands, thankfully not soaked in any blood. A childish giggle tickled in her, but she wasn't sure it was the time or place. The owl head was suddenly beside her and her bones liquefied with its proximity. If she hadn't died yet, she was sure whatever was left of her had definitively vaporized into oblivion the instant the creature's head was level with hers. They studied her, not yet making a move to pulverize her in their ivory beak. They shut their eyes slowly, their holographic lids scintillating with moving colors. Her whole body was a hammering heart, and she hadn't ever felt so alive yet non-corporeal. Though she didn't know what or how to decipher it, she had a strange inkling that maybe, just maybe, the creature might not be after her flesh at all.

She heard herself ask the beast if she could touch the enchanting, muted brilliance that were their eyelids. When they didn't flinch or acknowledge her question, she tentatively reached out, grazing them with the lightest possible touch.

Their eyelids felt like the crumpled, delicate, gold wrapping paper of chocolate bars she used to save flattened between book pages, for use in fantastical crafts in a future that never arrived.

"Your beauty is scary yet divine," she whispered. Her mind and mouth seemed disconnected from each other and she was starting to mind the discord less and less. The eyelids stirred so she drew back her palm. They opened to amber glass circles alive with literal montages.

She ought to have been shocked, but she was way beyond horror or disbelief at this point. At first the pictures were blurry, as if seen through an opalescent film, and all she could make out was an unlit room with box-like shadows. The montages shivered and something exploded. With the tremor, there was light. The cloak of yolk yellow slid off the creature's eyes and everything was now crystal clear. A man with a torch clamped sideways in his mouth crawled up from what seemed a hole in the ground. He wore a backpack and a bunch of tools hung from the pockets of his double-breasted shirt and cargo pants. His face was sheathed in a balaclava and in the illumination of his white torch light, Naina recognized the boxes as treasure chests, with intricate and ancient-looking motifs carved on them. The man then proceeded to burn the side of the chest with some sort of electric cutter. As a rectangle of it came off, a mountain of sparkle tumbled out. The view by now was getting farther and farther away, the man still somehow in focus as his surroundings dwindled in size, as if the capturing eye was zooming out.

The robber pounced at the jewels and gold with an urgency that bordered on madness. He stuffed handfuls of treasure into his pockets like a madman, despite the limp backpack he carried on him. Something made him turn around and his eyes widened as far as they'd go. The next sequence was a blur. The creature's familiar foot, weirdly much smaller than the present, stamping and clawing at the man, kicking down the wall of the basement or whatever the place was, the robber, blood squirting out his thigh and abdomen, attempting to stab the creature's feet. The sight curdled Naina's stomach with disgust and mirrored pain. The foot with the barely-lodged knife sent the man flying into the midst of what looked to be a temple procession, the crowd parting and screaming at first, then collectively zeroing in at the sight of the temple jewels dangling from what remained of the robber's pockets, a hive of civilians and a couple of policemen obscuring the man from sight.

The shots then sped up, getting more and more aerial with each step, traversing and trampling walls and thatch huts and trees, until it slowed to the scene that iced and singed Naina's heart at once: it was her, at the front door of the house, eyebrows mashed together, mouth a circle, her face zoomed in on like someone had stuck a camera right before her, followed by a side profile as she smiled at the cat in the kitchen.

Her eyes welled, and she didn't know what to make of any of it.

"Do you have a home other than the temple vault?" she choked. "Where will you go now that you no longer fit in an egg or even a room? I would keep you if I could, I swear, but how do I keep you from vile people, or people in general?" she asked, as if expecting an answer. When the creature closed their lids once again, Naina placed her palm on their feathery forehead. "If you could be around I'd name you, you know. I'd call you Maya for your illusory eyes, and Mayur for the most of you that's a peacock. I'd call you Mayamayur," she said, her fingers trying to stroke her love in, the name in.

When Mayamayur's eyes opened, they played a new montage as if in answer. A green tropical patch in a deserted expanse, sky and land teeming with more of Mayamayur's kind, rubble like piles of prisming stones and jewels scattered over the landscape of their world, eggs the size of ostrich eggs crated in the soft sand. Naina sighed with relief and the tiniest resentment that she'd never see her giant again. Mayamayur would be okay, they needed no petting or protection, they had their own ilk and land, she consoled herself.

Mayamayur's eyes shut again and this time they disappeared before Naina's eyes, gradually growing invisible until their eyes remained like a constellation-pricked night. She smiled. A blink and Mayamayur was gone. No draft or movement suggested their exit and yet something hard plopped on her head as if dropped by a bird mid-flight. She picked the red velvet satchel off the ground, pulling apart its mouth to find ancient hand-hammered gold coins and a couple of gems; a rainbow-refracting feather the size of her palm was stuck to the felt exterior of the pouch. She hoped there was an anonymous donation box for bigger gifts at the temple, as she wasn't sure the gems would slip past the ordinary box slits meant for currency notes and coins. Of the two things she held in her palms, Naida liked to think one was a mistaken drop and the other a deliberate gift. She closed her fist around the latter, smiling at the ceiling of night.

Nain Rouge Appreciation

CARMAN C CURTON

"What the hell was that?"

"What was what?"

"I just saw a really small guy?"

"Like a Little Person?"

"No. Just a really tiny guy. Over there, by the door."

"*No.* You did not see nothin."

"Yeah. Right over there."

"You did *not* see *nothin.* Say it, college girl."

"I didn't see anything."

"Shit. Prolly too late," Crystal mumbled, turning her green cap backwards. "Take off your shoes and socks," she barked.

"What the–" Kami leaned against the cold case, stripping off her footwear.

"Okay. Shoes back on. No, shoes first. Socks over them. Do it!"

Kami plopped on the actual floor, stretching her socks over her shoes, while Crystal wiped the specials off the chalkboard, scribbling:

Cream=10¢

Boogers=free

"It's the Nain Rouge," Crystal said, talking fast. "S'posed to have a kind of Halloween parade next week to keep him happy. No time now. We got to do the tricks and dress up right away."

"Why?"

"I dunno. Auntie says keeps him away."

At Kami's blank look, Crystal sighed. "Girl, don't you have an Auntie?"

"Uh, she's in Santa Barbara."

"Well, it's what you gotta do. Or bad things happen. They canceled the parade in 2020. Remember that year?"

"That doesn't make any sense. Why would a very small man in an ugly red suit do that?"

"Maybe to make you appreciate your Auntie," Crystal said, dumping a handful of giant rubber eyeballs into the tip jar.

Kami grinned, flipping her name badge upside down so it read: IWAK. "Always appreciate your Auntie!"

The Heart of Gervascio

GEORGE IVANOFF

Fortescue Smythe hacked his way through the undergrowth, swinging the machete in a manner he felt behooved a seasoned adventurer. An elegant sweep to the left. An ineffectual flourish to the right. Progress was slow.

A sound from somewhere in the darkness made him pause. Was that the call of the hidden beast? Or a cry of distress from his quarry?

He resumed his struggles with the vegetation as his mind pictured his nemesis, his obsession – Ricardo Maitea Gervascio. Marquis. Scientist. Academic. Adventurer. And now…damned debunker! He was also the sort of man who precipitated socially unacceptable desires. Tall and lean. Dark and handsome. Suave and alluring.

Gervascio had been a vociferous proponent of The Society and its work, having inherited his place on the board, and his legendary quest, from his maternal grandfather, Lord Robert Caractacus, Marquis of Lorneview, one of the Society's founding members.

When they had first met, Fortescue had been in awe of the man. He had practically worshiped the ground upon which Gervascio trod, each footstep instilling an increased yearning. But then everything changed.

Smythe seethed with ineffectual fury, taking out his frustrations upon the undergrowth, recalling the extraordinary meeting of The Royal Society for Cryptozoological Explorations that had taken place mere months ago. The meeting that had changed everything and set him on this new course of action.

"There you have it!"

Gervascio slammed a large, leather-bound folio onto the table as he strode into the meeting, having made haste from the port the moment his ship had docked. "Every scrap of evidence I have accumulated on the legendary beast." He paused for effect, his intense gaze surveying first the board as they sat, faces aghast at the mahogany table, eyes locked onto him; and then the rank and file membership, expressions ranging from stunned to disbelieving. How could one of their own, grandson of a founding member no less, turn against them in such a way?

"Folly!" He almost shouted the word which, coupled with his unkempt appearance, made some worry that he had become unhinged. "Utter folly! That, gentlemen, is what we are engaged in here. The unmitigated waste of resources and, dare I say it, the erosion of reason."

There was an audible gasp from the membership. Lord Thunderland, the chairman (thunderous by name and by nature), harrumphed through this mustache of extraordinary size, the other board members grunting their support of his position.

"My grandfather, God rest his tormented soul, was a fool."

"You go too far, Sir." The chairman was on his feet now, a storm blazing in his eyes, mustache aquiver, trembling finger pointing with all the power of inherited privilege and entitled self-assurance.

"I do not go far enough," countered Gervascio. "Out of respect for my dear mother's lineage, I hold short of accusing Grandfather of deliberate obfuscation."

The chairman's face took on a scarlet hue and the vein at his temple throbbed as if ready to burst.

"Let me state this as plainly as I can manage," said Gervascio, lowering his voice. "The beast does not exist. It has never existed. My grandfather's pursuit of it was in vain." He hung his head in apparent sadness. "I extrapolate from this that no other cryptids exist either. A stretch of logic, you may say." He held up a hand to hold back the expected outrage. "This creature has for many years been held up by this society as the most likely cryptid to be found and classified. If it does not exist, and I am certain it does not, then how can anyone put faith in the existence of any others? And so I say it again…no cryptids exist! None has ever existed. And so this society's pursuit of said creatures has been futile. And, therefore, the existence of this society is not only futile, but an abomination upon all reasonable thinking." Gervascio slammed his first onto the table. "And therefore…I resign! I renounce the aims of this society. And I rue the day my grandfather colluded with others to establish it."

The meeting had then devolved into an uncontrollable shambles, with many raised voices competing in unseemly fashion and much grandiose posturing; all of which achieved very little.

Sometimes, Smythe still had difficulty believing that these events had taken place. He even fantasized about Gervascio returning to the fold, to The Society…to him. But it was not to be.

Gervascio's diatribe had made all the newspapers. Outrage followed. Outrage at the waste of money and resources. Outrage that Crown funds were being spent in pursuit of non-existent creatures. Outrage at the very existence of The Society.

Within days, His Majesty had withdrawn the Royal Charter. His predecessor, and late mother, had bestowed her favor upon The Society many years past in the expectation of them eventually providing her with a new addition for her menagerie of rare beasts – one that none of her royal rivals would possess. The new king hated his mother, who had ruled her family as she had her kingdom, with an iron fist and a quick temper, playing favorites and following whims. No sooner had her corpse been laid to rest in the royal mausoleum, than he had followed his own whims and sent her precious beasts, one by one, to his table. Each had been a personal triumph. For him to take another stab at his mother's legacy was a welcome diversion that he grabbed with both hands and much eagerness.

So The Royal Society for Cryptozoological Explorations simply became the Society for Cryptozoological Explorations. And a society without royal approval, or, more importantly, patronage, could not effectively function.

Resignations quickly followed.

Those with positions at court, including the chairman (mustache still trembling), were the first to depart.

Other Lords and titled gentlemen were next, thus leaving the Society without a board to oversee matters.

All that were left were what the papers called "those with pretensions of aristocracy and delusions of competency."

It fell to Smythe to take action. He may not have had a place at Court or an inherited title, but he did have money. *Bucket loads*, as the riffraff would say. His family's position among the industry-lead nouveau riche, pumping smoke, soot, and coal dust into the skies, meant that he had the resources to pursue his interests, no matter how out of favor those interests might be.

And so he put his finances to work. First in bolstering up the Society. But that was merely delaying the inevitable. He needed to reverse public opinion in the hopes that a Royal Charter might be reinstated. And to do that, much as it pained him, causing his heart to ache beyond measure, Ricardo Gervascio would have to be discredited.

And thus he hired a consulting detective, and by extension, his unspoken network of street urchins, to follow Gervascio and report back on his every move.

He also hired Lady Madeline Busyworth (not a real Lady), gossip columnist for most of the prominent newspapers under a variety of pseudonyms, to dig the dirt on Gervascio and his family.

Meanwhile, Smythe buried himself in the archives of the Society, pouring over Gervascio's evidence as well as all their records of his grandfather, the esteemed Lord Caractacus, and his quest.

The archives divulged little that he did not already know. Gervascio's evidence seemed tenuous, a collection of academic papers on the unreliability of primitive oral culture, reports on the scientific unlikelihood of The Interior being able to sustain such a creature, and an unverified analysis of skin samples purporting to belong to the beast.

Lady Busyworth found nothing of use, merely rumors of

the Marquis' new obsessive infatuation with person or persons unknown.

But the consulting detective reported on Gervascio's clandestine arrangements for travel back to The Interior.

Why was he going back to the jungle if there was no creature? Smythe had wondered. He had to know the answer. And so he determined to follow him.

The indigenous people called it Krah, their word for heart. The newspapers referred to it as the Beast of The Interior. Gervascio's grandfather named it the Corbestia, a term borrowed from a dead language that only scholars read.

The Corbestia supposedly lived in the jungle domain known as The Interior, held within the grasp of that most untamed and godforsaken of continents, often referred to as Diabolus Terra. The locals all had legends, dating back many hundreds of years, about a hidden creature, a demon beast of unspeakable appearance, living at the continent's exact geographic center. Two expeditions were prepared, financed, and sent. But the environment was harsh, the locals uncooperative, and thus success eluded them. The first expedition barely managed five miles into The Interior before turning back. The second, lead by the perky young Lord Perceval Brenville, fared somewhat better, making it to the geographic center; an area of jungle so thick that it almost turned day into night, and concealed bog-like areas that when stepped in would not let go of a man for all the treasures of heaven, inexorably drawing him down into their depths. Those of the expedition who did not meet their muddy doom, returned with madness. Brenville alone retained his sanity, albeit with a distinct lack of perkiness, and a grim determination that no hidden creature was worth the deaths and minds of so many men.

It was thought that Brenville's report, coinciding with the deaths of Gervascio's grandfather and shortly thereafter of Her Majesty the Queen, would see an end to pursuit of the Corbestia. There were, after all, many other hitherto unclassified creatures to be pursued the world over — from the Albino Man-Devil of the world's highest peak, to the Serpentinia of the ocean's depths.

But then came Ricardo Maitea Gervascio.

Fortescue Smythe's attacks on the vegetation were becoming more and more wildly aggressive. Nostrils flaring, he huffed and puffed as he hacked and slashed. Momentarily caught on a branch, he unhooked the thorns from his jacket, wrenched the woody appendage from the gnarled tree, and threw it to the ground. His eyes widened as, not two feet ahead of him, that branch slowly disappeared beneath the leaf litter with the horrid slurping-sucking sound of boggy, unstable earth. Terra infirma!

Breathing deeply of the moist jungle air, Smythe calmed his thoughts. Wresting another branch from the tree, he used it as a blind man would a cane, prodding the ground before him, testing its stability. And so, with instrument of navigation in one hand and weapon in the other, he continued with greater caution and calmness of mind.

"Perhaps I can still turn him back to our cause?" he thought, as his mind again held Gervascio in its embrace.

Ricardo Maitea Gervascio had made his first appearance at The Society by striding into a meeting and claiming his privilege of bequeathed board membership. He towered over the rotund Lord Thurderland, only just appointed as replacement chairman, and demanded, not only recognition of his place on the board, but entitlement to pursue the Corbestia in his grandfather's name. Thurderland had little alternative but to grant him both.

Inheriting the complexion of his father's ethnicity rather than his mother's socially-preferred pallidity, Gervascio was a sight to behold. And while some more old-fashioned members held their regard for him in check because of it, Smythe found it part of what made him so alluring. Of course his desires were impossible. Even the most socially progressive of people would balk at condoning such an attachment. A Marquis could never be seen to have intimacy with anyone outside of aristocracy. Nevertheless, Smythe hoped for the unseen.

A hope that was to remain unfulfilled.

Gervascio held him at arm's length rather than how he yearned to be held – close. So Smythe admired from afar, following his progress as he prepared for his quest, spoke at conferences, and even appeared at Court (on a day that His Majesty was in absentia). Smythe applied for a position with the exploration team but was rejected.

Finally, Gervascio's expedition set sail. Within twelve months they had returned…significantly depleted in number and without Gervascio himself. Telling tales of frightened locals, terrifying sounds, and mysterious vines, they reported that despite all their pleading, Gervascio had walked into the bogs unaccompanied, with nothing but the clothes on his back and his grandfather's pistol. They waited as long as they dared, then, leaving two of their number in a nearby village in case he emerged from the jungle, set sail for home.

Smythe proposed a rescue mission, but it was the no longer perky Lord Brenville who, with a few handpicked men, crossed the seas and ventured into The Interior.

They were never heard from again.

The Society was on the verge of sending another expedition, this time to be led by Smythe (considered a more expendable member), when news arrived of Gervascio's miraculous reappearance.

Smythe lowered his machete as he emerged from the vines and undergrowth into an area of a relative clearing. A gasp escaped his lips. There! At last! Spread-eagled upon the ground, entangled in vines, smeared in mud, was Gervascio; shirtless and disheveled, trousers ragged and feet bare, eyes closed, chest heaving as he softly moaned.

"Ricardo?" Smythe whispered the name on an exhaled breath.

Gervascio's eyes snapped open. As he lifted himself into a sitting position, the vines seemed to withdraw from him, falling away and disappearing beneath the ground.

"You should not have come here, my friend." There was genuine sadness in his voice. And resignation.

Smythe stopped himself from running towards the man as he realized that, like the vines, Gervascio was sinking. Being consumed by the earth. Already his feet had been taken, the rest of him slowly following.

Smythe tested the ground with his branch. It shifted and sludged as the wood sank into it. He tried to pull it out, but it held fast and he had to give up, watching it disappear into the mire. His eyes darted back to Gervascio and he almost considered plunging forward in a vain rescue attempt. Instead, in desperation, he reached out towards the man, knowing he was too far away to be of any use.

"'Tis not toward me that you should direct your concern." Gervascio stood, rising from the bog to walk across the ooze like Christ upon water. "'Tis you who are in mortal danger."

Mouth agape, Smythe could not move. He looked down. Vines held him in place. Struggling, he found them tightening their grip, entwining his wrists and ankles, pulling upon him, stretching him out as if upon the royal rack that had on so many a public occasion provided the former Queen with amusement at her enemies' expense. His thoughts turned to Brenville, as his muscles stretched to breaking point, his joints ready to pop. Had this been his fate? A yelp of pain escaped Smythe's lips.

"No!" Gervascio called, his voice strong and clear and true. "This man…a fellow of my damned species…is my responsibility, not yours. You should not be the one to bear the guilt…to have his blood on your conscience. As always, I shall protect you, my love."

Who was he talking to? Smythe would have wondered, had he not been in so much pain. But then the vines relaxed their grasp, still holding him in place but loosening the tension upon his body. His relief was short-lived, for a new terror took its place.

The earth around Gervascio frothed and bubbled as a mass of tangled vines lifted from the ground behind him. No! Not vines! They were tentacles. They writhed and undulated from a central core that held mesmerizing eyes and a gaping maw, simultaneously exquisite and horrifying.

Corbestia! Though he mouthed the word, no sound passed his lips. So the cryptid did exist. And Gervascio knew of it. Had concealed its existence from The Society. Why?

One of the tentacles snaked around Gervascio's waist and he stroked it tenderly. "Fear not, my dearest, for I shall protect you." Another tentacle began to caress his face and he closed his eyes as he pressed his lips to its wet, leathery skin.

"What?" Tears slid down his cheeks as Smythe's confusion turned to understanding. "You…it…no!"

"Yes." Gervascio opened his eyes and unclipped the worn holster still attached to his ragged trousers. Turning his attention to Smythe he said: "I knew you would come eventually. So I have prepared myself."

He drew his grandfather's pistol. "It saddens me that I must do this." He took aim. "But she has my heart. Has had it from the moment I laid eyes on her. And I will do whatever it takes to protect her. I truly hope that you understand."

The creature behind him made sing-song, gurgling sounds, her tentacles trembling as more and more of them wrapped themselves around him…stroking him, caressing him.

Gervascio sighed and slowly squeezed the trigger.

But Fortescue Smythe's heart was broken even before the bullet found its mark and rent it asunder.

The Hundred Dollar Fortune

ROBERT BAGNALL

He flicked the tent-flap back, pausing, adjusting not merely to the dimness.

Saudari was used to looks of disdain, disgust even, often little more than the briefest flaring of the nostrils, a flicker around the eyes, but she knew what it meant. "Come," she purred vampishly, beckoning the man in. "For Madame Cassandra to read your fortune, you must cross my palm with silver." She uncurled one finger at a time, revealing skin leathery and lined, the color of over-creamed coffee. Wiry russet hair encroached from the back of her hand, circled the wrist that emerged from her sleeve. It made her palm look like cleared jungle, slash and burn.

He was a heavy-set man who moved carefully, as though every joint caused mild discomfort. He adjusted the stool across the card table from her, then sat slowly, bracing his thighs with his palms. His suit was narrow and tight, and he wore a black bow tie despite the June warmth. He removed a stiff derby hat, revealing thinning hair, slicked back above a furrowed brow. Tired bags hung under his eyes, eyes that seemed to ask for a moment more to think. He'd got over the initial shock of her appearance. Outside, through the canvas, could be heard the clack-clack of the coconut shy. A lairy cheer went up. At this time of day, families returned for their suppers and the atmosphere became febrile and combative.

He unbuttoned his jacket and reached into a waistcoat pocket, producing a fob watch. Even Cheiro, Saudari's calico cat, feigned interest from where she was curled in the corner.

"I have this," he said.

Looming down, he put it in Saudari's tiny hand. It was plain, with an empty loop for a chain, some scratches on the crystal, and a case with bronzed smears of wear, indicating some cheap tin-rich alloy. It had an outer bezel that could be rotated, but the strangest feature was…

"Forty-seven."

"What?" Saudari asked.

"Forty-seven. You were about to ask how many hands it has."

Thin ones, short ones, some little more than needles. More than could be easily counted.

"Why forty-seven?"

"Forty-seven is reckoned to be the number when 'many' becomes 'more than many'," he said gnomically, like a brush salesman in his grandfather's clothes, speaking in runes.

Saudari studied the timepiece, searched for any way of adjusting the mechanism, held it up to her ear. She used the moment to study his face studying hers. He couldn't help it, his gaze flicking between her flat nose, almost as wide as her mouth, her high forehead, the mat of hair that came up to her cheekbones. Again, she was used to it – contempt giving way to curiosity. She knew there were not many of her kind.

He only became animated when she tried to turn the bezel, as if she were about to light a match to read the instructions on a can of gasoline. "You be careful with that."

"But it doesn't work," she told him, the watch held cold against her ear, hearing only the music of the carousel and the steam organ outside. She had slipped, she realized, no longer Madame Cassandra of the elongated vowels. She had reverted to Saudari, the orang pendek.

He smiled, a smile that said she had no idea how far from the truth she was. "It doesn't tick-tick-tick tell the time, I'd agree with that. But as for it not working…"

"What does it do, then?"

"I'm hoping it'll buy my fortune."

Saudari pondered. Perhaps she could pawn it in the next town. A curio, it may bring her a dollar. A human would probably get two.

"Very well," she said, laying the mitteleuropean on thickly, compensating, ridiculously so now her mask had slipped, and dealt the six tarot cards.

The first card she turned over was the chariot. To those who thought the card itself important, it could mean triumph, vengeance, or trouble. To Saudari, it was merely a divining rod, channeling and directing… Nothing.

Saudari had never felt nothing before. Not true nothing. Not just an absence of any feeling, but a distinct presence of void. A vacuum, but a vacuum as if it were something she could hold in her hands. Her mouth dried.

The wheel of fortune. To the credulous, luck, success, abundance. But to Saudari… She found herself straining to see beyond a simple image on a paper card. But for once that was all there was: a poorly printed picture of a woman on a throne wearing a crown with twelve stars, holding a scepter. It hurt to swallow.

There followed the moon, the tower, the hermit, the empress. All with the same result, a sense of standing before an abyss on a moonless night. A cavity where there should be content, so close at hand, but so out of reach.

The stranger broke the silence, joking his surprise Madame Cassandra had not turned over death. "Or the fool."

"I think I am the fool in this case. I cannot see your future."

"Now, why would that be?" he asked quietly, ignoring the watch Saudari proffered back.

"Please. I am not a charlatan." *Why would he not accept the return of his watch?*

"Why do you think you can see no future for me?" he persisted.

"Because you do not have one."

She was barely aware of what she had said even as she spoke, as if they were words spoken not by her but through her. She felt as though she had just hit the canvas trying her luck in the boxing booth, *go three rounds with Peppercorn Jack Tate.*

The man nodded, twisted his hat in his hands. "That's what I figured too." And then he put the hat back on his head and used his meaty palms to lever himself up from the stool.

At the tent-flap he paused. "Why 'Madame Casandra'? It…"

He left his reasoning hanging, shook his head sadly and departed, but Saudari knew full well what he meant. *It doesn't go with a four-foot hairy cryptid primate from the Kerinci Regency of central Sumatra.*

Was it all an act? Was it hokum? Even Saudari herself no longer knew. All she knew was the cards revealed a sense of…the future. She had never attempted to put into words what that meant, never been challenged to explain. *I see you going on a great adventure…* She never saw anything. It did not happen in her mind, it happened in her heart and stomach and bones. It felt like an itch you couldn't scratch, two thoughts that should mesh but refused to fit together, a face in the crowd you knew you knew but could not place. She would say words, words that often surprised her as much as the person across the card table, with a visceral sense of their veracity.

Because you do not have one. The truth. Instinct told her so.

Outside, Saudari scanned the crowd, already thinning, for the burly man in suit and derby, walking like it made him ache. She looked past the stares, but he was nowhere to be seen. The only evidence he had ever been there: the strange forty-seven-handed fob-watch she held.

He was smaller than she expected, standing at the threshold in an elegantly understated herringbone three-piece suit which seemed to mold itself to him. Underneath the white starched collar was a silk tie in a two-tone blue diamond pattern, a pearl tie-pin just below a Windsor knot. His face was neutral, his impassive eyes expert in giving nothing away, whether in a Wall Street boardroom or here, in a Bronx boarding house. It was those eyes that added to his five feet six inches, that made you forget he wasn't yet thirty.

"Miss Saudari?" Vanderpetter said flatly, easing loose black silk gloves.

Saudari, sitting at a table in the corner of the single room, her legs swinging from the stool like a child, bade Vanderpetter enter with a sweep of her hand. Vanderpetter took in the bed, neatly made with Cheiro curled up asleep atop, the gas ring, the sink with the single tap, the table with two chairs, one pulled out for him. He chose to remain standing, his gaze dallying on the small washing tub propped in a corner and, by it, drying undergarments hung from a clothes horse. Then to the windows, grimy on the outside, but clean inside. A small bunch of flowers sat in a highball glass, a flash of bright freshness against an abiding accent of third-hand bathwater.

He was good, she had to concede. He had looked past her, through her, as if an orang pendek in a New York tenement was utterly unnewsworthy.

"This counts as good living on this street, Mr Vanderpetter."

Vanderpetter pulled his gloves off a finger at a time, nodding as he did to an unseen presence in the hallway outside. It was a clear signal he had not arrived alone – and that he did not see Saudari as a threat. He quietly shut the door.

"I'm not used to being blackmailed, Miss Saudari."

"I'm delighted, Mr Vanderpetter, because I have no intention of blackmailing you."

Vanderpetter drew a piece of paper from an inside pocket. He unfurled it and held it out by his fingertips. "Then what exactly is this?"

"It's a page of a book. I hate ripping up books, but it's hard to find something convincing, a present-day detail only you know. Please," Saudari said, again indicating the stool opposite.

He sat, tugging at his trouser creases. As he did so, Saudari slipped down off her own seat and went about searching for something in a low cupboard of paper packets, tins and jars.

"If you intend to offer me tea, Miss Saudari, I can assure you I am fine without."

"Mr Vanderpetter, I used to travel around county fairs, traveling shows, pitch a tent between the two-headed woman and those things where you hit a thing with a hammer and a bell rings." She glanced back at him, cracked a smile, as if taking in his tailoring for the first time. "It's not quite opera at the Met, I admit. Anyway, I was Madame Cassandra, fortune teller. I know what you're thinking: why 'Madame Cassandra'? Not very Indonesian. It came with the tent. Literally. Embroidered on. I'm Madame Cassandra right now. I'm not here to blackmail you, Mr Vanderpetter. I'm here to give you your fortune."

From its hiding place she extracted a brown paper package within which was a hard-backed book, a glossy dustcover quite unlike any of the leather-bound, gilt-picked tomes she suspected sat on the shelves of Vanderpetter's library. She held it up to him and smiled as his eyes widened at the cover photo of himself. *Vanderpetter: Wall Street Man.*

"I don't recognize that photo. It's me, but…I look…older."

"I don't think it's been taken yet," she breezily explained.

"You'll have to speak more plainly, Miss Saudari. Everything still points to blackmail."

"Mr Vanderpetter. This book is from the future. It hasn't been written yet. The page in your hand – thank you," she reached up and took it from his fingers as if dealing with a sleepwalker and went about slotting it back in place, "is torn from this book. The stuff on the page: you know about. The stuff in the book: most of it hasn't happened yet. I'm offering to tell your fortune, not the usual *you will go on a long journey and meet a mysterious woman* for a quarter, but a detailed, highly specific account for one hundred dollars. Take it or leave it. It's not blackmail."

His face creased with incredulity. "If this a joke…"

"If this is a joke, whose? Who knows about the baby? Think about it, Mr Vanderpetter, is this how *you* would go about blackmail?" She slid the book back into its brown paper bag.

Vanderpetter was silent for a long time. Cheiro woke, stretched, jumped off the bed and stalked by the door to be let out.

"A hundred dollars? I don't think I've ever paid a hundred dollars for a book," he said, extracting a snakeskin billfold from an inside pocket. He counted out the bills, pushed the notes towards Saudari, and reached for the book. She gently held on to it.

"A question, Mr Vanderpetter. Is it possible for you to do your job too well?"

He held her gaze and said nothing, the negotiator's way of getting their opponent to keep talking, to give themselves away.

"I would have thought not, Mr Vanderpetter. Maybe I'm being naïve, but I assume a banker can never make too much money. But a fortune teller…we should never do our job too well because knowledge of the future *alters the future*. Absolute, detailed, crystal-clear knowledge of the future is almost certain to ensure that future never comes to pass. Think very carefully before you start to read the book, Mr Vanderpetter. Think carefully indeed: do you even want to take this out of its wrapper?"

He pulled the book out from under her fingers, tucked it under his arm, and stood up from the table, his cold eyes never once leaving hers. "I think our business is done, Miss Saudari. I don't know whether you've escaped from some institution or the Cabaret Voltaire, or–" For the first and only time his mouth curled into a sneer. "–the jungle, but I still think this is blackmail, so please treat it as such yourself. In other words, if a word is breathed about baby Thomas, there will be consequences for you. Consequences which will not involve writs and lawyers. I hope I make myself clear. Good day."

"Mr Vanderpetter," she said softly. His hand paused on the door handle. Cheiro rubbed herself against his shins. "On reflection, you may think a select few of your circle of friends and associates would appreciate a similar service, with a ten percent fee for yourself, of course." And then she added coyly, "I'd be happy to pay it directly to baby Thomas' mother, if you prefer."

She took a moment to compose herself – time travel had a one-too-many-whiskeys aspect to it, plus you never knew what you were going to arrive in the middle of. The first time she stood in Union Square, *her* Union Square, and clicked the bezel forward, she found herself stifling an involuntary scream as a youth in shapeless clothes swooped towards her on some kind of monopod's roller-skate, before veering away. He essed past at speed, glaring back with an amalgam of concern and annoyance.

Her first moments in the twenty-first century – she had never heard of a 'skateboard.'

Flash Gordon at the nabe theater was fresh in her memory. She was disappointed the sky was not filled with men wearing rocket packs on their backs. But what surprised her more, every time she journeyed forward, was that each future New York differed, as if a house's fixtures, fittings, and furniture had been packed away then placed back from memory, almost but not quite. All the buildings would be the same, except one. Or, where, she would ask herself, had all the Studebakers, Oldsmobiles, and Packards gone? Once, she arrived within hoardings, surprising workmen, the blockwork being renewed. She had swiftly twisted the bezel back.

A June afternoon. As it was every time. The scent of food-stalls, exhaust fumes, a hint of salty, muddy river, East or Hudson, all depending on the breeze. She immediately registered the park's streetlamps as different, thick cast iron trees, each with five large glowing globes like monster fruit. Last time, they had been more delicate, art deco swirls, lamps like apples. The scrolling pattern on the paving: similar but different. And, across 14th, a building, end-on, its entire face an artwork, a deep maroon circular pattern of furrows, a gold explosion in the middle, a rocky projection and a single arm, like the second hand of a watch…

A watch. She reached into her haversack and felt for the fob-watch-that-wasn't, making sure it was still where she'd stowed it, tucked under Cheiro. The cat shifted in her sleep. Saudari smiled. What other feline could be put into a bag with a bottle of soda and two rounds of sandwiches wrapped in wax paper and not show the slightest interest?

She had by now learned what caused the cityscape to alter. The first time she saw it, she had swooned, panicked, spun the bezel back, to make sure there was a back to get back to. Now she just smiled wryly. It meant one of Vanderpetter's associates had failed to resist temptation and had read his biography. It was hardly surprising. This was the dilemma she presented them with: a book about themselves they could not read. A book that was true, every word of it – unless they tried to verify that truth. The moment they started to turn the pages it would become about some parallel them, their doppelgänger, their fates diverging from that point on. There is a limit to fortune telling, a point where prophesy turns to fiction. Fortune-tellers, the true fortune-tellers, have always understood this. The skeptical have forever missed the point. She admitted to enjoying the frisson, dangling temptation in front of men who denied themselves nothing.

Down Broadway, two blocks to the Strand Bookstore, and fifteen minutes later Saudari was on the second floor, in amongst the loaded tables and polished wooden shelves, higher than a human, let alone an orang pendek, could reach. Vanderpetter had given Saudari more names, secondary characters in his life. If their biographies existed, the Strand would have them. Her finger ran along the spines, her head tilted, before snapping up straight at a familiar name and a title that caused her heart to miss a beat, the bottom of her stomach to drop. The name of the book: *The Hundred Dollar Fortune*. And the name of the subject: her own.

She had already unwittingly discovered what happened if she attempted to move in time to a place that had gained solid mass. Like being swatted out of the way with a wrecking ball combined with a moonshine hangover. This was oddly similar. And this was how all those who had taken up her hundred-dollar offer must feel the moment she revealed their book. She knew all the arguments against, but…

She riffled through the bright white pages. Sentences jumped out at her, phrases chimed like bells with memories. The dustbowl years. Cletus at the traveling fair, Argus the Strongman, the twins. All there. She dwelt at a section, that night at the boarding house.

…she sat on the edge of the bed, took the watch-that-wasn't in her hand, turned it over twice, felt its weight, and then turned the bezel, gently at first, but with increasing force. It gave with a metallic click. She fell backwards onto a warm, unforgiving surface. Pain lanced from a scraped elbow, a jarred hip. Empty night surrounded her, the flophouse gone, bright lights in the distance that a moment ago had been a curtained window. The hard, level, pocked

surface under her was tacky to the touch. Blacktop, she realized. She'd gone from sitting on a chintz bedspread to being sprawled on asphalt. The dazzling lights in the distance were getting closer, accompanied by an ever-escalating roar. She rolled aside. A behemoth vehicle rushed by in a wail of engine and banshee-shrieking siren pulling a trailer the size of a building. She glimpsed a man at the helm, up high, on the bridge of the vessel glaring down at her…

She flicked forward.

…Saudari was first invited to meet the President in secret…

The President? What was this?

…the crisis with China had escalated. The call came direct from the Oval Office…

She read on hungrily, then turned two pages at once.

…cannily Saudari had invested all the spare cash from her dealings with Vanderpetter and his circle into Coca Cola shares. Now a millionaire…

Well, that hadn't happened. She turned back, returning to her dealings with the President, how she solved the diplomatic crisis in Asia.

"Saudari," the President cried down the line. "America needs you."

"I'm on my way, Mr President," the monkey-woman answered, wondering what to wear, and how much to tell Rhett, who lay smoldering beside her…

What the hell? What was this? This wasn't on the page a moment ago. Monkey-woman? Where did that come from? She felt giddy. She needed to sit down, she needed water.

Slowly it dawned on Saudari that she was no longer on the second floor. She was on the first, at the back, in fiction. She could see traffic moving outside the windows, level with her. The book in her hand was a novel, smaller, shabbier, with a more lurid cover, a chimpanzee having their clothes ripped off. Whose idea was it to show her as a fucking chimpanzee? That wasn't her. She looked utterly different: bigger face, a definite nose rather than crescent slits in a fleshy upper lip, rich auburn fur. It was still called *The Hundred Dollar Fortune*, still authored by a Robert Bagnall, but now remaindered at a dollar ninety-eight.

She needed to get out, to escape. The walls of books loomed down at her, the building's cast-iron supports, like soldiers on parade, had become an impenetrable forest. She stumbled towards the doors, conscious of gasps and stifled screams, dropping the novel on the floor before almost falling through the doors on to the sidewalk in the fetid summer air. A taxi blared its horn. The nausea passed leaving her cold and shivering.

She reached into her bag. Cheiro looked up, wiped a paw across an ear. Still underneath the sandwiches, the fob-watch that wasn't. With shaking fingers she tried to turn the bezel back. It wouldn't give. It wasn't just stuck, it was as good as welded on. She crouched, braced herself, twisting until her fingers hurt. Nothing. She examined it. Not welded on; never separate to begin with. The bezel was now purely cosmetic, the metal continuous except for a slight groove. She had worn the thin brass gilding, revealing the darker metal below. It matched the wear marks on the device when the stranger handed it on to her. She had given herself a blister in the process. The skin on her fingers was as thick as leather, nature's defense against the impenetrable jungle. She had never had a blister before. She gazed at the bubble of separated skin, tentatively thumbed the soreness, fascinated.

Only then did she see the people staring at her, gathered around at a safe distance. She had stopped traffic.

What the fuck…

What the hell is it?

Is that make-up?

Is this somekinda movie stunt?

Their wariness held a lurid voyeurism, unwilling to approach, unable to look away. She had become an exhibit.

Phones were out and up, filming. Somebody stepped forward to take a photograph.

"Do you mind?"

"Fuck. It talks. It talks English."

A small girl pressed herself against her mother and started to cry. An unspoken understanding went through the crowd. Stances stiffened, smiles softened. Whatever this animal-in-clothes was, it was a threat.

Belly-tall to most, Saudari had no difficulty slipping the net, running, lolloping back towards Union Square. Cheiro mewled from the confines of the bag. Hot with tears, her eyes were fixed on the monotone checkerboard of the concrete sidewalk slabs. She ignored the shouts, the cries, the sudden exclamations, the whistles, the blaring horns. Each one seemed to declare *freak, freak, freak.*

She did not have to be told. Not only had she suffered the fate of those tempted to read their futures; she found herself in a world *without orang pendek.* A world where they were unknown. To these people she was an anomaly, an abnormality. She may as well have dropped from another planet. A freak.

How could this be? How could she change her timeline but find herself in a reality where time had been changed *long before she had been born*? It made no sense.

By some miracle she went to ground in the ornamental undergrowth of Union Square, disturbing a squirrel that unwittingly became her savior, sending it bowling, panicked, through the shrubbery, the outer fronds of bushes magnifying its blundering. She heard voices disputing claims that it had just been a squirrel – *like fuck it coulda been* – while she curled into a ball, all the time whispering calming nothings to Cheiro.

After some minutes, the voices went away. She peeked out. Abraham Lincoln looked down at her from his plinth.

What to do? This was like nothing she'd ever faced.

She took an inventory of her possessions. Two sandwiches. One cat. A bottle of Coca-Cola. The clothes she stood up in. A key to a tenement block that had been demolished four decades earlier, assuming it had ever stood in this timeline. A thick roll of banknotes – she always kept them close – *there better have been a President Pinckney* – and a pack of tarot cards.

She slipped out of the bushes, over the low metal railing – which was still a climb for her – and sat herself with her back against a tree near the base of the Lincoln statue. She knew she was being stared at, people glancing at others as if to say *are you seeing this too*, not sure what to make of a four-feet high, russet-haired hominid in New York City. But now she was ready for them. A glare cut off a comment before it was made. She shuffled the pack and laid six cards out, face down, before her.

She turned the first over…

…and smiled.

By the time she had revealed the last she was practically laughing. She had a future, a bright, lustrous, incandescent future. But she needed to make it happen herself – if she weren't to give herself up to fate. Baby steps. She needed to find her way in this strange, dazzling, kinetic world. She needed to start with what she knew best.

The crowd – and it was now a crowd – was entranced, intrigued at her joy. Time had stopped for them, a bubble keeping out the traffic fumes and the horns and the frenetic city.

"Come," she called, emphasizing the rolling mock-Slavic in her voice, beckoning, her long hairy fingers presenting the cards. Cheiro glided back and forth against her legs. "Come. For Madame Cassandra to read your fortune, you will need to cross my palm with silver."

Huffenpuff

MIKAL TRIMM

1.

"So he's deformed, is that it?"

Dr. Peters-Thompson, his name declared on a rusty nameplate and several yellowing, curling diplomas on the walls of his office, coughed while simultaneously sneering in a bold display of arrogance. "I don't think that word is appropriate, Mr. Plumb. I would argue, in fact, that the *intricacies* of the boy's condition might be more of a *friendly challenge* for the adoptive parents than an–" and here he cleared his throat in such a way that anyone in hearing distance would feel they'd be spit upon soon, "–an issue of, shall we say, *inconvenient abnormalities.*"

"Yeah, like you said, but his hands are what, umbrellas? Sorry, doc, but what would *you* call them?"

Dr. Peters-Thompson shuffled some items on his desk, sighed, pulled out the adoption papers. "You know how lucky you are to get a healthy white baby, Mr. Plumb? Sign *here*, and *here*, and *here.*"

Driving home, Gary tried to focus on the road while completely failing to ignore his wife's interactions with the little web-fest known as his newly-adopted son. He watched Darlene peripherally as she put one of the baby's hands up to her face and blew, the child's little umbrella-segments puffing out like flesh balloons, then collapsing again into oddly-dense filaments or ligaments or whatever they were, and the worst part, the weirdest worst part of all as he drove and semi-watched, was the baby giggling in a loud and unabashed way at his wife's huffenpuff game.

Yeah, that's what he'd call it. *Huffenpuff*. Creepy. He mumbled something, not expecting her to glom onto it, but *damn* her ears were sharp. "What was that Gary?"

Crap. "Just wondered why he said *white* baby. We never asked for that. We just wanted *healthy*, right? I don't remember ever specifying race, or even gender, thank you very much. So what's up with this guy that he thinks we're racists or something that can't love a different-colored baby? Why a white baby with, um–"

Darlene held the baby to her chest, covering his ears. "Don't say it. And you weren't listening, Gary. Read the literature."

He'd been married long enough to know when to shut up, but inside all his thoughts tumbled around until he saw umbrellas opening and closing, dammit, just some alien version of hands, just something his wife would fall in love with without him.

He drove, and he watched the Great Balloon Bonding Show out of the corners of his eyes, and he tried to believe he wasn't feeling jealous.

And what was that about *literature?*

With the addition of the baby, home life changed.

No, not good enough, Gary thought. *Home life just relocated to an unknown universe and failed to forward my mail.* He wandered his house at times, seeing new elements his wife added seemingly in defiance of the laws of real-time: childproof locks on the drawers and cabinets in the kitchen, closeable gates in every possible chokepoint between living areas in the house, and even an annoying little plastic gadget holding the toilet seat down for those toddler years Darlene could apparently see in the immediate future, despite the inability of said child to hold his head up without a surrogate hand to replace his floppy neck muscles.

Seriously, though, all of that was just mechanics, really. Changes, sure, but merely minor annoyances to be added to your daily routine and eventually forgotten. Gary understood baby-proofing, he really did, *I have a degree and everything, I can get used to this, this is* nothing.

Naming the child, on the other hand, placed Gary into his own private Twilight Zone Hell, and he realized what a close and personal bond he had with Dorothy Gale.

This damn sure ain't Kansas *anymore...*

Gary lost the first skirmish of the war he never realized he'd be fighting with the Battle of Son's Name. In his first – and, historically, tragic – foray into the battle, he'd jokingly suggested they name the boy Edward.

Darlene got the reference. Darlene did not find the reference funny. Darlene banned him from future naming sessions with the unsaid-but-understood caveat that any future attempts by Gary to attempt a nomer (mis- or otherwise) would be met with a punishment doled out in the dungeon-slash-torture chamber their bedroom would become.

When she named the boy Ryan ("and don't even ask, it's for me!"), Gary waved the white flag and retreated to the safety of his Netflix account, waiting for a fight he might win.

2.

Gary decided Ryan was an alien when the boy's baby-fine hair thickened, darkened, and reacted to itself, one strand addressing another with each encounter until they learned to trust each other and play well together. It was a slow process, and anyone not paying attention at this point would just see a pre-toddler with more thick lustrous hair than one might expect on such a small child. How odd, but how pretty.

Gary *paid attention*, though, and as he spent more and more time with Ryan while his wife went back to work, he watched that hair, and those nails (which seemed pretty damn tough for a baby, especially after Gary broke a set of 'baby's first nail clippers' on his initial attempt to blunt those little machetes). Ryan wasn't speaking, but he gestured a lot, usually pushing his tiny hands up to Gary's face and then puffing his cheeks out hopefully.

"Yeah, huffenpuff, I get it," and once in a while Gary would give a desultory puff in Ryan's general direction, but it just didn't seem right. *Surely there's more to child-rearing than this?*

He even tried to start a conversation with Darlene about it one night. "You ever wonder who his parents were?" Gary sat with Ryan, idly running his fingers through the boy's, well, *tentacles*, for want of a better word. "I mean, sure, some kids have a distinguishing mark or two, but *this?"* Ryan's hair clenched Gary's fingers, sensing his confusion, then began caressing, one finger at a time, playing his fingers like keys on a piano, calming, soothing. "I mean, don't get me wrong, I don't care if they were–" (*SPACE INVADERS!* his inside voice screamed) "–you know, different in some way, but shouldn't we find out for, I don't know, *medical* reasons or something? I mean, God forbid something happens where we–"

"Oh, look!" Darlene noticed Ryan blowing on his own hands with a healthy lack of success. Ryan held them out to Gary, wiggling his fingers as if Gary'd never noticed them before. Darlene chortled in glee.

Conversation, or at least the attempt at, over.

So, nothing to be done but to man up and take matters into his own hands.

And make sure Darlene never found out.

The adoption agency looked a bit more, well, *daunting* when Gary returned. Ryan hung out in his little papoose-carrier, knocking his head back against Gary's chest every now and again to make sure it hadn't caved in or disappeared, apparently. Whenever this happened, Gary would take a deep breath and puff it out slowly, which kept Ryan abreast of the situation and, judging by his burblings and gurglings, content.

If Darlene knew I was doing this, I wouldn't be able to make those noises; more like moans and strangled begging sounds.

Gary didn't like sneaking around behind Darlene's back, but some things just didn't add up here. He designed games for a living; he hated when something went buggy – it gave him an extremely OCD-like need to fix said bug. Also, conveniently, it let him work from home, which gave him time to be with the baby when Darlene worked and, more importantly, time to *hunt down bugs.*

Not that *Ryan* was a bug, perish the thought. But that Dr. Tom Peters or whatever his name was, the one that thought everyone was some kind of racially-insensitive jerk?

Well, Gary sensed some bad code there.

A couple with a baby stroller passed him, arguing in harsh whispers. Gary tried to catch a glimpse of the baby inside, but the angle was wrong; he could only hear a slight whimper from within, as if the child could sense the negative vibes in the air. The couple noticed Gary, or more to the point, Ryan hanging happily from his chest, and they pushed the stroller further along.

Gary heard them resume their hushed argument as the agency's doors closed behind him.

"I need to talk to Dr., uh, something with a Tom and a Peter, I think?"

The receptionist parsed his gibberish at an alarmingly professional rate. "Dr. Peters-Thompson no longer works with FAA, but if you'd like I can see if Ms. Seelie's available?"

Gary mouthed his next line silently, as it involved at least one veiled threat toward the missing doctor's future health, then recovered brilliantly. "Ms. Seelie?"

Big receptionist smile, no wait. "Our director. She cares about each and every placement we make. If you're having issues..." and here she gave the tiniest nod in Ryan's direction.

"Issues? Oh, nothing like, well, not so much, um, okay maybe some tiny – like, teeny-tiny – little questions I have? If she has the time?"

The receptionist (whom Gary now thought of with 'from Heaven' permanently appended to her title) made her giggle sound like "sure," or "sure" sound like a giggle, he couldn't be positive, typed something short and (he just knew) sweet on her laptop, nodded at an apparently instantaneous reply, and told Gary to go on in. "The door with the rainbow on it."

Gary smiled and walked down the hallway, idly wondering what the Federal Aviation Administration had to do with Dr. Peter-Tom-whatever.

The receptionist (from Heaven) meant it when she'd mentioned the rainbow. Gary wasn't sure how they'd achieved the effect, but the door didn't sport some kitschy rainbow sticker – it looked like the end of a rainbow somehow met the doorway and stuck there. Colors washed across it in a hypnotic prismatic display, and Gary nearly forgot his purpose until Ryan knocked his head back and coughed, just in case the blow to the chest didn't command enough authority.

Ryan may have touched the doorknob before the door opened – his fingertips tingled, so the possibility existed – but it seemed as if the door opened to his *desire* to enter. And it closed behind him by itself. No mistaking that, but it closed slowly, patiently, and it shut with a gentle click. Nothing to make him feel he'd been, say, *locked in.*

Ms. Seelie (and that must be her name, it said so right on her nameplate) smiled, stood, and held her hands out in welcome–

–to Ryan, who clapped delightedly and held his hands out in return.

"Oh, what a lovely child! You and your wife must be so proud!" Ms. Seelie clutched Ryan's hands in her own, gave an odd little twist and shimmy that looked like some clever baby handshake code, and released him slowly, her face illustrating 'wistful' for the inevitable dictionary image. Gary reached out a hand, belatedly, but Ms. Seelie instead committed to a hug, trapping his unacknowledged arm between her and Ryan. The kiss on the cheek made him forget the arm and worry about lipstick traces instead, so *well played, ma'am.*

Ms. Seelie, now back behind her desk – and Gary totally saw it happen, she didn't just *swoosh* over there, he'd verify with Ryan later – asked him the Million Dollar Question. "So, Mr. Plumb, what brings you and your lovely son here today?"

"Well..."

"W-I-G-H-T, Mr. Plumb. He said your son was a *wight* baby. I can understand your confusion to a point – Dr. Peters-Thompson suffered a bit in the warm fuzzy department – but still, I'm confused. Didn't you read the literature?"

That's what my wife said. "I saw some pamphlets in the lobby, but there was an old issue of National Geographic I'd never seen, so, um–"

Ms. Seelie pressed the advantage. "But you came to the Fae Adoption Agency; surely you must've had some inkling?"

Gary, just now realizing he'd botched his acronyms earlier, decided to play poker. "I thought Fae was the owner's name?" Well, *that* didn't up the ante. "And anyway, what do you mean Ryan's a wight? What, he's an undead baby or something?" Gary, a long-time addict of role-playing games, mentally upgraded his hand to a Royal Flush.

"Oh, dear, Mr. Plumb. You played D&D as a child, didn't you?"

Gary folded his hand. *And, by the way lady, the 'as a child' comment stung a little, not gonna lie.*

Ms. Seelie, having won the round while showing commendable largesse, came around her desk (in normal speed this time, no need to consult with Ryan), took one of his hands in hers, and spoke to him like a slow-witted-but-beloved child. "Mr. Plumb, a wight is a supernatural being. As is a leprechaun, or a boggan, or a gnome, or – well, they once were legion."

Gary stroked Ryan's hair with his free hand. "Once?"

Ms. Seelie dropped Gary's hand and reached out to stroke his hair in a strange, intimate echo of Gary's actions. "They're dying off, Mr. Plumb – or Gary, do you mind if I call you Gary?" A slight shake of his head, and she continued.

"It's all about *belief*, Gary. Once, everyone believed in the Fae folk, never mind what they called them, but people knew that a network of otherworldly creatures existed beside them, almost invisibly. They set out food and saucers of milk for the helpful, made wards against the spiteful, and avoided the mischievous as best they could.

"That was then, Gary." She moved her hand to Ryan's head. "This is now." Her hand grasped Gary's, both of them entangled together with Ryan, and Gary saw

death upon death, frail wings torn off in savage winds of apathy, hosts of knightly warriors choking on the rust of their crumbling armor, Kings and Queens crushed into dust by the sudden weight of their own impossible crowns, and the children the children disappearing like soap bubbles like the fading memory of dreams on awakening and all for lack of someone to believe in them,

and he wanted to cry out, but Ryan seemed calm so he merely wept silently.

"Are you all right, Gary?" Ms. Seelie, back behind her desk, but still within easy reach, still available to touch, if needed.

"I." *No, not that, Gary.* "He." *Better, you're going in the right direction.* "How." *Not a question, good job. You might just have a crack at getting this right.*

"Believe," she said. "There are so few places left for the children of the Fae. Pockets of stubborn lovely folk in Ireland, in Hungary, in hidden corners of the Appalachians – but not enough to keep them alive for long. Not nearly enough...

"You're actually in an enviable position, Mr. Plumb. Most people tell their children, 'Oh, you can do anything, I believe in you'. In your case, though, it's not just a pep talk."

"Because if I – if Darlene and I don't believe–"

Ms. Seelie shook her head slowly. "Pop."

Gary felt the urge to clap for Tinkerbell, but Ms. Seelie needed more. "So, this whole thing with his hands? I'll believe, trust me, but in what? What's this about?"

"Maybe he'll be a very good swimmer, Gary. Who knows, maybe he'll fly. What do *you* think? Or rather, what do you *believe?*"

"Fly?" And Gary pictured tossing Ryan in the air, and Ryan spreading his suddenly-webbed arms and taking to the skies, joyous, amazing, loved.

"Ms. Seelie, you know what *I* believe?"

She smiled, she nodded, *she knew*. He could tell, somehow.

"I believe we're going home."

Ryan might have approved, but he'd fallen asleep.

Smiling, though. He was definitely smiling.

Leaving the FAA, Gary noticed the baby stroller he'd tried to look into earlier, still parked around the side of the Agency, no parents in sight.

It was empty.

3.

Darlene came home from work that evening to find Gary and Ryan in the midst of an intricate charade, one so intimate that neither noticed her enter the house. The play went like this:

Gary, recreating an old fairy tale: "Then I'll huff..."

Ryan, hands thrust out to hold Gary's mouth closed for a heartbeat, then dropping back to his sides...

"And I'll puff..."

Ryan, hands up, beat, hands down...

"And I'll blooow your house down!"

Ryan's hands to Gary's mouth, Gary's breath filling both hands' worth of Ryan's tiny umbrellas, Ryan chortling with more glee than one child could possibly contain.

Darlene, feeling the need to make her presence felt, clapped. "Bravo, boys!"

Gary noticed her, gave a twisted grin, then made a tiny bow in his chair. "Thanks. We've been practicing."

Ryan, not ready for his final bow, crowed "Huffenpuff, Daddy, more huffenpuff!"

"Gary! Is Ryan *talking*?" Her expression, in Gary's mind, made Darlene's face as beautiful as he'd ever seen it.

One hand nestled in Ryan's hair, the other beckoning to his wife, Gary said, "Why yes. Yes, I do believe he is."

Falling for Her

G V PEARCE

"Wow, you're strong!"

Those were not the first words Eleanor had intended to say to her crush, but she also hadn't planned on falling into a lake today either, so blurting something embarrassing was the least of her problems right now.

"I'm tall, too," her Valkyrie-like rescuer replied with a grin, shaking her short silver hair back from her eyes. Even the water droplets caught the light of the sun as they fell, like diamonds glittering around her head.

"And pretty," Eleanor replied, "don't forget pretty."

"I think you might have hit your head," the woman scoffed quietly, as she adjusted her grip under Eleanor's shoulders. She had the darkest eyes Eleanor had ever seen, with irises so big there was hardly any white around them. "I run beginner lessons on the weekends, you know, you didn't have to jump right in."

"Oh, I know, I've seen you," Eleanor said before she could stop herself. Maybe she had hit her head.

"I only meant," she backtracked, "that I've noticed you, your lessons I mean, when I've been walking by everyday. I haven't been watching you or anything. I didn't even see you in the lake just now, I was looking at something else–"

The woman cut off Eleanor's panicked rambling with a laugh. "You certainly weren't looking where you were going. I've never seen anyone just walk off a path like that. Except maybe in a cartoon."

Eleanor shivered as the water dropped away beneath her and the cold air hit her limbs. She hadn't expected to be carried right out of the lake like this. Her teeth were chattering too hard to make another witty retort, even if she had been able to come up with one.

Survival instincts wanted Eleanor to snuggle closer to her rescuer for warmth, but embarrassed attraction kept her paralyzed.

As if reading her thoughts, the woman adjusted her grip again to hold Eleanor's body closer to her own neoprene-wrapped chest. There was a tiny silver seal charm attached to the zip of her wetsuit that Eleanor couldn't help but stare at – it glittered just like the woman's hair.

"It's all right," she murmured. "We'll get you inside and you'll soon warm up."

The cadence of her steps changed, the slosh of shallow water giving way to the slap of wet feet on wooden boards. She was carrying Eleanor towards the diving school, which had to be several minutes away, even under normal circumstances.

"Oh, you don't have to carry me that far, I can walk," Eleanor protested weakly, her cold limbs making absolutely no effort to prove her right.

"Don't be daft. You're hurt, and besides – I do like to show off how strong I am, especially to those who appreciate it," she winked, and Eleanor hoped she couldn't feel the way her heart rate jumped against her chest. "I'm Niamh, by the way."

"You're Irish?" Eleanor closed her eyes against the embarrassment of yet another obvious statement.

"That too."

"Sorry, I just…hadn't noticed the accent before," Eleanor realized that wasn't a good excuse even as she was saying it.

"While you definitely weren't watching me teach classes?" There seemed to be a teasing edge to Niamh's voice, but Eleanor didn't want to open her eyes in case she was just imagining it.

"It's not every day you see people diving in a lake. Well, I hadn't seen it before I moved here." She sighed. "There were only shopping trolleys and plastic bags in the river where I grew up."

"Ah, well, I was in the sea before I could walk, so I won't judge you on that count. However, I might judge you a little on the whole 'not looking where you're going' front."

Niamh tightened her grip on Eleanor's shoulders, making

her open her eyes just as Niamh kicked open the door to the diving school. The young man behind the reception desk sat up, blinking hard as if that would hide the fact that he'd been asleep in his chair.

"I was distracted by something strange in the water," Eleanor admitted as she was lowered carefully onto a bench. "I guess I walked right into the lake."

"Oooh, another victim of the Howden Hydra?" The receptionist asked, with far too much glee in his voice. "Did you see the beast? Did it grab you?"

"Don't be an eejit." Niamh snatched a towel and foil blanket from his hands. She looked like she wanted to shoo him away but he was holding the rest of the first aid kit against his chest like a shield. "Ignore him, he's talking nonsense."

Eleanor wasn't really listening to him anyway.

She was too busy looking up at her rescuer and falling in love all over again.

Niamh was a head taller than the receptionist – who was at least six foot – so she hadn't been lying about being tall. Tall and strong. Her wetsuit must have been custom made for her powerful build. No wonder she'd been able to carry Eleanor all that way without complaining.

"Thank you," Eleanor murmured as Niamh bent close to wrap the towel around her shoulders. She really would have liked to lean in and kiss her, but the receptionist was still loitering beside them with a manic look in his eyes.

"It's okay, I couldn't just leave you there–"

"You'd have been eaten!" The receptionist chimed in, gleefully.

"Martin, how many times have I told you to shut up about that?" Niamh snapped. "You're going to cost us business! This isn't Loch Ness! There's no ancient monsters in there, it's not even a natural lake."

"It could be the ghosts of drowned villagers."

"Oh, for…" Niamh pulled the first aid box out of Martin's hands – almost toppling him over in the process – then pointed firmly at his desk. "Go away! Go back to sleep and leave the poor girl alone."

"Don't worry," she continued to Eleanor once he was gone. "There are no 'drowned ghosts' down there. They made the valley into a reservoir during the war. Everyone was moved out of the area a long time before they let the water in. Now we use the old buildings for advanced diver training – the most you'll find in that lake is a dummy or two."

"It's okay, I'm not worried. I think it was a dog anyway – the thing I saw." Not that she'd seen much – she'd caught a glimpse of something moving through the water before she fell in there herself. It could have been anything. "Or maybe it was a cow. Can cows swim?"

"I don't know, I've never asked one."

"Probably a dog then." Eleanor laughed. "It was definitely too big to be an otter, and seals don't live in fresh water, do they?"

Niamh blinked slowly. "Only in Russia. Not in the north of England."

Her solemn tone took Eleanor by surprise, but before she could say anything Niamh was opening the first aid kit and gently pushing Eleanor's hair back from her forehead. Niamh grimaced at whatever she saw there.

"I guess you'd notice if there was a seal in the lake with you," Eleanor said, trying to break the tension. "I mean, they're pretty big."

"I take care to know who is in the water with me. Good thing too, I'm not sure you would have made it out on your own after a bump like this," Niamh's tone didn't change much, but her face softened a little as she pressed a piece of gauze to Eleanor's brow. The contact hurt more than expected.

"Thank you again, I hope I didn't interrupt any of your lessons."

"No, I was just training today."

"Oh, training for what?"

"I'm a triathlete."

"Oh, uh," Eleanor stumbled as a lifetime's disinterest in sports came back to ruin her day. "That's uh, good? I'm more of a try-athlete, you know, because I don't really…try…"

Niamh's smile returned, and grew with every awkward syllable out of Eleanor's mouth.

Heartened by the shift back to good humor, Eleanor decided to go for broke. "Or I guess you could say I'm a bi-athlete–"

"Because you're bi?"

Eleanor blushed, and bit back a grin of her own.

"If that was meant to be a clever way of signaling that you're not straight, I appreciate it, but I promise you, I could tell." Niamh winked.

Once again Eleanor's heart tried to do a flip inside her chest.

"That's good to know," she said. "Usually I just wear a shirt with 'awkward bisexual' written across the front, but its in the wash."

Niamh's laugh was so sudden it was almost a bark.

At the reception desk Martin jolted upright again – apparently he'd followed the instruction to go back to sleep.

"You'll have to tell me where you got it sometime," Niamh said, easing the gauze away from Eleanor's skin with a worried look. "We should get you showered and changed. It's no good staying in wet clothes like this."

"Oh, I don't live far away, I–"

"It's no bother," Niamh waved away her objections. "If I lend you some spare clothes, I won't worry about you getting sick, and you'll have to come see me again to return them. So, win-win."

If Eleanor blushed any harder her clothes would be dry soon anyway, but she couldn't argue – Niamh had made a good point.

"Besides, a doctor should have a look at this head wound. It might only need tape, but I'd hate for you to go home and pass out, or end up with a scar." Standing from her crouch, Niamh offered a hand. "Come on, I'll show you through to the locker room."

The hot shower had been a blessing for Eleanor's cold bones, though it brought attention to all the cuts and scrapes she'd been too distracted to notice until the warm water got her blood flowing again. At least the cut on her head was the only one that seemed serious, and didn't everyone say that head wounds looked worse than they really were?

Still, she kept a corner of the towel pressed to it while she waited awkwardly on the couch in Niamh's office, more worried about getting blood on her borrowed clothes than anything else.

To distract herself from the pain, and the sounds of Niamh in the shower on the other side of the wall, Eleanor looked with interest around the room.

She didn't know anything about diving – in fact, she could barely swim herself – so most of the objects were a mystery to her, but there were still personal touches to paint a picture of the woman she'd been crushing on for so long.

Niamh had a lot of awards and trophies on display, along with an almost equal quantity of seal-focused memorabilia. Photos, drawings, plushies, glass figurines – there was even a mug with a cartoon seal with the words 'I give this coffee my seal of approval.'

The seal charm on her wetsuit made more sense now – of course a diving instructor would love an animal that was so good at swimming.

Almost as if her train of thought was heading right towards it, Eleanor found her eye drawn to the blanket thrown over the couch she was sitting on. She'd barely registered it before – just a big piece of soft gray fabric, the kind of thing seen on sofas everywhere to either hide or prevent stains.

Except, now that she was really looking at it, she realized it was actually fur.

Short, soft fur, that glittered like every strand of hair was made from silver. Eleanor had never touched real fur that wasn't still attached to a living animal, so she had no idea how to tell if it was real, but it felt vaguely oily and the edges were uneven.

Standing up, she saw that the fur had been thrown haphazardly onto the couch rather than neatly spread out.

The shower sounds had stopped, but a quick glance into the

corridor assured her that the door to the locker room was still closed.

Why she felt nervous about handling this thing, she couldn't say. Maybe years of 'fur is murder' rhetoric had got into her head. With that in mind, she had to know whether it was real. She hadn't asked Niamh out on a date yet, but if she was the sort of person who owned fur, then Eleanor wanted to know the story behind it.

With one edge held between her fingertips, she did her best to shake it out. She had always been a short woman, so even with her arms outstretched she couldn't keep it from trailing on the floor.

There was a *face* at the end closest to her hands.

A large flat face that hung distorted without a skull to give it shape. Wide. Dog-like. Earless.

Two clawed flippers protruded from the middle, while another pair of flippers were poking out from the pool of fur still resting on the carpet.

It was unmistakably a seal skin, and a damaged one at that – several long wide stripes of hairless scar tissue ran diagonally across what had once been the creature's back.

Part of her wanted to scream and throw the thing as far away from her as she could, but the impulse was being drowned out by a nonsensical urge to hold it close.

That feeling was stranger than anything else she'd experienced today. It was like a craving, a bone deep certainty that the fur was important and she should keep it for her own.

She had never once in her life wanted to own part of an animal, but here she was, thinking about taking this glittery silver thing that didn't belong to her.

That word seemed to shake something loose in her mind.

This pelt didn't belong to her.

She had no *use* for it. She didn't *need* it.

She had no idea why Niamh had it – that wasn't even her business – but it *belonged to Niamh.*

Moving with the quick sharp gestures of someone who had once spent a summer folding returns in a High Street bedding shop, Eleanor folded the pelt into as neat a rectangle as she could manage. That was a trickier task that she had anticipated since the flippers got in the way.

Once she was finally content that the bundle was as neat and regular as it was going to get, she smoothed out the oddly empty face, ensured that the whiskers were all pointing in the correct directions, and set the whole thing carefully on the couch.

Despite the lack of eyes it seemed to be looking at her warily.

"Thank you for folding that," Niamh said quietly from behind her.

It was only due to a building headache that Eleanor managed not to jump from fright. She had not heard her come into the office. How long had she been standing there?

"I uh," she stammered, lost for words.

Niamh stepped around her, picking up the bundle of fur with one hand while the other reached for a set of keys that had sat unnoticed on the arm of the couch.

"Are you ready to go?"

"Why do you have a seal skin?" The question tumbled out of her mouth of its own accord, surprising Eleanor almost as much as it seemed to surprise Niamh.

"This isn't a seal skin."

"It isn't real? It's synthetic?"

Niamh blinked, her big dark eyes reflecting Eleanor's own image back at her. "Well, it isn't from a dead animal, no."

"Oh, thank goodness," Eleanor sighed with relief. "Sorry, I just… overreacted. I think maybe I did hurt my head worse than I realized."

"Understandable. You've had a hard day."

Niamh's car was the usual run-down, all-wheel-drive beast seen everywhere in England's rural Peak District. The bundle of silver fur was even more out of place on the backseat than it had been in the office.

Eleanor couldn't shake the feeling that it was watching her in the rearview mirror.

"Thank you again, for everything, I don't know how I can repay you…" she said, trying to fill the silence.

"You could give me your phone number," Niamh smiled to herself as she maneuvered the car onto a busier road. "And you still haven't told me your name."

"Oh! Damn, I'm so sorry. It's Eleanor, but not after the song," the explanation came automatically, the result of a lifetime of being asked that question immediately after giving her name.

"Nice to meet you, Eleanor," Niamh said. "I promise not to hum the tune at you, if you swear that you don't keep your face in a jar."

Eleanor found herself glancing into the back seat again. Nothing about the fur had changed in the last ten seconds.

Rolling her eyes at her own foolish thoughts, she reached for her phone. "I don't know my mobile number, but if you give me yours I can call – oh, damn."

"What's wrong?"

"I don't have my phone."

"Could it be in your wet clothes? I can call the school and ask Martin to check."

Eleanor shook her head while she patted at the pockets of her borrowed clothes, knowing already that they were empty.

"No, I have my keys – it was in the same pocket." She sighed. "I guess it's at the bottom of the lake."

"Probably not at the *bottom* – you only made it a few feet from the shore."

"Same difference." Eleanor knew she sounded petulant, but it had been a relatively new phone in a fancy case – it was a lot of money to lose all in one go.

Niamh pushed her hair back from her eyes to give her a reproachful look, but all Eleanor noticed was that her hair dye perfectly matched the pelt on the backseat.

"Eleanor, I run a diving school – I can look for your phone."

"Thanks, it's probably not worth it though. Water damage and all that. I can get a new one."

She sighed again, then shook herself. The woman she'd had a crush on for months had saved her from drowning, this was the perfect excuse to spend time with her – she couldn't sulk.

"How did you become a diving instructor?" she asked, turning in her seat to focus properly on the answer.

"I was clipped by a speed boat when I was younger, nearly died." Though her tone was light, Niamh's fingers had tightened on the steering wheel. "*Would* have died if someone hadn't pulled me out of the bay. They got me the help I needed, and that inspired me to help others."

"Oh, I'm so sorry, I didn't know."

Eleanor felt terrible for bringing up such a traumatic memory, but Niamh just reached over the handbrake to squeeze her knee reassuringly.

"It was a long time ago, don't worry about it," she said. "I've always been in the water, as long as I can remember. A few dozen stitches weren't going to put me off going back in. Now I teach police divers, coast guards, even the occasional cave diver. It's good work."

"Why here? Why not in Ireland, or at least somewhere on the coast?" Eleanor hesitantly placed her hand over Niamh's, hoping the gesture would convey that the question was just an innocent one and not a judgement.

"Lakes don't have tides, and this one has no secrets. It's just easier to teach new skills when there are fewer unexpected events, such as beautiful but distracted women appearing out of nowhere…" With one last pat of Eleanor's knee, Niamh freed her hand to point ahead of them. "Anyway, here we are. Let's get you to a doctor."

Under Eleanor's hand the warmth of their contact seemed to linger.

The hospital's accident and emergency department had been unusually crowded for a weekday afternoon, so Eleanor had sent Niamh home with her thanks.

As much as she wanted to get to know her rescuer, a waiting room filled with sick people wasn't the place to do it. A first date should involve candles and good food, or at least be free from the sound of anyone vomiting in the background.

She regretted that choice the next day, when she realized how hard it would be to track Niamh down without a phone. It had been years since Eleanor had been forced to do anything without that helpful rectangle of plastic and glass; apparently she'd forgotten how to be a person without it.

Niamh didn't have any classes scheduled until the weekend, and Martin – the odd diving receptionist – didn't know anything about her training schedule. He was sympathetic to Eleanor's plight, and promised to pass on a message, but even he was sensible enough not to give out a colleague's address to a stranger.

So she set off around the lake, hoping to run into Niamh again. Preferably without falling in this time around.

Without the distraction of her phone, and the many entertainments it contained, the world seemed stranger somehow. She had been so used to filling time with a podcast or a playlist that the countryside's constant birdsong felt disorientating.

The absence of her phone stung most when she looked up at a movement in the water, and saw the creature in the lake again.

She would have appreciated the chance to rewind a video of the last thirty seconds just to be sure she wasn't going mad.

In the water the animal could have still plausibly been mistaken for a dog. A very large, short-haired silver-gray dog with no ears, but definitely a dog-like creature, that leapt heavily out of the lake onto a rock a dozen yards away, where it pushed itself up on very un-dog-like flippers.

There were three long, pale scars running diagonally over its back.

It was a seal.

A seal holding a mobile phone gently in its mouth.

A seal that was looking directly at her with big dark eyes.

Eleanor blinked first, rubbing at her eyes like a child waking from a dream.

When she looked again, the rock was unoccupied. Only a few ripples in the surface of the water suggested there had ever been anything anywhere near the rock.

Within a breath or two even the ripples had vanished.

She'd watched that empty rock for far longer than she cared to admit – so long that the sun had set and a squirrel had run across her shoes without realizing she was a person.

Had she really seen a seal in a landlocked lake sixty miles from the nearest coast, or was she just a love-sick fool with a head injury?

She was still pondering that question when her slow walk home was interrupted by a shrill whistle.

Sadly it wasn't Niamh standing in the doorway to the diving school. It was Martin, waving something white over his head.

"We found your phone!" He shouted.

As she walked closer, he held out what turned out to be a bag of uncooked rice, with Eleanor's phone nestled in the middle like an incongruous meatball.

"Well, Niamh found it, but I fixed it!" he added cheerfully, turning the bag to show her that the phone was turned on, her lockscreen glowing behind the grains of rice.

When she took it from him the screen reacted to her touch, allowing her to type in her passcode without complaint. For some reason it unlocked to the camera app, which she hadn't been using when she lost it.

"Looks like you were really lucky," he continued, though she wasn't really listening.

There was a preview of an unfamiliar photograph in the corner of the screen. Eleanor swiped to open the gallery, and immediately hid the phone against her chest.

"Niamh said it had ended up further into the lake that she expected–"

Eleanor peeked at the screen again, angling the bag so that

Martin wouldn't see the photographs she hadn't taken. The last picture contained a familiar figure, and rather more of that figure than Eleanor had been expecting to see just yet.

"–so she had to dive pretty deep–"

The photos seemed to have been taken by accident – four very unflattering up-nose selfies of a gray seal that must have been holding the phone in its mouth, one image from the same angle but showing Niamh's face, and finally a naked woman's torso half wrapped in a seal skin.

Eleanor deleted the last picture with her eyes closed. It wasn't right to look at it when the subject didn't know it had been taken.

"–are you okay?" Martin asked, possibly for a second time.

"Oh, uh, yes, I'm fine, thank you." Eleanor knew she was babbling but staying calm was out of the question right now. "Is Niamh inside?"

"No, sorry, like I said a second ago – she went home."

"Sorry, I don't know where my head is at right now. Can you tell her I said thanks? Oh, and thank you for putting it in rice too, of course."

"Sure," Martin nodded.

She'd almost turned away when she remembered why she had missed her mobile phone in the first place. "Actually, do you have a pen? I promised to give Niamh my number – I might as well write it down and leave it with you."

"Oh, of course, I'll make sure she gets it."

Trying to ignore her phone where it sat silently on the kitchen counter – still undisturbed by either calls or texts during the full week since Martin had returned it – Eleanor opened her laptop and typed in the search term that she'd so far managed to resist investigating.

'Woman Seal Skin Magic'

The words stared back at her from the search bar, the cursor blinking like it dared her to press enter.

Eleanor refused to be bullied by a few pixels, and jabbed that key so hard her finger hurt. The things she was willing to do for love.

The first result began with the words – 'In Celtic folktales and mythology, *selkies* or *seal folk* are mythological beings able to change from seal to human form by shedding their skin.'

She should probably have looked that up sooner.

As plans went, this was a foolish one. Which was the point, really.

If it had been a clever plan there would be no need for Eleanor to be rescued from it, and Eleanor really wanted to be rescued right now.

Perhaps doing it at night was a poor choice, but at least this way no one else would notice her from the shore until morning. If the plan worked, she would have been rescued by her target already. The internet said that seals had good night vision and great hearing, so…

Of course, she *was* assuming that Niamh would be somewhere near the lake at night, and not at home, watching TV and completely oblivious to Eleanor's efforts. She had a car, so she probably had a house, or at least an address. No one was going to send employment documents to a rock, or just 'in the lake,' right?

Leaning back, Eleanor stared up at the stars – which were always so bright above the peaks – and hoped she was being just the right kind of foolish.

"Where did you even manage to find a flamingo-shaped dingy around here?" A voice asked from the darkness in a tone that definitely implied it thought she was being very foolish indeed.

Eleanor tried and failed not to grin too widely as she looked around. She couldn't see far into the darkness, but a pair of reflections just above the water could have been eyes.

"I think it's supposed to be a pool float. The previous owners of my house left it in the attic with a set of unworn stag party t-shirts."

"Sounds like there's a story there, but this isn't a pool."

"I know."

There was a huff that could have been a sigh. "Those things are dangerous on open water."

"I know, but it's been a week. You never called me, and Martin started hiding under the desk so I couldn't give him any more messages for you." Eleanor pouted. "I just wanted to thank you in person, even if you don't want to see me again."

A pale hand caught hold of the side of the float, just beside one of the gaudy plastic wings of the flamingo. It was definitely a human hand, attached to a human arm, which led to the naked (and also human) shoulders of the woman she'd been looking for. She was holding a piece of silver-gray fur against her chest. It glittered with more than reflected starlight.

There was no sign of the wetsuit she had been wearing the first time they met.

Eleanor blushed and turned her eyes to focus on Niamh's hand.

"It's not that I didn't want to see you," Niamh began, "I just…"

"Didn't want to explain that you're a seal?"

"Selkie." The correction came quickly, but without ire. "Don't go trying to pull the skins off any old seal you find on a beach – most animals don't like it, and if you do happen to find one of my folk, they'll be just as liable to bite as the rest."

The image of someone walking along a beach trying to unmask random seals made Eleanor giggle, but she tried to suppress the sound.

"I won't – that would be rude," she replied instead. "I wouldn't try to take your skin, well, anyone's skin really. They lock people up for that kind of thing. Even if yours is more like a coat, that would still be stealing."

"There are plenty of stories about people taking our skins to make us marry them," Niamh sighed.

Moving carefully – to avoid startling the woman in the water or tipping herself out of the float – Eleanor placed her hand over Niamh's own.

"I'd rather win you over with my wit and charming personality," she said.

Niamh's laugh still sounded a little like a bark, but it was cute all the same.

"I deleted the photographs," Eleanor went on, "from my phone, I mean. I didn't want to hang on to anything that could end up being evidence for Martin's 'Howden Hydra' theory, though I guess it'd be the Peak District Pinniped since you're a seal…"

"Selkie. And there's no way Martin knows that word. But thank you. I realized it was taking pictures, but I couldn't delete them without your password, and, well, I guess I panicked."

"You didn't have to give it back to me, you know, if you were worried about your safety."

Niamh shrugged. The tall, inflated head of the flamingo bobbed slightly, tapping Eleanor on the shoulder as it moved.

"I promised."

"And I promise I'll never trap you in anything you don't want by stealing your skin."

"But you will trap me into rescuing you for a second time?" Niamh winked.

"You don't have to rescue me; you could leave me here and let someone from the diving club pull me in tomorrow morning. I just wanted to talk to you, and maybe *ask* you to come on a date with me, entirely of your own free will, no strings or skins attached."

The float shook more wildly as Niamh leant over the side to press a kiss to Eleanor's lips. "You know it's the weekend tomorrow? So, I'd still be the 'someone from the diving club' rescuing you?"

Eleanor grinned against Niamh's lake-cool skin and kissed her again. "Maybe?"

"Do you have your phone with you?" Niamh asked. "Or anything else that might fall out of your pockets?"

"No, I left those at home, why?"

"Well, if I have to rescue you again, I'd rather do it the fun way."

Before Eleanor could ask what the 'fun way' meant, the flamingo-shaped pool float had already jerked out from under her, tipping her over the side and into the warm arms – no, *flippers* – of the waiting seal.

At least she got the chance to be carried out of the water in Niamh's strong arms for a second time, and they had something to talk about on their date – Martin's new conspiracy theory about the mysterious pink monster he'd seen in the lake.

Baba Yaga's *Apprentice*

LOUIS EVANS

Two women sat across from each other in a booth at the back of a bar. Both were old, but in vastly different ways. The first was old in the way of a wealthy woman from a modern, industrial nation: graceful and well-supported. She wore an antique bomber jacket and a surprisingly adventurous pair of jeans. The jeans looked as if they'd been pulled from a back closet after years of disuse, and in fact they had been.

The second woman was ancient beyond days and wizened like a peasant whose teeth had never known fluoride and whose face had never known sunscreen. Her gray hair had wrinkles, and from her wrinkles sprouted endless gray and bristly hairs.

"Baba Yaga has not had a customer in many years," said Baba Yaga, her accent Slavic, her voice creaky. She was perfectly capable of using the first-person pronoun, but she liked the sound of her own voice saying her own name. "How did you find Baba Yaga?"

"It's what I do. I'm a journalist. Or I was." The other woman, whose name was Grace, smoothed the front of her shirt, feeling naked without her press pass. She'd worn this outfit to cover the Democratic Convention of 1968; the smells of weed and tear gas and hippie blood were still baked into the jacket.

"And you want Baba Yaga to return you to the heights of your profession, yes? A scoop, a Pulitzer, an editorship? This can be done, but be warned – all Baba Yaga's spells come at a price."

"No. No, I gave up on that years ago. I'm not here for me. I'm here for the kids."

"Kids are Baba Yaga's specialty! She has done this since *before* the Old Country. Your sons and daughters, Khans and Tsarinas!"

"Not *my* kids. I don't have kids like that." Grace was not looking for a love potion.

"Speak, child. Baba Yaga will stop jumping to conclusions."

"I'm a political journalism professor these days. And I'm worried for my students."

Baba Yaga nodded. The process – chin down, chin up – took the better part of a minute, and produced the creaking of a wooden ship in a hurricane as her wrinkles, wattles, and warts rearranged themselves tectonically.

"The newspapers have been dying for two decades now. No ads, no subscriptions. And all everyone wants to read is lists of quizzes about period dramas set in Imaginary England. Even the surviving papers are only hiring television critics. No jobs for political journalism, real journalism.

"And the news itself is just as bad. Do you remember the debt crisis?"

Baba Yaga cocked her head thoughtfully, then spoke, "In the third year of the reign of Ivan the Irritable, Baba Yaga loaned him an emerald the size of a boar's heart on the promise of repayment in four chests of pure gold, but when the prince's treasure fleet–"

"You don't remember it! Precisely my point. The debt crisis was the biggest political news last year and nobody cared. Because there was no story there, no villain. Just a bunch of unmemorable squares in suits shooting themselves in the foot for reasons the reading public doesn't understand and then pointing at each other and shouting 'he did it.'"

Grace took a huge swig of the beer in front of her. "Ahh. Now Watergate, that was a story. Crime! Lies! Secrets!"

Another swig. "Not that I want another Nixon! That bastard was too clever by half. Too clever."

Another swig. These microbrews were surprisingly strong. "What we really need is some utterly bankrupt idiot. Morally bankrupt. Too egotistical to really *hide* anything. That would do it. Gravy train for the journalism school class of twenty fifteen, woo!"

Another swig.

"Ah, I'm full of shit. Forget it."

"Is not shit, and Baba Yaga does not forget. You will have your spell."

"Really? I don't have to like, find wing of bat and eye of newt? Newt Gingrich once gave me the elevator eyes in this jacket, does that help?"

"Is not necessary, and please do not mention Gingrich again. Some things Baba Yaga does not touch."

"Just to be clear, Grace didn't touch him either," said Grace.

They shared a firm nod, two female professionals at the top of their respective fields, each one knowing the price she had to pay to reach this point and guessing that the other's price was just as high.

"Baba Yaga is the greatest witch in the world," said Baba Yaga. It was a statement of fact, not a boast. "All she needs is intention, power, and faith. Three ingredients, three participants to make the spell. Let it begin."

Baba Yaga was silent a long time, and when she spoke again her pitch was not a crone's high rasp but the deep bass of good jazz.

"What is Grace's intention?"

"To create successful careers for graduating political journalists."

"Whatever the cost?"

"Whatever the cost."

"Good. What is Baba Yaga's power? It is the power of ice and snow, of bear and hawk. The power that moves the thrones of the world like a child moves his toys." Grace was nailed to her seat. Nothing physical was happening but the spell was *working*, throwing off more power than an atom bomb.

"And faith. Not Grace's faith, for a journalist turns her face from faith to seek the truth. Not Baba Yaga's faith, for a witch cannot trust in the gods. The faith of another. The sublime, self-confident man who was born to riches and believes he has Midas' touch, who lies in ruins and claims they are a great palace. That faith of man's privilege, called hubris, called arrogance, this spell binds thee–"

Baba Yaga's voice gave out. She panted in the whirlwind, and then, all at once, the spell dissipated.

"It is done," said Baba Yaga.

Grace smiled, not sure what she believed. But hundreds of miles distant, in a green room in a taping studio, which bore the name 'The Apprentice,' in a skull with unnatural hair like fool's gold, the spell struck home. A single whisper split the silence.

"It'll be *yuge*."

Life and Limb

EVAN BAUGHFMAN

Even though the Arizona sun did its best to wear him down, Rafe hardly slowed his pace. He ran along the Sonoran Desert trail, between brittlebush and ocotillo, daring the heat to vanquish him.

If he wanted to compete in the Boston Marathon again, his mind had to be stronger than his body. With the Mesa-Phoenix qualifying race only a month away, Rafe needed to ensure that every step of every workout carried him closer to success.

In the past, Rafe had been a machine, nearly impervious to self-doubt and pain. His slim frame and competitive nature had made him a college cross-country and track star. After graduation, he'd earned medals in 5Ks, 10Ks, and more. Rafe always finished a footrace near the front of the crowd, no matter the distance.

Now, a decade later, and after a car wreck, Rafe had a carbon fiber prosthesis secured below his left knee. Though he'd mostly gotten used to his adopted gait, he still had trouble with backaches brought on by an unfortunate bout with thirtysomethingitis.

Rafe's C-shaped running blade often invited stares, so he trained out in the wild, away from other people. In the middle of the desert, there were no stoplights or bad drivers, no baking asphalt or noisy construction crews. There were awe-inspiring canyons and riverbeds, cacti and clear skies, vibrant scenes lifted from art gallery walls.

There were rattlesnakes, too.

The sun didn't give Rafe much pause, but the venomous serpent now lounging in the dirt directly ahead of him brought Rafe to a standstill.

The snake, coiled in the center of the trail, shook its tail. It warned Rafe not to get any closer.

Damn. Rafe hadn't planned to double-back so soon. But he

knew there was no safe way around the warning reptile. He'd be hospital-bound if the snake struck anywhere but his prosthesis.

Rafe assured the reptile that he was leaving and retreated a few steps. Once out of the snake's strike zone, he turned away from the animal, zooming back the way he'd come. Rafe knew that, about ten minutes ahead, the trail branched off into an alternate path, one he had explored a couple times before.

Two-and-a-half minutes into his rattlesnake retreat, Rafe found himself approaching a massive saguaro, the columnar cactus standing six meters tall. A spiny arm bulged on either side of the plant, each appendage mimicking a body-builder's limb.

Had the tree-like titan been beside the trail when Rafe passed by before? How could he have possibly missed such a monster? And ignored its impressive shade?

Indeed, the cactus cast a generous shadow across the footpath, and Rafe chose to pause inside its gloom. If nature was offering him respite from glaring daylight, he might as well take advantage of the opportunity.

He pulled his hydration pack's straw into his mouth. As Rafe gulped water, he studied a trio of empty cavities in the cactus' front. At one point, they had been home to woodpeckers or owls, but now they looked like the eyes and mouth of a malformed jack-o'-lantern.

Above the 'eyes,' a pair of smaller protuberances had begun to sprout from the saguaro's flesh. They curved upward, away from the cactus' 'brow,' resembling rising devil horns.

Suddenly, the plant reached for Rafe with one of its side arms. He ducked the attempted grab, the straw falling from his jaws, cactus spines nearly scratching his skin.

Had it been the wind? Had a gust bent the branch, giving it the sudden appearance of life?

No breeze blew. The desert was perfectly still.

The saguaro swiped at Rafe again, its body creaking as it strained for its prey.

Once more, Rafe dodged the attack. Dumbfounded, he

stumbled away from the cactus, backpedaling in the opposite direction of the beast.

The plant's roots extracted themselves from the earth, whipping around its base like tentacles. They turned the cactus counterclockwise, bringing Rafe face-to-face with its Halloween grin.

Rafe ran. He sprinted down the trail, back toward the rattlesnake. He'd rather confront the reptile than this crazy cactus creature.

Perhaps the snake wouldn't even be there anymore? Maybe it had already slithered off into the sand?

Rafe's legs propelled him closer and closer to a definitive answer. His hamstrings screamed. His heart hammered. His sweat spilled.

Hopefully he was putting real distance between himself and the sentient saguaro. Hopefully, its roots had given up and chosen a separate route.

But, on second thought, was Rafe even fleeing an actual entity? Could the cactus have been some kind of heat stroke-induced illusion?

Rafe did something that runners were never supposed to do. He looked over his shoulder to determine the proximity of his opponent.

He was rewarded with a terrifying sight: the cactus was chasing him, gaining ground on its own pair of thunderous feet. The thing's roots had twisted into human-like legs, carrying the creature after Rafe, its lower extremities pumping as powerfully as pistons.

Rafe yelped. If he didn't somehow channel the college kid competitor slumbering inside of him, that bipedal nightmare would soon be hugging him tighter than an iron maiden.

Rafe raced forward. He learned that his prosthesis was a piston, too. And so was his will to win, his desire not to be shish kabobbed under a grueling sun.

If he could lose the cactus somehow and find safety, then he could slow down and use his phone. He could call a friend or the Forest Service and try to explain what the hell was going on.

Up ahead was where the rattler had rested. Thank God, it seemed to have moved on.

But, as Rafe approached the empty spot in the trail, he heard the snake's warning call. It hadn't gone far, after all. Just barely into the brush.

Too late, Rafe noticed the camouflaged critter sitting there, within reach. It sprang for him.

To miss the strike, Rafe contorted mid-stride. The snake missed its target. Rafe lost his balance.

He tumbled off the footpath and end-over-ended down a steep slope. He slammed to a stop in the middle of an unwelcoming patch of cholla.

More specifically, an unfriendly cluster of 'jumping cholla,' the desert's most vicious vegetation. This particular cactus species was known for its aggressively clingy, spiky bulbs. Once they got ahold of something, they refused to let go.

Rafe groaned. "Shiiiiiit." Dozens of barbs pierced his skin, accentuating the agony brought on by blooming scrapes and bruises. "Christ!" His prosthesis had broken free during the fall; it was now discarded in the dust, halfway up the incline.

Rafe yanked himself away from the cholla, but a number of its bulbs detached as well, holding firm to his arms and neck like needy parasites. They dug deeper into his spasming muscles.

Someone giggled. "Fine, take me with you. Because I'm not going anywhere. No, no, no."

Was the cholla taunting him? Were auditory hallucinations symptoms of a concussion?

The saguaro appeared at the top of the crest. Fucking hell.

Rafe screamed, "Go! Leave me alone!" Wincing, he forced himself onto his lone leg. He began to hop for his running blade.

Behind him, the cholla said, "Aw, crap. The big dude."

The giant gingerly began its descent, stepping over rocks, lizards, and flowers. Rafe had zero chance of getting to his prosthesis before the monster saguaro did. Stubborn as he was, he still tried.

A frightened tarantula fled the moving cactus. The spider scurried in Rafe's direction. He hopped over the bug but then slipped on a jutting stone and landed on his tailbone.

The saguaro stood beside his blade. Examined it.

"That's mine!" Rafe shrieked. "Don't fucking touch it!"

"I understand." The beast spoke from its lowermost orifice. "You have no reason to trust me." Its speech, unlike the cholla's, was a booming baritone. "But I'll be gentler than my cousin."

"What the fuck *are* you?"

The saguaro scooped the prosthesis up into its arms. It brought the limb to Rafe, who hurriedly secured the thing to his knee, despite every little movement exacerbating the cholla barb pain.

"I've watched you," said the saguaro. "You've been here many times before."

"Don't worry," Rafe said through gritted teeth. "I won't be coming back."

"You're frightened. I'm sorry."

"Plants don't walk…and talk."

"Because those spines have stuck to you, we're now connected through our suffering. And we can communicate."

"These needles hurt you too, huh?"

"Sharp things don't tickle, human. For the time being, as long as you share in our pain…you and me…my cousin…together, we are cact*us*."

"Don't want to be cactus. Just want to be me." Rafe glowered at the cholla. "Asshole!"

The saguaro turned to his cousin. "Release him. But leave some spines behind."

"Yeah, whatever you want, big dude," the cholla was quick to reply. "No problem."

"Yes, problem!" Rafe staggered to his feet. "Leave *zero* spines behind! How about that?"

"Then I'd have to give you some of mine," said the saguaro. "You don't want these. They're much larger."

Rafe could see that was true. He moaned as the cholla bulbs retracted from his skin.

"All done," confirmed the cholla. "Left him with three." The bulbs returned to their homebase, jumping like kangaroo rats.

Indeed, Rafe's right elbow still stung. He asked the big dude, "What's this all about? Why'd you come after me?"

The monster said, "I want to make you an offer. Give you my help."

"Help?"

"It's in my nature to help others. My body's been home to a variety of animals over the years. It's provided shade…comfort… to countless passerby. And then there's my fruit…"

"What fruit?"

The saguaro reached into one of its eye sockets and removed a bulbous, pink orb. "It doesn't sprout often," the cactus explained. "I store whatever grows for safe-keeping."

"Okay…" Rafe didn't take the fruit.

"You look quite uncomfortable. Miserable, if I'm being honest."

"I just fell down a hill!"

"Eat this, and it'll put you into a never-ending state of euphoria."

"Excuse you?"

"Desert life's rough. How else do you think I manage to stay so cheery out here with spines extending from my flesh? Eat this fruit, and my happiness will pass on to you."

"I…I don't need some kind of weird psychedelic *drug* to make me feel like… Listen, I'm not even unhappy, okay?"

The saguaro gestured to the prosthesis. "Weren't you just running away from something?"

"Yeah, you!"

"Before that."

"I run for fun."

"Humans run for *fun*?"

"Some of us do."

"How is it fun? You grimace, breathe heavily, and sweat profusely."

"I don't expect a cactus to understand, but… Running keeps me healthy, and it also gives me a little break from whatever difficulties I might be dealing with at a given time."

"Difficulty means unhappiness." The cactus offered the fruit again. "You should eat. And also inherit my ability to survive the sun without much water."

Speaking of water… Rafe was feeling faint. He drank from his hydration pack.

Was this thing telling him the truth? If so, and he ate its fruit, he'd be close to his old self again. Classic college Rafe, a guy with very few worries.

Plus, if he didn't have to drink a lot of water and lug around a hydration pack every time he hit the trail, the future could be bright. Rafe could qualify for fifty Boston Marathons if he wanted to!

The saguaro added, "I've helped someone like you before. A slightly younger human. This was in another place, long ago, where a different part of me was planted. I can regenerate from parts of myself that break away." The beast smiled. "This slightly younger human called me Pokey Man."

"Great name."

"He visited me after. 'Hey, Pokey Man,' he said. 'Thanks for choosing me.'"

Rafe was silent for a while. Then: "Well, I don't need to be chosen. Don't need to be helped. I'm fine."

"But you said you have difficulties…"

"A difficulty isn't necessarily a bad thing. Overcoming an obstacle makes you a better, stronger person. You don't build character by taking shortcuts. By taking handouts. You've got to put in the work."

Pokey Man was puzzled. "You really don't want my assistance?"

Rafe shook his head. "Losing this leg a few years ago taught me the importance of adapting to difficult situations." He stared at the fruit in Pokey Man's grasp. "Your offer's generous. Part of me wants to take it, but I…I just can't."

"Frankly, I never thought a human would turn this down."

"Every advantage I get in life, I want to earn through hard work, okay? Perseverance. It's taken me a while to get as comfortable as I am with all of this. To truly get back on my feet." Rafe rapped against the prosthesis with his knuckles. "This reminds me that I can do anything, if I'm smart about it… If I'm honest about it."

"This is surely a surprise, isn't it, cousin?"

"Yeah," said the cholla. "Not the choice I would make."

Rafe replied, "Being lucky…being in the right place at the right time…doesn't sit well with me. I've got to earn all my happiness. Thanks, but no."

He removed the final cholla spines, tossing them into the dirt. He then jogged back up to the trail, hearing the words of cacti no more.

Rafe made sure to enter the footpath away from where the rattlesnake had lain. He ran again. After making sure Pokey Man wasn't following him, Rafe eased his pace. His adrenaline was fading.

If he was being honest with himself, he felt horrible. Bloody and beaten. The sun felt more like an enemy than it had before.

He was still pretty far from his car. Could he even make it back to the vehicle on his own?

Walking now, he took the phone from the hydration pack pocket.

Fucking fantastic. The device was cracked. The screen wouldn't function.

Something stepped onto the trail ahead. A coyote. Followed by another. And another. All three animals yipped. Only fifty meters away.

Rafe stopped. Groaned. "Seriously?" He knelt down and palmed a fist-sized rock.

More yipping behind him. Two more coyotes. Forty meters away in the other direction.

"Fuck off!" Rafe hurled the stone at the encroaching pair.

No coyotes were harmed in the making of that fastball. It sailed wide, skipping into the desert.

Rafe roared. He cursed. He wildly pitched stones, again and again. He even flung his phone.

The entire pack remained, unflinching. Then, as one, the five hunters trotted toward their kill.

Rafe veered off-course, into soft sand. Christ, no! It was like running at the beach. He wasn't built for this, not anymore.

He grew slower by the second. The coyotes glided over to him with ease.

He shouted for help. The carnivores brought him down.

Two of them clamped onto his legs. One tore the prosthesis free. A third leapt onto Rafe's back, attempting to bite into his shoulder. Instead, its teeth punctured the hydration pack. Water sprayed.

The mini geyser burst startled the canines, preventing the final pair from darting for Rafe's throat. For a few moments, the confused quintet watched their crawling prey flee at sub-tortoise speed.

Before they could resume their attack, Pokey Man arrived, clutching nasty cholla bulbs. The saguaro threw its cousin's bits. Thankfully, the cactus had better aim than Rafe. The cholla connected with a trio of coyote hindquarters. The wild dogs yelped.

The other two snarled and snapped at Pokey Man. The friendly monster pummeled one of them to the ground with an angry arm. The last coyote was punted across the sand with powerful roots.

The entire pack scampered off, bellies empty, cholla holding strong.

"Thanks," Rafe squeaked.

Pokey Man brought the prosthesis over. Before Rafe could re-secure his appendage, the cactus gripped his hand, stinging Rafe with sizable spines.

"Ow!"

"Are you okay?"

Rafe stared at his pierced palm. "Not a fan of this form of communication."

"Those animals," said Pokey Man. "Did they harm you?"

"Mostly, just hurt what was left of my ego. Thanks again."

"You're welcome. I'm here to help." The saguaro held its fruit out to Rafe once more. "Yes?"

Rafe gently pushed the gift away. "I'm plenty happy with just being alive. Still have plenty of places I'd like to visit before I'm gone." He put on the prosthesis.

Pokey Man smiled. "That sounds nice. 'Visiting places.' Can I go, too?"

"'Go' how?"

The cactus removed one of its 'horns' and now offered it to Rafe instead of the fruit. "Take this with you? Please? Over time, this piece can develop into another me and experience another place. Plant it someplace beautiful? Where humans abound?"

"Why don't you go into the city? All of you, I mean."

"That's a long journey, isn't it? Besides... Do you think I would be accepted there?"

Rafe imagined Pokey Man traveling on Mill Avenue, offering happy fruit, and people screaming down the street. He imagined a militarized police force arriving on scene with machine guns and flamethrowers.

Rafe said, "You're probably better off here."

"I'd like at least a part of me to thrive elsewhere. I'd like to be more helpful, if I could."

Rafe took Pokey Man's puny protuberance. Perhaps Rafe could propagate the plant at a botanical garden. Or even his own front yard.

He unzipped his tattered hydration pack and placed Pokey Man, Jr. inside.

"Thank you!" The cactus beamed. "Need any further assistance?"

"Know where can I find some water?"

"Yes. Walk with me? It's not far."

Rafe then followed Pokey Man to a favorite oasis, saying hello to a variety of chatty cacti along the way.

Flash of Fin

ATLIN MERRICK

The stone is dirty. Of course it is, I dug it up with a dozen others. They're meager little things, but in a pile round the fire they help hold the wood in place and I can roast the herring I catch from the river. They're big fish, silver when you catch 'em, but they go red when they're…well I say ripe, but Maebh just rolls their eyes each time I do. I know they're hiding a smile.

After we eat, we poke at the stones, get them far from the simmering coals. When they cool a bit Maebh puts a couple by their feet. I stuff several under my shirt and I'm warm right through, even though they sting a little.

It's all good. We have everything we need, here by the river. More than enough while we wait.

The runan-shah, she'll come for us soon. We've seen flashes of fin and scale a couple times, the water roiling. There's a war going on under there, one we can't help her fight, what with our puny little air-hungry lungs. But we'll be here when she rises, when the war gets run to ground.

We'll be ready.

Meantime, I also use the stones to sharpen our blades.

Author Bios

ALI HABASHI *(Landlocked)* graduated from the University of St. Andrews, Scotland with a degree in English and Management, and currently works in Boston. She generally spends her days marketing for publishers, writing about monsters, and galivanting through Salem dressed as a witch. Her short stories have been featured on The Other Stories podcast (Hawk and Cleaver), on The NoSleep Podcast, and in the Flame Tree anthology *Footsteps in the Dark,* among others. She also came in first in the Creature Feature category for *The Asterisk Anthology Vol II.* Learn more by visiting her website at alihabashi.com.

ALISON MCBAIN *(The Development)* is a Pushcart Prize-nominated author with work in *Flash Fiction Online, On Spec,* and *Abyss & Apex*. Her debut novel *The Rose Queen* received the Gold Award for the YA fantasy category of the 2019 Literary Classics International Book Awards. When not writing, she is the associate editor for the literary magazine *Scribes*MICRO*Fiction.* Find more of her writing at medium.com/@amcbain and alisonmcbain.com or follow her on Twitter @AlisonMcBain.

AMY LYNWANDER *(PG at the Park)* works as an administrator and co-owns Baltimore Ghost Tours, a haunted history walking tour company. Her short fiction has appeared in Unidentified Funny Objects, Speculative North, and others. She lives in Baltimore, Maryland with her family.

ANGEL WHELAN *(Healer's Song)* grew up in the British countryside, where she developed a taste for the macabre. She currently lives in Philadelphia, USA with her childhood sweetheart and their three children. She likes to write the kind of stories that kept her awake long after dark, afraid to close her eyes. Her author page can be found at https://www.facebook.com/DelectablyDark/.

ATLIN MERRICK *(Flash of Fin)* is the commissioning editor for *Dark Cheer: Cryptids Emerging* – this anthology – as well as for Improbable Press. She's the author of hundreds of articles, features, and essays, as well as two short story collections: *Sherlock Holmes and John Watson: The Day They Met* (writing as Wendy C Fries) and *Sherlock Holmes and John Watson: The Night They Met.* Atlin is beyond excited by the amazing stories Improbable received for this anthology. She can be found on Twitter at @atlinmerrick, same goes for Tumblr and just about everywhere else.

BRIAN TRENT *(Love Song of the Wendigo)* Brian's speculative fiction appears regularly in Analog, Fantasy & Science Fiction, The Year's Best Military and Adventure SF (winning the 2019 Reader's Poll Award), Terraform, Daily Science Fiction, Apex, Escape Pod, Flash Fiction Online, Galaxy's Edge, Nature, and numerous year's best anthologies. The author of *Ten Thousand Thunders,* he lives in New England, where he works as a novelist, screenwriter, and poet. His website and blog are located at www.briantrent.com.

CARMAN C CURTON *(Post Card from Roswell, New Mexico, USA; Nain Rouge Appreciation; Adopt A Human)* consumes caffeine while writing a series of microstories called QuickFics, which she leaves in random places for people to find. You can find her on Twitter and Facebook @CarmanCCurton.

CARTER LAPPIN *(Road Trip)* has a bachelor's degree in creative writing. Her writing experience includes placing second in the 2021 Parsec Ink competition as well as being scheduled to appear in an anthology with WorldWeaver Press. She lives in California with her family and her three-legged cat. You can find her on Twitter at @CarterLappin.

DOMINICK CANCILLA *(Mysterious Travelers)* As the author of *Disneyland for Vampires, Zombies, and Others with VERY Special Needs,* Dominick considers himself the country's foremost expert on Disney vacations for sentient non-humans. To be fair, there's not a lot of competition for that title.

ELIZABETH WALKER *(Pics or it Didn't Happen)* is a writer, a swing dancer, a business operations person at NASA, and definitely not three velociraptors hiding in a trench coat. Writing as E.D. Walker, she is the author of the *Fairy Tales of Lyond* Series that begins with *Enchanting the King*. As Elizabeth Walker, she has had short stories published in the USA Today Bestselling Pets in Space anthologies as well as Zooscape and the Toasted Cake Podcast. She lives in Southern California with her husband, two small children, and one housecat. You can find her online at www.edwalkerauthor.com and on Twitter and Instagram as @AuthorEDW.

ERIC SHLAYFER *(The Kyivan Song)* is a very queer person writing about queer characters finding their queer joy. He lives in Kyiv, Ukraine, where he spends all of his spare time either reading or writing. He writes as "need_more_meta" on ArchiveOfOurOwn, making sure that his favorite characters have the sweet, wholesome romance they deserve. You can find Eric on Twitter as @need_more_meta where he posts his stories and writes about fandom life in general.

EUAN LIM *(The Beauty in the Unexpected)* is a genderqueer, Chinese-Romanian author and a first-generation U.S. citizen born and raised in Minneapolis. He's currently a sophomore at the University of Minnesota; when he's not doing dreadful homework, daydreaming, or panicking about the future, he writes contemporary and fantasy fiction with the hope of one day publishing a series of novels. His work has also appeared in an anthology by TL;DR Press. He can be found on Twitter @euan_a_lim.

EVADARE VOLNEY *(New Song for the Old Canary)* is a bisexual bi-ethnic Appalachian expat, has published erotic fiction in *Heart, Body, Soul* (New Smut Project 2015) and *Journey to the Center of Desire: Erotic Tales of Jules Verne* (Circlet Press, 2017), Erato (New Smut Project, 2020), and forthcoming in *The Queer Adventures of Sherlock Holmes* (Carnation Books) and *Cunning Linguists* (New Smut Project, 2022). She can be found on AO3, Twitter, Tumblr, and Dreamwidth as Vulgarweed, and is currently working on a full-length Holmes/

Watson novel. She divides her time between Chicago and North Carolina. Her daemon is a turkey vulture named Heurtebise.

EVAN BAUGHFMAN *(Life and Limb)* Much of Evan Baughfman's writing success has been as a playwright, his plays finding homes in theaters worldwide. Many of his scripts are published through Heuer Publishing, YouthPLAYS, Next Stage Press, and Drama Notebook. Evan has also found success writing horror fiction, his work found recently in anthologies by No Bad Books Press, 4 Horsemen Publications, and Black Hare Press. Evan's short story collection, *The Emaciated Man and Other Terrifying Tales from Poe Middle School*, is published through Thurston Howl Publications. His novella, *Vanishing of the 7th Grade*, is coming from D&T Publishing in 2022. More info available at amazon.com/author/evanbaughfman.

FRANCES PAULI *(Original Activist)* writes books about animals, hybrids, aliens, shifters, and occasionally ordinary humans. She tends to cross genre boundaries, but hovers around fantasy and science fiction with romantic tendencies.

GEORGE IVANOFF *(The Heart of Gervascio)* is an Australia-based author who usually writes for kids and teens. He's written over 100 books, ranging from the interactive fiction of the *You Choose* series, to the nonfiction *Survival Guides*. Sometimes he has a go at writing grown-up stuff. So far he's done okay, with stories appearing in numerous magazines and anthologies, including *Midnight Echo*, *Belong*, *Dead Red Heart* and *[untitled]*. Check out George's web site at: georgeivanoff.com.au.

G V PEARCE *(Falling For Her)* is the author of the queer supernatural romance novels *Ghost Story* and *Strangest Day So Far*. Several years spent working in animal welfare have left Gen with an endless supply of tales too ridiculous to be fiction. Perhaps one day they'll put those stories into a book. In the meantime, Gen can usually be found wandering the Yorkshire Moors in search of cool rocks, inspiration, and a decent cup of coffee.

JEFF DAVIS *(Old Friend)* Born in Upstate New York, Jeffrey spent many years in Boston before returning to his hometown. He still likes to travel whenever and wherever he can, including Japan. Developing a love for the country and learning Japanese. Though he has had a long career as a programmer and database administrator, he now spends much of his time writing as well. His first short story was published in the anthology *The End of Dragons: A Collection of Short Stories.*

JULIE ANN REES *(The Grundylow)* holds a first class master's degree in creative writing from the University of Wales Trinity Saint David. Her short stories have been published both online at horla.org and in print with Parthian books, Sliced Up Press, Black Shuck Books, and a forthcoming anthology with Honno Press. Her first book, a memoir entitled Paper Horses, will be released by Black Bee Books in December 2021. She is a single mother and works at a busy rural library in Wales. When not riding her horse over the wild Welsh hills she can be found on https://www.facebook.com/julieAnnRees and https://twitter.com/JulieRe36071199

KEYAN BOWES *(Chicken Monster Motel)* is frequently ambushed by stories and took the Clarion Workshop for science fiction and fantasy writers in self-defense. She's a member of SFWA. Normally peripatetic but San Francisco-based, these days Keyan can be found online or somewhere near Puget Sound. Her most recent publication is *Honey and Vinegar and Seawater*, a short poem in Mermaids Monthly. More of her work is linked here: https://keyanbowes.com/publications-page-2/. Website: www.keyanbowes.org; Facebook: www.facebook.com/keyan.bowes; Twitter: @KeyanBowes.

LOUIS EVANS *(Baba Yaga's Apprentice)* would never sign a deal with a magical entity without having an attorney review the contract. Or vice-versa. His fiction has appeared in *Nature: Futures*, *Analog SF&F*, *Interzone* and many more. He›s a member of the Clarion West ghost class of the plague year. He›s online at evanslouis.com and on twitter @louisevanswrite.

MADELINE V PINE *(Loud Came the Rain)* is a hydro engineer, a genderqueer author, and what happens when little kids never stop asking "Why?" Their favorite hobbies include taking things apart to understand how they work and setting out on research dives for increasingly random subjects. When not writing, investigating, or slipping the results of their investigations into their novels, they can be found on abandoned logging roads, asking "Where does this lead?" One day they'll end up in a parallel universe or a portal fantasy. In the meantime, you can reach them on Twitter: @Madeline_Pine.

MARLAINA COCKCROFT *(Leviathan)* writes modern-day stories about folklore and misunderstood monsters for children and adults. Short stories have been published in Strange Horizons and Daily Science Fiction, as well as the anthology "Strange Fire: Jewish Voices from the Pandemic." She lives with her family in New Jersey. You can find her online at marlainacockcroft.com or on Twitter at @mdcroft.

MARSHALL J MOORE *(Lakers)* Marshall (he/him) is a writer, filmmaker, and martial artist who was born and raised on Kwajalein, a tiny Pacific Island. He has traveled to nearly thirty countries, once sold a thousand dollars' worth of teapots to Jackie Chan, and on one occasion was tracked down by a bounty hunter for owing $300 in overdue fees to the Los Angeles Public Library. He lives in Atlanta, Georgia with his wife Megan and their two cats. His stories have appeared in collections from Flame Tree Publishing, Mysterion, Tyche Books, and many others. Find him at: twitter.com/kwaj14, facebook.com/kwajmarshall, or Instagram.com/kwajmarshall.

MERINDA BRAYFIELD *(From the Ashes)* has always loved telling stories. She has appeared in several anthologies and has recently published her first novel, *Timepiece*. She lives in Texas with her two cats and enjoys spending time on Twitter, where she can be found @merindab.

MIKAL TRIMM *(Huffenpuff)* has sold over 50 short stories and 100 poems to numerous venues, including Postscripts, Strange

Horizons, Realms of Fantasy, and Ellery Queen's Mystery Magazine. He's also on Facebook, because he's old, and that's where old people congregate.

NEETHU KRISHNAN *(Fireflies and Thieves)* is a writer from Mumbai, India. She holds postgraduate degrees in English and Microbiology. She writes essayistic nonfiction and (occasionally) poetry. Her creative nonfiction has appeared in The Spectacle. You can connect with Neethu on Facebook at https://www.facebook.com/neethu.krishnan.944.

NORA BAILEY *(The Beast in the Deep)* is a writer and PhD candidate living in Chicago with her pet rabbits, Pippin and Fíli. By day, she studies astrophysics and the movement of planets. By night and various other times, she writes fiction, primarily science fiction and fantasy. She can be found at http://nora-bailey.com or wherever there is a good cup of decaf coffee to be had.

PARKER FOYE *(Grim Up North)* Parker (they/them) writes queer speculative romance and believes in happily ever after, although sometimes their characters make achieving this difficult. An education in Classics nurtured a love of heroes, swords, monsters, and beautiful people doing foolish things while wearing only scraps of leather. You'll find those things in various guises in Parker's stories, along with kissing, explosions, and more shifters than you can shake a stick at. Parker's most recent novel is Foxen Bloom, a queer fantasy romance featuring old gods, new tricks, and a bit with a goat.

RICK HODGES *(The Goat-Boy Paradigm)* Not quite a superhero, Rick is a professional writer by day and author by night. His other fictional works include the novel *To Follow Elephants* (Stormbird Press), winner of a Nautilus Book Award. See more at rickhodgesauthor.com or facebook.com/RickHodgesAuthor.

R L MEZA *(Skrunch)* is an author of horror fiction. She lives in a century-old Victorian house on the coast of northern California with her husband and the collection of strange animals they call family. Learn more at rlmeza.com.

ROBERT BAGNALL *(The Hundred Dollar Fortune)* was born in Bedford, England, in 1970 and now lives in Devon, between Dartmoor and the English Channel. He is the author of the novel '2084 – the Meschera Bandwidth', and the anthology '24 0s & a 2', which collects two dozen of his fifty-odd published stories, both of which are available from Amazon. He can be contacted via his blog at meschera.blogspot.com.

ROBERT PIPKIN *(The Jackalope)* developed this story by telling it many times over many campfires for family and friends. He lives with his family in North Carolina, USA, where he has a day job and writes weird stories when he finds a quiet moment. This is his first anthology publication. Follow him on Twitter @PipkinRobert.

SARINA DORIE *(A Guide for the Lover of Jorogumo)* has sold over 180 short stories to markets like Analog, Daily Science Fiction, Fantasy Magazine, and F&SF. She has over sixty books up on Amazon, including her bestselling series, *Womby's School for Wayward Witches*. A few of her favorite things include: gluten-free brownies (not necessarily glutton-free), Star Trek, steampunk, fairies, Severus Snape, and Mr. Darcy. You can find info about her short stories and novels on her website: www.sarinadorie.com.

SHAWNA BORMAN *(The Water Horse)* holds an MFA from the University of Southern Maine's Stonecoast program. Though she dabbles in all genres, her true love is horror. Whether dealing with your average socially-awkward serial killer or an angel/demon/mortal hybrid entering the terrible teens, Shawna is most at ease visiting with the voices in her head. She resides in Texas with her father. For more information and links to her social media profiles, please visit www.snborman.com.

SIMON KEWIN *(The Monster)* is a fantasy and sci/fi writer, author of the Cloven Land fantasy trilogy, cyberpunk thriller The

Genehunter, steampunk Gormenghast saga Engn, the Triple Stars sci/fi trilogy and the Office of the Witchfinder General books, published by Elsewhen Press.

He's the author of several short story collections, with his shorter fiction appearing in Analog, Nature and over a hundred other magazines. He is currently doing an MA in creative writing while writing at least three novels simultaneously. Find him at https://simonkewin.co.uk/.

TOM VELTEROP *(Nights Without Dreams)* is a writer of short stories and children's books, as well as a freelance illustrator. His other works include *Blacktooth* and *The Wolves of Desolation*, published in the sci-fi anthology *Tales to Survive the Stars* by Greenteeth Press, *Nico's Nightmares*, a children's ebook self published to Amazon, and the illustrations of *A Trip to the Zoo*, written by Mohammed Umar. He is currently studying a Creative Writing MA at the University of Bristol.

YVETTE LISA NDLOVU *(When Death Comes to Find You)* is a Zimbabwean sarungano (storyteller). Her debut short story collection *Swimming with Crocodiles* (University Press of Kentucky, Spring 2023) won the 2021 UPK New Poetry & Prose Series Prize. She is pursuing her MFA at the University of Massachusetts-Amherst, where she teaches in the Writing Program. She has taught at Clarion West Writers Workshop online and earned her BA at Cornell University. Her work has been supported by fellowships from the Tin House Workshop, Bread Loaf Writers Workshop, and the New York State Summer Writers Institute. She received the 2017 Cornell University George Harmon Coxe Award for Poetry selected by Sally Wen Mao, and was the 2020 fiction winner of Columbia Journal's Womxn History Month Special Issue. She is the co-founder of the Voodoonauts Summer Workshop for Black SFF writers. Her work has appeared or is forthcoming in F&SF, Tor.com, Columbia Journal, Fiyah Literary Magazine, Mermaids Monthly, and Kweli Journal. She is currently at work on a novel.

Dark Cheer: Cryptids Emerging (Volume Blue)

Tales for those who never outgrew goosebumps

Here are stories for lovers
of chupacabras and hulders,
griffins and gargoyles.
Here be darkly cheery tales
of ancient creatures
beneath still waters, in the attic,
or the shadows right by the bed.

Herein an autistic hiker meets a cryptid
who wants her camera;
a Japanese tanuki seeks his fox daughter;
and two women fall in love, never
mind one's a swamp monster.

Here be stories of changelings, nix, and
demons adopted, of hungry kraken
and cryptids we'd see if only, if only
we looked into treetops, behind doors, or in
our own back gardens.

Here there be monsters.

Thank all the gods.

Tags: Speculative fiction, LGBTQIA+, BIPOC, disability, urban fiction

Order Volume Blue, the first in the Dark Cheer anthology, at: https://improbablepress.com or online from most book retailers.

www.ingramcontent.com/pod-product-compliance
Lightning Source LLC
Chambersburg PA
CBHW030603310726
48979CB00003B/556
* 9 7 8 0 6 4 5 2 8 9 9 2 3 *